KINGS OF AMERICA

Also by R.J. Ellory

Candlemoth
Ghostheart
A Quiet Vendetta
City Of Lies
A Quiet Belief in Angels
A Simple Act of Violence
The Anniversary Man
Saints of New York
Bad Signs
A Dark and Broken Heart
The Devil and the River
Carnival of Shadows
Mockingbird Songs

Novellas

Three Days in Chicagoland:
1. The Sister
2. The Cop
3. The Killer

KINGS OF AMERICA

R.J. ELLORY

First published in Great Britain in 2017 by Orion Books,
an imprint of The Orion Publishing Group Ltd
Carmelite House, 50 Victoria Embankment,
London EC4Y 0DZ

An Hachette UK company

1 3 5 7 9 10 8 6 4 2

A CIP catalogue record for this book is
available from the British Library.

ISBN (Hardback) 978 1 4091 6862 1
ISBN (Export Trade Paperback) 978 1 4091 6312 1

Typeset at The Spartan Press Ltd,
Lymington, Hants

Printed and bound in Great Britain by
Clays Ltd, St Ives plc

www.orionbooks.co.uk

This novel is dedicated to my editorial director, Jon Wood, and my editor, Jemima Forrester. Without their routinely unreasonable demands, this would have been something else entirely. I owe them a debt of gratitude for their enthusiasm, their creative input and their guidance.

Also to my agent, Euan Thorneycroft, for those times when I needed to be told to get back in the ring and slug it out.

To my wife, Victoria, for her endless support and encouragement.

Finally, I would like to acknowledge my grandmother.

She had no idea how to look after a little kid, so she sat me in front of the TV with the understanding that I could watch any film made before the year of my birth.
It was she who introduced me to the Golden Age of Hollywood, and thus initiated a love affair with film that has been true and faithful throughout my life.

FOREWORD

The quantity of research undertaken for the *Kings of America* project was both fascinating and very extensive. I consulted authoritative works on the history of Hollywood, also memoirs, newspapers, magazines and a wealth of other anecdotal information. The vast majority of things I learned have not been included in the book. This was never intended to be a history of Hollywood, per se, but rather the story of individuals and their experiences during an evocative, influential and significant time period. This book begins at a time when the magic of film was still utterly magical, and the foundations of the film capital of the world were being built by pioneers and forward-thinkers. As with all works of fiction there has been an element of creative license. If there are errors in time and place, then these were either unintentional, or they were deemed necessary for the continuity and flow of the narrative. I trust that those who have a far greater comprehension of the history of Hollywood will forgive me.

ONE

Ireland–November 1937

If you're born to hang, you'll never drown.

The thought crossed Danny McCabe's mind like a cloud shadow across a field. Something his father used to tell him, like *Fate has you by the balls,* but with a poetic lilt.

Then Danny thought, *We are so feckin' brave,* and he knew they were all thinking the same thing as they lay there in the mud watching the Garda station. The mud sucked and dragged and hungered, and he could feel the damp and dirt in his bones. There was himself and Jimmy O'Connell and Micky Cavanaugh. No one dared say the truth, but he could hear it loud like chapel bells. He knew there was no bravery here, not a shred of it between them. Sure enough they were pure stupid, fueled by blarney and poteen and the raw edge of unbridled youth. What would Danny's nail-tough ma say if she could see him? She'd grab a fist of his hair and bring him to his knees; she'd look right down into his damned and everlasting soul and tell him the truth as it was.

Ye're an eejut, lad. Didn't bear all that pain and heartache to raise an eejut. Get back to the house.

Danny thought of his sisters—Brenda, Deirdre, and the little one, Erin, the light of his life. He felt a chill sense of terror through his bones and beyond.

"Here we go, lads," Micky Cavanaugh said, his voice an urgent whisper.

The three of them hunkered a little further into the black mud as the last of the Garda left the small police station and walked to the car.

It was Friday; even shades craved a drink ahead of the weekend.

A dark devil of a night, no doubt about it. The mud was rotten, and the rain fell straight down like stairposts and stank like black piss. Danny McCabe, a born fighter in his hands, heart, and head, clutched a whiskey bottle filled with gasoline, and he wanted nothing more than to be home and away. But there was no turning back. Not a prayer.

Danny looked left at Micky; he could see the ghost of fear in his eyes. Long gone was the memory of all those big words from small mouths, acting the maggot, out on the lash, making believe their hearts were as big as their egos. They'd crossed paths with Johnny Madden, and he'd said, *Where the tongue slips, it speaks the truth*, and he'd looked at all three of them in turn, eye to eye, looked right through them, in fact, and they knew well enough he was a Fenian.

I know you, Madden had said to Danny, singling him out with a flinty stare. *You're Clancy McCabe's boy. Heard word you were a fighter like your father. Another one plannin' to bust out of Clonegal wit' your fists. Good luck's all I can say. Drag yourself as far away as ye can. This place'll forever drag ye back.*

Johnny Madden and his kind carried a fierce national pride, a sense of disbelieving indignation, a red-hot hatred for the heathen bastard English and all they represented. Folks said Madden and his fellows were Irish Republican Brotherhood, but they were more like some half-crazed illegitimate offspring, buckled with drink, never anything but ready for a fight.

Madden went on at them, saying, "Ye gotta do ye own growin', lads, no matter how tall your father." There was a glint of shamelessness in his eyes as he added, "Now let me buy ye fellers a drink."

Three drinks in and it was, "You want a job, I can get it for you... that's unless ye fellers're nowt but a scatter o' gowls wit' nary a backbone between ye."

Cavanaugh was drunkest and spoke first. "If it's a fight, we'll take it," he said. "Clonegal boys don't run from a fight."

"That they don't," Madden said.

Danny McCabe and Jimmy O'Connell didn't shed a word.

"I got a fight for ye... a wee skirmish if ye're up for it," Madden said.

"Sure as shite is shite," Cavanaugh said.

And then he gave them details, and they bantered together. *Yes, we can do it. Feck the shades. Burn the place out, sure. Send them a message they won't forget.*

"Be in touch wit' ye, then, I will," Madden said, and he got up from the table. He looked down at the sorry gang, gave a crooked smile, said, "Remember this, lads... whoever keeps his tongue keeps his friends," and then disappeared into the smoke-filled hubbub of a Friday-night pub.

And so it was, lying there in the stinking mud with bottle bombs in their hands and good intent in their hearts. Johnny Madden had given them this job with the promise that it'd make heroes of them to a man. Johnny Madden, mad bastard that he was, had become their leading light and mentor, and now they were ready to shit their pants.

Danny was the youngest, a mere eighteen years of age. He was a dreamer for ropes and rings, the smack of leather, the roar of crowds. The threat of another's fists lit a fire inside him, and he was all set to burn a road out of the past into a legendary future. Alongside him, neither leading nor following, were Micky Cavanaugh and Jimmy O'Connell, twenty-four and twenty-two respectively, both of them fathers, Micky twice over, wee babes lying at home with wives who were none too wise as to what was afoot.

The Garda car was gone, the station was empty, and out of the mud and shadows they came. Micky was up ahead, keen to show his true colors. Danny hung back a little, eyes left and right for signs of anyone who might share a word with the law. Most folks carried their tongues in their pockets, just as Johnny had said, believing it was against God and nature to share even the narrowest of truths with the shades. Rather die a squalid and terrible death by poison before telling a copper who done the poisoning.

The station was up ahead no more than fifty yards. It was a lonely stretch of road between nowhere and nowheres else. They were coming upon it fast, even on foot, and with the nearness of the place the tension and the tremors came on strong for Danny.

Micky glanced back toward Jimmy and Danny, motioning for Jimmy to head around the other side of the building, for Danny to approach from the rear. Windows on all three sides, a blessed Barrowside cocktail set to fly through each of them, and the place would rage like a hole into hell itself.

Danny's heart was a derailed train. He felt dizzy, too, like he'd drunk way more than he had. Jimmy was white as Dublin snow, eyes dark and round like ferryman pennies. Micky was twenty yards from the outer wall, jumping it now, hurrying across the last stretch of ground before the station itself. Danny saw him dip his head, and he was then out of sight until he flattened himself against the stonework and motioned for them to hurry the feck up, for Christ's sake.

Danny knew he was going to be sick, but no sick came.

He looked at the bottle in his hand, the rag stuffed in the neck, the furious stench of gasoline intoxicating his mind, watering his eyes, there on his lips, in the back of his throat.

It was only a feckin' building, Jesus's sake. Nothing but bricks and mortar.

"Come on!" Micky hissed.

Jimmy started across the grass. Danny willed himself beyond all resistance and went after him.

Micky had a light going, was ready to fire up all three and send each of them to their positions.

Danny wondered if the thing would explode in his hand, if the bottle would bounce away from the glass and shower him with flaming gasoline, if he would burn down to a cinder right there and then as a penance for his sins. If not now, then when? Someday we all paid the piper.

"You pair of feckin' arseholes are gonna get us busted," Micky said, his voice a punch to the gut. "Hold out them bottles, for Christ's sake. Jesus, Mary, and Joseph, I don't know what the feck ye pair are doin', I tell ye."

Jimmy's hand was out, the rag snatching at the flame like a hungry thing, and then it was alight, burning bright like a torch.

"Away!" Micky urged, and Jimmy went around the side of the building.

Before Danny even realized what was happening, the bottle in his hand was flaming, too.

"Go, go, go!" Micky said, and almost shoved Danny over.

Danny lost his footing for a second, and the sudden movement caused the flame to flare wildly. He was frightened then, truly frightened, more than he'd ever known, and hurried on to the window at the back.

Danny heard the glass breaking before he realized that he'd let the bottle go.

Almost as one, those three bottles went through their respective windows. A trio of dull crumps came from within as they broke and exploded.

It was not the sound that Danny had expected. He'd not have been able to say what he expected, but this was not it.

He imagined he felt the heat, but he could not have done. He saw the light, of course, and it was mere seconds before the three of them were howling back across the grass toward the low wall, vaulting it like the kids they once were, vaulting bowed backs in games of leapfrog.

"There's a bold feckin' message to the tans," Micky said, but Danny didn't feel it was so bold. He felt it was cowardly and pointless, would serve no purpose but to aggravate the Garda, inspire them to be even more random and vicious. This was the south. The north was where they needed to be, fighting the English direct, not down here making noises that would be nothing but faint echoes by the time they reached London.

Jimmy was the first to move. He wanted to be away from the scene. Soon as word was out that the place was burning, it would be crawling with shades. Johnny Madden hoped there would be nothing but cinders and ash by the time they got there, but a roaring furnace would suit just as well to make their point.

Danny could smell nothing but the gasoline on his hands and clothes. That would be as good as any written confession.

The three of them watched as the fire took hold, licking out through the busted windows, curling up against the walls, and finding the eaves despite the rain. Would take a flood of biblical proportions to put the thing out now.

"Good job if ever I seen one," Micky said. "Let's be away now, eh? 'Fore they get wise and send some gunfighters to kick our arses."

Micky started away, Jimmy on his heels, but there was something about the flames that entranced Danny, and he hesitated for a moment.

Had he not done so they would not have known until morning.

But Danny did hesitate, and when he saw that ghost of movement behind the very window through which he'd thrown the bottle, he *knew*. Not so much something he clearly saw, but something he perceived, something that was almost preternatural in its intensity.

There was someone inside, someone right there inside the Garda station, and the flames were billowing from those windows and the glass was cracking and snapping in the heat, and the brickwork around those apertures was blackening with soot, and whoever was in there was consigned to the hereafter, whether he deserved it or not.

"Th-there's s-someone in the b-building," Danny said, and his voice cracked, and he could barely hear himself above the sound of the rain and the sound of the flames.

"Danny!" Jimmy hollered. "Get off there . . . Be away with you, for Christ's sake!"

Danny looked back at Jimmy and Micky, and the expression on

Danny's face must have said all that needed saying, but still Jimmy asked.

"What're ye doin', lad? Get out of there, will ye?"

Danny shook his head. He looked back toward the station. His heart was like a clenched fist, and every drop of blood in his face had drawn away into hiding. He was washed-out and wasted, nothing but a ghost of himself.

"S-someone . . ." he whispered, and then it was Micky who was asking, taking one step backward, turning, looking at Jimmy as if Jimmy held a clue to what was going on.

Neither of them spoke, but Micky started walking and Jimmy followed on his heel.

Danny heard him first. He heard the screaming. It wasn't the sound of a man. Couldn't have been. It was the sound of a terrified beast, a creature from some other godforsaken place that had nothing at all to do with what they'd done.

Micky heard then, Jimmy too, and their eyes were wide with horror and they started running toward the place.

Danny was last in line, and even as they reached the side of the building, the fierce heat drove them back.

Micky and Jimmy backed away.

Danny stood there, could not avert his eyes from those flames.

"Get the feck away!" Jimmy shouted, and his words were swallowed as the roof started to give. It creaked and moaned like a ship gashed and twisted upon rocks, and there was a deep yawing sound as beams and rafters bowed beneath the weight of scorching-hot slates.

"Oh, Jesus!" Micky said, and for the first time the blarney was gone. He stood for a moment, and then he turned and ran backward. He stopped suddenly, walked back the way he'd come, and then started for the wall once more.

Something caught Danny's eye, out and to the left beyond the turn in the road. Was that a light? Was that headlights?

"Shades!" Micky said. "Feckin' shades are comin'!"

Danny looked toward the road. It was the shades for sure, behind them the fire engine, bell ringing so loud, and Micky Cavanaugh and Jimmy O'Connell stood and watched as their fate approached them from the road that ran adjacent to the Whelan farm.

Jimmy thought of his baby girl and started crying. It was involuntary, barely more than a physiological response, but he dropped to his knees and the tears streamed down his face. Danny could see the smoke on his skin, the faint layer of soot through which the tears coursed.

He glanced back, saw Jimmy and Micky readying themselves for flight.

He could not go. He could not leave the man to burn.

He took a step forward.

"What in God's name are you doin'?" Jimmy asked.

"Go," Danny said, his voice low and urgent. "Go now, both of you," he said.

Micky looked perplexed. "Wha—"

Danny hurried toward them, feeling something other than fear now, feeling a strength inside of himself that was as much a stranger as joy.

"Ye have wives and little 'uns. Get away now. I'll run. They won't catch me. They'll see me go, and I'll be distant 'fore they get here. You go that way . . ." Danny said, and he pointed back over the other side of the building. If Micky and Jimmy hightailed it for the trees down past the river, they'd be a memory before the cars even reached the station.

Micky hesitated.

"Go for feck's sake! Go now!" Danny said, and the punch of his tone just sent them charging away toward the grove of willows. They were in and among those branches and shadows within a handful of seconds, and Danny turned back to the road and saw the first police car reach the long drive that wound its way down to the station.

Danny didn't look back again. He started around the building and reached the front door. The heat was like nothing he could have imagined. He felt the sweat dry up on his face and hands. He felt his hair begin to scorch, the moisture gone from his eyes, his lids unable to close.

And then he charged that door, head down, right shoulder forward, every ounce of strength he possessed brought to bear upon that wood.

Danny collided with the front door of the Garda station like a thunderous cannon. He felt it give, but it did not break. It had been locked, and locked from within, and he could not understand why. He backed up and went again, faster, harder, summoning from some deep well of terror an even mightier reserve of force.

And this time it went through, the doors bursting open and flying backward against the inner walls.

The man within was down on his hands and knees. The smoke

was thick and hot and acrid. The crook of his elbow around the lower half of his face, Danny staggered forward and grabbed the back of the man's collar. He felt his hair crackling, his skin tightening, the heat tearing every breath from his body. He turned back, head down, each footstep he took an impossible challenge.

He knew that if he didn't make it out they were both done for. He knew that if they did, he was done for anyway, but he could not leave a man to burn, no matter who he was or what he represented.

Danny fell out of the front doorway of the station, his eyes streaming, his chest heaving, the sick rushing from his stomach as his body fought to repel the filth he'd inhaled.

The man behind him crawled forward and collapsed, but he was far enough from the doorway to be safe.

Micky and Jimmy were long gone. They were nowhere to be seen.

The sound of bells and sirens now filled Danny's head. He ran then, ran away from the flames, the smoke, the creaking building, away from the man on the ground, away from the certain knowledge that there was never a hope of running fast enough.

He knew before he crossed the pathway near the wall that they'd caught sight of him. There was more than one car, and while the first car pulled up with the fire engine and spilled four coppers into the rain and heat, the second car came after Danny.

His heart leaped and burst. He felt the heat of the burning building and the heat of his own breath and blood as he flew headlong into the evening darkness, desperate to make it away, knowing even as he stumbled, gathered his feet again, pushed himself harder and faster, that there was no way on God's green earth that he could ever outpace a car. Even the fence he hurdled gave him no advantage, for that car just plowed right through it, barbed wire and post trailing after it like some macabre wedding festoon.

The lights had him, and then he heard a gunshot, and he knew that one of them coppers was leaning from a window with a Webley and hoping to wing him. Didn't want to kill him. Oh no, for that would mean he'd never see the bowels of a tan jail.

Danny ran like a man crazed, like a man imprisoned and suddenly freed, but his legs couldn't move faster and his heart could beat no more blood, and when he finally skidded sideways in the filth and mud, he knew it was all over.

The car slid to a staggering halt merely feet behind him, and before he had a chance to right himself they were upon him, fists flailing, feet flying, hands tearing at him, wrenching him from the ground, an elbow into the side of his head, another to his ribs. He tried to get to his knees, but he was forced down again, his face into the mud, gasping for breath, the taste of dirt in his mouth, the stench of gasoline on his clothes, the smell of smoke and the coppery haunt of blood on his tongue and lips and in his throat.

"Bastard!" one of them said.

"Bastard fucking filth," another said, and he was kicked again and again and again.

He started screaming for them to let him up. Let him up they did, but only to kick him down again. By the time he was dragged from the ground and shoved into the back of the car he was broken and bloodied and covered in shite.

He sat between two of them in the back. He thought to tell them what he'd done, that their man was alive because he'd broken through those doors and dragged him out of the station, but he knew such words would be meaningless. They would take it as some desperate lie to mitigate his situation. There would be no mitigation. They slammed him with elbows, and then the one in the passenger seat just turned and looked at him with an expression of such disgust and hatred it was impossible for Danny not to feel the shame right to the core of his soul.

That one then let fly with an almighty fist to his face. Danny felt his nose crack, and he went out like a snuffed candle.

TWO

As a child, Danny McCabe remembered being stricken with a fever so desperate and fierce he knew it was merely a matter of minutes before his lungs would fill no more. No matter how hard he sucked and wheezed it was never sufficient; his face white, his fingernails near punched through his skin as he grasped and clawed at the bedsheets, his eyes lit with pain, his frail body running with sweat. Each time it happened he knew he would die, and each time he did not. Once or twice he'd almost hoped it would end. Such a thought could only be a cousin to pure wickedness itself, a devil thought that would scratch and scurry about the corners of his conscience, and then—finding guilt for nourishment—would gain confidence and strength and consume him whole and complete. But that thought had never been anything of substance. Truly, he'd never wished himself dead, not from the day he was born to the very evening he left after supper with a plan for drinking with Jimmy O'Connell.

That wish changed on the night of November 12, 1937.

He knew that his fate was in the hands of God or Lucifer. It was merely a matter of who got there first. He'd been battered and bruised by his father, by sparring partners, by opponents in the ring, but what he was subjected to that night was the worst pain he'd ever experienced.

Administering his formal interrogation were two fellows by the name of Jack Carey and Bobby Durnin. One of their own had almost burned to death at the hands of terrorists. They knew there was more than one guilty man in Clonegal, and Daniel Francis McCabe was going to tell them the truth, even if they had to kill him to get it.

Bobby Durnin was once a welterweight champion, little more than county angling for national, but a busted wrist put paid to any dreams he might have harbored. Some said the bitterness he felt for seeing that aspiration snuffed like a candle set him on a queer course for hatred of humanity in general. Others said he was always a twisted knot of bitterness, seeing himself hard done by, as if fate had dealt him a bad hand out of spite. He went to the Garda for the same reason as Jack Carey, simply a means to get even with folk who aggravated him without ever being held to account.

Durnin and Carey had the McCabe boy handcuffed to a simple wooden chair in the cellar of Clonmel. Already his wrists were raw, his arms pulled tight to the lower crossbeams beneath the seat. Stripped to the waist, his nose bloodied, one molar cracked from a sideswipe Durnin landed before he was even seated, Danny knew that there were three ways to make this stop: He told them what they wanted to hear, they tired of beating him, or he died right where he sat. There was one other chair in the room, and here Carey sat and watched while Durnin used Danny's upper body like a punching bag. They were experienced, the pair of them, knew how to hurt without raising bruises or breaking skin. Kidney punches, a hard fist wrapped in a wet towel, elbows into the top of the spine, knuckles to the top of the head, twisting bones in sockets until the pain tore through every nerve and sinew.

"A man is never alone," Carey said, leaning back in the chair, front legs off the ground, a cigarette burning in the corner of his mouth. He seemed relaxed, nonchalant even, content to spend the rest of the night eliciting whatever information he could from Danny McCabe. It was already two in the morning, Saturday the thirteenth, and there was more than enough bitterness and black coffee to keep the Clonmel Garda fueled. Politics aside, John Carmody was a known and respected man, a family man, father of three, and to see him laid up in hospital with his burned hands and face was unconscionable.

"No, a man is never alone," Carey repeated. "He doesn't drink alone or work alone, no matter what he might be doin'. Now we have a good mind as to who was wit' ye, lad, but we need to hear it from your own lips, so we do. That way we make it all official and straightforward."

Durnin fetched a long length of damp cloth that was hanging on the door handle. He wound it around each fist and let it hang loose between his hands.

"So, are we gonna start cooperatin' wit' one another, or do we have to keep beatin' at ye until ye give it up, eh?"

Danny looked back at Carey through the slits of his swollen eyelids. He didn't say a word.

Carey nodded at Durnin. Durnin looped the cloth around Danny's neck a couple of times and started to draw it tight. The cloth was damp to avoid abrading the skin, the width of it sufficient to encircle his throat from collar to chin. There would be no bruising or lesions, nothing to suggest that the hacking, desperate gasp for breath that Danny now suffered had ever taken place. His feet kicked, his hands tugged mercilessly at the cuffs that held him to the chair, but the pressure didn't ease.

Carey didn't flinch. He leaned back a little further and allowed the chair to meet the wall. He smoked his cigarette and he waited.

Durnin eased up and Danny's head slumped forward for just a moment. Barely had he time to fill his lungs before the tightening began again.

His eyes bulged, his face reddened furiously, and he had visions of his mother holding him, trying to help him breathe, trying to ease the terror that he'd felt so many times as a child.

Durnin released him. Danny tried to suck as much oxygen as he could. His head pounded, his eyes hurt, he was dizzy, sick, disorientated, but even as he heard Carey's voice he knew that whatever they asked of him would get no answer.

"Stubborn bastard," Carey said. "Give ye that, little man. Stubborn like most o' them dumb boggers. Witnesses put three o' ye there. Madden won't be among it. Never gets his hands dirty, just convinces people like you to do his dirty work. So we'll be needin' them names, Daniel McCabe. Two names and it all goes away."

Danny sat still. His chest heaved; his wrists burned like fire. He'd already pissed himself. The stench of his own urine filled his nostrils and shamed him.

But he didn't say a word.

Durnin rapped his knuckles sharply on the top of Danny's head.

Danny howled in pain. Durnin did it again and again, and Danny felt consciousness sliding away from him.

Carey, still leaning against the wall, said, "We know who ye are, lad. We know your father, too. Family of fighters ye may be, but everyone breaks, even the toughest ones. Doesn't have to be like this. You might have shot to hell your chances of ever bein' a boxer, but you don't have to take the blame for these others. Tell the truth and the hurtin' stops, lad."

Danny tried to fill his mind with nothing but thoughts of his youngest sister, Erin. The fact that there was every possibility he might not see her for years was far worse a torture than Durnin and Carey could ever inflict. Without him, she would be lost.

Danny pictured her face, her smile, the way she laughed when he played the fool for her. Now she would barely recognize him, his eyes bloodshot, his crooked smile indiscernible due to the swelling of his lips.

"Hit the little fucker again, Bobby," Carey said, and Bobby stepped around the back of the chair and let fly with a right hook into Danny's kidneys.

Danny howled in agony.

"Again," Carey said.

Bobby was on his knees then, his fist like a stone, jabbing repeatedly into the small of Danny's back. The pain was close to unbearable, worse than anything he had ever suffered against the ropes, but Danny forced himself to believe that the pain was something else, some other feeling, something he could bear. He tried to breathe slowly. He tried to focus his mind on something other than what was happening to him. And even as the blows kept coming he knew it would be only so long before he passed out.

Eventually he did, but only for a short while. Durnin was slapping his face, urging him to wake up, shaking him by the shoulders and screaming into his face.

"Maggot! Feckin' maggot bastard! Wake up, ye feckin' maggot bastard!"

The cloth around his throat again, the desperate gasp for breath, and Danny couldn't hold on any longer. He passed out once more, this time into some deep hole of shadows and painlessness that welcomed him with open arms. The last thing he recalled was the feeling of pain against his tongue from the tooth that had cracked and broken.

After that there was nothing.

THREE

By the time it was over, Johnny Madden was dead. Spoofer and toe rag and bullshitter he may have been, but when it came to the raid on the Clonmel Garda station there wasn't a man who could've said a harsh word about him.

Madden had told Danny McCabe's confederates Micky Cavanaugh and Jimmy O'Connell that the situation needed to be taken care of, even if he had to do it himself. Danny McCabe was to be rescued, and that's all there was to it. Frankie Doolan was recruited to drive, and the four of them headed on up through Bennettsbridge to Clonmel.

Perhaps they saw it as a simple act of defiance, an act of loyalty for a fallen brother. Perhaps Madden needed no excuse for further violence. Here would be the force majeure for events that not only crossed the Atlantic, but generations yet to be born. What transpired no one could have foreseen, but the storming of the Clonmel Garda station marked an auspicious and notable beginning for a far greater history to come.

Madden was not the only one who'd crossed swords with Carey and Durnin. Frankie Doolan knew them, too, had himself been a guest at Clonmel, and they knew that building like their own homes. The ease with which four masked and armed men overtook that station defied explanation, but they did. There were merely three Garda on duty, Carey and Durnin still in the basement with Danny McCabe, and when Micky Cavanaugh and Jimmy O'Connell burst through the door of that interrogation room all hell broke loose.

"Bastards!" Micky hollered, and he charged forward like a mad thing. With one almighty hook, he leveled Bobby Durnin. The man went over like an empty bottle, and Micky laid in with a few kicks to the ribs.

Jack Carey had still been sitting on his chair, front legs off the ground, back against the wall. In a desperate move to get up, he lost his balance and the chair keeled over. Carey was on his back, the chair still beneath him, when Jimmy O'Connell dropped a whirlwind of fists on him.

Carey fought back wildly, his arms thrashing, but Jimmy was down on his knees, sending a few swift hooks to the face and neck. Carey curled up, knees into his chest, and made it clear he wouldn't be doing any more fighting.

"Keys!" Jimmy screamed at him. "Give me the feckin' keys!"

Carey gave up the keys, and Jimmy let Danny out of the handcuffs.

"Up we go, lad," he said, lifting Danny bodily from the chair and making his way to the outer hallway.

By the time they reached the end of the corridor Danny had found his own feet. Every bone in his body, every muscle, every nerve and sinew screamed with pain, but he was standing and he was not going to fall again.

It was then that they heard the gunshot from above.

Everything stopped for a second, and then Micky Cavanaugh gave both Durnin and Carey a half dozen more kicks and fled after O'Connell.

The three of them charged headlong up the stairs, found Frankie Doolan holding the remaining Garda back with a pistol. Johnny Madden was on the deck, his head in a pool of blood that was ever-widening.

"Jesus, Mary, and Joseph, what the feckin' hell happened?" Jimmy asked.

"Bastards shot him," Frankie said. "He's dead, for sure."

"We're away," Micky said. "They can account for their own mess, so they can."

Frankie aimed his pistol at the Garda back against the wall, and then he raised it and fired a couple of shots into the ceiling.

"Follow us and ye're dead fuckin' meat, so ye are."

They backed away—Jimmy O'Connell, Micky Cavanaugh, and Frankie Doolan, all of them still masked.

Danny hesitated then, looking down at Johnny Madden, seeing that brash grin, that blarney, that bravado, that fire in his eyes . . . all of it extinguished.

"Come on, for feck's sake!" Frankie Doolan hollered. "Get the hell out of there!"

The sound of footsteps pinned Danny to the spot.

Someone was coming up from the basement.

When Bobby Durnin appeared, gun in hand, that gun pointed directly at Danny's head, he knew that this was what they wanted.

They'd wanted Madden dead for a long time, and now Danny McCabe would join him, and the shades would make an example of them for all the world to see.

Danny was not going to let that happen. He could not let that happen.

He heard the car revving outside, someone shouting his name. Beyond that he heard nothing else, saw nothing but Bobby Durnin walking toward him, in his eyes the trademark glint of malice. The last Garda hesitated, and then he flattened himself against the wall and sidestepped his way along to the staircase. He disappeared as fast as he could, and Danny believed he'd make good his escape.

"Wee bastard, ye are," Durnin growled. "Ye've had it now. You'll swing, Danny McCabe. You're gonna die right here like Madden, or I'm gonna see you swing."

Durnin took another step forward and kicked Madden in the side of the head. The final ignominy.

The gun in Durnin's hand was unerring and steady.

Danny felt the rage boiling in him. Durnin was a bastard, a maggot. The man took three or four rapid steps forward, and the gun was up in Danny's face.

"Ye think I won't?" Durnin asked. "Ye think I don't have the nerve?"

Danny was not ready to die. The will to survive consumed him, possessed him. This was between himself and Bobby Durnin, and one of them wasn't walking away.

Durnin prodded the barrel of the gun in Danny's face.

Danny smacked Durnin's hand aside, but the gun was back in his face within a moment.

Durnin sneered. The fire in his eyes was fierce. He was a fighter, and a good one. The man was once possessed of a fearful reputation, and had it not been for that broken wrist so many years ago, he'd have been a champ. Danny knew the man could let loose, for only a matter of minutes before he'd been tied to a chair while Bobby Durnin pummeled hell out of him with his bare fists.

The world stopped. A hiatus, a vacuum that excluded everything but two men facing each other, and Danny knew—one way or another—that this was where it would end. If he went down, so be it. He would not die in a jail cell; nor would he die running away.

Durnin stepped back. He took another step, three, four, and then he took a sly glance at Danny.

"I see where your mind is going, Danny McCabe," he said.

Durnin took the bullets from the gun and put them in his pocket. He set the gun down and kicked it toward the wall. He pushed his shirtsleeves further up his arms and assumed the stance. He was a southpaw, and his weight was heavy on the right. He stood too high for his center of gravity, and Danny saw the weakness.

Danny leaned back a touch, felt the bruising and muscle damage that had already been inflicted upon him. He knew he couldn't take much more, that he could not let Durnin strike low in his solar plexus, that he had to keep his kidney and the small of his back out of the line of fire.

Durnin came forward. He was agile, quick, and despite his inaccurate stance and tenuous balance, there was something altogether forbidding about the man's certainty. So much of it was the certainty, the lack of inhibition, the speed with which the first strike was delivered. Catch a man unawares, deliver that blow to the face, the stomach, and not only did you unsettle him physically, but you unsettled his self-assurance.

"Let's be gettin' about it, then," Durnin said. He started weaving, and his center of gravity settled. The immediate weakness was gone, and Danny knew he had a fight ahead of him.

The first strike was delivered, and it came fast and furious and straight out of the sun.

Durnin launched a rocket into the side of Danny's head. Danny went sideways, lost his step, skidded on the outer edges of the ever-widening pool of blood that had escaped Johnny Madden's head. He looked up to see Durnin advancing on him, a grin on his face that said victory was all but a strike away.

Danny was up on his feet, skipping backward, avoiding further blood, and he came around Johnny Madden's spread-eagled body and returned to the fight on Durnin's right.

Danny knew the others were set to leave without him. He sensed it. He could feel their desperation. But he would not be leaving. Not now. He would not back down. He cared not if it was blind stubbornness or muleheaded stupidity. Durnin was not going to shame a McCabe.

"Come on, then, ye little bastard . . . Let's see if you've got anything worth tellin' the girls about," Durnin said.

That smirk, that sneer, that condescending expression.

Danny raised his defense. He took a breath, paused for just a second, and then he went for Durnin.

Durnin was stunned by the first blow, if not by its force then by its speed. The fist that collided with the side of his head was done and home before he'd even seen it coming. He stepped back, his eyes losing focus, and Danny was back again. A right to the center of his face, a left beneath the rib cage.

Durnin grunted awkwardly, and he found himself against the wall. How long it had been since his last competitive round Danny did not know, but the agility and precision that marked a frequent fighter was already visibly lacking.

But the man was strong. Bobby Durnin could take a punishing as well as anyone, and he'd not be going down until there was nowhere else to go.

Bobby pushed himself away from the wall. He used the impetus it gave him to rush Danny. Danny stepped back, lost his balance, and went sprawling.

Bobby was over him like a hurricane, and it was only Danny's rapid turn to the left and the speed with which he regained his feet that saved him from a brutal fusillade of knuckles.

"Bastard!" Bobby howled as Danny disappeared from beneath him.

Danny came around to the side, caught Bobby in the side of his body before he'd had a chance to get up.

Bobby grunted painfully. Then he let loose some primeval roar and charged Danny.

Danny sidestepped again, and he knew that the urge for revenge had gotten the better of Bobby's emotions. That was the primary flaw of the fighter, the one place from which it was impossible to return. Vengeance was like quicksand; it gripped you, would not let go, and the more you tried to resist it, the more it swallowed you.

Danny saw it in Bobby's eyes.

This was it now. If Danny missed this chance, it was all over. He was bruised and tired and unsteady on his feet. His shoes were slick with Johnny Madden's blood, and if he took two or three more of Bobby's bruising roundhouses, then he doubted he'd be able to stay upright.

Bobby's defense was strong, his balance good, and there was not a flicker of fatigue in his eyes.

Danny held his ground. He raised his fists. He knew the next blow would count for everything, and he hesitated just a moment longer than he'd have done in a competitive match. This was no match; it was a battle of wills, a battle for life, and if he did not put Bobby Durnin down, then he knew Bobby would kill him. To hell with recrimination, penalty, the right of law or anything else. Revenge alone would put those bullets back in the gun and the muzzle to Danny's head. Danny knew that Bobby would not hesitate, even if Frankie and the others came charging back to kill Bobby for what he'd done.

The first jab could have been stronger. It could have been a killer. Danny gave it all he had, but his arm had been weakened by handcuffs and the strain they had exerted against the muscles in his upper arm. Notwithstanding the fact that it was limited in its force, it collided with Bobby's temple as Bobby turned his head to avoid it. That was a bad move, and Bobby knew it even as his balance was thrown. He threw out his arm toward the wall, hoping that the wall would curtail the fall, but he misjudged the distance. The wall was a good six inches farther away than he needed, and his hand slid down it as he went to one knee.

Danny was over him. The second blow caught Bobby Durnin full in the face. Danny heard the man's nose break. Blood rushed from both nostrils like a tap.

Bobby howled in agony.

Danny saw red, and his mind was full of mist. Scarlet mist, blood-red mist, and the sound rushed in his ears and the blood was behind his eyes, and he could feel something like a tourniquet around his throat, and he knew that if he didn't let loose with everything he possessed, he would somehow implode and disappear in that very moment.

His rage and anguish boiled furiously, and before he had a moment to think, he was firing one blow after another after another into Bobby Durnin's torso, his throat, his face, the side of his head.

Bobby was on his side then, his knees tucked up to his chest, his hands over his head in self-defense, but it was hopeless. Danny's temper was raging, and that rage found vent in every single fist that was released, withdrawn, fueled once more by sheer fury and let loose again.

Danny was outside of himself. His body worked ceaselessly, the sweat leaping from his brow, his breath like a train, the pummeling relentless and rapid and savage.

Those fists kept pounding down into Bobby Durnin's body long after whatever light had fired the man's temper was extinguished.

When Micky Cavanaugh and Frankie Doolan finally dragged Danny away from the bloodied, motionless form that was Bobby Durnin, Danny was rambling and out of control.

Danny did not resist their efforts to hold him back, but when he looked at them each in turn they saw that the focus was gone from Danny's eyes, that he was no longer there, that Danny himself had somehow vacated the body and left behind nothing but a fierce and uncontrollable animal. But the force was spent, and they carried him away from that awful scene with no resistance.

Danny said not a word that made sense, and even as they bundled him wholesale into the back of the car, it was as if he'd been drugged.

Frankie Doolan took the driver's seat, headed away toward Kilsheelan. Johnny alone had known the full details of the plan, but Johnny was dead. Frankie knew enough to get Danny out to Waterford, where Johnny's cousin was waiting for them. Frankie guessed it was onward to Rosslare Harbour and out of the country, maybe get him to Pembroke Dock and vanish him into the Welsh countryside. Frankie didn't know, didn't care to know; Johnny Madden was lying in a pool of his own blood at the Clonmel Garda station and they needed to be rid of Danny McCabe.

In the backseat, Danny remained delirious and incomprehensible. He sat between Micky and Jimmy, the pair of them doing what they could to hold him upright as the car tore around corners and bends.

Danny was groaning and moaning; at one point his head slumped forward and he stopped breathing.

"Get his feckin' head up, will ye?" Frankie said. "Get the bastard breathin', will ye? Jesus, all that to get him out o' there and he dies in the feckin' car."

They got Danny's head up straight, but whatever he was saying made no sense.

In truth, none of them knew what to say. What had happened was not to be undone.

They didn't speak of Johnny Madden, didn't want to speak of him, didn't want to think of him. The man would be a martyr to the cause, for sure. Maybe that's what he'd wanted all along.

It was now all so much history, especially for Danny McCabe.

The law wouldn't rest until they had him.

As for any life he'd imagined, he was as good as dead already.

FOUR

New York–March 1938

"Always be unsure of where you might be tomorrow. If you don't know, then no one else will," Julie said. He laughed. "Doesn't even make sense, like most everything else I say!"

Julie was Giulio Bessami. He was the counterman at a lunchroom favored by the Italians on 116th. Perhaps his ears had heard more deals go down, more death sentences issued, more oaths uttered and promises made than any other man in New York, but ask him straight and he'd seen nothing, heard even less, and that was the way it would always be.

Nicky Mariani had run a couple of books for the guy, earned his trust by returning his winnings pronto and not one red cent short. As far as Julie was concerned, Nicky had a long way to go, but he was respectful and obliging; he had all the time in the world for someone trying to make the bigger leagues.

"You're a bright kid," Julie said, and he looked at Nicky, all of twenty-two years old, a firework in a bottle. "How long you been here?"

Nicky shifted on the barstool. "Ten weeks."

Julie laughed. "Oh man, how I wish I was your age."

"It sucks," Nicky said.

"You'll say different when you're fifty or sixty, trust me."

"Sure, Julie, but this is not how it's supposed to go. I need to get in there. I need money. I need some—"

"What you need is to slow down," Julie interjected. He set down the dishtowel and put his hands on the counter. He smiled, and there was wisdom, experience, and reconciliation in those eyes.

"They call me Little Nicky, like I'm some sort of joke."

Julie sighed and shook his head. "You understand even less than I give you credit for," he said. "Hell, you ain't even Italian. You're Corsican, for Christ's sake. Thank your lucky stars they even talk to you."

"I need money, Julie. I need to get a foot in the door. You know how it is. If you ain't running you're standing still, right?"

Nicky shifted on the stool. He straightened his jacket and tugged his sleeves. The suit he wore was secondhand, a size too big, but somehow he felt like he was bursting out of it. He stood up. He sat down again. His father used to say that he never stopped moving, that even when he walked he'd taken his second step before he'd even finished his first.

Julie closed his hand over Nicky's. "Let me tell you something, kid," he said. "You got your two buddies . . . what's their names again?"

"Piero Altamura and Freddie Cova."

"Right, right . . . Piero and Freddie. Good kids, both of them. They've been around a while. People know who they are. You stick with them, keep listening, don't talk so much, calm down a little. You'll find a way in, okay? You're smart, but watching you is like waiting for a bomb to go off. You'll make people edgy."

"I gotta make some money, Julie. I gotta get my sister out to California. I promised her, promised my folks."

Julie gripped Nicky's hand even harder, almost as if he was trying to quell the agitation that seemed to flow off him in waves.

"You push this thing, it'll blow up in your face, Nicky. You got a ladder here. You don't even know where the first rung is. Bide your time. It won't take long. Have some patience—"

Julie looked up at the sound of the bell above the door.

"Speak of the devil," he said. "Your buddies . . . say their names and they show up."

Nicky turned and greeted his two friends. He hardly knew them, but they seemed like the sort of people he should know. They were both second-generation and possessed all the hallmarks of wannabe Americans. Piero was a head taller, narrow in the shoulders, wiry, and tough. He gave off an air of menace without even being aware of it. Freddie was heavier, and his shock of black curly hair gave him the appearance of someone younger. Nevertheless, Freddie Cova was the voice of reason, always had a measure for things, whereas Piero Altamura was headstrong and opinionated. Piero was nineteen years old, had spent much of his childhood in the backstreets of Salerno. Whereas more fortunate kids had gone to school and gotten at least two squares a day, he'd survived by running errands for pocket change, stealing anything he could. Like Nicky Mariani, he saw America as a horn of plenty just waiting to be plundered.

"We got a thing," Freddie Cova said.

"*Maybe* we got a thing," Piero added.

"What's happening?" Nicky asked.

"Got to meet a guy who can maybe get us in on some smokes from Canada. It won't be a lot of money, but it's something."

"How much?" Nicky asked.

Piero looked at Freddie. Freddie shook his head.

"You don't know?" Nicky asked.

"That's why we go and speak to him now," Freddie said.

"Eight o'clock in the morning," Julie said, "and you guys are meeting someone in a bar to talk about smuggling cigarettes from Canada?"

Nicky was off his chair and halfway toward the door.

Julie smiled and shook his head. "Kid'll be three weeks early for his own funeral if he carries on this way."

The bar was a half dozen blocks away, and even though Nicky didn't know the way, he was ahead of Piero and Freddie by some distance.

Two blocks down, Freddie had to holler at him to turn around and come back.

Nicky hurried to meet them, did a little two-step thing like a fighter coming into the ring. Fists up, punching air, laughing. "World moves too slow," he said.

"Take it easy on this one," Freddie said. "This guy is connected. He ain't big-time, but he knows a lot of people. We get in with him, then we're getting somewhere, okay?"

Piero put his hand on Nicky's shoulder. "Freddie's right. You gotta play it down a little."

Nicky laughed in his own infectious way. "Everything's good," he said. "We can fetch cigarettes from Canada. We can do whatever they want. I just need to get that money rolling in fast, okay?"

"Yeah sure, but—"

"Hang in there with me," Nicky said. "Gonna make a fortune. Gonna shake the world, boys. That's what I'm gonna do. And I'm gonna get my kid sister to Hollywood and she's gonna be a big movie star. Light up the town, you know?" He grinned, did that little boxer's two-step again, and clapped Freddie on the shoulder. "So let's go," he said. "What are we waitin' for?"

Fifteen minutes in and Nicky was saying, "This is bullshit."

"Hey, people have things to do, you know? He's late. No big deal. Just be patient."

An hour they waited, and whoever was meant to come was a no-show.

It was past nine thirty, and already the winos and deadbeats from the Strip were coming down.

"Look at these people," Freddie said. He indicated an old guy making his way to the bar, his clothes filthy, his shoes torn, his features displaying the ravages attendant to a lifetime of drinking. "What the hell—"

"Leave him be," Nicky said. "He ain't doin' anyone any harm."

"Stinkin' the place up, that's what he's doing."

Nicky slid out from the booth. He looked down at Freddie. "Someone's son that was, and maybe he's someone's father. So he lost his way. What you gonna do, eh? You gonna go around being an asshole to everyone?"

Freddie didn't respond.

Nicky turned and approached the bar.

Freddie and Piero watched as Nicky shared a few words with the old man. He put his hand on the man's shoulder, laughed at something, and then he waved the barkeep over and bought the guy a drink.

Back at the table Freddie and Piero looked at him like he'd lost his mind.

"What?" Nicky asked. "He's a good old boy."

"I don't get you sometimes," Freddie said.

"You don't gotta get nothin'," Nicky said, grinning. "I am what I am. Take it or leave it. Anyways, let's get out of here. This cigarette guy ain't showin'."

Out on the sidewalk, Freddie went left and was almost knocked down by another drunk on his way into the bar.

"Christ almighty, feller," he said. "Look where the hell you're going!"

The man was young, perhaps younger than Freddie himself, and he stood there with an expression on his face like he hadn't heard a word. He swayed a little to the right, and then he smiled from ear to ear. "To hell with you," he slurred. Then he started laughing and tried to push his way past Freddie.

Freddie already had a switchblade in his hand.

The young man looked at Freddie, looked at the blade, and shook his head. "You plannin' on doin' somethin' clever with that, or do you want me to show you a good hidin' place for it?" He laughed again, took a step backward, nearly lost his balance.

"What the hell are you doing?" Nicky asked.

The man hesitated, took a little time to focus on a new face, and said, "What the hell does it look like? I'm gonna get me a drink."

"Is that so?"

"It is at that."

Nicky frowned, smiled a little cruelly. "What the hell kind of talk is that? Where are you from?"

"That'd be none o' your business."

"You disrespect my friend here," Nicky said.

"Is that what I'm doin', is it? Disrespectin' him?"

"Yes, it is, and now you're going to get a lesson in manners."

The young man raised his eyebrows as if amused. He seemed relaxed, nonchalant almost, and he looked at the three men facing him and shook his head.

"And who's goin' to be teachin' that lesson, me fine Italian friend?"

Nicky sneered.

Freddie Cova held out the knife. He advanced on the young man. The young man, still smiling his crooked little smile, seemed to be asking a question with his eyes.

That question was never asked, and Freddie never got a chance to say a word as he walked into what appeared to be a whirlwind of knees and elbows.

Before Nicky even understood what had happened, Freddie was spread-eagle on the ground. The young man was still standing, still smiling, seemingly unconcerned with whatever might happen next. He went to kick the switchblade over to the edge of the sidewalk, almost lost his balance, righted himself again. He started laughing again. He was as drunk as hell and still he'd put a knife-wielding man on the floor without breaking a sweat.

"You next?" he asked of Piero Altamura. "Or is Mr. Eye-talian Teacher here gonna deliver his lesson personal-like?" He tugged his jacket sleeves and stood like a boxer, one leg slightly behind the other, fists raised.

Piero was quicker, tougher, far more adept at street-fighting techniques than Freddie, but he was no match for the young man.

Seconds, barely, and Piero found himself advancing back toward Nicky, his arms pinned behind his back, his feet almost off the ground with the sheer force that was being applied to him. The pain he was experiencing was evident on his face, but he did not cry out. That would have been far too shameful.

"Seems your boys are in need of a little practice," the man said to Nicky.

He shoved Piero forward; Piero stumbled, fell, and found himself on his knees. He rose awkwardly, looked back at the young man with such hatred in his eyes.

"Who are you?" Nicky asked.

"And who might be askin'?"

"My name is Nicolas Mariani."

"My name is Francis. Francis Madden. My friends called me Frankie."

"And where are you from?" Nicky asked.

"From a country a great deal older and wiser than this one... and I guess yours is the same. You're Italians?"

"I'm from Corsica," Nicky said, "but my friends are Italians."

Frankie Madden smiled. He looked back at Piero, even now getting up from the road and brushing down his pants.

"Well, I guess we made our introductions, didn't we?" Frankie said. "And now I'll be about my business, so I will."

Frankie took a step toward the doorway of the bar.

"Wait," Nicky said. He looked at the young man, still off-balance, still wearing that crooked grin. He saw what he saw, and it was unmistakable.

Piero shook his head. "No, Nicky... leave him be."

Nicky paid no attention to Piero. The man was fast, a natural, and whether he was trained or not, he'd still dropped both Piero and Freddie without missing a beat.

"You're a fighter?" Nicky asked.

Frankie smiled his crooked smile. "I'm Irish, my friend. We're all fighters."

"That so?" Nicky could see it already. He could almost smell the money.

"Born that way, die that way," Frankie said. "Only question is how many years in between. Now, if you're done with your questions—"

"You ever earn money as a fighter?" Nicky asked.

"I earned money doin' a lot o' things," Frankie said, "but never fightin'. Only thing I ever got from fightin' were some pretty ribbons and a good deal o' trouble."

"You want to?"

"Want to what? Fight?" Frankie looked closely at Nicky, and in that moment he seemed to sober up. "That's a different story for a different day." The bravado had vanished, and Nicky felt that he was looking at a completely different man. There was a ghost of something around him, as if here was a man carrying something too old for his years.

"It's better than drinking yourself to death," Nicky said.

"Is that what you think?" Frankie Madden asked, but the question was rhetorical and seemed to be for himself alone.

"So?"

"Is that what you do? You some kind of fight organizer?"

"I do a lot of things," Nicky said, "and that includes anything that will make some money."

Frankie nodded. "Well, that's one thing I'll never turn down, so I won't."

Nicky laughed. "You have a strange way of talking."

"As do you," Frankie replied.

"So, are you interested in some work, Mr. Irishman?" Nicky asked once more.

"Fightin' the likes of these fellers here? If that'd be your business, then it seems I'm in the wrong league." Madden looked at Piero and Freddie. "No offense, fellers, but you'd be doin' yourselves a favor if you worked on your stance, your defense arm, and you've got your balance all wrong... Get knocked down in a flash, you will."

"No, not fighting these guys. Real fights. Proper fights. Organized, paid for, people betting hundreds of dollars," Nicky explained.

"And how much'd I be lookin' to earn in this racket?" Frankie asked.

"The sky's the limit," Nicky said. "Good fighters can make anywhere between twenty-five and fifty bucks a fight."

Frankie put his hands in his pockets and took out a handful of coins.

"This is what I have in the world," he said. "Been here three days. Off the boat on Wednesday, and all the promises I was given seem to have been made from nothin' but dust and dreams. I'd be interested in what you're offerin', my friend, but I'll not be lookin' to get my head kicked off, mind."

Nicky laughed. "I like you, you crazy son of a bitch. I think we could make a lot of money together."

"Sounds like the kind of music I could dance to," Frankie Madden said.

FIVE

Lucia Mariani awoke to the plaintive yowling of a dog, and for a moment—just a brief and breathless moment—she believed she was home in Corsica. For a few seconds she could see the forests, the peak of Monte Cinto against the aquamarine skyline, the aromas of *l'Immortelle d'Italie* and *ciste velu* in the maquis scrubland that ran from the coast right up into the mountains. Closing her eyes tight, she could remember the last time she and Nicky had sat in the small garden behind her parents' house in San-Nicolao, her mother bringing freshly baked *falculelle,* that unmistakable smell of chestnuts in the air, her father's laughter, the pipe smoke, the glass of *aquavita* in his hand.

But it was a dream, and nothing more. Lucia knew precisely where she was. The hubbub from the street below, the damp, spiderwebbed plaster ceiling above her, the crowded desperation that seem to fill every run-down tenement and cramped sidewalk of this wretched Italian Harlem. Not only was this place gray and shadowed and filthy, it was also inhospitable and fierce and lonely.

She turned and sat cross-legged on the mattress. She wondered where Nicky was, how early he'd left, what he was doing. No matter what happened, she would always worry about Nicky. He was headstrong and impulsive, and people took it the wrong way. They thought him arrogant and aggressive, but he was simply desperate.

They'd been here over two months, and despite all her dreams and expectations, America had proven to be little more than a nightmare. Nicky said it was the price they needed to pay, and she knew he was right. What she wanted lay at the end of a long and difficult road. She was pragmatic enough to understand that Hollywood was a dream. Since first she'd seen those faces light up a screen the dream had possessed her, and she could not let it go. She didn't want to. Her head was in the stars, and it was near impossible to keep her feet on the ground. Every reality began with a wish. She knew the harder she wished, the faster it would happen, but in this moment, sitting on a thin mattress and looking at the damp-stained walls, it all seemed a million miles away.

From their first encounter with officialdom at Ellis Island, the harsh reality of what she and Nicky had done in leaving Corsica had become ever more present. It had been so much more difficult and challenging than she'd imagined. She was twenty years old, Nicky two years older, and already it felt like they'd reached the lowest point imaginable. There were moments when she really questioned their ability to make it.

"Our fortune is here," Nicky kept reminding her, and he smiled in the way only Nicky could smile. That light in his eyes, that spark of mischief, and you knew he could sell wood to a forest. "I'm brave and resourceful and you're young and beautiful, and we just need to get to California, Lucia. We just need to get there and the world will be ours."

Nicky wasn't driven by greed. People may have thought this, but Lucia recognized something far deeper; she saw Nicky's fear that he would become his father, a small man with small dreams, possessing nothing but a parcel of scrubbed earth from which he barely wrenched sufficient crops to feed his family. Nicky was a dreamer, too, reality and pragmatism supplanted by the belief that charm and confidence alone could carry him to the top of the world and beyond. Maybe it would. Maybe that was the real irony. In truth, the ease with which he saw only what he wanted to see, heard solely what he wanted to hear, was perhaps his greatest asset. He had come to America like a man starved; he did not care what he ate, just as long as he never again knew hunger.

Lucia rose and walked to the window.

She looked down into the street. Already it sprawled with people, the sidewalks like arteries, all of them connected, and yet somehow everyone still appeared to be lost. Compared to home, this was a young city, and yet the streets and sidewalks and buildings seemed exhausted with the effort of making a different future. Smoke from chimneys, the hubbub of voices in the air, the smell of food, the sound of motorcars, and what seemed like a million people crowded together, all of them desperate to find something known only to themselves.

She told herself that people were all the same, not only looking and sounding alike, but feeling the same rough edges and sharp corners of reality.

But she knew that this wasn't true. She knew that most of them never thought beyond today, tomorrow, next week.

Sometimes she wished she had not been cursed with a dream. To want for something more was both a blessing and a curse.

She turned away from the window and walked to the sink. Above it was a cracked and spotted mirror. She held her hair up at the back, smiled, tilted her head, laughed a little.

"Why, yes, Mr. Berkeley," she said. "Of course we can do another take."

And then she let her hair down and closed her eyes for just a moment.

Even as a child, she'd known that where her life had begun was not where it would end. She could sing, she could dance; she was rarely happy unless the limelight found her. Lucia knew she was beautiful, and the world seemed intent on reminding her again and again. She believed what she was told. She was destined for a life of wealth and fame and adoration. She knew it in every ounce of her being. That was the life she was meant to live.

Nicky believed in her, too. Believed with everything he possessed. Sure, he was proud, bullheaded, impulsive, but how much he cared for her was never in doubt. He'd come to America to make his fortune, to do whatever it took to support her. Nicky was one of those rare individuals: bright enough to aspire, sufficiently unaware to acknowledge obstacles. *If you think you can, you can*, he would say. It was as simple as that. But he was impressionable, and Lucia knew how easily he could be seduced by anything that promised money. Temptation was always there, and temptation had so often undermined and overtaken his common sense.

Nicky had found work easily enough, but Lucia didn't much care for the people who'd employed him. They assumed he was Italian, and Nicky let them believe their assumption. Nicky was prepared to do anything they asked. The need to survive so often circumvented morals and honesty. Whatever he was trying to escape, he could not escape his heritage and his blood. He was Corsican, half of him believing the world thought him inferior, half of him knowing he was better than any man alive. Corsicans did not give loyalty easily, but once given it was never taken back. Sons drowned in the blood of their fathers for age-old vendettas. Lucia feared that money would become the sole thing to which Nicky would give his allegiance, and it frightened her. Corruption and crime was rife, and it promised great wealth to those willing to walk that road. She held her tongue, however. Since they'd arrived in America, Nicky had provided for them both. She tolerated, but she did not intend to tolerate long. Getting out of New York and making it to Hollywood was not only the substance of her dreams, but it was also a way to extricate Nicky from New York and all the shadows it harbored.

East of Lexington between 96th and 116th, it seemed that half of Italy had crossed the world looking for something that wasn't there, never had been, and never would be. She and Nicky were not Italian, and had anyone taken the time to consider their history, it would have been all too evident that calling them Italians was the worst kind of insult. That they now spoke French did not make them French; that they had endured five centuries of Genovese rule did not change what they were: Corsicans, in mind and in heart, and fiercely proud of their heritage. Working for the Italians here in Manhattan, Nicky told her, was nothing more than a means to an end.

"They don't need to know who I am. They just need to know that I can do what's asked of me and keep my mouth shut, eh?"

Nicky would smile his Nicky smile, and he would pull her tight until she struggled away.

"Patience, Lucia, patience. The money is coming, I promise, and when it does you'll need to hire people to carry it for you. You just have to trust me, and everything you ever wanted will be yours."

She let it go. She always let it go. He could do that. That was his secret weapon against anyone. Nicky Mariani and his artless charm.

She looked at the clock. It was past nine, and she knew she'd slept so long simply because she couldn't easily face the day.

Crossing the room, she drew the makeshift curtain that hung between her own mattress and that of her brother.

Surveying their squalid quarters, an all-too-familiar sense of disillusionment overcame her. The impulse was to run home, and yet she knew she could never return. The life that awaited her in Corsica was a life that would kill her in the same way that poverty would kill Nicky.

They had yet to gather enough money for a clean and dry place to sleep, let alone the money to buy a car that would take them west. For now it was simply a matter of endurance. She would not complain, for complaining served no purpose at all. She would fetch groceries from the market, she would endure the catcalls and wolf whistles that were the soundtrack to her life. She would set aside her frustrations and disappointment and once again ask anyone she met if there was any hope of work. She could wash clothes, clean houses, mind children. She was neither proud nor entitled.

Lucia dressed in clothes that took so much time to keep clean and pressed in such a place. The simple cotton slips and dresses that were suited to a Corsican summer climate were scant protection against the bitter breezes that seemed to find her wherever she walked. The Saturday-morning market would be finishing in an hour or so, and prices were always better at the end. A handful of dollars, that's all they had between them, and unless Nicky brought some more money soon they would starve.

Lucia went down two flights of stairs, the squawling of hungry babies, of arguments, of life in all its raw and awkward madness seemed to spill from every half-open doorway, every landing and window. The smell was indescribable: sour milk, toilets, rotting food, unwashed men, and liquor. She held her hand across her face, but nevertheless it crept through the pores of her skin.

Out through the door and into the street she went, at once experiencing some small relief. The sky was bright, the day cool, and she hurried up toward the corner of Second.

Here a million lives intersected a million more. Harlem was a world all its own, and even though she knew she would never belong, there was something about the atmosphere that made her wish she could. Family was everything, community too, and it seemed that in the most difficult of circumstances people found the greatest reserves of kindness.

Children played in the street. They ran and laughed, their clothes nothing better than ill-fitting hand-me-downs, but they were so very much alive. Mothers stood talking in doorways and on stoops, some of them pausing to smile at Lucia. There were the obligatory wolf whistles and *Ciao, bella!* as she passed the gatherings of men at street corners, smoking, arguing, joking with one another as they waited for the cars and trucks that came down to fetch them for piecework and day-rate laboring jobs. They were good people, people who'd come here with the dream of a better future, still holding on to those dreams as if to let go would see the end of all hope. What they wanted was simple—enough food, enough money to take care of their families, a fair wage for a fair day's work.

Lucia reached the market and was in luck. She started gathering her vegetables— tomatoes, onions, fresh garlic. She was fortunate to find a man selling pork chops that were still pink and bloody.

She paid for the meat, dropped the package into the bag with the vegetables, and headed back toward the apartment. She hurried, conscious that unaccompanied girls had often been robbed of their groceries. Work was scarce, money was scarcer; the devil danced in empty pockets.

The thought gave her a sense of unease, and she was relieved to reach the corner of 106th.

She could see Nicky down near the front door of the tenement building. Freddie and Piero were with him, and she hoped that they were not all expecting to be fed. Nicky was so often generous with no thought for consequence. It was an endearing trait, but you couldn't survive on traits. And then she saw a fourth man. He was young, perhaps even younger than herself, his fair complexion and pale eyes suggesting something other than Italian. The Italian boys sculpted their hair flat to the scalp with Vaseline or Murray's or Dixie Peach. They wore secondhand shirts and silk ties and suits a size too big that gave them broader shoulders. This stranger was out of place, lost perhaps, incongruous in his rough tweed trousers, his collarless shirt and cap.

Even as she neared the small gathering the young man looked up. Whatever words he'd been sharing with her brother became unimportant. He just looked at her, as if it was impossible for him to look away.

His intensity made her uncomfortable. She felt awkward, hollow.

Nicky turned and saw her, too.

"Lucia!" he shouted.

Lucia approached the steps. She smiled, greeted both Piero and Freddie. Nicky grabbed her and hugged her, kissed her cheek.

"This is a new friend of ours," Nicky said.

The young man took off his cap. "Miss," he said.

"This is my sister," Nicky said. "Lucia."

Again the young man bowed his head respectfully. "Miss Lucia."

She did not recognize his accent. He wasn't Italian, that was certain; nor did he sound American. There were a handful of Scots and Canadians in the neighborhood, though differentiating between them was all but impossible.

"This is Frankie Madden."

Lucia smiled. "Mr. Madden."

"Frankie is a fighter, born and bred," Nicky said.

Lucia's expression noticeably changed. Her thoughts ranged somewhere between aggravation and disbelief. What was Nicky up to now?

"Nicky, you said—"

Nicky raised his hand. "Not now," he said. "We're talkin' business with Frankie."

Lucia looked at Frankie Madden. "You're a fighter?" Immediately she knew her reaction to the appearance of this stranger was justified. Nicky was concocting some wild plan again, something irresponsible, if not illegal.

Lucia looked at Frankie unerringly. He seemed uncomfortable, as if her presence alone somehow intimidated him. "Yes, miss, I am," he said.

"Then you're as stupid as my brother and his two stupid friends."

Frankie made no attempt to hide his surprise.

"What the hell, Lucia!" Nicky exclaimed. "You can't just call people stupid. What are you doing?"

"I'm wondering how much crazier you could be, Nicky. You said that you weren't going to do this anymore—"

"There's money in it, Lucia, and you know it. Last fight, our guy went away with twenty-five bucks—"

"And half a dozen stitches in his face, a broken hand, a cracked skull," Lucia interjected. "Nicky, you promised me that—"

Nicky turned to his sister with a look of dismay. "Lucia, seriously. Enough of this. This is business, okay? This is nothing for you to be concerned about."

She shook her head. "You're such a fool, Nicky. Sometimes you are such a fool."

Lucia gave each of them—Frankie Madden included—one more disapproving look, and then she left them where they were, the four idiot men, and went up the steps to the door of the tenement.

SIX

To Danny McCabe, it all seemed an age ago. His memory was uncertain, images here and there appearing as if through smoke. He remembered Liam Banwell's voice: *They say we never forget, but them English bastards have as long a memory as anyone. They catch him, they're gonna do their worst, no doubt about it.*

And another voice, a younger man.

So, after Pembroke, where's he goin' then?

God almighty knows, but wherever they send him, hell ain't gonna be too much farther along the road, that's for sure.

And then slipping away again, losing all sense of time and orientation.

He remembered struggling to sit at some point, the pain of his cracked ribs lancing through him like fire.

The younger one—Brendan—gave him whiskey, told him to keep still.

Ye've done all the fightin' you'll be doin' for a good while yet. Stay down, feller. Stay down.

Danny closed his eyes. He thought of Erin.

When he woke again the pain was less.

"You know what happened back there?" he asked.

"Your mate tells me you done busted up a copper," Liam Banwell said. "Said you were a man possessed."

He asked about Jimmy O'Connell and Micky Cavanaugh.

"They're off and away, mate. Gone like the mist. You kept your tongue, and Johnny Madden's dead now, so no one will ever know who was there in Clonegal."

"Johnny is dead?"

"Aye, he is. Shades put a bullet in his head. Dead 'fore he hit the ground. He was the one who got ye out o' Clonmel. Owe him your life, you do."

Brendan brought more whiskey.

Danny sat up slowly.

Liam raised his glass. "May the devil make a ladder o' your backbone."

They drank. Danny coughed, winced with pain. Brendan returned with bandages, and he and Liam bound Danny's torso even more tightly so he could move without such discomfort.

"Be a while to heal, it will," Liam said, "but I think you're gonna have a good deal more troubles to care about than a busted rib. At least for the time being."

"Where you after takin' me?" Danny asked.

"The harbor, boat over to Pembroke Dock, and then I don't know... don't want to know, if truth be told."

"Wales?" Danny asked.

"Closest place that's somewheres else. We just gotta get you out, lad. That's all there is to it."

Danny did not want to, but he understood perfectly.

This was a war. He was a terrorist and a fugitive—inadvertent, perhaps, but that changed nothing. He didn't know how long he'd be running, nor if he'd ever be able to stop.

He couldn't clearly remember what had happened after facing up to Bobby Durnin, and in that moment he didn't want to remember.

He closed his eyes, pictured Erin's face.

Danny confronted the strong possibility that he might never see his sisters again, never see Clonegal or his ma. None of this.

Whatever past he may have had, he'd now smashed it to pieces and there was no hope of repair.

From the freezing cold night he'd spent hunkered in the stinking bowels of the fishing boat ferrying him from Waterford to Pembroke Dock, on to the cramped claustrophobia of steerage aboard the SS *Excalibur* between Genoa and New York, Danny had been living as if in a dream. That dream, however, was haunted by all the colors of a nightmare.

He was berthed in a cabin with five other men—all Italian, none of whom spoke a word of English. The Italians talked quietly among themselves and made no effort to include him. They sensed Danny's anger and despair, and many times he would simply pull his knees to his chest, roll onto his side, and weep for all he was leaving behind. It was a torment and a penance, a premonition of the sentence that awaited him when he finally had to face what he'd done. He was going to hell, and there was nothing to be done about it.

Danny's restless sleeping hours were invaded by images of

Carmody, of the flames that had torn so ferociously through that building, the roiling smoke, the insufferable heat. He didn't know what had happened to the man; nor did he know what had happened to Bobby Durnin. And then came thoughts of Erin and his sisters, thoughts too of his father, holed up somewhere with a gang of friends who would stay friends as long as the whiskey lasted. Lastly his ma, the way she'd look at him. *Eejut,* she'd say. *I raised up an eejut, so I did.* Open his mouth, twitch a muscle to respond, and she'd clatter his ears with calloused hands and leave him deaf for a week.

Somewhere in amid all the images and emotions and disturbing thoughts, he would drift away into yet another vague and restless sleep, murmuring to himself, agitated and disturbed.

The fear that gripped him was a powerful and relentless thing. It seemed that everyone who looked at him could see what he'd done. He was transparent, a phantom, his sins there for the world to behold, consigned to fight with demons that were set to tear him apart.

When daylight crept through the thin curtains over the porthole of his berth, he leaned close to the glass and looked out at the endless sea. Once or twice he thought of just hurling himself into the ocean, of being done with all of it, of making everyone's life so much simpler by just vanishing into the depths of the Atlantic. But he did not. Suicide was not only a mortal sin, it was also an admission of defeat.

Irish Nationalist sympathizers had paid his way. Without ever telling him what they wanted in return, they'd fed him, clothed him, provided him with the paperwork to support a new identity, then secured him a berth on a transatlantic vessel and sent him to America. He went under the name Francis Madden; that had been his choice, a tribute and an acknowledgment to the man who'd saved his life.

The journey to America was in itself surreal. Steerage was crammed with those wishing to escape their past in the hope that an unknown future would be better. It was a gamble, as were so many things in life, and Frankie Madden, as he now had to think of himself, was perhaps gambling most of all.

It wasn't long before he found some other Irish emigrants, huddled there along the plain deal benches in the dining area. They had come from all over the country, their eyes and voices bright with hope, defying seasickness, bad food, the rolling and lurching of the ship, the breathless confinement of the lowest decks. Their belief was strong; it had to be. Different words perhaps, but the prayer was the same from every mouth. It would all come right in America. America was El Dorado, land of milk and honey, a paradise in the making. If a man was willing to work, then that man could own the world.

"And for you?" a woman had asked him. "What's out there for you?"

Danny had looked at her, his eyes wide, his mind empty, his heart swollen with heartbreaking loss, and he had not been able to say a word.

"Whatever it is, it'll find you," she said. "You can be sure of that."

He could interpret her words as nothing but some dark premonition of whatever he might find on the other side of the Atlantic.

It was on the evening of the third day that Danny got a glimpse of his true situation.

He'd taken a walk on deck, stood there by the rails for a while and watched the waves lash against the side of the ship, a strange sense of vertigo and nausea disorientating him further. He'd spent just a few minutes watching the rich folks as they promenaded along the covered walkways before turning away. Inside it was warm and well lit; gentlemen sipped brandy and enjoyed fine cigars; women sat in groups playing cards and sharing anecdotes.

This was the world of the Smoke Room & Bar, the Country Club Veranda Café, an invitation to dinner with Captain Groves and Chief Officer Stevens, berthing on A Deck, looking forward to a fine view of the New York skyline. The *Excalibur* would dock on the morning of Wednesday, 23rd of March, 1938, and someone would be there to carry bags for these people, to open the doors of a limousine . . . and Danny wondered for just a little while how it would feel to be important, influential, to be somebody that mattered. No sooner had he imagined such a thing than reality crept around those thoughts and snatched them away. The ghost of his past would always be there, and he knew no matter the efforts he made to forget it, it would never forget him.

With an all-too-familiar sense of despair haunting him, he returned to the door, to the long and narrow staircase that would return him to his berth. It was as he reached the bottom of the second flight that they came for him. They came without warning, two of them, and even though he resisted with everything he possessed, it was futile. The men that held him were far greater in size and strength than he, and they quickly subdued his protests and frog-marched him away.

"What the hell? Where are you taking me?" he yelled. He heard the fear in his own voice. His breathing was constricted, his chest tight.

"We go through this door now," the one to his right said, his accent anything but Irish. "Say a word, put up any struggle, and you'll be overboard, you understand?"

Danny didn't answer.

The hand around his throat was an iron vise.

"You understand?"

Danny nodded, already struggling to breathe.

They went through the door. Danny did not resist, even when they let go of his arms.

A further corridor, a short flight of steps, and then they were outside a cabin door.

As far as Danny could work out, they were on the upper landing near the prow of the ship.

The man on the left knocked once, and without waiting for a response, the door was opened and Danny was manhandled through and pushed down to his hands and knees.

A pillowcase was forced over his head, and he was once again hauled to his feet.

His heart thundered. His ribs hurt with such a fierce pain. His arms were pinioned. They walked him several steps and pushed him down into a chair.

The hands that had held him so tightly let go. He sat there breathless, utterly stricken.

"Mr. McCabe," a voice said.

The voice was calm, measured, immediately identifiable as English. The diction was precise and succinct, that of an educated man.

"Perhaps we shouldn't use your given name anymore. Mr. Francis Madden is the name you've chosen to employ, or so I understand?" The question was rhetorical.

Danny's hands were sweating. He could sense the two men behind him, knew that any movement would serve no purpose. They could kill him right where he sat, throw his body over the side of the ship and that would be the last anyone saw or heard of him. Who were they? Perhaps English police or a private agency intent on returning him to Clonmel. The Garda had their contacts, their informants, their allies—even deep within the IRB—and discovering where he'd gone had only ever been a matter of time.

"You got yourself involved with some Fenians, didn't you, my friend?" the voice went on.

And then, almost as an aside, he said, "Take it off."

The pillowcase was removed, and it took a while for Danny's eyes to adjust to the darkness of the room.

A seated figured, a lampstand behind him, over which had been placed a scarf to shade the light.

The man—nothing more than a silhouette—was smoking a cigarette. Beside him on a low table was a bottle, from which he poured an inch or two into a glass. He extended the glass toward Danny, and one of the men came from behind to fetch it. He handed it to Danny. Danny took it without question.

It was Scotch, and a good Scotch at that.

"Are we . . . what do you call them? The shades?" There was a smile in the man's voice. "The answer to your question is no. We are not the shades. We are the people who took you out of Ireland and put you on this boat, young man."

Danny tried to say something, but his throat was dry. He took another drink and coughed.

The man facing him was still and silent. He let Danny settle.

"I'm in your debt," Danny said.

"That you are, my friend. That you are."

"John Carmody," the man said. "That was the name of your man in the Garda station, correct?"

Danny hesitated.

"Answer the question."

"Yes," Danny said. "That's right. John Carmody."

"He's going to be okay. That's the word I have right now. His burns will heal, and he'll recover quickly enough from the smoke inhalation."

"Thank you for telling me," Danny said.

The man then leaned forward and lowered his voice. "Your copper in Clonmel," he said, "is a different story, however."

"I don't remember what happened. I remember fighting him, but after that it all seems to have disappeared."

"I'll tell you what happened," the man said. "You beat him to death. You beat that man to death with your bare fists."

Danny felt the color blanch from his face.

He remembered Durnin, he remembered the gun in the man's

hand, he remembered how Durnin had set the gun aside and they had gone at it like hurricanes, but somewhere within that furious clash of fists everything had just vanished.

The images, the feelings, the awareness of what had happened was nothing but a blank.

"I . . . I don't know—"

"You don't need to say anything," the man said. "We knew Durnin. We knew what he'd done, what a vicious bastard he was, and he had it coming. Had it not been you, it would soon enough have been someone else."

"But—"

"But nothing. You are here. We will soon arrive in America. You have ceased to be Daniel McCabe, and you are now Francis Madden. We have paid your passage, and we will give you money to find somewhere to live in New York. But we own you, Mr. Madden . . . We own you."

The man fell silent. The words sank in, and Danny felt a cold hand around his heart.

"Your hometown of Clonegal," the man eventually said. "*Cluain na nGall* in your mother tongue, if I'm not mistaken. That place has seen its fair share of horrors, has it not?" There was a lighter tone in the man's voice now, yet somehow edged with cruelty. "Meadow of the Foreigner, Cromwell's soldiers called it. Confederate Wars. Routed your people, massacred every man still breathing."

Danny knew the history, as did every man in County Carlow.

"Someone will come to you," the man said. "When, how, it doesn't matter, but they will come. They will tell you they're from the Meadow of the Foreigner. Whatever they ask you to do will be toward the debt you owe us."

Again, the man paused to let the true significance of his words arrive.

"Do we understand each other, Mr. Madden?"

Danny just stared at the dark shape in the corner of the room. The aftertaste of Scotch burned in his throat. He felt light-headed, and when he opened his mouth to speak, there were no words forthcoming.

"Tell me you understand, Mr. Madden."

"Y-yes . . . Yes, I understand you," Danny replied.

"Rest," the man said. "You need to get your strength back. You have a good deal of traveling ahead of you."

Danny leaned back and looked at the ceiling.

There was no other way to describe how he felt... as if something other than himself was inside his body. He had saved John Carmody only to kill Bobby Durnin.

He closed his eyes. The guilt and shame drowned him. He would always and forever be in debt to these people. More than that, he knew he would never be able to go home.

Caught between the devil and something worse, his life—whatever he might have made of it—was no longer his own.

It was like a bullet through his heart, and his world collapsed.

"We will be in touch, Mr. Madden," were the last words Danny heard, and then the pillowcase was over his head once more.

"Stand up," one of the men behind him said.

Danny did as he was asked, and then a train collided with the side of his head.

He went out like a light.

SEVEN

Four months had elapsed between that terrible night in Clonmel and the moment Danny McCabe first shared words with Nicky Mariani.

Whatever remnants of his life might still have remained in Clonegal had to be forgotten forever.

Danny had to think of himself as a man without a past. His name was Frankie Madden. He had to believe himself to be nothing other than who he'd become. Even in his mind, even within the privacy of his own thoughts, he had to forget the name McCabe, forget his home, his sisters, everything of his earlier life. If people asked, he was an East Coast native, second-generation Irish-American. He was allied to the Irish-American faction of the Republican Brotherhood, as fiercely nationalistic as those at home, perhaps even more so due to the simple fact that those abroad rarely had to put their words into action.

As to what would be asked of him, he had no idea. The mere thought of it silenced his mind and hurried his heart. Was he now to help raise funds for the cause? Worst of all, did they think him capable of killing people?

He'd tried to believe that America would give him a second chance: a new name, a new country, a hope for the future. He could always fight—that had been a mainstay and an anchor for as long as he could remember—and yet knowing the truth of what had happened in Ireland now threatened everything.

Upon disembarkation he'd been given a small amount of money and the address of a two-room apartment over a butcher's shop on East 99th Street. His anonymous sponsors had paid the rent for six months in advance. The money had vanished before he even knew where it was going. He was broke, in need of a job, and awaiting instructions for whatever duties he was destined to fulfill. Maybe those instructions would never come. Perhaps these people enjoyed the sense of rebelliousness and notoriety that came with harboring and helping a fugitive from the law. Perhaps they were filthy with money, had some gripe with the British government, so allying themselves with Irish nationalists and German socialists alike was a way of saying *Fuck you* to the government without ever needing to spill blood or dirty their hands.

But Frankie Madden had no way of knowing who they were or what they intended, and would not find out until they contacted him again.

Someone would come from the *Meadow of the Foreigner*, and he would have to face the consequences of his past.

That late Saturday afternoon, Frankie Madden sat in a bar on 104th with Nicky Mariani, Piero Altamura, and Frederico Cova. Whatever hatchet needed to be buried between Frankie and Nicky's two compadres was buried quickly. They could tell Frankie was a born fighter. There was no shame in getting your ass kicked from a man whose business it was to kick asses; any such bitterness would have been akin to grieving over a lost game of Irish Poker with Clancy McCabe.

The four of them drank and talked, and the talk was fighting talk. From what Frankie understood, Nicky Mariani and his friends were part of some underground bareknuckle-fighting circuit. This was Italian Harlem, and here the Italian-American families ruled the roost. Nicky—despite being neither Italian nor part of any organized crime family—had ingratiated himself into the machinery of the thing. It was known as the *bullpen*, an ever-changing makeshift venue where illegal fights were staged, wagered on, won and lost. There was money to be made, but it was a brutal and unforgiving way to make it.

"There are people here you don't wanna get involved with," Nicky explained. "The shit that goes down here is like nothin' you ever seen. Last year, May, right? That thing with that shadow guy."

Piero nodded.

"This guy," Nicky went on. "Name was Ferdinand Boccia. They called him the Shadow. He gets himself killed by two guys, Willie Gallo and Ernest Rupolo. This guy, Rupolo, they call him the Hawk."

"Genovese family," Freddie said. "You heard of the Genoveses, right?"

Frankie shook his head. "I don't know anything about these people."

"Well, okay, so Vito Genovese is one of the big bosses here," Nicky explained. "These are one of the five families that run the show. They take a piece of everything that happens in New York, even when there ain't a piece to give. Taxicabs, garbage, bookmaking, gambling, coffee shops, lunchrooms, hair salons, hotels . . . Everyone who takes a dollar gotta give a piece of that dollar or they get themselves closed down. That's just the way it is, and either you pay up or you move someplace else."

"And you work with these people?" Frankie asked.

Nicky smiled. "We do what we got to. Lot of money here. Better to have a little of something than all of nothing."

"So you want me to fight in this bullpen. That's what you're asking."

"The offer's there, Frankie. Looks like you know how to take care of yourself. Looks like you got what it takes. Most of these clowns are muleheaded giants, all beef, no smarts. They lumber around the place thumping people, knock a few down, win some fights, but they got no style. They got no grace, no panache." Nicky laughed. "Learned this word yesterday. 'Panache.' It's a good word. Means—"

"I know what it means," Frankie said.

"Well, okay," Nicky said. "Mr. Dictionary here knows what the freakin' word means."

Frankie glanced at Altamura, then at Cova; neither of them seemed to know where to look.

Frankie didn't yet know what to make of Nicky Mariani. He certainly didn't appear stupid, but who was he to judge? He'd angled his way through school, did the best he could, but he was no university professor. Given the choice between books and boxing, there had never been a contest.

Maybe Nicky's attitude was borne out of some sort of insecurity. A little fish in a big pond. He was older than Frankie, but not by a great deal, and yet there was something impetuous in his manner, like he was hurrying toward something he didn't fully understand. He possessed a manic quality that Frankie had seen before. Back in Ireland there were those who said the right thing, made all the brave noises, but when it came to doing something . . . well, then it was quite a different story. Maybe Nicky was one of those guys. Only time would tell. Nevertheless, it was almost impossible not to like him. There was something contagious about his manner; energy and enthusiasm came running off of him and you were caught up in it whether you wanted to be or not.

"I'll take a shot at it," Frankie said. "What the hell, eh? What's the worst thing that could happen?"

"Could get your head knocked off," Freddie said.

"Sure I could, but it wouldn't be the first time. My head screws right back on anyways."

Nicky laughed. "You're a funny guy."

"I ain't even started," Frankie replied. "So when do we do this?"

"You need time to get yourself straight for this?" Nicky asked. "You need to get ready?"

Frankie shook his head. "It's only a fight. What would I need to do? Get a drink in me, maybe."

"You have no idea, my friend. Some of these guys are fucking animals."

"I was raised in a zoo."

"Tomorrow," Freddie said. "I know where."

"What? You can just show up uninvited?"

"You can show up if you're invited by us," Nicky replied. "We gotta ask Don Casale. Don Casale is the one who puts this together. Nothing happens without his okay. Meet us here. Five o'clock tomorrow."

"You boys'll not be gettin' yourselves to church then? You'll be fightin' on a Sunday?"

Nicky laughed again. "Oh man, you are gonna kill me with this shit."

Frankie watched the three of them get up and leave half-empty glasses on the table. Sure as hell, these people were from a different world.

Later, alone in his apartment, Frankie stood at the window and looked down into the darkening street. The lights flickered, and people walked beneath them and then vanished like ghosts. It was cold, and the shadows beyond the window seemed to beckon to him.

He thought of Nicky's sister, Lucia. Something inside of her was on fire. She was going somewhere. She possessed some quality he recognized in himself. Nicky was driven, too, but driven by money, perhaps by the need to be taken seriously among his contemporaries. Were they good people to get involved with? He didn't know, but he felt there was no choice. He wanted to fight, *needed* to fight, and if this was the only way to do that, then so be it.

Thoughts of home and family filled his mind. He only had to think of the little one, Erin, fifteen years old in a little more than three weeks, and his heart started to crack. She would be missing him terribly; he knew that with certainty. They had been so close, and the age gap between Erin and her elder sisters was such that she would now be alone. Though she could be a wild one with the best of them, Deirdre had a big heart and would perhaps take Erin under her wing.

And then came thoughts of his father—the drinker, the liar, the finest friend a man could have until the whiskey ran dry—and he wondered what he thought of all that had happened.

Frankie Madden needn't have wasted his time, for Clancy McCabe had been dead the better part of three months. He'd lived long enough to see his only son arrested, charged with arson, grievous assault, and murder, escaped and on the run, but the drink had already done its worst. In the first week of January 1938 he'd fallen down dead in the street. Though a good many folks were relieved, none were surprised. Some said his heart gave out. Some said he never had a heart in the first place. His last words, perhaps nothing more than apocryphal, were from the Shawnee chief, Tecumseh: *Sing your death song, and die like a hero going home.* Why Clancy McCabe would even know Tecumseh's words, and why he would quote an ally of the British would be a mystery going with him to his grave. The prevalent question among those who actually knew the man was why it'd taken this long to see the back of the drunken bastard. He was a man neither well loved nor well respected.

Grania McCabe had lost the only two men in her life within a matter of weeks, and there was nothing to be done about it. Loss was inevitable; grieving was not. She had her three daughters, and they needed all the support and guidance she could give. Erin was not well. That was altogether clear. When Grania looked at her face she saw something; when she looked in her eyes she saw something else entirely. Grania took time to speak to the older two. She told them to keep an eye on their little sister. Deirdre did the best she could, but the age gap was a ravine. Erin was tough. She had survived her father living, just as they all had, and she could survive her father's death. The bruises he'd left behind lay deep beneath the skin and did not easily show themselves. Grania couldn't answer Erin when questions were asked of Danny. Danny was gone, could well be dead. That fierce bastard Johnny Madden was in his sorrowful grave and could shed no light on anything, least of all Danny's whereabouts. Rumor had it that Danny had gone to the mainland, that people sympathetic to the Irish struggle were taking care of him. That told her both everything and nothing. That could well have meant that he'd been quietly done away with to avoid embarrassment and later complications. Bobby Durnin was dead, the blood was on Danny's hands, and now he'd vanished. It was all so much history, and history belonged nowhere but the past.

Frankie Madden closed the curtains and lay down on his bed. He hoped the dreams would not come tonight. He did not want to see Bobby Durnin's broken, bloodied face leering up at him through the darkness to frighten him awake. Most of all, he did not want to hear Erin crying in the dark, pleading for him to come home.

EIGHT

Early on Sunday morning, Nicky left Lucia sleeping and headed out to see Julie at the lunchroom on 116th.

He would get some breakfast and wait until the Italians were done with church. These people were a contradiction: Sunday-morning mass, lunch with the family, spend the afternoon collecting debts, breaking fingers, and hammering holes in people's heads. In the evening they'd watch men thump one another stupid, then head home to kiss their wives and kids good night.

Nicky wasn't opposed to violence. For some people it was the only language they understood. He had a problem with hypocrisy, however. If you were crooked you were crooked. It was that simple. Especially now, work as scarce as it was, you had to do whatever it took in order to get by. If that meant affecting an Italian accent to get your foot in a door, then so be it. If survival required holding on to some guns, losing a couple of knives in the murky depths of Hell Gate, then this was just the nature of things. His father would have understood. Saveriu Mariani, as Corsican as they came, was old-school. He wasn't a gangster, far less a drug dealer, but he was a staunch nationalist. He did what he could to aid and abet the nationalist movement, but had you asked him about it you would have met nothing but silence. The look in his eyes would communicate volumes to those who knew how to read such an expression.

Saveriu Mariani's blood ran through the veins of his son. Yes, he would most definitely have understood.

Lucia, however, was a different story. Lucia wanted the world to be some way it would never be. Nicky loved her for her who she was, for her passion, her imagination, but sometimes she refused to see what was right in front of her eyes. She was a dreamer, which was all well and good, but dreams did not put food on the table.

Nicky knew that the bullpen was where he needed to be. He held coats, fetched coffee and sandwiches, carried money, anything they wanted. This was a world Lucia would never understand. These were old-timers, been in New York for years. They knew their business.

As Julie had told him, you had to climb a ladder from the first rung, no matter how high it went. Determination was everything. Every single one of these guys had begun the same way, no doubt about it. So if they called him *Little Nicky*, maybe he didn't like it, but he sure wasn't going to argue. He followed orders, and followed them good.

Down in the derelict warehouses and stockyards, in the parking garages and basements, these guys would be shepherded in. They all looked the same. Two hundred pounds of horsemeat shaped like a man. Prominent foreheads, fists like ham hocks, half a dozen teeth between them. They were fighters, sure, but only after a fashion. A real fighter had grace and style. A real fighter was quick of foot and quicker of mind. A real fighter could see where an opponent was headed before the opponent arrived, and have a devastating roundhouse for a welcoming party. If Nicky was right in his estimation, then Frankie Madden was like that. Freddie Cova and Piero Altamura were not altogether useless when it came to a street fight, but Frankie Madden had floored them drunk. Hadn't even broken a sweat. And he didn't shame them either, which was the sign of an even better fighter. There was no preening or gloating. It was just business.

Nicky knew what needed to be done. He had given his word to their parents. He would look after Lucia. He would take care of everything. He would get her to Hollywood just as he'd promised. The end justified the means. It was not complicated.

Frankie Madden would go to the bullpen. He'd knock a few heads apart and make some money. He was a meal ticket, a bus ride, and that was all there was to it. The more men Frankie put down, the closer the Marianis would be to California.

Of course, Lucia didn't want Nicky anywhere near this territory. But what was he to do? Did she have a better idea? No, she didn't. If she knew a better way, then he would listen, but she hadn't said anything worth hearing.

So, today was the day. Sunday evening, a debut fight, Frankie could crack a couple of skulls and made some pocket change. Nicky would make ten times whatever Frankie made, but he was the manager, the one with the introductions, and if Frankie proved himself as good as Nicky believed, then there was going to be a great deal more money to follow.

"You been in church, kiddo?" was Julie's greeting for Nicky at the lunchroom.

"Tried to get in. They told me to go away. Said I was a lost cause."

"Then you need to pray to Saint Jude, my friend. Patron Saint of Desperate Cases and Lost Causes. He'll take care of you."

"You got his number?"

"Someplace for sure. I'll give him a call, put in a good word for you."

Nicky took a seat at the counter. Julie made him an espresso.

"So, what's happening today?" Julie asked. He wiped down the counter with a rag and then tucked it into the pocket of his apron.

"Got a fighter I want to bring in," Nicky said. "Figured maybe I could speak to Mr. Casale."

"Oh, you did, did you?" Julie said, his eyebrows raised.

"I gotta get a foot in the door sometime."

"Most guys try to get their foot in the door end up losing their toes."

Nicky drank the coffee. He reached for cigarettes, lit one, said nothing.

"You're serious, aren't you?" Julie asked.

"Serious as night follows day."

Julie laughed. "You gotta stop sayin' shit like that, kid. That doesn't even fuckin' make sense. Serious as night follows day. You mean *sure* as night follows day."

"Whatever, Julie, you know? I just need a break here."

"You really wanna have a sit-down with Luca Casale."

"You know any other way to get new blood into the bullpen?"

"You got a point."

"So he comes here after church, right? He always comes here after church, regular as clockwork."

"Sure he does."

"So you can have a word, see if he'll give me a minute."

Julie didn't respond. He took the rag and wiped the counter once more.

"I'll owe you," Nicky said.

"Owe me what?"

"What d'you want?"

"You give me your sister—"

Nicky was off the counter stool.

"Hell, take it easy, kid . . . Jeez, you are such a hothead. I am kiddin'! You know I'm kiddin'."

"You don't kid about that, Julie. Seriously, man, she's my baby sister."

Julie reached out and gave Nicky's forearm a conciliatory squeeze. "Lighten up, Nicky boy. These guys say the most outrageous shit, believe me. They ain't serious. She's a great-looking girl, and there's gonna be hound dogs lining up on your porch once they get her scent. You gotta relax a little. You get uptight around these guys, they're gonna chop off your fingers and throw you in the West Channel. You wanna do business in this neighborhood, you gotta be smooth as silk."

Nicky listened; Julie was worth listening to, and the man could get him in front of Casale.

Julie made Nicky another espresso.

"So, tell me about your fighter."

"An Irisher. Dumb as a fence post, but took my boys down in a flash."

"You know it's gonna cost you plenty. You use Casale as an introduction, then he's gonna take twenty-five percent of whatever you win."

"Twenty-five percent of something is better than a hundred percent of nothin'."

"Well, that's true, kid, but when you deal with these kind of people, you ain't only payin' in dollars. You pay in loyalty, as well. They want something done, then it gets done. They say you take somethin' someplace, you better just take it and don't be askin' what it is or where it came from, know what I mean?"

"Sure I do. Business is business. I'm prepared, Julie. This two-bit bullshit isn't for me. I don't wanna stay down here. I wanna good place to live, wanna be able to get my kid sister out to Hollywood—"

"Is that what she wants? She a movie star now?"

"You seen her, man. She's a natural."

"I'll give you one thing, kid. You is a big thinker. No small dreams for you, eh?"

"You know where I come from, Julie?"

"Sure I do. Some island in France or something."

"Corsica. That's where. You know who else came from there?"

"Go on, tell me."

"Napoléon Bonaparte. You've heard of him?"

"Sure I have."

"He said, 'Death is nothing, but to live defeated and inglorious is to die daily.' I ain't gonna live and die down here in these backstreets and tenements, Julie. I got a big dream, sure, but better to have a big dream and work for it than get to the end of your life and ask yourself where the hell it all went. I didn't come all the way to America to be a nobody."

"You knock yourself out, kid. You're gonna be a star, for sure."

"I am, Julie. Lucia too. She's gonna have her name in lights and her face on all them billboards in Hollywood."

"So, we start with the bullpen. Time we got?" Julie glanced at the clock on the back wall. "Be back here in an hour. I'll speak to Mr. Casale. You come give him your pitch. We see what happens, okay?"

"I owe you, Julie. I really do."

"Well, you can pay me back by getting you and your pretty kid sister out of here and then go cause some trouble in Hollywood, okay?"

"I'm gonna do it," Nicky said. "You just wait and see."

NINE

The spirit returned. There was no doubt about it. There was fire and life in him, and he felt it coursing through his veins and strengthening his bones and he knew there was nothing in him but railway sleepers and tire irons and awkward jags of dark slate cut right from the face of a mountain. He was a rock, and he was indestructible.

Frankie stood resolute and ready, stripped to the waist, his laces tied tight and tucked inside his boots, socks pulled up over the cuffs of his pants, his face smeared with Vaseline, his fists like hammers. This was the bullpen, and the atmosphere was charged and fierce and electric.

The man confronting him was slight and short, but every inch of him was muscle. He looked to be constructed from sinew and little else. His eyes were glazed, as if he saw nothing beyond three feet, and Frankie had yet to enter his line of vision. His hands were calloused, the knuckles toughened by repetitive smacks against hard flesh and harder bone, and there was no doubt in Frankie's mind that the man was a contender. There was also no doubt in Frankie's mind that he could win.

Frankie kept right on with that belief until his opponent—a seasoned veteran of the bullpen called Stanley "Wasp" Gallagher—hit him broadside and sent him reeling into the crowd. The crowd pushed him back, jeering and hollering, and Frankie dodged to the left as another fist whistled past his ear. The man could fight, but that glazed vacancy in his eyes was worrying. It unnerved Frankie, as if he was fighting someone who was all but physically absent. Wasp was quick, no question, but Frankie could be quicker.

Frankie weaved back and forth, but Wasp followed him like bonfire smoke. Frankie took one strike after another, felt his nose bloody up, his lip cut, and there was a sense that he might have called this too soon. Wasp had done this before, Frankie was a newcomer, and this was a world apart from the Carlow County Trophy matches he'd fought at home.

Second round, Wasp barely bruised, Frankie's head was swimming. He thought of Erin, how she would cheer him on, screaming at the top of her lungs for him to finish it. Frankie found the well of resolve, and he drew deep from it. This was his debut, his first fight in New York, and every doubt he'd had, every moment of despair he'd felt in Clonmel, in Pembroke, even as he crossed the Atlantic about how he would never fight again, was banished from his mind.

Danny did not think of Carmody, nor of Durnin. He did not think of his past or the ghosts that would forever follow him. He kept his mind where it belonged, right there in the moment, and he went back like fury.

When he took yet another punishing strike from Wasp's cast-iron right, he thought of Lucia Mariani. Something happened in his thoughts. He imagined her watching him, imagined her standing right there at the edge of the makeshift ring, her hands grasping the rope, her knuckles white with tension, and he asked himself what the hell kind of fighter he was.

Frankie Madden came into the third round a different man. He gained some ground, stunned Wasp with a couple of merciless kidney punches, and when the fourth round began he could see that Wasp was now wary of this teenager from nowhere.

A minute in and Frankie lunged back, evaded a killer swipe, and used the impetus of his return to connect with Wasp Gallagher's face. Frankie had a right hook that could put a horse on the deck, and Wasp got right in the road of that and felt the reverberations through every inch of his skeleton. The man was not going to take it easily, and he roared back, the rage visible in his eyes. He stung with that left, just as his name implied, and Frankie was back against the ropes, hands on his shoulders pushing him back into the fray, merely thirty seconds of the fourth remaining.

A low crushing blow into Wasp's solar plexus and the man was winded. Wasp stepped back, dropped his guard, Frankie let loose another right and connected with Wasp's left lower jaw. It was a bombshell, a missile, and Wasp staggered back.

Urged by the roaring crowd, Frankie went after Wasp, striking relentlessly anywhere he saw unguarded, and it was as good as done.

A last flailing roundhouse caught Frankie's nose and sent a rush of blood out across his face, but that was all that Wasp had left.

The referee called it, pulling Frankie away from Wasp as Wasp lost his footing and fell on his ass.

Frankie felt the rush of victory. He was a fighter. He was a winner. He was back home in more ways than could ever be described.

*

Lucia was waiting for her brother, heard the sound of footsteps and voices below, and went out to look down the stairwell. What she'd anticipated was not what she saw.

Piero and Freddie were shouldering the Irishman between them, awkwardly making their way up toward her. She knew it was bad before she even saw Frankie's face. When they reached her, she realized how bad it was.

Despite her sense of shame and displeasure toward her brother, her instinct and maternal nature came to the fore and she hurried the men into the cramped room.

Frankie dropped to the mattress on the floor as if wounded deadweight. Lucia fetched water, a cloth, and she started to clean away the blood that had welled beneath his eyes, around his lips, even undoing the upper buttons of his shirt to clean the lower half of his neck and his chest.

"What happened was this—" Nicky started, but Lucia shot him a bullet glance that silenced him.

"What happened," she said, "was that you and your two idiotic monkeys took this fool down to one of those illegal fighting matches and let him get beaten half to death."

Frankie started laughing.

Lucia looked at the Irishman on her brother's mattress and didn't know what to say.

"Hell of a fight," Frankie said. "They know I'm here, right? They know Frankie Madden has arrived in New York!"

Piero started laughing.

"Go!" Lucia said. "Out of here, the pair of you."

Piero and Freddie glanced sideways at each other, hesitating for just a moment.

"Now!" Lucia snapped, and they hesitated no more. The pair of them fled like scalded cats.

Frankie eased himself up on his elbow, then to a sitting position. He gingerly touched the swelling on the right side of the face. He winced momentarily and then grinned.

"Tough guy," Nicky said. "You beat him fair and square, Frankie, and that was a tough guy for your first fight."

"First and last," Lucia said. She looked at Nicky. "Does a promise mean nothing to you?"

Nicky shrugged. "There are promises and promises."

"Meaning what, exactly?"

"Meaning that I promised to take care of you, promised to get you out of here. Those are real promises. Telling you I ain't gonna get into a fight, that I ain't gonna do whatever it takes to get the money so we can head west . . . those are little promises, and they sometimes get broken on the way."

Lucia shook her head, went back to administering to Frankie's bruised and bloodied face. She didn't know what to feel then, caught somewhere between a native caring instinct and an intense dislike for what was happening. There was truth in what Nicky was saying, and yet she could not bring herself to admit it. As for this Irishman with his hammered and bloodstained face, there was a second when he looked at her, his eyes so clear and bold, and she felt something she did not understand. Perhaps she felt a momentary kinship with him, as if the pair of them had been unwittingly manipulated into this by her brother. She knew it was a foolish thought, that Frankie Madden was more than capable of causing plenty of trouble by himself, and yet she could not accept the notion that she had somehow started to like him. She had to explain it away, and that was all she could think of in that moment.

Frankie took the cloth from her and wiped his own face.

"This ain't nothin'," he said. "Me own father gave me a kickin' far worse than this more times than I can remember." Frankie laughed again. "Christ almighty, maybe that's why I can't remember!"

Lucia did what she could to suppress the smile that took over her face. There was something incorrigible and awkward about the man, but at least he did not take himself seriously.

"So, I trust you have learned your lesson this evening," she said.

"And what lesson would that be?" Frankie asked.

"That trying to make some money in this dreadful fighting circuit is just a fast way to an early grave."

"Hell no, woman," Frankie replied, and struggled to pull a bundle of creased and bloody dollar bills from his pants pocket. He held out the money. "We only just got started, didn't we, Nicky?"

Nicky didn't speak.

"So what are you saying . . . that you and my brother are going to do more fighting?"

"Well, I wouldn't be ratin' your brother much as a fighter, but I'm not averse to getting' back in there and thumpin' a few more heads. There's money to be made, and looks like you're gonna need as much as you can get if you're headin' to Hollywood."

Lucia turned to Nicky, an expression of dismay on her face. "You told him?"

Nicky shrugged. "We were just talkin', you know. It's no big deal."

"Our business is our business, Nicky—"

"No harm done," Frankie said. "Who am I gonna tell? You are the only people I know."

"So why are you here, Mr. Madden?"

"Same reason as you, sweetheart. There's fortunes to be made, and I wanna be one of those makin' 'em."

"Don't call me sweetheart. I'm not your sweetheart."

Frankie looked up at Nicky. "She's a firework, this one. Just like you said."

"You ain't seen nothin' yet, my friend," Nicky replied.

"Hey, what is this? All of a sudden you're best friends? You met each other yesterday. Nicky . . . you're telling him about me, telling him about our plans."

"Take it easy, lady," Frankie said, and he gave her his most disarming smile.

"I will not take it easy, Mr. Madden, and if you think that talking to me like this is going to win me over, then think again. I don't like you, not from the moment I saw you, and everything you have said and done since then has just confirmed my first impression."

"Well, I am sorry for that," Frankie said. He eased himself up off the mattress and got to his feet. "Maybe I am a dumb Irish bogger with no more sense than a plank o' wood, but I have a good heart, and I'm no liar. We all got a past, lady, and some of it ain't so wholesome. You don't know a thing about me, and yet you're makin' judgments and tellin' me how you don't like me and that everything I say just makes it worse. Well, here's the truth . . . you don't have to like me, and I don't have to like you."

Lucia was surprised at the Irishman's retort. She felt ashamed of herself.

"I'm sorry—" she started.

"For what?" Frankie asked. "For being yourself and havin' an opinion? Don't ever be sorry about that, lady. You start being sorry about who you are and ye're already fucked."

Her eyes widened.

Frankie grinned. There was blood on his teeth. "I'd apologize for the language, but I'm a dumb Irisher with no manners." He turned to Nicky. "I'll see you tomorrow, my Corsican friend, and we'll see what can be done about winnin' some more money."

Nicky opened his mouth to speak, but Frankie raised his hand.

"You don't need to say a thing," Frankie said. "Seems your sister done all the sayin' that's gonna be needed for a time."

With that, Frankie crossed the room, opened the door, and headed downstairs.

Once his footsteps were nothing but an echo, Nicky said, "I can't believe you'd talk to him like that."

"Like what? You can't tell me what to say, Nicky."

"And you can't tell me what to do! I'm going to do what's necessary to get us out of this shitty little place, and that's all there is to it."

"Even if it means getting involved with bad and crazy people."

Nicky sighed and shook his head. "The world is full of bad and crazy people, Lucia. There are more of those than anyone else. Just go out there and take a look. If you don't deal with them, then who do you deal with? The losers and schmucks that work every hour there is and still go home with nothing?"

"Losers and schmucks?" Lucia asked. "Since when did you start talking like this?"

"Since I stopped pretending I was still in San-Nicolao. This isn't Corsica, Lucia. This isn't home. There's no beignets and fiadone. There's no bottles of Patrimonio breathing before dinner. Wake up, eh? Look around you. We live in one room, we have barely enough money to eat, and you want to go to Hollywood and be a movie star."

Her eyes flashed with hurt.

Nicky's expression softened. "I'm sorry," he said. "I love that you have this dream. You know that. I want to see your name in lights as much as you do, but California is nearly three thousand miles away, and we ain't gonna be flyin' first class with Transcontinental and Western. I gotta get a car, I gotta make some money, and there aren't that many ways to make that kinda money around here."

Lucia looked at her brother. She knew he loved her, and she knew he was right. If this was what it took to get out of New York, then the end would have to justify the means.

"I'm sorry," she said. "I really am." She took a step toward Nicky and they hugged. "What can I do to help?"

"You can be a little kinder to the crazy Irisher," he said. "That man has a head made of stone, and he may very well be our ticket out of here."

TEN

Frankie Madden got busy. He was back on track. He'd been given a second chance to take something he believed he'd lost forever. He knew he would never outrun his own memories. The past was a country he could never escape, but he drove his body to help his mind forget, if only for minutes at a time. Those minutes were precious beyond belief, and he savored them.

In the early hours of the morning Frankie ran beneath the freeway overpasses near Jefferson Park. Nicky found a makeshift gym, nothing more than the basement of an empty building, a ramshackle boxing ring, a few punch bags, a half dozen hopefuls knocking each other senseless in the vain belief that the big ticket was right around the corner. Frankie worked hard, gathering strength, building speed, and he watched the bruisers and also-rans with a keen eye. Frankie knew he was different from these guys. Fighting was in his blood. And he could take a kicking, for sure. Maybe all those beatings he'd taken from his drunken father had served some kind of purpose after all. McCabes were a tough breed, tough and contrary, and—when it came to the fighting spirit—it seemed the fruit had fallen not so far from the tree. Once or twice Frankie had seen someone fired up to challenge his father. Clancy would let loose the fury, raging with fists as hard as hooves until there wasn't a single word of contradiction left in the challenger's mouth. Had Clancy not fallen headfirst into a bottle, he could have been a champion, too. That was one thing that always held true with Clancy McCabe: Disagree with him and he'd be breaking your nose before there was time to take off your cap.

All the while Frankie trained—dodging, weaving, working on keeping up the left while striking hard and fast with the right, punching and twisting his fists into enamel bowls filled with coarse sand. He thought of home, his ma, his sisters, but he thought more often of Lucia Mariani. He did not know the girl at all, and yet somehow she'd invaded his thoughts.

Frankie possessed sense enough not to speak of it with Nicky.

They became close, spent hours together each day, returning to their respective rooms merely to sleep, to eat, and then meeting once more the following day to work even harder. As a result, Frankie had come to know a little of Nicky, and he liked the man. There was no escaping the fact that he was hungry, driven, oblivious to any idea of failure, but he was smart, perhaps even smarter than he gave himself credit for. His mind was quick, and he always came back with a sharp line, something that made people laugh, and the more people he met the more people liked him. He was also obsessively devoted to Lucia, and felt it his God-given right to protect and defend her from anything the world could bring to their door. In her own way, Lucia was similar in temperament. She was passionate, her naïveté and lack of experience masked by the sheer drive she possessed to achieve her aspirations. All three of them were so very different, and yet they were all so alike. Frankie couldn't help but feel that fate had somehow played a part in bringing them together.

The subsequent Thursday night, Frankie's face healed almost completely, he took on a Scandinavian in his thirties. The man was lithe and quick, but his defense was weak. Frankie caught him three successive blows to the kidneys and the man went down. Lashing back furiously, he caught Frankie's already-battered nose a sideswipe and the blood was torrential. Later Frankie spent an hour snorting warm salt water to loosen the clots.

Saturday morning, Nicky took Frankie to a doctor recommended by one of Luca Casale's people and they cauterized Frankie's nose. He wouldn't bleed any more.

Casale had seen the Scandinavian fight. He was interested in the young Irishman. He had potential, no doubt about it, but it would be a while before he could play tough in the major league. Smaller fights, sure, and there were bucks to be made even in those makeshift setups. Friday night, Saturday night if he could take two in a row, Frankie and Nicky were walking away with fifty or sixty bucks between them. It didn't seem a great deal, but it added up, and by the time May rolled around Lucia had more than a hundred and fifty dollars hidden away. They were frugal and cautious. The more they spent on living, the farther away lay their life.

Mid-May, and Nicky Mariani was in a different class. Even on the street, he was acknowledged by Casale's button men and runners. They knew who he was, they knew the Irishman, and there was talk of a fight on the last Saturday of May where some real money could be made.

The Monday evening before, Frankie and Nicky had to go see some people together. As was his usual routine, Frankie waited down on the street.

Lucia was on her way back from visiting a friend. She slowed on the opposite sidewalk and watched Frankie for a moment or two. Then she crossed directly to the steps and spoke with him.

"You always wait down here for Nicky," she said.

Frankie had been elsewhere, was taken by surprise. He took off his cap and smiled awkwardly.

"Miss Lucia," he said.

Lucia smiled. No one called her that but Frankie.

"Why don't you ever come up and knock the door?" she asked.

"Don't want to bother you," Frankie said. "I can wait down here."

"You don't like me, do you?"

Frankie laughed suddenly, a little embarrassedly, and could not hide the fact that he was overreacting. "I like you just fine," he said.

"Did I really upset you that much . . . that we can't even be in the same room as each other?"

Frankie shook his head. "Never worried me, it didn't, but you made your thoughts clear as day."

"That was—what?—two months ago, Frankie. You're still holding on to that?"

Frankie smiled. "You know what they say about the Irish, right? We never forget."

"I was angry with Nicky," Lucia explained. "I was mad at him because he'd promised not to get involved in all this fighting business, but we talked afterward and we straightened everything out."

"Strange how money seems to straighten out most things, isn't it?"

Lucia paused before she spoke, her expression a giveaway. "If that was supposed to make me feel guilty for what I said to you, then it worked."

"The guilt is yours, Miss Lucia. Like me, it's probably a great deal more to do with your Catholic upbringing than anything else."

"Are you trying to make me angry again? Revenge? For how mean I was to you."

"You should hear what your brother's Italian friends say about revenge."

"And what do they say?"

"You plan for revenge, better dig two graves."

"And these friends of my brother's, they're your friends, too?"

"I don't have any friends. I'm just making my impression on the world the best way I know how."

"And how long does this go on for? You can't fight forever."

"We'll see what the weather brings."

"I really don't know what to make of you, Frankie."

"Who says you have to make anything of me? I am who I am. Take it or leave it. Once Nicky has enough to get you out of here, then you'll never have to see me again."

Frankie could hear himself; he was trying hard not to be mean to the girl, but there was something about her that invited it. He had worked hard to convince himself that she had a heart of stone, no passion at all, but he knew that was untrue. He'd told himself time and again that thinking about her was nothing but a waste of time and energy. Why that inspired him to tease her in this way, he did not know. Perhaps there was a taste of bitterness on his tongue, and all his words were flavored so.

Lucia smiled then, and smiled with such warmth and humanity that Frankie felt all his hard work undone. Defenses fell like Jericho walls.

"I really have made an enemy of you, haven't I?" she said.

"We're not enemies, Miss Lucia. We don't know each other well enough to be enemies."

Lucia paused. Her expression was thoughtful. "Perhaps I misjudged you," she said.

"You ever consider that you didn't need to judge me at all?"

"Okay. You win. This goes around in circles—"

The sound of someone coming down the inner stairwell interrupted her words.

"That'll be Nicky," Frankie said. "We gotta go someplace, see some people."

"Until next time, Mr. Madden."

Frankie put his cap back on. "Until next time, Miss Lucia."

Nicky and his sister shared a few words in the hallway, and then Nicky came out onto the steps.

"You ready?"

"As ever," Frankie replied.

They spoke little as they walked. Frankie thought of his exchange with Lucia. What he'd told her was true; he'd made no definite plans for what would happen next. He'd see what the wind brought in and go with it. There was always the possibility that he'd get himself hit so hard in the head that he'd forget his own name, and then there'd be no decisions to make. There were mumbling, stuttering remnants of men at every fight, carrying pails of water, mopping up blood, standing near the money guy ready to thump anyone who tried a funny trick. These were the ex-fighters, capable of half a conversation and little else. You had to know when to stop, but therein lay the problem. The rush, the energy, the fierce nature of competition were all addictions. They drove you on for more and more, and you ignored the signs. You had to make sure your thirst for glory didn't overwhelm your common sense. There was a balance in everything. The trick was to get it right.

Then there was the thing of which he would never speak—not to Nicky, not to Lucia, not to anyone. One day someone would come. They would demand their pound of flesh, and he would have no choice but to give it. There were strong Irish connections here on the East Coast; only the devil himself knew all the pockets and how deep they were. If the Italians got wind of the truth, they would sell his soul faster than taking an espresso. Frankie owed these people no loyalty, and he could expect none in return. He would do what was asked of him. If he did not, he'd find himself dead where he stood or on the way home to Clonegal. If he went home, he'd be going back merely to hang.

These thoughts kept sleep at bay. These thoughts invaded Frankie's mind as he ran and sparred and fought, as he listened to Nicky and Freddie and Piero joking among themselves, as he ate dinner, took a bath, cleaned his shoes.

These thoughts would never leave him. However hard he worked to be rid of them, they followed him relentlessly. They were as good as his shadow, though twice as long and three times as dark. There were moments of respite, but always the battle between past and future was raging in his mind.

Nicky and Frankie crossed 106th and headed for Second. Behind the school down on 105th there was a little Italian restaurant called Casa Lontano da Casa, "Home away from Home." Nicky had set up a meet with Casale's people about the big-money fight. To Frankie, these people seemed crude and brutish. They drank too much wine, talked too loud, made promises he doubted they'd keep.

Upon arriving, they were shown to a back room. Half a dozen men sat talking about Mussolini. Frankie had been keeping an ear open for the situation in Europe. Before he'd left Ireland there was word about the national socialists in Germany, how they might be an ally in the fight against the British. He'd also heard word that de Valera might be calling a general election. Thoughts of Ireland stirred thoughts of home, of his ma, his sisters, and he pushed those thoughts away.

One of the men at the table rose and shook Nicky's hand. As he did, three of the men moved through to the front of the restaurant. Evidently they were not invited to the meeting.

"This is your hitter, eh?" the man said.

"He is," Nicky said. "Frankie, this is Rafaello Anzelmo."

"Raffi," the man said. "Everyone says Raffi . . . except people who piss me off, and they say, 'No please, please, please don't fuckin' shoot me!' "

The men laughed; Frankie laughed with them.

The others were introduced—Dante Carlino and Enzo Maletta, men with eyes that raged with awkward secrets. They gave tempered smiles, little more than an acknowledgment of the guests.

Frankie could so clearly see that these people were Nicky's role models. They wore tailored suits and jewelry. Their hair was barbered slick. They wore cologne and gold wristwatches and socks that matched their shirts. Frankie doubted that any of them could remember the last time they'd taken a razor to their own face.

Nicky sat down, indicated for Frankie to take a seat as well.

"You wanna eat with us?" Raffi asked.

"Sure we wanna eat with you," Nicky said. "My boy here needs all the pasta he can take."

Frankie nodded in thanks. Perhaps the myth was true, that you could take an Irishman out of the country but never take the country out of the man. The smell of loam and peat and poteen would never really leave the nostrils; no matter the clothes, they would never be finer than a Donegal tweed; oysters and a bloody hanger steak could never satiate hunger like boiled ham and colcannon. He certainly didn't much care for pasta, but he knew better than to decline. From observation, there was much similarity between the Irish and the Italians: the Catholic influence, the importance of family, the unwillingness to forgive or forget those who broke promises or betrayed agreements.

Raffi called a waiter. He ordered linguini, ravioli, various sauces, a plate of veal. The food came, wine also, and they ate as they talked.

"Don Casale is interested in a real fight," Raffi told Nicky. He glanced at Frankie and smiled. "He says you are ready for a war."

"Does he have a date in mind?" Nicky asked.

"Saturday."

"This Saturday?"

"Sure," Raffi said. "You not ready?"

"I'm ready," Frankie said.

Nicky nudged Frankie. *Let me do the talking,* that gesture said.

"He wants to pitch your boy against the Pole."

There was a moment's silence. Nicky glanced back at Frankie.

"*The* Pole?" Nicky asked.

"*The* Pole," Raffi echoed.

"We can do that," Nicky said.

"Be a lot of money on the other side of the table."

Frankie leaned forward. "You're settin' me for a fight and bettin' against me now?"

Nicky looked back at Frankie, opened his mouth to speak.

Frankie smiled. "I'm the one gettin' thumped here, my friend... Seems I have a right to ask a few questions."

"He has a point," Raffi said.

"So who is this guy?"

"His name is Bodak. Aleksy Bodak. He is a good fighter, seasoned, experienced, and he has a very hard head."

Carlino smiled like he knew something.

"Like a tree... The guy is a fuckin' tree," Maletta said.

"Trees fall," Frankie said. "Hit 'em with an ax, and they fall."

"Bodak fights for us," Raffi said. "Hell, everyone fights for us, even the ones who think they fight for someone else. Here we can't lose. Either one of you wins, we win. That is the game we play."

"Good game," Frankie said. "As long as we get a piece."

"You get a piece. Two hundred bucks is a good piece."

"Each," Nicky said.

Raffi smiled. "Greedy fuckin' Corsican. Of course each. What do you think this is?"

"A turkey shoot."

"Maybe, maybe not. Bodak is a big guy, but like your Irishman says, the big ones fall hard. I seen it before. Maybe everyone will get a surprise, eh?"

Nicky turned to Frankie. He spoke low. "This guy is a beast, Frankie. He ain't so tall, but he's wide and solid. It's gonna be like thumping a fire station."

"Two hundred bucks each, Nicky," Frankie replied. "One fight, two hundred bucks, even if I lose. You think we can afford to turn it down?"

"You're sure? You ain't even seen the guy."

"What do I need to see? Even if I get all beat to hell, I'll come out of there with two hundred bucks."

"Or you won't come out."

"Chance I gotta take, Nicky."

Nicky turned back to Raffi. "We got a deal," he said.

Raffi smiled. "So eat, drink, let's talk about something else. You get yourself in shape for Saturday night. I'll have one of my guys tell you where it's gonna happen." He paused for a moment, his fork raised, and looked at Frankie Madden. "Word of advice?"

"Sure thing."

"Bet against yourself and take a fall. Third or fourth round, make it look good, but take a fall."

Frankie didn't say a word.

Nicky opened his mouth to speak, but Frankie nudged him silent.

ELEVEN

Since the meeting with Raffi and the others, Nicky and Frankie had focused on Frankie's training. Nicky found an old bruiser who'd done the bullpen circuit for a few years, and he worked with Frankie from dawn till dusk over the four days. His name was Ron Gerhardt, but everyone called him Manhattan Red.

Frankie asked him why.

"Don't ask," Gerhardt said, and that was that.

Red was a taskmaster, no bones about it. He got Nicky paying for steak and eggs, fatback bacon, potatoes, pork ribs, pancakes, anything that would build some weight on Frankie. He had Frankie pounding sidewalks, Red following on a bicycle down East 112th to the park, back along First to 115th, then all the way up to Lexington before starting again.

Utter a word of complaint and Red would say, "Shut the hell up, Frankie. Your mouth ain't for nothin' but eatin'."

Lucia surprised Frankie during the days running up to the fight. He would go over there in the evening to see Nicky, all set to wait on the street until Nicky came down. When Lucia found out he was down there she would call him from the window. She started making food for three, and though she didn't include herself in their conversations Frankie knew she was hearing every word. Naive she was not, not by any stretch of the imagination, and he started to wonder if she wasn't the driving force behind Nicky. Every once in a while she would simply ask a question, and in that question it was obvious that she grasped every angle of what was going on.

On Thursday evening Lucia mentioned a film director called John Ford.

"Irishman," Frankie said.

Lucia frowned. "He is not."

"Sure he is. One of eleven children. His real name is Feeney, John Feeney, and his father was from County Galway. And he won an Oscar for one of his films, you know?"

Lucia looked at Frankie and didn't know what to say.

"What?" he asked her.

"Er . . . nothing. No, nothing at all."

Frankie smiled. "You think I'm too stupid to watch a film."

Lucia laughed suddenly, inadvertently.

"Here's the sort of feller who'd go to the picture house and sit the wrong way 'round. That's what she was thinking."

Nicky laughed.

"I never said that," Lucia replied.

"May not have said it, but I see it in your eyes."

"I'm sorry if I—"

Frankie raised his hand and she fell silent. "Never be sorry for having an opinion, even if it's wrong."

"Every time I speak to you I feel like I've misjudged you."

Frankie smiled and the Irish light was in his eyes. "Said it before, say it again. I never felt the need to make a judgment."

"Now you're making fun of me."

"Me? Would never dream of it."

She didn't respond. He was goading her, and she knew it.

"Enough of this chatter," Nicky said. "Movies and directors and whatever, who cares? Only movies I'm interested in haven't been made yet because Lucia isn't in them."

"Hell of a line," Frankie said. "Wish I'd thought of that." He looked at Lucia. He did not smile. She did not look away, and she did not smile either. The air snapped between them.

"We have two days," Nicky said. "Two days and we're almost there for money."

"Do you have an idea of where we're going to buy a car?" Lucia asked.

"I have ideas all the time."

"A *good* idea, Nicky. We need a good car, a car that will get us all the way, and we need to work out where we are going to stop on the way and where the cheapest hotels are and everything like that."

"Take the train," Frankie said. "Grand Central to La Salle Street in Chicago, Chicago to Denver on the *Zephyr*, which takes about fifteen hours because that's one hell of a fast train. Then go Denver to Los Angeles . . . or you could go Denver to San Francisco and buy a car there and drive down the Pacific coastline."

Lucia started laughing. "You're doing this on purpose."

Frankie frowned, honestly bemused. "Doin' what?"

"Saying things that make me look foolish."

"I ain't doin' nothin' to make you look foolish. You'd be doin' that all by yourself. I'm just sayin' maybe you should take the train. Take a Pullman, you know? A sleeper carriage. Would cost a hell of a lot less than three thousand miles worth of petrol and motel rooms."

"Petrol... you mean gas."

"Petrol, gas, same thing."

"So how do you know this... getting from here to Los Angeles by train. How do you even know how to do that?"

"I was just interested. I went down to Grand Central and asked someone. Surprised me how little it costs."

"What do you think?" Lucia asked her brother.

"About what?"

"About going to Los Angeles on the train!"

"Sure, whatever you say. Can't say I'm too excited about driving three thousand miles."

"Then that's what we'll do. We'll take the train from here to Hollywood."

After dinner was done, Lucia gathered up plates and dishes and washed them in the small sink. Frankie offered to help, but she declined. There was a tension between them, an awkward edge to her own emotions. She did not feel the same as yesterday, the day before, and she wondered if this wild Irishman hadn't found a way under her skin. He had blown in like an Atlantic squall, and now he seemed to have become part of their lives. He was more than just a fighter. There was a weight to his presence, as if he was somehow burdened and lost. She did not know why he was in America, and she wondered whether he was escaping from something in his past. Questions concerning his family were evaded, and he never spoke of his future plans. In truth, she knew nothing but her own preconceptions, and it seemed that with everything he said he somehow proved those preconceptions wrong.

It was obvious that Nicky had taken to Frankie, or at least made the pretense. For all his charm and humor, Nicky was self-serving. He very seldom took off his business head. He'd made it clear that Frankie was a way to earn money, a fast ticket out of New York.

The way it seemed, this fight against the Polish man was the last fight Frankie and Nicky would undertake. With the money they earned they'd be able to leave the city. Lucia knew the kind of people with whom they were now involved, and she knew they'd be attending the fight. The question in her mind was whether or not Nicky and Frankie would even be permitted to leave the city. If

Frankie won, surely these people would want to keep him on their circuit. Nicky had never mentioned any such possibility, and she didn't want to raise it.

Lucia didn't wish to tempt fate, for fate appeared to be on their side. Somehow they had found Frankie, and it looked like Frankie was going to get them out.

However, to leave her future in the hands of her brother and this Irishman was something she could never do.

That was why she had to be there.

The way Lucia announced her intent to attend the fight caught Frankie off guard. His surprise was evident in his expression.

"I've told her already," Nicky said. "She won't hear a word of it. She says she's coming and there's nothing I can do to stop her."

"I agree with your brother," Frankie said. "I really don't think it's a good place for you to be."

They sat at the small table in the window. She had made coffee, asked Frankie to join them before he and Nicky left.

"I'm coming," she said. "You can't stop me."

"Defiant, stubborn, hardheaded . . . a real Corsican girl," Nicky said.

"Why do you want to be there?" Frankie asked.

"My reasons are my reasons."

"I can't chaperone you—" Nicky started.

"I don't need a chaperone," Lucia interjected. "I've made my own arrangements."

"Your own arrangements?" Nicky asked. He leaned forward, concern in his expression. "What the hell's that supposed to mean?"

"It means what I say. You don't need to chaperone me. I've made my own arrangements."

"Lucia," Frankie said. "I've no place tellin' you what you should and shouldn't be doin', but this is a bad idea. Believe me, this is a really bad idea."

"Then it's a bad idea," she replied. "That doesn't stop me from having it."

Frankie looked at Nicky. Neither of them spoke. They knew well enough that this was a war they could not win.

"Whatever the hell you've got planned, I don't like it," Nicky said.

Lucia laughed at her brother. "How can you know that you don't like it if you don't know what I'm doing?"

"You see?" Nicky said to Frankie. "You see what I have to deal with?"

"I see," Frankie said, and didn't dare say another word.

They left soon enough, and as they crossed the street Frankie looked back and saw Lucia looking down at them from the window.

"What's going on?" he asked Nicky. "What's she doing?"

Nicky shook his head resignedly. "She lives in a drama all her own, Frankie. What can I tell you? The girl has been playing parts her whole life, like everything is some sort of theatrical event. She used to drive me crazy, but I decided a long time ago that this was just who she was and nothing would change her."

"What does she think's going to happen? She's never been to a fight before."

"She's not stupid, Frankie. She knows there will be important people there... people with money, people with influence. Los Angeles may be the place they make the movies, but New York is where they find the money. That's all I can think. Besides that, she knows that this will be our ticket out of here."

"If I walk away," Frankie said.

"You do what they say, Frankie. That's the truth of it."

Frankie looked askance at Nicky. He frowned.

"You take the fall," Nicky said. "What the hell, Frankie? You think you're gonna beat this guy? You do anything but take a fall and you're gonna get killed."

Frankie laughed. "You're kiddin', right?"

Nicky stopped dead in his tracks. "You wanna get out of New York?"

"Sure I do."

"Then you give a good show, Frankie, but you go down, my friend... you go down."

Frankie looked at the ground. He took a deep breath. He clenched his fists and held them up. He turned them over, watched as his knuckles whitened. He could feel his heart racing then, challenged not only by the fight itself, but the fact of being told to do something he could never even consider.

He lowered his fists and smiled at Nicky. He knew better than to say anything.

Nicky, translating that smile the way he wanted, seemed satisfied.

Nicky reached out and gripped Frankie's shoulder. "Hell, even if I have to carry you myself, we're getting out of New York, my friend... We are getting out of New York."

Frankie glanced back one more time, but Lucia was gone from the window.

He felt a ghost stir in his heart. He thought once more of Erin, of all that he'd left behind. He'd saved one man yet killed another.

What he felt in his heart was nothing but contradiction, as if there were two sides of him battling for dominance. He could find neither resolve nor redemption. And now, as if he didn't have sufficient to cope with, he was feeling something for Lucia that he did not understand. What was he hoping for? That she would reciprocate that feeling without ever understanding it herself? Was it merely loneliness that impelled him toward her?

It seemed that he'd somehow escaped the prison of the past only to build a new one for the future. Guilt and conscience were so much stronger than any steel bar or locked gate.

His brief experience with the American-Italians, behind them families with legendary names—Lucchese and Colombo, Gambino and Genovese—said all that he wished to hear. These people were far better organized and far more dangerous than any republicans or nationalists back home. The history here spanned merely a century— the Bowery Boys, Corcoran's Roosters, the Hudson Dusters, the Slaughter House Gang—but a century was enough to make its mark. The names that were invoked—Mose the Fireboy, Monk Eastman, Cyclone Louie, and One Lung Curran—were invoked with awe.

Not only did Frankie feel that his hidden past demanded a constant need to keep moving, but he was aware that staying in New York could only become a greater and greater liability. New York was where he'd been sent. That made him all the easier to find. Perhaps he could never move far enough or fast enough to evade those who held this debt over his head, but America was a vast country. He was sure the Marianis had no intention of taking him with them to California, but that didn't mean he couldn't choose his own escape route. If he went three thousand miles west, how much time would he buy for himself? The farther he went, the more tenuous the connection, the more difficult he would be to trace.

Beyond that, he was walking a fine line between bareknuckle fistfighter and soon-to-be Mafia strong-armer. From what Nicky had told him, the guys who showed real prowess in the bullpen were often recruited into the ranks of the families. A boss liked to have a man with a name looking after him when he walked the streets.

These questions troubled him, and for now he could see no simple resolution to any of them.

His first order of business was the fight. Without the money they were due to earn, all questions were meaningless. That's where he had to focus his mind, and he had to focus his mind on it to the exclusion of all else. Even Lucia Mariani.

TWELVE

The venue was a near-derelict warehouse on the east side of Jefferson Park, there in the shadow of Franklin Roosevelt Drive. The air was rich with the ammoniac taint of rat runs and damp, rotted seeds. Lucia could smell the river, too, the filth from the Triborough swelling and rolling in the Little Hell Gate inlet; it haunted the atmosphere like the ghost of something long dead.

The people who crowded the warehouse were people from another world. Crass and foul-mouthed, drunk, angry, laughing, aggressive, but the money flowed back and forth as if sourced from a never-ending stream.

The setting itself was a circus, a Roman amphitheater, a makeshift arena for liquor and bloodshed.

Lucia could not have felt more out of place, and yet she could not have felt more alive.

She had come for Nicky, for Frankie, too, but most of all she had come for herself. She had paid attention; she'd heard names, even recognized some of them, and she knew all too well that agents and talent scouts were all over New York. That they might very well be connected to those for whom Nicky worked was altogether possible. Wealth and power were inseparable, and all it took was one word, one brief conversation at the right time and in the right place and her name could be one to remember.

The gown she wore was borrowed. It was a sheer pearl-colored silk creation. It draped her as if tailored for her frame and hers alone. Off one shoulder, it clung to her body like a second skin, and in her hand she held a matching clutch purse. That it had been made for someone else entirely was something no one needed to know. For this moment, for this day, it was hers. One of the women in a lower apartment had helped her. Her dark hair had been pulled back from her face, the arrangement of curls and twists on her head sculpted like a bouquet of rare flowers. The makeup she wore accentuated everything that could be accentuated—her cheekbones, her finely arched mouth, the aquiline nose and almond eyes. She knew who she was. She was Lucia Mariani, no doubt, but it was a Lucia Mariani that neither her brother nor Frankie had never seen before.

For this performance she'd not only spent money she could ill afford, but she had recruited Freddie Cova and Piero Altamura. She'd told them that Nicky had specifically asked that they accompany her. They were to chaperone her. That was Nicky's request. They were to find dinner suits, clean shirts, bow ties, and they were to make sure she came to no harm.

She was convincing. They did as she asked, and they entered that warehouse, one on each arm, and gave the impression that here had arrived a starlet, a true doyenne of the silver screen.

Lucia was aware of how heads turned, how people stared, how people whispered to one another. It was like a drug, a lifeline, and she could not get enough of it.

Lucia Mariana made her grand entrance, and already those with influence were asking who she was, to whom did she belong, and whether or not she could be stolen away with the promise of even finer clothes and greater fortunes.

And then she caught Nicky's eye. Those eyes widened, his mouth dropped open as if to catch flies, and after a moment's hesitation he came hurrying toward her.

"What are you doing? What the hell are you doing, Lucia?" He looked at Freddie and Piero. He grabbed Freddie's lapel. "And what the hell is this? Where did these clothes come from? What game are you playing here?" His tone and manner was of a man angered and betrayed.

"Nicky," Lucia said. "Settle down. Freddie and Piero came because I asked them to." She leaned close to her brother's ear and whispered, "Don't make a scene. People are looking at you. They're supposed to be looking at me."

Through the throng she caught sight of Frankie, and then Frankie saw her.

He looked as if someone had sideswiped him. His eyes as wide as Nicky's, his mouth wider, he didn't know where to look, and when she smiled at him, he assumed the expression of a man unsure of his own senses.

"I'm here for you and Frankie," Lucia said. "See how they stare."

With that, she leaned forward and kissed her brother's cheek. Leading Freddie and Piero like screen extras, she started walking toward Frankie.

The fight had yet to start, but already there were people cursing, shouting, throwing wild punches at one another. It seemed that most everyone was drunk or intent on getting there as soon as they could. But as she moved through those people, the crowd separated. Voices quieted down. People wanted to know who she was. Women glared enviously. Men gawped with hungry eyes.

Lucia reached Frankie. She looked at him for just a moment, and then she extended her hand and touched his face.

Frankie looked back at her as if he were seeing a ghost.

"I came to wish you luck, Frankie," she said, and then she leaned forward and kissed his cheek.

You came to be seen was all Frankie could think, and wondered what ulterior motive or vested interest she was seeking to accomplish by making such an appearance.

She held his gaze for a moment more, and there was something strangely distant in her eyes, as if waiting for the next line in this unscripted play.

"Thank you," Frankie said, but the words came involuntarily.

She smiled and turned away, Freddie and Piero following her without a word.

She found a place for herself and her two escorts at the edge of the ring. Within moments other men were navigating their way through the hustle of people to get closer to her. Lucia watched as a tall man with a cruel scar on his face tried to elbow Piero away, but Piero turned and looked at the man with such forthright aggression that he backed down.

Lucia felt her heart beating rapidly. She had never been to such a thing before, and was immediately shocked by the rough and brutal nature of what she was witnessing. She watched Frankie and Nicky together. There was another man there, older, a beaten face, one eye half closed. He seemed to be encouraging Frankie, telling him what to expect, what to look out for. When Nicky was in earshot, Lucia asked who the man was.

"Manhattan Red," Nicky replied, and then he was gone again, taking just a moment to glance back at her with that telltale expression on his face. He was not pleased.

And then Lucia saw Aleksy Bodak, and her heart nearly stopped. Had she possessed a mirror she would have seen the blood drawn from her face as real fear took hold.

Bodak was more animal than man. His shoulders were scarred, his face asymmetrical where bones had been broken and incorrectly set. His upper body was like some sort of primate, broad and muscular, and he leaned forward as he walked. The expression in his eyes was that of a man looking for someone to hurt. This lent him an even greater potential of aggression than was communicated from size alone.

Frankie was no bantamweight, but compared to the Polish fighter he was a sapling.

Lucia watched Frankie. Frankie stared at Bodak. He did not take his eyes off him for a second. It seemed like Frankie was trying to absorb everything he could—the way he moved, every detail of his body language—as if this would somehow give him an advantage.

The promise of their escape from New York did not assuage the feeling of fear in her stomach.

Before they faced each other, Frankie shared words with Aleksy Bodak. Lucia—from where she stood—could hear them both clearly.

There was no mistaking the threat and aggression in Bodak's challenge. In pidgin English he told Frankie that he was going to beat him senseless, that when he woke up it would be the middle of next week.

Frankie came back with, "Well, you're either a joker or a liar, and right now I don't see no one laughing." The wisecrack seemed to confuse Bodak and he just sneered.

Lucia's heart raced faster than ever as she saw those final bets laid down, as the crowd gathered around a roughly marked square, as a man angled his way through the throng and stood center stage.

This was the referee. He introduced himself as Monty Leonard. He raised his arms and the crowd hushed.

"Ladies and gentlemen . . . welcome to the bullpen!"

The roar was deafening. Lucia stepped back, found herself jostled and pushed, and then used her elbows to work her way back to the edge of the square. With the imminent start of the fight, whatever attention she may have garnered by how she looked was less than insignificant in the face of the real reason these people had gathered. They were here to see gladiators kill one another.

"Put your money down! Put your money down! Get those bets placed! Fight starts in five minutes! Five minutes, ladies and gentlemen!"

Sawdust was layered on the floor, and a rope was strung between four weighted posts.

Lucia felt nauseous and terrified, and the fight had not even begun. She feared for Frankie, his lack of experience, the brash attitude that had brought him here perhaps insufficient to get him out.

Bodak walked to the edge of the rope and people started cheering. Hands reached out to touch him, to acknowledge him, and Lucia wondered if this was nothing more than a ritual execution. Surely Frankie didn't stand a chance against this man. It was then she became truly aware that he'd worked his way among her feelings and found a place to stay. It was not love. It was not even respect and admiration. It was something altogether different. The Irishman had made himself an ally. Somehow he'd accomplished this in the handful of weeks they'd known each other. But she didn't *know* him. That was the truth. Still waters run deep, they said. He seemed so distant from everything, as if to feel anything was already too much. He was so unlike the preening, self-conscious Italians with whom Nicky associated. Frankie, it seemed, felt no need to prove anything to anyone, least of all to her. Blunt and uneducated he may have been, but that seemed to make him all the more honest, all the more real.

She looked once more at the Polish fighter and then back at Frankie. The money was against him. There was no question in her mind. He was being paid to take a beating. These people—these loud, aggressive, drunken people—wanted to see a slaughter, and Lucia was deeply concerned that their collective wish might be granted.

Frankie stepped away from the rope and stood for a second. He looked Bodak up and down, and then he smiled in that unmistakable Frankie Madden way.

And then Frankie looked at Lucia, and the smile he gave her was very different indeed. She felt transparent, as if he saw right through the glamorous facade she had worked so hard to create. A borrowed dress and shoes, the purse paid for with money they could ill afford, the convincing it had taken to get Freddie and Piero to accompany her, all of it like some surreal fantasy. What had she hoped to accomplish? Had it been nothing more than the vain need to be the center of attention? And for what? Nicky was mad, Frankie was confused, and now there was nothing but the blunt truth of what was about to happen.

Lucia felt her cheeks color. She returned Frankie's smile as best she could.

"So, we're to business, then?" she heard Frankie say to his opponent.

"Ready to break, little man?" Bodak said in heavily accented English.

"Ready to have you try, Polack."

Bodak grunted dismissively.

"Ladies and gentlemen!" Leonard shouted. "Bets are closed. Bets are closed! You ready for a fight?"

The crowd roared.

"Then let the fight begin!"

Again, a coarse bellow erupted from the crowd, and to Lucia it seemed nothing less than a wave of bloodlust. She hated what was happening, and yet she could neither stop it nor drag herself away.

Bodak took a step forward, Frankie echoed that step, and the pair of them faced up to each other like lions vying for dominance of the pride.

For a second there was breathless silence, and then it began.

THIRTEEN

Bodak did not come hurtling away from the rope, fists flying, intent on overwhelming his opponent by sheer size and force. He did exactly the opposite of what Frankie had predicted. He hung back, and those thin legs immediately danced and shifted, the strength in them more than adequate to cope with Bodak's upper-body weight. The man was a fighter, seasoned and proven, and Frankie Madden, skilled though he was, would need a great deal more than self-belief and bloody-minded stubbornness.

Frankie went in tight and close, his elbows tucked, his left in defense. Bodak swung, but wide, and Frankie saw a pocket and filled it. He was beneath Bodak, a sharp jab to the side of the man's ribs. Frankie heard him grunt. The man could hurt, but could he hurt enough?

Bodak's left swung in response, and Frankie felt air whistling past his right ear. He kept his head back and down, taking his weight and leaning toward the rope, skirting another ham hock fist that would have crashed into his shoulder.

Bodak smiled. It was like chasing a rabbit. It was merely a matter of time before one of his roundhouses connected, and one alone would be sufficient to send this Irish son of a bitch home in the mail with no return address.

Frankie sidestepped another haymaker but misjudged his footing. He stumbled to the left, and Bodak was quick.

With that first punch, he felt like he'd been hit by a car. Frankie saw stars exploding in his left eye. He tasted blood at the back of his mouth. He did not fall, could not dare to fall, and he went backward to the rope and snatched a second of respite.

People behind him pushed him forward. He felt hands urging him into the fray.

"Fight! Fight! Fight!"

He glanced to his right, tried to see Nicky, Lucia, Manhattan Red, but the faces of the onlookers were nothing but a blur.

He saw a flashing image of Erin. She was laughing about something.

Then he felt Bodak's shadow over him, and Frankie scuttled sideways, lost his balance, and was on his hands and knees.

The fist that reached the small of his back set off a series of nervous explosions that charged all the way to his skull. His head reverberated like a church bell, and once again the sense of losing all bearings and orientation overtook him.

His hands on the sawdust, feeling its texture, the dust in his nose and mouth, and Bodak was coming at him again. A minute into this thing and he was already on the way out.

Frankie pulled himself up by sheer will alone. Less than three weeks to his nineteenth birthday, and if something didn't change there was a strong possibility he might not make it. He had to make it. He had to survive this thing.

"Fight! Fight! Fight!" the crowd urged, and when Frankie spat sideways he saw red. Blood hit the sawdust, and the crowd roared even louder. They'd seen it, and they wanted more.

When Bodak swung, Frankie ducked and punched. He reached the left side of Bodak's solar plexus. He winded the man, but only for a moment.

Bodak was enraged, and here Frankie saw a real advantage. If not his upper-body weight and high center of gravity, then perhaps the man's temper.

Frankie dodged another killer punch and stepped to Bodak's right. Frankie brought his fist around and connected with the side of Bodak's face. Even Frankie felt the force of it as it sent ricochets through the man's head.

Bodak roared and swung again, and this time Frankie wasn't quite fast enough. The momentum of his evasive maneuver toppled him into the arc of Bodak's swing, and the side of the man's fist caught Frankie's left shoulder. He was sent sprawling once again, tasted that sawdust a second time, and then he was up on his haunches, on his feet, stepping backward and sideways once more as Bodak roared toward him.

Frankie let fly with everything he possessed. A right roundhouse, a left jab, right again, again, a desperate fury of motion. Even though his reach was too short, his movements too awkward, it was as if some force as profound as gravity drove him relentlessly forward with a hurricane of fists. Bodak came back with greater fury, and there was nothing Frankie could do to temper or assuage it. The man was easily as fast as Frankie, his reach longer, that ferocious right hand like a baseball bat into the side of Frankie's head. As soon as Frankie believed there would be a moment's respite, it was merely his opponent taking a small step backward in order to lunge and strike again and yet again, each time with greater deliberation.

Frankie was losing it. He knew it. Whatever he anticipated, Bodak moved another way. Whenever he dodged a right, he flew headlong into a left. He was bleeding from the nose, coughing back gobbets of blood and trying to swallow them. He knew if he spat them the crowd would be fired with even greater bloodlust, and that would encourage Bodak into an even wilder frenzy of violence.

And then he heard Lucia.

Frankie heard her voice. He was sure of it. Looking to his right he saw her, and the expression on her face was so pained, so tormented, it was as if a fire had been lit inside him. Standing there like some silver-screen vision, her expression shattered all illusions and fantasies. She was utterly terrified for him, and there was no way for her to hide it.

Bodak lunged, right shoulder down, and Frankie moved fast.

Bodak hit nothing but air, and his own weight and impetus sent him sprawling to the ground.

Now Bodak got a mouthful of sawdust, and before he even had a chance to understand where his opponent had gone, Frankie was over him.

Frankie Madden's fists were hoof hard, just like his father's. They rained down a torrent of punishment on Bodak's face and upper body. Bodak's arms were up in defense, and it was here that the size and mass of his torso played against him. He tried to turn left, but Frankie was there, those fists like a tornado of pain. He turned right, but Frankie was there again, and those fists came back a second time, a third, a fourth.

Now Bodak's blood boiled. He kicked out desperately, and even though his feet connected Frankie did not fall. He staggered backward but retained his balance.

Monty Leonard should have called a foul, but he did not. Monty Leonard was nowhere to be seen. It was in that moment that Frankie realized that Manhattan Red was not there either. He saw Nicky, he saw Lucia, but no one else he recognized.

Frankie stood firm. He raised his fists. Bodak was up now. He charged again, and once more Frankie stepped sideways at the last second.

Bodak flew into the crowd. Someone howled. The onlookers pushed him back forcibly. They wanted to see a man killed, and they didn't much care which one.

Bodak paused, perhaps gathering himself, focusing, trying to let go of the rage in his eyes. It did not dissipate, and when he rushed Frankie again it was with the same desperate hatred.

Frankie thought he had him again, but Bodak was too fast.

Bodak hit him fair and square, and Frankie went down.

Now it was Frankie's turn to writhe and twist beneath the flurry of fists that came at him. Those hands were big, those punches interminable, and Frankie felt the sense knocked out of him again and again.

"Frankie!"

He heard Lucia. There was no doubt in his mind.

"Frankie . . . get up!"

Frankie scuttled backward like a crab, and then he was on his side, his elbow beneath him, somehow managing to get himself away from Bodak for just a heartbeat. It was enough. He was on his feet, throwing his head and shoulders back to get himself away from another blistering haymaker.

Monty Leonard had vanished, no doubt about it.

Had this been the plan all along? A setup for him to get beaten to death by this Polish monster? Was this Casale's doing? Had Casale set him and Nicky up for a guaranteed lose?

Frankie went in low and tough, fists like a jackhammer, finding Bodak's belly, his kidneys. He knew he'd hit pay dirt when he heard something give. A rib perhaps, and Bodak looked down at the source of whatever excruciating pain had assaulted him.

Frankie didn't miss a beat. He leaped at the man, an over-arm flier that caught Bodak's head broadside.

Bodak looked stunned, dismayed, and Frankie hit him again.

Bodak took a step backward. He seemed to be losing his balance, and Frankie was there to help him.

Frankie hit Bodak in the throat, the upper chest, the face, the neck. Bodak kept going backward until he found the rope. He was pushed forward by the crowd, and it was that push that gave Frankie the edge, but only for a second. He got one more roundhouse under the wire, and then Bodak let loose a cannon that broke Frankie's nose. It was not the pain; it was the shock. Immediately he could not breathe. His mouth was filled with blood. He spat furiously, tried to clear his air passage, but it was no good.

The crowd was frenzied.

Frankie found Lucia. He wondered if it would be the last time he saw her.

And then he caught sight of Nicky, his expression desperate with fear, and he knew that there was no money for them here. He knew what had happened, how they'd all too easily fallen for it. Their greed had been their undoing. Frankie was going to die right here in a derelict warehouse, choking on blood and sawdust while Raffi Anzelmo and Luca Casale laughed behind their backs.

No, Lucia mouthed. *No, Frankie*, and Frankie looked up to see Aleksy Bodak lumbering toward him, his lip split, a wide bruise already visible across the side of his abdomen, and he knew that it was now or never. Was he going to let this happen? Was he going to die right here amid the noise and fury of this wretched place?

Bodak was unrelenting. He came charging at Frankie and caught him broadside. Frankie went down like a stone. His forehead connected with the floor, leaving him dazed, unable to think. Bodak possessed even greater advantage. He threw himself at Frankie, got down on his knees and pounded those huge fists into Frankie's chest, his abdomen, his shoulders.

Frankie was weak, his breathing fast and shallow. He was not getting enough oxygen and his vision was blurring.

Bodak kept on and on. Frankie twisted, but no matter which way he went he found himself on the receiving end of another fusillade of knuckles that had been sharpened and tempered precisely for this occasion.

Frankie bellowed with everything he possessed and lashed out with both arms simultaneously. The suddenness of Frankie's response took Bodak by surprise, and Frankie's right fist connected with the man's lower jaw. Bodak spun sideways and lost his balance. He landed on his side, the weight of his body on Frankie's left leg, and Frankie brought the side of his fist down on Bodak's temple.

Now it was Bodak's turn to be disorientated, and Frankie had a moment to wrench his leg free. He was up on his feet before Bodak had moved, and Frankie went back at him with everything he could muster.

His vision blurred. Sounds seemed to slip away from him. He saw the brick wall at the back of the house where he had chalked the outline of a man, where he'd practiced his stance, jabbing at it with gloved fists, all the while imagining that he was in the ring, the roar of the crowd, the adrenaline rush overtaking him as the battle ensued. He saw his father, he saw Erin, and then there was a red wave of images that came too fast for him to identify.

Somewhere he believed he was losing consciousness, but this was nothing he'd experienced before. He was right there, but he was elsewhere. He was facing up to Aleksy Bodak in the crowded guts of some broken-down New York warehouse, but he had simultaneously escaped, if not in body then in mind and spirit, and he was looking back at himself as if it was all a distant memory.

Frankie rained down blow after blow, connecting time and again with Bodak's face and the side of his head. There was a second crack, and he knew from the sudden rush of color to Bodak's face that it was the cheekbone. Blood welled from Bodak's mouth.

"Frankie!" he heard Lucia scream, and he glanced sideways.

She was there, no more than ten feet away, and in her eyes he saw a desperate plea for him to keep going, to finish this thing, to win. There was something else there, a hunger, some inherent need for justice. She wanted to see the Polack punished for what he'd done.

Frankie saw nothing. He felt nothing. There was no pain. There was no hatred, no need for vengeance. There was just the matter at hand, and he dredged from somewhere deep within himself a reserve of strength and perseverance that had lain dormant. The Frankie Madden that returned to the fray came with more fury than even he knew he possessed.

Bodak's arms were up, but Frankie's fists found their mark. Time and again, he connected with that shattered cheekbone, and he did not let up.

He could feel Lucia urging him on, could feel the force of her intention, and it was so very potent and so very powerful. The woman possessed a volatile, dangerous streak, and it lit a fire in Frankie's mind.

The fire became an inferno. He could no longer see, and he did not care. His fists found their mark, and he did not stop, even when he felt blood spraying up against his face, his chest, his upper arms. He was outside of himself. He was hell unleashed.

Eventually they had to just pull Frankie away from Bodak. Blood everywhere, Frankie's chest and face spattered, Bodak unconscious, blood pouring from his nose, his mouth, his ears. Bodak was a rag doll, beaten and broken, and Frankie stood over him, his heart thundering, his vision blurred, his eyes almost closed with swelling. His nose was broken, his left wrist dislocated, bruises covered his upper body, and yet he'd never felt more alive and energized.

Lucia was there. He could sense her even if he could not see her, and then Nicky was holding him up, and he was being hustled away from the scene, voices everywhere, hands grasping at him, losing all sense of reality as he staggered out of the ring and made his way toward the edge of the warehouse.

Frankie did not hear the outcry. He did not understand what had taken place until the following day, and by then he was already halfway to Chicago.

New York behind him, he would never know of the consequences of what had happened.

Bodak hemorrhaged and died before Frankie Madden even came to his senses.

Casale had lost his best fighter, and he was aggrieved. Monty Leonard took his payoff and kept his mouth shut. Manhattan Red wouldn't see the end of the following week. Raffi Anzelmo would kill him personally under orders from Casale himself.

The fight had been rigged both ways. Casale made a fortune, but money could always be made. To keep Frankie Madden in New York would have been an insult. Nevertheless, you don't kill a man for surviving. Frankie Madden and Nicky Mariani just needed to vanish, and fast. If he saw one of them, Casale told Anzelmo, then he saw both, and both would drown in Hell's Gate. He gave his word.

Three weeks short of his nineteenth birthday and Frankie Madden was twice guilty of murder under two different names. More than that, he knew—no question—that whatever dreams he might have possessed to be a champion of the world had been shattered beyond repair. He'd been given a second chance, and that chance hemorrhaged and died on the floor of a derelict warehouse somewhere in New York. What had really happened, he could not remember. This scared him most of all. Put him in a fight, face him with an opponent, and one of them would die. The fury was deep inside him, perhaps inherited from his father, but it was a demon that could not be controlled. If it took him, it took all of him, and there was no coming back from whatever abyss of madness that swallowed him.

Frankie Madden knew he would never raise his fists again, and thus he recognized the end of any life he might have imagined for himself.

They went—Frankie and Nicky and Lucia—out of New York on the first westbound train.

It was now as good as any blood oath.

Whichever way the dice fell, the three of them were in it together.

FOURTEEN

Los Angeles–May 1938

The City of Angels: Sometimes it seemed like everything, other times like nothing at all.

For Detective Louis Hayes, late of Cleveland, before that the distant memory of a childhood in Pittsburgh, he didn't know whether Los Angeles was less a birthplace and more a cemetery for the dreams of the young and hopeful.

Once upon a time he'd had dreams of his own. Once upon a time—a thousand years before—he'd been all on fire for jazz piano. While other kids rode bikes, copped cans of beer, smoked cigarettes, and dismayed girls, Louis practiced scales and Hanon exercises. By the time he reached seventeen he showed a great deal of promise, and then a freak accident took much of the ring finger and pinkie from his left hand. Now he could barely stretch an octave, let alone a ten or twelve.

His father, a characteristically sensitive Pennsylvania steel worker, said, "Guess that piano business is all shot to hell, then. Time to think about a real job."

In a way, Hayes Senior was relieved. He'd always viewed the music thing as kind of suspect.

Pittsburgh didn't have much to offer, so Louis headed out to Cleveland. He considered the army, opted for the police. If he was going to die in the line of duty, he wanted it to be on American soil.

By December of 1930 he was on Cleveland PD beat patrol, worked his way up through sergeant to detective in less than five years.

In March of 1935, a relationship breakup still feeling like a kick in the balls that wouldn't ease, he moved out to LA.

Central Division was happy to take him. He was young, just twenty-five, but he was smart and hardworking and honest. Frank L. Shaw was mayor, James "Two Guns" Davis was chief of police, and already the press were on their backs. It would get worse before it got better. A great deal worse. New blood gave the LAPD some hope of cleansing the system.

At first Hayes saw nothing but wide streets, palm trees, and sunshine. The houses were pastel-colored adobe haciendas with manicured lawns and flower boxes. Even the pebbles on the pathways seemed to have been handpicked for size and hue. The difference between LA and Cleveland was sufficient to jettison him out of the funk he'd dug himself into. It had been a deep funk, blue and morose, and he was relieved to see the end of it.

After a surprisingly short while, however, the cloudless sky was simply featureless, the once-comforting throb of nighttime cicadas rasped on his nerves, fueled insomnia, and he longed for a rain that never fell.

And then there were the people.

Los Angeles—specifically Hollywood—was a magnet for the gifted and beautiful, but in their wake—as convinced of their own brilliance as it was possible for a human being to be—came the crazies and obsessives, the delusional dreamers, the *If-you-wish-upon-a-star* farm girls and cowboys out of the corn belt who believed that silver-screen stardom was simply a matter of showing up. It was safe to say that those who imagined the most wound up with the least. It was a brutal, fearsome, ugly business, and the ones who survived were few and far between. The ones who made it were even rarer.

Louis Hayes had seen them all and went on seeing them every day. Some of them were close to dead; some had already made it. The lines between bit-piece actress, dinner companion, escort and hooker were pencil thin and so very easily erased. *I'll do it for the money, you know, just to see me through* was the oft-incanted swan song not only of a career, but to any vestige of morals or integrity. As was the case with so many things, once a line was crossed it had a habit of disappearing.

Back in Cleveland he'd seen the money and the graft, the vice, the corruption, even skirted the edges of syndicate gambling and racketeering. It was back there that he'd first heard of Mickey Cohen. Acting as one of many hired hands for the likes of Lou Rothkopf and Moe Dalitz, both of whom would be instrumental in the creation of Las Vegas, Cohen sidelined his burgeoning boxing career with some part-time employment. It was the kind of casual work that sent late payers and deal breakers to the emergency room. Cohen was a little guy, a cartoon thug, face like a bag of pork chops. But irrespective of looks, Cohen was dangerous. Short guys with short fuses gave little but short shrift. Here in LA, here in Central, right here in front of him, that name was being uttered again.

For the third time in as many weeks, Hayes had picked up a Hollywood street star of a different kind. Freddie Fishbait. That's how he was known, and that's how he wanted to be known. Pimp, lowlife, dealer, killer, Freddie earned his name with the simple threat that if you crossed him you'd be fishbait. It was that simple. His given name was Alfredo Cova, and Hayes had brought him in for an unofficial face-to-face. Word had it that Freddie was the bankroll behind a series of jobs carried out by persons unknown that had stricken terror into the wealthier community. A masked and armed gang had invaded homes of producers, directors, even movie stars, looking for cash, jewelry, weapons, and drugs. Of course, no one had reported the theft of the guns and the drugs, but it was clear as day.

That morning, Hayes sat in an interrogation room with Freddie and asked him over and again the same questions, questions that he knew Freddie would never answer. Freddie—mid-fifties, receding hairline, hair grown long in the back, the kind of man who made a three-hundred-dollar silk suit look like a thirty-dollar off-the-rack piece of shit—sat quietly, a faint smile on his face, forever cleaning his fingernails with a cocktail stick.

"The thing is," Freddie said. "The thing is, Mr. Hayes, that we all know you got a hard-on for Jack Dragna. Los Angeles is Mr. Dragna's city. I know that. You know that. The whole freakin' world knows it. Now, if that wasn't trouble enough, Mr. Dragna has a special friend, you see? You know Ben Siegel? You heard that name before, Detective Hayes? People call him Bugsy. Does that ring a little bell someplace?"

Hayes sat patiently. It was the same story—always had been, always would be. Misdirection, diversion, send you looking someplace else for something that didn't exist. People like Freddie had five different versions of everything that happened, and even those versions changed in the recounting.

"I'll tell you who he is," Freddie continued. "He's a big shot from New York. He's come over here to help Jack Dragna sort out all the infighting and the street-corner wars, and between them they're gonna tie everything up nice an' neat with a pretty pink bow. Anyone who doesn't toe the line is gonna have to deal with a nasty little son of a bitch called Mickey Cohen."

Hayes looked up. He could not hide his reaction.

Freddie smiled. "Oh, so you know of Mickey Cohen, do you?" Though Mickey Cohen would not have known Louis Hayes from Adam, Hayes remembered Cohen. Remembered that he was crazy.

"Why the hell are we talking about Bugsy Siegel and Mickey Cohen?" Hayes asked.

"We're not," Freddie replied. "Not unless you want to talk about Bugsy Siegel and Mickey Cohen."

Hayes smiled. There it was, the stock-in-trade of all such characters. *Let this slide, maybe I'll give you something worth a great deal more.*

"You wanna know something, Freddie?" Hayes said. "I spend my life listening to people like you spin such fabulous stories. I listen to the lies, and then I listen to the other versions of the lies, and I go home at night and I think about what it must be like to be you."

Freddie shrugged his shoulders. "Sorry if it disappoints you, but I never think about you."

Hayes ignored the mocking tone of Freddie's comment.

"Are you telling me that these robberies, robberies that have your signature all over them, are something to do with Mickey Cohen and Jack Dragna?"

Freddie leaned forward. "You've been here plenty long enough to know that anything that goes on in this city has something to do with Jack Dragna."

Freddie was right; LA was Dragna's city, no matter what anyone said. Dragna had been in LA since Prohibition. He made a fortune alongside his brother and consigliere, Tom. They raked money in hand over fist from the bookies, the gambling ships, even smuggling heroin. Dragna was everywhere, intrinsic in the very woof and warp of the city itself. It was tight and breathless, the air was dirty with corruption, and Mayor Frank Shaw turned a blind eye, washed his hands, and then used those hands to take the bribes and payoffs. If there was one man who personified everything that was wrong with Hollywood, it was Dragna. And now, if Freddie's implication was true, Bugsy Siegel, heavyweight representative of the American-Italian syndicates in New York, and Mickey Cohen, one of the nastiest thugs ever to walk on American soil, were collaborating with Dragna. But for what? What was being planned?

Hayes leaned forward. "You have something to tell me, Freddie?"

"You got something to charge me with, Mr. Hayes?"

Hayes smiled. "Why d'you call me 'mister,' Freddie? Why not 'detective'?"

Freddie smiled his lizard smile. "You people ain't no better than us. No matter how white you say it is, it's always some shade of gray. Take your mayor, old Frank Shaw there . . . His hands are dirtier and bloodier than anyone's. You know what makes it worse? What makes it worse is that he's pretending to be something he's not. Jack Dragna, even Siegel and Cohen . . . hell, even me, Mister Hayes, even I count in this lineup. We are who we are. We say it how it is. We're crooks, we're thieves, hell, every once in a while we might even bruise our knuckles on some poor schmuck's face, but we never pretend to be something else. You think we're lowlifes, and you have a right to your opinion, but when it comes down to it we have a sense of integrity that you can never recover. We never bullshitted about who we were, and we never will. You people are trying to fool yourselves and the rest of the world with every breath you take. So, to me, you're not a detective. You're just another guy in a suit with a mouthful of lies."

Again, patiently, Hayes listened and did not rise to the bait.

"In answer to your question, Freddie . . . no, I don't have anything to charge you with."

"But you're gonna keep your eyes open, right?"

"Right."

"And when you got something on me, you're gonna drag me back in here and we'll have a talk about Jack Dragna and Bugsy Siegel and Mickey Cohen, right?"

"Maybe."

Freddie pushed back his chair and stood up. "That's the deal right there, Mr. Hayes. Whatever you can find to charge me with, I can give you something bigger and better to file on someone else."

Hayes got up. He walked to the door and opened it. "You've been here enough times to know the way out, right?"

"Second home, Mister Hayes," Freddie said with a self-satisfied grin on his face. "Second home."

With Freddie gone, Hayes sat down again. He closed his eyes for a moment and took a deep breath.

Los Angeles had not made him a cynic or a pessimist; it had made him a realist. Dreams and reality were neither blood-related nor neighbors. In most cases they were natives of a different country with neither language nor law in common.

Harsh but true, many of those who came to Hollywood did not make it. The smart ones realized it fast and moved on. Those who mistook stubbornness for perseverance often persevered their way to desperation. Some persevered all the way to the grave. Routinely, and almost without exception, those graves were dug by Dragna and his cohorts. Drugs, prostitution, gambling, pornography—every vice imaginable was right here for the taking, and there were plenty enough prepared to pay. Dragna's business was supply and demand, and the supply seemed never-ending.

Hayes was haunted by a handful. Most of the dead, the missing, the lost and lonely he could forget, but there were some names—perhaps no more than half a dozen in the three years he'd been on the West Coast—that nudged the edges of his conscience. With one or two exceptions they were all girls—bright-eyed, high-spirited, equally convinced of their own magical Hollywood destiny as they were terrified of failure. But they came anyway, wearing clothes that were out of fashion in 1930, lugging cardboard suitcases, somehow undaunted and resolute. Most of them lasted a month and headed home.

Those who stayed wound up waiting tables, holding on to their hopes as best they could, building up a wall of defensive cynicism and bitterness that aged them faster than bourbon and Lucky Strikes. They took cheap rooms in cheap motels; they bussed it from one audition to the next; they kept smiling and reciting their monologues; they prayed to the God of *The Next One Is Mine*. And then they got hungry. And then they got frightened. It all began with a bad decision. It inevitably ended in a cheap motel room or flophouse, their clothes dirty, their hair unwashed, their eyes dead and wide and staring at the cracked plaster ceiling, the smell of damp and human degradation forever in their breathless lungs.

Sandra Mayweather. That name kept coming back. Sandy to anyone who had known her. Sandy Mayweather. Had she been able to speak, her words would have been the same as all the others.

Look at me. I've got what it takes. I could have been somebody. I really could have been somebody.

But when he'd found her in that motel room—a room that looked so much the same as every other broken-down and dilapidated flea pit—he had been struck by the utter pointlessness of it all. For some reason the vision of the girl—naked, her right arm back behind her head, her hair splayed out across the pillow, the expression on her face one of almost reconciled relief—had seemed so familiar, yet so incongruous. Six months on and the image was as clear in his mind as the moment he'd seen it. Girls like this didn't die like that. Girls like this stayed back in small Midwestern towns; they married decent guys, and they raised good-looking kids in picture-postcard houses. It was as if Sandy Mayweather had somehow come to represent every single one of the lost and lonely, forgotten before they were even buried.

Hayes had never shared a single word with the girl, and—however hard he might have wished—he could not hear the words of the dead. Hayes did what he could, but—in the main—there was very little he could do. He cared, of course, and yet was growing ever more reconciled to the knowledge that he cared alone.

Maybe, one day, if he lived here long enough, he would finally open yet another motel room door to find yet another wasted life, and feel nothing at all.

He hoped such a day would never come, but somehow he knew it was inevitable.

Meantime, Hayes went about his business. He took calls, visited folks, asked questions, filled out paperwork. Every once in a while he skirted the edges of Hollywood—the parties, the drunken brawls, the on-set squabbles that became off-set vendettas. Perhaps the real truth of the City of Angels was that it possessed an endless capacity for demons. Everyone had them, everyone carried them, and the worst of all seemed to be the belief that success was somehow dependent upon the failure of others.

It would be some time before Louis Hayes crossed paths with Nicky Mariani and his beautiful sister. The Marianis had only just arrived. For now they were nothing more than two other names and faces in the vast ocean of names and faces that poured off the Greyhounds and Pullmans into LA every week.

Perhaps, had Hayes known what would happen to Nicky, to Lucia and to Frankie Madden, he would have told them what his father had once told him as he wrestled with his own uncertain future. "Son, in the words of William Jennings Bryan, 'Destiny is not a matter of chance. It is a matter of choice.' "

Detective Louis Hayes believed that to be true. Maybe destiny was indeed the hand you were dealt, but in every game he knew there was an option to change your cards.

FIFTEEN

Lucia Mariani awoke to the plaintive crying of a baby, of someone gunning an engine down in the street below, and close on the heels of this the sound of both her brother and Frankie Madden snoring in the adjoining room. She knew where she was and she knew why. The emotion that accompanied this swung wildly between hopeful anticipation and a sense of desperation.

The room within which she lay was at least dry, the air breathable, and the smell of rotting food and human ablutions was—thankfully—behind her in New York.

They were living in Lincoln Heights, supposedly the oldest suburb of Los Angeles, now crowded with Italians, French, and Mexicans. Over the Los Angeles River was yet another Little Italy, and it was here that Nicky had spent their first weekend *making connections*. That's what he'd said. Leaving early in the morning, returning late at night, he'd told her that progress was being made, that LA really was all they'd dreamed it would be, that opportunities were everywhere and it was simply a matter of finding the right ones.

"A man can have too many choices," he'd said, though she had yet to see him make a choice about anything save the dingy hotel where they were living.

Their epic train journey had taken the better part of a week. The memory of what had happened in New York was all too evident in the damage to Frankie's face, and they had stood like lost children on the platform of La Grande Station. The Pullman conductor had been eager to tell them that La Grande was once the most beautiful train station in the world, bar none, until the Long Beach earthquake back in '33. Then they'd had to take down the Moorish domes to make it safe for travelers. "Of course," he explained, "we're going to lose all our passengers to the new Union Passenger Terminal next May, but that's progress for you. Gotta leave history behind or you don't go nowhere."

It had seemed a fitting commentary to their present situation. New York was behind them, as was Corsica, and even though they weren't in Hollywood, they were at least on the right side of the country.

"We'll get to Hollywood," Nicky had assured her with his characteristic bravado. "Trust me . . . it's gonna happen. I can already see your name on the billboards."

And so he'd gone out into the big city, meeting people, talking to people, establishing contacts, and she'd been left behind in the hotel with Frankie Madden.

The previous day, a doctor had come by to take a look at Frankie's nose. It was busted all right, but it wasn't as bad as it could have been.

"It'll be a little crooked," the doctor had told Lucia, "but that'll probably serve your husband well."

Lucia laughed. "Oh, he's not my husband," she said.

The doctor seemed momentarily puzzled.

Lucia then understood how it appeared.

"My brother's business partner," she said, and even as the words left her lips she knew they sounded contrived and fictional.

"Indeed," the doctor replied, as if he did not believe her for a moment. He had seen everything, and those things he'd not seen had been seen by someone he knew. He worked in Hollywood, after all.

Lucia was struck by her own sense of self-consciousness. Even though the exchange of words was awkward, she was surprised at how much she felt—a sense of indignation that the doctor would think of her in such a disreputable way, and close on the heels of that a feeling that she had every right to be with whoever she wanted, that it was none of his business. As for his assumption that Frankie was her husband, she didn't even dare consider how she felt about that.

"Well, as I was saying . . . your friend here. His crooked nose might get him some walk-ons in some of these gangster movies they're making nowadays."

The doctor had gone on to explain how much he loved those gangster flicks, more an effort to make small talk and circumvent any further awkwardness.

"I saw *Kid Galahad* with Edward G. Robinson and that Bogart feller. You seen that one?"

Lucia had explained that she hadn't been to the movies for a good while.

"Well, you're in the right place for movie theaters, that's for sure.

Saw *The Last Gangster*, too. James Stewart was in that one. Great movie. Westerns, too. You like Westerns?"

"Sure," Lucia had said. "I like most kinds of films."

"Good one couple of years ago. *Texas Rangers*. Fred MacMurray. You know Fred MacMurray?"

"I know who he is, yes."

"I got his autograph." The doctor had seemed very pleased with himself. "At the Musso & Frank Grill."

"That's a restaurant?"

"Yeah sure, a restaurant. Up on Hollywood Boulevard. All the stars go there. Hell of a place. I'm up there one time, some old guy has a heart attack, and there I am doing what I can to help out and Fred MacMurray is seated at a table not ten feet from me. Helluva nice guy. Anyways, the ambulance comes and off the old guy goes, and Fred comes over and tells me that I done a real good job helping the old feller. I ask him for an autograph and he says it's the least he can do. Such a nice feller."

"Actually, I want to get into the movie business," Lucia had said. "That's why we're here."

"Is that so? The movies, eh? Well, you sure are pretty enough for the movies."

Lucia had blushed.

"And now I must get going. Your friend here is fine. He'll probably sleep for a week. Make sure he eats and doesn't get dehydrated. It's hotter than it feels—humid, too. People forget."

The doctor had taken five dollars for his trouble, and Frankie Madden—having barely slurred into semi-wakefulness even while the doctor examined him—had gone back to sleep.

Lucia had sat for a while and watched him. His nose was still blocked with blood and he had little choice but to breathe through his mouth. It was not a pleasant sound, but nevertheless it made her smile. She could imagine how he'd looked as a boy, that pale Irish complexion, the fierce shock of almost-black hair, his eyes like watery aquamarine. He was a handsome young man, no question, and she hoped that the broken nose would not make him look like the hoodlum the doctor had predicted.

The following day the washed-out early-morning Californian light woke her and she lay there for a time. Cracks spiderwebbed the ceiling, and she followed them like lines on a palm to the edges. She did not know how long Nicky would be *making connections*, but she had no choice but to trust him and wait.

She was frustrated and impatient. She wanted to see everything—the Hollywoodland Sign, Grauman's Chinese Theatre, this restaurant the doctor had spoken of where it was possible to sit ten feet from Fred MacMurray. Had Frankie been strong and well, she might have gone into the city with him and taken a look for herself, but he may as well have been in a coma for all the good it did. She had resolved her awkwardness around him. He did not make her angry anymore. Every once in a while he would look at her as if he expected to be thumped, and that made her smile. The big tough Irish guy was intimidated by a petite Corsican girl.

Lucia rose and dressed. She thought of dresses she'd left behind in San-Nicolao. She thought of the beautiful gown she'd worn that day in New York. She owned only what she could carry, and there was no hope of anything more until they had money. What little she did possess was clean but tired. She looked exactly as she was—a poor immigrant—and it spurred her on to further resolve and determination. This was not the way she was destined to live, and she would not let it stay this way for long.

The vista from her window was a great deal different from that of New York. In New York she'd barely seen the sky. That was what she now realized. No wonder she'd been miserable. At least here she could see the sky, the palm trees along the streets, and though she didn't much care for Lincoln Heights, it was still preferable to anywhere else she'd been in America. Cars passed by and disappeared, and down on the sidewalk people gathered in twos and threes to talk on stoops and in doorways. Children entertained themselves with games that required nothing but imagination, and even though this was America, even though this was exactly where she'd wished to be for as long as she could remember, it was still a million miles from where she needed to be.

She wanted to think of tomorrow, next week, of where she would be at Christmastime, but she did not dare. Tempting fate, perhaps, but even more than that, she did not want to set herself up for disappointment. It was all very well to believe in miracles; it was something else entirely to depend upon them.

When Nicky woke he came through and said they should go out for breakfast. She could see the change in her brother. He would recover, of course, and swiftly, but for now he looked exhausted, perhaps even a little afraid. What had happened in New York had shaken him. Despite his bluff and bravado, he would take what had happened seriously. When it came to Lucia, he did not shoulder his responsibility lightly. If Lucia was unhappy to be living in such a wretched place, then Nicky would be more than desperate to leave. Just as was the case for Lucia, this was not the America he wanted.

"I don't think we should leave Frankie here alone," she said.

"He'll be fine. He ain't gonna do nothin' but sleep anyhow. Come on. We'll just be gone a half hour. I'm so damned hungry I'd eat a dead dog if there was ketchup."

Lucia scowled disapprovingly.

"What?"

"You don't have to talk like that around me, Nicky."

"Like what?"

"Like someone with no manners. Like one of these gangsters. Out there you can be anyone you like, but here it's perfectly all right to be yourself."

Nicky laughed. "Is that how a gangster talks? You been watchin' gangster flicks and you know everything there is to know now, eh?"

"I know you sound like a fool. Now go... If we're going, let's go."

Fifteen minutes later, seated in a diner a block and a half away, eggs ordered, coffee in front of them, Nicky told Lucia things she didn't so much want to hear.

"All sorts of things going on," Nicky explained. "Last year the city bought a place called Mines Field. It's the Los Angeles airport, basically, but they're gonna build it real big now. Looks like it's gonna be the biggest airport in the country."

Lucia looked out of the window. She knew where Nicky was going, and she knew she wouldn't like it.

"People I'm speaking to are involved in construction, real estate, transport, everything you could imagine. They're spending millions, Lucia, tens of millions, and there's slices of the pie everywhere."

Nicky paused for a moment. He did not have Lucia's attention, and he knew it was because she didn't want to give it.

"Listen to me," he said. "This is not what you think, okay?"

Lucia looked back at her brother. He was hungry, just as she was, but she knew they would never eat from the same tables.

"Just this February, there was a storm right here," Nicky went on, determined that Lucia would hear him out. "There were two storms, in fact, coming in from the Pacific. Swept right across the basin, killed more than a hundred people, and they say there was maybe forty million dollars' worth of damage. Five thousand buildings gone, whole towns washed away, roads and everything all gone. Those roads and buildings all gotta go back up, and someone's gotta do the building. Then they gotta put a whole load of dams around to make sure it don't happen again."

Lucia smiled. "All of a sudden you're a builder, Nicky. What do you know about building?"

"I'm not talking about being a builder, Lucia. Do you not see the possibilities here? Can you even begin to imagine how much money is gonna be spent on these projects?"

"And what does that have to do with us?"

"Frank Shaw, the Mayor of Los Angeles, has his hands in everything. There's corrupt politicians and councilmen, union people, bribes, backhanders, people buying into the construction contracts, all of it going on here. Just the craziest things, you know—"

"And you know all of this because of the people you've been talking to . . . in just the last two days?"

"I'm listening. I'm asking questions, that's all."

"Listening to the wrong people, asking the wrong questions, Nicky. I didn't come all the way here from Corsica so you could be a gangster."

Nicky laughed. "What are you talking about? I'm not going to be a gangster. You're overreacting. I'm trying to get us some money. We can't live on what we brought from New York forever. There's all sorts of things happening here. The law has changed. They're bringing in something called nonstop roadways. That means someone is gonna be building a lot of freeways over the next few years—"

"What do you know about freeways?"

"I don't know anything about freeways. Only thing I have to know about any of this is that someone somewhere's gotta pay for it, and it's a lot of money. I am talking a *lot* of money."

"Is that what you are now? Someone who is just interested in money?"

Nicky didn't reply. The waitress came with eggs, asked if they needed anything else.

When she was once more out of earshot, Nicky leaned forward. "Thing you have to know is this," he said, his voice almost a whisper. "Los Angeles is a big city. It goes all different ways . . . out to Pacific, the San Gabriel Mountains. Sixty years ago there were maybe ten thousand people. You know how many people live here now?"

"I have no idea."

"One and a half million. One and a half million people, Lucia.

All of them gotta live somewhere, all of them gotta eat, go to the movies, drink beer, drive cars, wear clothes. That's where the money is, my sweet naive kid sister. The money is in the things that people can't do without."

"And when you have all this money? What then? What are you going to do?"

"I am going to live the high life. *We* are going to live the high life. We are going to live in one of those mansions in the hills. We are going to send money home to Ma and Pa. Hell, we might even get them to come and live here with us. If there is an American Dream, Lucia, and I believe there is, then it's right here in the City of Angels."

Lucia could not help but be captivated by Nicky's enthusiasm, but there was a shadow behind her thoughts. Money was never easy; money was supposed to be worked for, earned with toil and perseverance. If money came fast, then it was all-too-likely dirty.

Nicky ate his eggs. He wolfed them down. Hungry for breakfast, but greedy in every other way. Greed was a cardinal sin. With it came envy and gluttony, other such afflictions of the soul. Lucia and Nicky had been schooled by nuns, nuns who taught them English and good manners and believing in Jesus, and Lucia knew all too well the depths to which man could fall in the vain search for mortal pleasure and material satisfaction.

"So, what business are you involved in?" she asked him.

Nicky smiled, as if here he kept a secret.

"Tell me, Nicky."

Nicky stabbed the last piece of egg and ate it. He sat back and looked at her with a knowing expression. "I'll tell you something, Lucia . . . I'll tell you something right now."

"What?"

"You've heard of RKO Pictures."

"Sure I have."

"I met a guy. A producer. He makes the money for the pictures. His name is Morris Budny. Good guy. Knows a lot of people. He and I were talking, and he says you should go over to his hotel suite on Wednesday morning and meet with him."

Nicky stopped talking. He was watching her expression. She colored up, her eyes wide, but she was utterly incapable of speech.

"You understand what I'm saying?" Nicky asked. "I got you a meeting with an RKO producer. Two days in Los Angeles, and already you're meeting with a Hollywood big shot."

Lucia nearly exploded with enthusiasm. She started laughing. There were tears in her eyes, and she came around the table to hug her brother.

"Oh, Nicky! Nicky, you are incredible! I don't know what to say!"

"Calm yourself," Nicky said, playing it down. "It's a meeting, that's all. I told him about you, said you could act, sing, dance, whatever, and he said there was no harm in taking a look at you and seeing if there was maybe an audition he could get you into. Nothing is guaranteed, you understand. It's just a meeting."

"I know, Nicky, I know... but it's exciting! I am going to meet a Hollywood producer!"

"You are indeed, and you better not screw it up."

"Nicky," Lucia said, her expression one of surprise and dismay.

"Kidding," Nicky replied. "Eat your breakfast. We gotta get back and see your boy."

Lucia frowned. "He's not my boy."

"I see what I see, little sister."

"Meaning what?"

"Meaning that there is something going on, and even if you don't know what it is, I can sense it."

"You're talking nonsense, Nicky. There is nothing going on between me and Frankie."

"Well, if you say so, but you need to be careful. I think he's maybe getting sweet on you, and he ain't the boy for you. You need a man with prospects, a man with some money and influence behind him. He can chaperone you for now, but I don't want to be dealing with any complications, you hear?"

Lucia took her seat again on the opposite side of the table. "I am not going to fall in love with an eighteen-year-old bareknuckle-fighting Irish boy, Nicky."

"There is a lot more to him than that, and you know it. And besides, he ain't gonna be fighting anymore, not after what's happened."

"I am not listening to you."

"Sure you are," Nicky said, and smiled. "We three are joined at the hip, Lucia. What happened in New York—"

"Is part of our history, Nicky. As far as I'm concerned, it was nothing to do with us."

"Well, I don't think Luca Casale or Raffi Anzelmo or the New York Police Department would agree with you."

"They are three thousand miles away—"

"Sure they are, but that don't mean they'll forget. That Polish guy is dead. Frankie killed him, and we were there. That's all there is to it."

"I was happy, Nicky, and now you're upsetting me."

"You go on being happy, sis. The world is nothing but rainbows and pretty flowers. You go see Morris Budny and get yourself in a motion picture."

"I will," Lucia replied. "That is exactly what I'm going to do."

The discussion over, Lucia got the waitress's attention and ordered some breakfast to go. Until he was capable of taking care of himself, Frankie was in her care. She did not want to think about what she might or might not feel for him. She was in Hollywood. This was where her future lay. It could even be better than she'd dreamed. Some sort of romantic entanglement with Frankie Madden would merely serve to complicate things.

They had escaped New York, and—in truth—Frankie was the only person who really needed to answer for what had happened back there.

SIXTEEN

The Hollywood Roosevelt Hotel was straight out of a movie, number 7000 right there on the Boulevard itself.

Frankie Madden and Lucia Mariani arrived before the appointment so they could see a little of this mythical place. Sunset, Santa Monica, La Brea, Melrose, and Cahuenga: streets that Lucia had read of in the dog-eared and worn-out copies of *Daily Variety*, *Silver Screen* and *Life* she'd managed to accumulate since she was a little girl. Those magazines now sat in a box beneath her bed in San-Nicolao, but she only had to close her eyes to recall every page.

In truth, those pictures could never have done justice to the reality. The first thing that struck her was the colors, as if some great creator had determined that every shade in the spectrum would be employed. Perhaps she viewed it through some haze of optimism and childlike innocence, but it seemed truly magical. The streets were wide enough to take several cars at once, dwarfing any road back home. The buildings were higher, their awnings providing ample shade, and outside the diners and restaurants people drank coffee and smoked cigarettes as if everything they did was an iconic scene in some movie. The promise of fame and fortune was in the very air, seeping up through the sidewalk, navigating its way between the buildings and storefronts to find her. She could sense it here, firing her imagination and reviving her lifelong dreams.

"It's just incredible," she said. "I've seen so many pictures, but I don't think I ever really believed that I would get here." She laughed for a moment. "I mean, of course I knew I'd get here, but . . . but this is so much more than I ever imagined." She turned to him with an expression of such childlike wonder that he couldn't help smiling.

Frankie was doing better. His nose was no longer swollen and clotted with blood. He could breathe properly, and the bruises had faded to a dull tallow-gray. He still looked as if he'd run into a tree, but his energy and appetite had returned. Irrespective of his physical recovery, there was still a shadow. It haunted him like a ghost. Lucia was unaware of its source, but Frankie knew all too well. Take away a man's dream and you take away his life. Had Lucia been denied any chance of acting, perhaps she would appreciate the sense of disillusionment and hollowness that Frankie Madden felt, but in that moment she was too self-absorbed to think of anything but the forthcoming meeting. Frankie hid it. He said nothing. With the death of Aleksy Bodak, a little of Frankie Madden had also died. Competitively, he would never fight again, and that was a pain almost too great to bear.

"It's Hollywood," Frankie said. "You got to where you wanted."

"I got here," Lucia said, "but that is only the beginning."

At nine o'clock that morning they sat in a bakery and coffee shop called Van de Kamp's on the corner of Ivar and Yucca Avenues. It was built to look like a windmill, and from the window seat Lucia could see the Knickerbocker Hotel.

Perhaps irony played a part, for the seat beside Frankie's had been occupied by none other than Detective Louis Hayes just half an hour earlier.

Lucia wanted to walk, to look, to see everything. She chattered incessantly about places she'd read about, buildings she'd seen in movies, and when she told Frankie that the hotel they were going to was where Elizabeth Patterson lived, it was all Frankie could do to smile and nod interestedly.

"Elizabeth Patterson," Lucia, her tone one of disbelief. *South Sea Rose*, *Secret of the Blue Room*, *Night of Mystery*. You must know *Dinner at Eight*... Jean Harlow and Lionel Barrymore were in it."

Frankie smiled patiently. "I'll tell you what I know, Lucia. If Jean Harlow and Lionel Barrywood were sat in the next booth I wouldn't know 'em from Adam and Eve."

"Barrymore. Lionel Barrymore."

"Like I said, don't know their names, don't know their faces. I come from a small town in Ireland called... well, no matter what it's called. I guess I must've seen two films in me whole life, and neither of them had any words."

"Silent movies."

"There was a whole load o' music, so they weren't silent, no. But no one said a darn thing from start to finish."

Lucia laughed.

"Hey!" he reprimanded. "Laugh at me and I'll thump you, Lucia."

"You'd never thump me, Frankie. You owe me for looking after you these last few days. And anyway, I'm not laughing at you. I'm just laughing at the situation."

"Right you are. That's what people say when they're laughing at you and they don't want to get thumped."

"You really don't know anything about Hollywood?"

"I've been busy with other things."

"Well, you're here now, and it's one of the most famous places in the world, and we're going to meet someone that Nicky knows and see if he can get me an audition."

"So you can be in one o' them silent movies with Lionel Barry-whatever."

"They don't make silent movies anymore, Frankie. They invented something called the talkies."

"Lot o' talkin' is there?"

"Yes."

"You'll be well suited for that, then, won't you?"

Lucia frowned, but couldn't keep the amusement out of her eyes. "You ever gonna stop teasing me?"

"You ever gonna stop talkin'?"

Lucia sideswiped Frankie's shoulder. "Such a pig, you are."

"Careful now, little missy."

Lucia did not take the bait. She went back to her coffee and pastries.

Frankie sat and watched the world through the window. Truth be told, he'd never imagined such a place. He could just imagine his sisters' reactions, their eyes wide, their mouths agape, hands shading against the bright sunlight, the brilliant colors, the flashy cars. Women wore Sunday best to fetch groceries. Chauffeurs hefted packages into cars as long as buses. Everyone smiled and shared words, but it all seemed like theater. To Frankie, ignorant though he was of such things, it seemed that to maintain such a life would be nothing but exhausting.

"So?"

Frankie turned. Lucia was looking at him.

He frowned. "So? So what?"

"You're not listening to me at all, are you?"

"I'm sorry, I was distracted. What did you say?"

"I asked you a question."

"So ask me again."

"This is where I want to be more than anywhere in the world. This is where I've been heading my whole life. I just asked you what you wanted, that was all . . . if there was somewhere you wanted to go more than anywhere else."

Home.

There was no other answer to Lucia's question, but it was an answer he could never give.

I want to go home, but home is the one place I can never go.

Frankie smiled. He tried his best to hide the welling of emotion that invaded his chest.

"Wherever you are," he said. "That's where I want to go."

Lucia looked shocked for just a moment, and then she saw the suppressed laughter in Frankie's expression.

She sideswiped him again. "You really are the worst person, Frankie Madden. I was being serious. It's an honest question."

"I don't have an answer for you, Lucia. I am a fighter, always have been, always will be. Now it's something I can't do anymore. I am a boat adrift. I guess I'll find a new direction, or maybe a current will take me someplace."

Lucia hesitated before speaking, and then she said, "Finding a direction is better."

"Maybe," Frankie replied.

"Tell me the truth. Tell me why you're here... in America. What happened to you?"

He looked out of the window. He saw a world that he did not understand, nor believed he ever would. He didn't feel lost because he'd never actually had a destination. A current had indeed taken him, and it had been strong.

One thing he knew for sure: The pull of home would always be there, as if he'd set his anchor and the chain that held him would drag forever.

"What about your family? You do have a family, right?"

Frankie turned and looked at her. He paused before speaking, and there was a sense of finality and reconciliation in his tone. "Not anymore," he said.

"Not anymore?" Lucia echoed.

Frankie shook his head and Lucia understood there would be no more discussion on the matter.

The meeting with Budny was at eleven; they stayed at the bakery until ten thirty.

Frankie walked over with her, said he'd come on up to the suite but would wait outside. He didn't want her to feel self-conscious while she talked to this producer guy. Maybe this Hollywood big shot wouldn't look twice at her. She'd made an effort, for sure, and as far as he was concerned she looked great, but she had very few clothes, and even the ones she had had seen better days. She was a Hollywood hopeful, just like so many others, and Frankie hoped she would not find her dream shattered before she'd even woken up.

The foyer was all marble and wooden floors, chandeliers, potted plants, and deep-pile rugs. The vaulted ceiling was like something out of a French cathedral, and centering the floor was a huge octagonal fountain. Back on the SS *Excalibur*, Frankie had taken a peek through the door into the opulence and grandeur of the Country Club Veranda Café. The Roosevelt made that look like a prospector's cabin.

The man behind the desk was conservatively polite, a little unsure what this young woman and her beaten-up companion were doing in his hotel.

"We're here to see Mr. Budny," Lucia explained. "Morris—"

The man smiled warmly. "Of course, miss. Mr. Budny. And may I ask your name?"

"Lucia Mariani," she said.

The man picked up the telephone and made a call, smiling altogether too much. Seemed that now he knew they had business in the hotel they'd all become lifelong friends.

Frankie didn't much care for airs and graces. People were who they were. Everyone deserved the time of day, no matter where they came from or how they looked. You trusted people until they gave you a reason to think otherwise. It wasn't complicated. Maybe it was different here; maybe everyone had a suitcase full of faces and they wore whichever one suited the occasion.

The man set down the receiver and smiled some more.

"Mr. Budny will send someone down shortly," he said. "Meanwhile, he asked me to show you something very special." Raising his hand, a bellhop appeared as if from nowhere.

"This is Tommy," he said, introducing a young man. Tommy couldn't have been more than nineteen or twenty, and despite the smart Roosevelt tunic, Frankie could see he belonged there no more than himself. His complexion was pale, his dark hair glued to his scalp with pomade, his manner one of practiced friendliness.

The man behind the desk said, "Tommy is going to show you the Blossom Ballroom. Mr. Budny says you will appreciate it. It was here, in 1929, that the first ever Academy Awards ceremony was held."

Lucia's eyes lit up. She looked at Frankie, but Frankie—evidently—had no clue as to the significance of this.

"The hotel was named after President Roosevelt, of course," Tommy said, leading the way. "It cost two and a half million dollars to build it, and the group that financed the building included the famous actors Douglas Fairbanks and Mary Pickford, and Mr. Louis Mayer, the cofounder of MGM Pictures. As Mr. Mayer used to say, 'Hollywood has more stars than there are in the heavens.' "

Frankie heard the lilt in Tommy's accent.

"You Irish, my friend?" Frankie asked.

Tommy smiled. "Got me," he said, and immediately that accent was stronger. "Where you from?"

"South."

"South is big."

"Originally Kilkenny, but I been all over. You?"

"Galway," Frankie lied.

Tommy extended his hand and they shook. "Been away more 'an a year now. Miss it somethin' dreadful."

"Ain't no better than when you left it, I'm sure."

"You off the boat recent?"

"Recent, yeah. Still not made me first million, though."

Tommy laughed. "Me neither. Let me show your girl this place, eh? Maybe we could get a pint sometime and you could tell me all the bad news."

The Blossom Ballroom was impressive. Even Frankie had to admit it. Arched doorways, balustraded balconies, a ceiling that was nothing less than a fantastic spiderweb of glass panels through which a beautiful blue light emanated.

Lucia was breathless and transfixed. She asked question after question about the awards event, and Tommy answered every one. Douglas Fairbanks was the host, and awards went to the likes of Howard Hughes, King Vidor, Gloria Swanson, Emil Jannings, and Charlie Chaplin. Frankie had heard of the Chaplin fellow, remembered some film at a picture house in Dublin when he was younger.

"*The Gold Rush*," Frankie said. "I've seen that one. That is one picture I have definitely seen."

Lucia seemed altogether too wide-eyed and starstruck to pay any mind to what Frankie had to say.

Frankie ventured nothing further. It was evident that this was a world to which he did not belong, though which world he now belonged to he could not have said.

Another fifteen minutes of chatter, and Tommy said he would take Lucia up to Mr. Budny's suite.

"If you'd care to follow me, miss," Tommy said to Lucia, and then he glanced back at Frankie and gave him a conspiratorial wink. *Lucky Irish bastard,* that wink said.

Frankie winked back. *If only,* he thought.

Budny's suite was on the ninth floor in the corner of the building. Outside the elevator was a lounge area with a leather settee and a table covered in magazines. Tommy walked them down to the room, knocked on the door, and waited.

Lucia glanced back at Frankie and Frankie got the message. He headed back to the elevator and sat down. He would wait there until her meeting was done.

It seemed that Budny wasted no time. Tommy was back and calling the elevator within a couple of minutes.

"I'm up and around and all over the place," Tommy said. "Like I said, we should get a pint sometime. I like to be reminded of home."

"That'd be good, so it would," Frankie said, and they shook hands again.

The elevator bell sounded, the door opened, and Tommy was gone.

Frankie picked up a magazine called *Hollywood*. Proudly announcing that it was the *Only 5c Movie Magazine in the World,* it showed a photo of a man and a woman, beneath which was the line *How an Ugly Duckling Became a Hollywood Star*. Frankie tossed the magazine aside. He was thirsty, wondered if he should head down to the lobby and get a drink. He decided against it. He didn't know how long Lucia's meeting would be.

Frankie thought about New York, about what had happened, about the man who'd died. Aleksy Bodak. Whatever anyone might have thought, Frankie didn't think of himself as a killer. It had been a fair fight. In truth, it had been a fight heavily weighted against him, and yet he'd won. And before, back in Ireland, Bobby Durnin. That had been a matter of self-defense. Manslaughter. Unintentional, no question about it.

Frankie held out his hands and looked at them. The bruising had gone, the stiffness in his fingers was a memory, but there was blood on those hands now. This was the kind of blood that never washed off. Eighteen years old and he had the deaths of two men on his conscience. Was this some kind of omen for the rest of his life?

It seemed a thousand years ago, yet less than six months had passed since that boat had come up to Pembroke Dock and the

English had been waiting for him. Now his own family would not recognize his name, and perhaps they would not recognize the man he'd become. He was harder. Harder of mind, harder of emotion. He knew that the life he'd envisioned for himself was not the life he was going to get.

Frankie understood that there was no point casting his mind backward and wondering what might have happened if things had been different. The faces of the others—Micky Cavanaugh, Jimmy O'Connell, the ones who'd sprung him from Clonmel—were imprinted on his memory. He only had to think of those days and their faces would be there. But the one that would haunt him forever was Johnny Madden—wild gypsy bastard that he was, all on fire for killing as many English as he could. Well, he got as good as he gave, and now he was dead and gone.

As had been said before, the past was a different country.

Frankie got up and paced the hallway in front of the elevator. He had no idea what would happen now. Could he even stay here in Los Angeles? Then again, if he kept on moving, where would he wind up? If you left home and kept walking, you inevitably wound up heading home again. Was that the life for him? Running forever, always looking over his shoulder, always worried about who might be watching him?

And Nicky? Nicky was brash and arrogant sometimes, but Frankie did not believe he was inherently bad. He aspired to some life that he didn't even understand, and Frankie didn't doubt that he was associating with people who would do him no good. But Nicky had his redeeming qualities, the foremost of which was his duty as a brother. He loved his sister, cared for her life and happiness as much—if not more—than his own, and Frankie could respect that.

And then there was Lucia herself. Frankie didn't even understand what he felt for her. He wondered if it was merely a symptom of loneliness. Was he beyond foolish to think that she might be interested in him? She was a dreamer, sure, but there was something beneath that. Maybe these Corsicans were just as tough as the people back home. That moment in the fight, the moment it looked like Bodak was just gonna beat him into the sawdust, there was something in Lucia's eyes, something cold and unforgiving that had driven him on. Had she not been there, he did not know what would have happened. She had motivated him to pull whatever deep reserve of spirit he possessed and give it everything he had. And so he had killed a man. Seeing Lucia Mariani had driven him to kill a man.

Was that in him, or was that in her? Was it something they created together, or was he imagining some fierce connection between them that was nothing more than delusion?

Frankie stopped pacing and sat down again.

Fifteen minutes elapsed, and Frankie became agitated. It was nothing more than boredom, but beneath that was a hint of anxiety. What was this meeting that was taking place? Who was this Morris Budny, and what kind of man lived in a hotel like this?

Frankie headed for the suite into which Tommy had shown Lucia, and he paused outside the door.

He tried to hear voices, a conversation, anything. There was nothing for a good minute, and then he heard something unmistakable.

Frankie Madden held his breath and pressed his ear to the door. Someone was crying out, as if both angered and afraid, and there was no doubt in his mind that it was Lucia.

Frankie knocked on the door. No response. He knocked again more loudly, called her name.

Behind the door everything went quiet, and then he heard a man's voice—low and insistent—and he knew that he had to find out what was going on.

Frankie took three steps back and then launched himself against the door shoulder-first.

SEVENTEEN

Hayes could not stop thinking about the conversation he'd had with Freddie Fishbait. The man was a liar and a thief, more than likely a killer, but despite his utter absence of conscience or morals, he was driven by the very same motivation that every human being possessed, no matter who they were or what they did. Everyone wanted to survive. Everyone wanted to see tomorrow. Everyone wanted to hold something in reserve in the event that their well-being was threatened.

Freddie would not have mentioned Dragna, Siegel, or Cohen without a reason. Maybe he knew that Hayes would finally nail him for the Hollywood home invasions, but even so, there was no logical reason for Freddie to have ventured a get-out-of-jail card unless he had a purpose. Knowing Freddie, that purpose would be for his own advantage and his alone. Unless . . . unless Freddie had been told to say something. And if he had been told to say something, then who had told him, and what was their reasoning? Why would someone want Central PD thinking there was something going on with Siegel and Dragna? Territory? Was Freddie working for the Jewish gang? Was it movie money that was behind this? Was someone at MGM or RKO afraid of the influence that could be brought to bear on the unions, and wanted to stir up trouble for Dragna's network?

Hayes didn't know. He could suppose and assume all he wished, but—as was the case with the robberies that had plagued the wealthier set—there was nothing he could do without evidence, without warrants, without names and faces and reasons to file charges.

Seated at his desk the same morning that Lucia Mariani and Frankie Madden attended their appointment at the Roosevelt, Hayes took a call from his lieutenant, Eric Fuller. It was a summons to the captain's office.

Hayes headed up there. He knew what was coming, and he knew there was nothing he could do to stop it.

Fuller was a good cop, long in the tooth and worldly-wise. He'd done the LA beat for years as a patrolman, worked his way up through the ranks and achieved a well-deserved reputation as a tough, fair, never-hold-a-grudge kind of guy. If you screwed up, you got a kicking, figuratively speaking, but once it was done it was done. Tomorrow was another day.

Look at Fuller and you'd see a man nailed together with two-by-fours and roofing studs. He was weatherproof, bulletproof, incorruptible, and tough. Never married, though word had it there was a woman in his life, he had given all for his job and asked for nothing in return.

Captain Edward Mills was less of a known quantity. Mills had come sideways into Central, hailed out of San Francisco, spent no more than three or four months as a lieutenant and then gained a captaincy when the last captain retired due to ill health. Hayes figured that the sheer speed of his ascension had made him light-headed. He was a political man, and he looked like one. He was a couple inches taller than Fuller, wiry and lean. His hair was cut short, his uniform ever pristine. When he donned a suit for mayoral committees, PR glad-handers, meet and greets, he looked like he was running for Congress. It was the same with most captains, but those that Hayes had known—both in Cleveland and here in LA—had recognized that politics ran second to getting the job done. Not so with Mills, it seemed, and Hayes often wondered whether his rapid departure from San Francisco had more to do with leaving something behind that needed to stay forgotten.

"This current case," Fuller began once Hayes was seated in Mills's office. "You had Fishbait in here, right?"

"Fishbait?" Mills asked.

"Alfredo Cova," Fuller said. "Street name is Freddie Fishbait."

Mills shook his head as if in disbelief. That was the first sign of a man who'd never pounded sidewalks in LA. A few months of that and nothing anyone did or said came as a surprise.

"I did, yes," Hayes said.

"And?"

"And nothing. No evidence, no charge, no reason to hold him."

Fuller shook his head resignedly. He'd known the answer to the question before it came, but he had to ask it for Mills's benefit.

"These people are Hollywood," Mills said. "They've got the money, so they are the city. We can't have people just bursting into their houses with guns and masks and robbing them."

"I do understand that, sir," Hayes said.

"How many now . . . eight?"

"Nine," Fuller said. "Nine in the last five weeks."

"And we have nothing but some guy called Fishbait, and we can't even hold him for questioning? Is that what you're telling me?"

Fuller nodded. "Yes, sir."

Mills looked at Hayes. "You have anything to say about this?"

"Nothing that I haven't already said."

Mills looked irritable. He leaned forward and placed his hands flat on the desk for emphasis. "You appreciate the awkwardness of the conversations I have with City Hall?" he asked.

Neither Fuller nor Hayes ventured a response.

"When I get calls from the mayor's office . . . well, you can imagine that this utter lack of result does not sound too heartening."

Again, neither Fuller nor Hayes spoke.

"So, tell me, what is it that you believe has to happen for some progress to be made on this matter?"

Fuller looked at Hayes. Hayes's expression said everything that Fuller was thinking.

"More people," Fuller said.

"More people," Mills echoed. "That's the best answer I can get?"

"That's the only answer you're going to get," Hayes said, knowing his tone would merely serve to aggravate Mills further. If he was honest with himself, he didn't care. Central was undermanned, underpaid, under-appreciated. He didn't want a fight, but sometimes a fight seemed to be the only way of expressing his frustration with the situations he faced every working day. He was not a special case. This was not a special precinct. It was the same story city wide, and though Mills might not want to hear those same words again, the fact of the matter was that reality would not change until someone or something changed it.

Mills looked away toward the window. When he turned back Hayes saw an expression that he had seen so many times before, not only from Mills, but from others in authority. The words were the same as well, so familiar that Hayes could have written them himself.

"My hands are tied," Mills said. "You understand this as well as anyone. We have what we have. There are no more people. Notwithstanding this, I need results. I need progress. I need something that I can take to the chief, to the mayor's office, something that will calm down the entire situation."

There was silence from Fuller and Hayes. There was nothing to say.

"You have my permission to assign whatever existing resources we have wherever you choose to assign them, Lieutenant Fuller, but I cannot give you any more. That is the bottom line."

"Yes, sir," Fuller replied.

"And Detective Hayes?" Mills added. "Whatever efforts you are devoting to this, which I am sure are considerable, I need you to double them. I need results, and I need them fast."

Hayes got up. The meeting had come to its very predictable conclusion.

Fuller walked with Hayes down to his office.

"You got absolutely nothing on Fishbait?"

Hayes smiled. "Ironically, he's anything but fishbait right now. He isn't even close to being on the hook."

Fuller smiled. "Comedy isn't your strong suit, Louis. Stick to the day job, okay?"

"He started talking about Bugsy Siegel and Mickey Cohen. It was inconsequential, the usual 'I've got something, but I'll only go there if I need a bargaining card' kind of deal. I doubt there's anything in it."

"I know Siegel's here," Fuller said. "Cohen too. Rumor has it that Dragna's pissed. Dragna wants everyone on their toes, everyone wondering if there's gonna be a war. It's all so much horseshit. They'll collaborate, and between the three of them they'll squeeze LA to death."

"I figured Siegel was Mr. New York."

"Not anymore. They've got money. Hollywood is the land of fame and fortune. Lot of profit to be made in this industry, and it's only going to get bigger and better, believe me."

"So what do you want me to do?"

"Do what you're doing," Fuller said. "Don't listen to that. I know you're busting your balls on this. Wish I had more like you. He has to deal with the politicians and the bean counters, so let him deal with them. We start worrying about his job then we'll start forgetting our own."

"I get it."

"So, I ain't lookin' to give you any holidays, and I sure as hell can't give you a pay raise, but I'll listen to any reasonable demands for extra men if you're onto something that looks good, okay?"

"Appreciated."

"Do your best, Detective Hayes, and let's hope it's better than the worst these assholes can do in return."

Fuller left Hayes at the office door. Hayes went inside and closed it behind him.

He sat down and took a jotter. He started listing the names of everyone he could talk to, everyone who had ever crossed swords with Freddie Fishbait, every man who ever voiced a grievance about Dragna, every man who owned him a favor. The list was long, and much of it would come to nothing, but most times the only way to get something done was to do it.

EIGHTEEN

Lucia Mariani was seated on the edge of the bed, her face red, the look in her eyes one of utter horror and rage.

It was evident that she'd been putting up a fight. She held Budny's right forearm in both her hands, was even then pushing him back, doing her utmost to stop him advancing on her any further.

This was the sight that greeted Frankie Madden as he burst into the hotel room. The door did not come off of its hinges, but the jamb broke and the door swung wide and slammed against the wall behind it. Budny turned suddenly, the look on his face quickly turning from perverse anticipation to abject outrage.

"Who the hell—" he started.

Budny didn't have time to finish the question.

Frankie Madden brought him down to the ground with a single roundhouse, and Budny scuttled backward on his ass until he reached the wall, his nose streaming with blood.

It was then that Frankie saw that Lucia's dress was torn at the seam. Anger overcame him, and he let loose with a kick that sent Budny sprawling sideways onto the carpet.

Frankie turned his attention to Lucia, helped her up, and walked her to a chair on the other side of the suite.

"You okay?" he asked.

Lucia was straightening her dress, catching her breath, and even though whatever had happened had not gone as far as Budny had hoped, she was very shaken up.

Budny was up on his feet, had his pants up, was fixing his belt. "How dare you come in here—"

"Don't say a fuckin' word, you little bastard!" Frankie shouted.

He walked toward Budny, stood over him, Frankie taller by a head, and he glared at the man.

Budny shrunk further.

Frankie grabbed the man's lapels and twisted roughly. Budny was near lifted off the ground wholesale.

"You little shite," Frankie said. "Who the fuck do you think you are?"

"Frankie!" Lucia exclaimed.

Frankie turned, saw Tommy in the doorway.

"What the hell—" Tommy said.

"This little bastard tried to . . . you know . . . well, he tried . . ." Frankie shook his head. "I don't even wanna say it, man."

Tommy closed the door of the room. He saw the look of fury and disgust on Lucia's face.

"Jesus man, what are you thinkin'?" Tommy asked of Budny. "How old are you? Old enough to be the girl's granddaddy."

"I didn't mean to—" Budny stuttered.

Frankie had his hand around the man's throat. "Didn't mean to what? Didn't mean to get that poor girl to do something disgusting? Is that what you didn't mean to do, ya wretched bastard?"

"I'm sorry," Budny pleaded. "I'm really sorry . . . I didn't mean to hurt anyone. You can't say anything. You can't tell anyone."

"I think it's too fuckin' late for that, ya little maggot," Tommy said.

Budny's eyes were wide with fear. Both Frankie and Tommy were considerably larger than he, and there was no way out.

It was then that Lucia stepped forward. Less than a minute had passed, but she had gathered herself together, and she now stood between Frankie and Budny, glaring at him.

"Do you know who I am?" she asked Budny. Her tone was direct, unflinching. The expression on her face was hard and unforgiving.

Frankie glanced at Tommy. Tommy's eyes widened fractionally, an almost-imperceptible flicker.

"I am the granddaughter of Mr. Guzzardo," she said coolly.

"Mr. Guzzardo?" Budny asked. He sounded weak. He wore the expression of a cornered rabbit.

Frankie got it immediately.

"Sure," Tommy said, quick to grasp where this was heading. "Mr. Guzzardo. You don't know Mr. Guzzardo?"

Budny frowned, and then he read into that statement exactly what Lucia intended him to. "I don't know him, no . . ."

"You don't *want* to know Mr. Guzzardo," Frankie said, and in his tone was something almost sympathetic, as if Budny had just decreed his own death sentence.

"Please—"

"Please what?" Frankie asked. "You don't want Mr. Guzzardo to know what you tried to do to his granddaughter?"

Budny—eyes wide, tears welling—looked from Tommy to Frankie to Lucia and back again.

"What do you want?" Budny asked. "You're not going to hurt me, are you?"

"Oh, you have no idea, my friend," Frankie said. "You have no idea how much we're gonna hurt you, and when we're done hurtin' you we're gonna make a phone call to Mr. Guzzardo and he's gonna send a couple of his goons over here and they're gonna take you up into the hills and—"

"I can give you money!" Budny said. "I can give you money. How much money do you want? How much money to make like this never happened?"

"You don't have that much money," Tommy said.

"A thousand dollars," Frankie said.

Budny looked like someone had driven a car through his house.

"No," Lucia said. "No one is going to hurt you, Mr. Budny. And no one wants any money from you." Lucia seemed as self-possessed as Frankie had ever seen her. The speed with which she appeared to have recovered from her ordeal surprised him, though on her face was an expression Frankie had seen before. Back in New York, back in that moment when she'd urged him to win, to beat Bodak, to really deliver some serious punishment to the man.

Frankie eased back.

There was something cruel in Lucia's eyes.

Perhaps Tommy saw it too. He took a step forward, but Frankie raised his hand and halted him. Tommy said nothing.

"You're a producer for RKO Pictures?" Lucia asked.

Budny, still stunned from the turn of events, shook his head. "No . . . well, yes . . . er, kind of a producer."

"Kind of a producer?" she asked.

Again, Frankie heard that very threatening edge in her voice. Lucia Mariani had the power to intimidate. There was no doubt about it.

"I'm an accountant," Budny said. "Just an accountant. I balance the books."

"You're an accountant?" Frankie said, incredulous. He could not restrain himself. He rapped his clenched fist on the top of Budny's head, and Budny yowled in pain.

Tommy smiled, seeming to find this scenario more than amusing.

"So what do you want?" Budny asked. "What do you want from me?"

"You don't want my grandfather sending anyone over to see you," Lucia said.

"No, no . . . please, I'm sorry . . . I'm sick . . . I can't help it. I'm sorry. There's something wrong with me, there really is—"

"You're going to help me meet some people," Lucia said. "You're going to give these boys fifty dollars each, and you're going to help me meet some people in the picture company. That's what you're going to do, Mr. RKO accountant."

"I don't know that I can—"

Lucia's eyes flashed. "Frankie, I think we need to make a phone call—"

"Okay, okay, okay," Budny whined. "I'll speak to some people. I promise, I'll speak to some people."

Lucia took a step closer to Budny. "We're coming back on Friday morning," she said, "or I'll speak to my grandfather, and . . . well, let's just say that you really don't want me to do that."

She was convincing. Had Frankie not known it was entirely fabricated, he might very well have believed her himself.

"I promise. I'll speak to some people," Budny said. His voice was plaintive, almost whining. "Friday morning. I'm sorry. I really will speak to some people."

Budny ducked sideways and hurried over to a desk on the other side of the room. He took money from a drawer, gave Frankie and Tommy fifty bucks each. Tommy stepped around the desk, took another twenty and stuffed it in his pocket.

"We'll be back," Frankie said, and the three of them left the room.

Tommy and Frankie were laughing before they reached the elevator. Lucia started to breathe deeply then, and behind the anger was a well of shock and grief from which she suddenly drew. Frankie sat beside her on the leather sofa, his arm around her shoulder, and pulled her close. Lucia turned toward him, said nothing, and he just held her until her breathing had once again settled and the color had returned to her face.

Had it perhaps been another girl, Frankie believed there would have been nothing but tears and disbelief, but Lucia surprised him once again. She was tougher than he'd given her credit for, not only immediately understanding the nature of the situation, but turning it to her advantage.

Tommy stood silently, didn't know where to look or what to say.

And then Frankie saw something else in Lucia's eyes. Confusion was the only way he could describe it. A profound sense of confusion and dismay. This was not what she had imagined. This was not the dream she'd wished for as a child. Maybe back home she was the golden girl, forever in the limelight, the girl that every other girl wanted to be, but here she was just another pretty face within an endless crowd of pretty faces.

Frankie knew how easy it was to see the goal of a lifetime become a vague and distant memory.

Lucia gathered herself together, stood up, said she was ready to leave.

Tommy called the elevator.

Not one of them spoke on the way down, and then Frankie and Tommy shared a handful of words before Frankie escorted her through the foyer and out of the building.

"Not a word to Nicky," Lucia told Frankie. "This never happened, you understand?"

Lucia Mariani looked at Frankie Madden, and her expression said everything that needed to be said. There was something within this girl, something fierce and strong.

At the same time, the child that she'd once been was buried deep inside, and what had nearly happened in that hotel room had terrified her.

"I understand," Frankie said.

"I know you do," she replied, and Frankie could not fathom what that was supposed to mean.

NINETEEN

Nicky Mariani spent that same Wednesday morning in the company of people for whom his mother would only have found disapproval. The people with whom *Little Nicky* was now breaking bread were seasoned veterans of the Hollywood scene.

There was more than one game on the West Coast, and these people played every side of them. Union fixers, shakedowns, rigged strikes, backhanders between supposedly competitive producers to keep such and such an option open, another option closed down, hookers, drug dealers, the sleazy freelance journalists and private eyes who blackmailed up-and-coming stars with photos of their indiscretions—the list was endless. All the way back to the decade-long bootlegging and racketeering heyday of Joseph "Iron Man" Ardizzone, Los Angeles had been a major player in the American-Italian organized crime family syndicate.

Known for his arrogant and bullish attitude, Ardizzone still managed to upset the National Syndicate, that tenuous and fragile agreement between the crime families that somehow held everything in check on the streets of New York, Chicago, and Los Angeles.

Ardizzone vanished without a trace in 1931, leaving his underboss—Jack Dragna—to take the reins. Dragna made peace with the Syndicate and got to work.

The connection between LA and New York went way back. Charles "Lucky" Luciano's personal Hollywood connection had started some years earlier. Lucky saw the potential in the West, put casinos in Capone's restaurants, and exacerbated the infamous Luciano-Capone war. That war didn't last long. Luciano went first to Sing Sing, then to Clinton Correctional in Dannemora, New York. Capone went to Alcatraz and succumbed to syphilis.

The families needed a man they could trust, and Jack Dragna fitted the bill. He and his brother, Tom, got real busy real fast. Hollywood—the jewel in the crown—was an amusement park, and they wanted to go on all the rides.

Though it would never really challenge New York or Chicago, Los

Angeles was still a haven for those who enjoyed a little sunshine and palm trees with their brutality and bloodshed.

By the time Nicky Mariani touched the edges of that world, Prohibition had been over for five years. With that income source gone, Dragna had turned to gambling and loansharking. He and his Chicago compadres drove established businesses out of the city. Dragna worked with Joe Shaw, the mayor's brother, to "clean things up". Bookies were shut down and kicked out. It didn't take long for Dragna to control every black-market gambling operation in LA, and his right-hand men, Frank Bompensiero and Jimmy Fratianno, were all too quick to send someone on a one-way trip to the Hollywood Hills.

And then came Bugsy Siegel, dispatched from New York to establish a wire service for the West Coast horse-racing industry. Buying out the Continental Press Service hadn't worked, so Siegel founded Trans-America. The relationship between Siegel and Dragna was rumored to be tenuous, even fragile, but in reality they worked together very closely.

Dragna had people everywhere. If he wasn't in your face then he was already in your pocket. Nicky knew Dragna's name, knew his business, and was ready to do whatever it took to get a piece for himself.

That Wednesday afternoon, as Lucia swore Frankie to silence about what had happened with Morris Budny at the Hollywood Roosevelt, Nicky was in a restaurant somewhere off La Brea. Al Fresco was a pizza and pasta joint owned by Dragna's underboss, Girolomo "Momo" Adamo. It was a sometime hangout for the rich kids of Hollywood's production elite, a late haunt for those who didn't want the hustle and bustle of the Strip. Most of all, it was a meeting place for Dragna's soldiers and button men. This information had not been hard for Nicky to come by, and he knew that here he would find people that had a rung on the Dragna ladder.

Three of the Al Fresco's regular customers were part of the Dragna new blood, kids in their early twenties who'd been recruited as collectors and runners for Siegel's wire service. Showing some small spark of initiative, they'd swiftly graduated to soldiers, and the Al Fresco was their oasis of choice until word came in on work. Their names were Anthony Leggiero, aka 'Tony Legs', Vince Caliendo, and Paulie Belotti, twenty, twenty-three, and twenty-four respectively.

Nicky was there taking an early lunch, while also minding other people's business. Behind him in a booth were Leggiero, Caliendo, and Belotti, unaware that their very private conversation was being eavesdropped on. All Nicky had to hear was *drop, payoff* and *fuckin' A*, and he knew that here were people with whom he could work.

That those who met him assumed he was from the old country worked just fine for Nicky Mariani. He let them keep their assumptions. He adopted New York Italian expressions and mannerisms, and the mere fact that he did know something of New York served him well. Mentioning street names and restaurants was more than sufficient for most to accept him at face value.

Nicky was smart in his own way. He understood the importance of first impressions and keeping your mouth shut. He also knew how to throw away a line that would get someone's attention.

As the manager, Lenny Falcone, was bringing coffee over to the three young men seated on the adjacent table, Nicky commented that his zeppole was as good as any he'd found in the city.

"The girl makes them," Lenny said. "She's from Naples."

Nicky took another from the plate. "Tell her she does better pastries than my ma."

Vince Caliendo glanced over at Nicky.

Nicky saw a young man much like himself, dark-haired, his Mediterranean origin evident in his complexion and eyes. He was dressed as well as he could with the money he had, another man trying to make a name for himself in a city crowded with names. He seemed a little shorter than his associates, but he was broad in the shoulders, looked like he'd have no difficulty taking care of himself.

"You from New York, kid?"

Nicky paused before replying, gave the moment a feeling of tension. "My old man calls me kid."

Caliendo nodded. "I didn't mean anything by it."

"Good to know," Nicky replied, and went back to his pastries.

"What's your name?" Paulie Belotti asked.

Nicky looked up at the second man. Again, he was much the same as the first, Italian origin, an old scar bisecting his left eyebrow, his skin pockmarked. His manner was more arrogant, as if he was trying his hardest to make his presence felt.

"Depends who's asking," Nicky said.

"I'm asking."

"And who are you?"

Belotti turned to his friends. "This one has a bad attitude," he said, and laughed.

Nicky didn't look away. "You think I'm some dumb fuckin'

goombah right off the fuckin' boat, or what?" He could feel anxiety in his lower gut, a sense that he may have already crossed a line, but what he wanted was a way into this business and this was the fastest route he could take. Risk nothing, win nothing.

Tony Leggiero had sat with his back to Nicky all this time. He glanced over his shoulder. Nicky took a good look at him. He wanted to know what he was up against. Of the three, this one seemed the toughest. He was the most relaxed, showing little concern for who Nicky might be and that he might pose any threat. He was heavier-set. His hair was cut shorter, black as ink, and his eyes were a deep shade of green. Back in his lineage were Romany people, perhaps even Turks. Nicky guessed that this one was the chief, the other two his Indians, whether they acknowledged it or not.

"What's your problem, buddy?"

"People mindin' their own business," Nicky said.

"And what business you got that you think we might be interested in?"

"Every kind of business, and I'm gonna tell any stranger I meet, that's what kind of business."

Paulie Belotti laughed. "You're an asshole. That's what you are."

Nicky smiled. "One asshole is better than three."

Now all of them laughed, and Lenny Falcone shook his head at the idiocy of American-Italian youth and went back to the kitchen.

"So you gonna eat zeppole and drink coffee all on your lonesome, or you gonna come join us?" Vince Caliendo asked.

"You gonna ask me polite?" Nicky said.

Again the three of them laughed, and Nicky laughed with them.

"You really are a freakin' asshole," Belotti said. "You really got a very fuckin' bad attitude."

Nicky picked up the plate of pastries and his coffee cup and walked to their table.

Belotti shifted sideways and Nicky took a seat.

Introductions were made. From first impressions, Nicky's initial assumption seemed to be confirmed. Leggiero, or "Tony Legs" as they called him, was the hub of this little wheel, self-appointed perhaps, or merely the result of his greater confidence and certainty. It appeared that Caliendo and Belotti followed his lead.

"So you're New York," Caliendo said, "but where you from originally?"

Nicky shook his head. "Tell you the truth, I don't even know. Earliest I remember is Corsica."

"That's old, old Italy, man," Belotti said. "French took it, right?"

"Sure," Nicky said, "but that don't mean we can't take it back."

"He thinks he's Napoléon Bonaparte, this boy," Caliendo said. "That's where Bonaparte was from. His family was Italian nobility."

"Didn't stop him fighting us, though, did it?" Nicky said.

"Confused loyalties," Caliendo said. "Sometimes it happens."

Belotti looked at Caliendo. "So, you a freakin' Italian history major or what, now?"

"Yeah, sure I am. I give lectures an' everything, but the classes are fuckin' closed for this term, A-hole."

The banter went on, and Nicky sat and watched the three men talk back and forth. Though he had met them only briefly, almost immediately he got a sense of who they were. Leggiero was a man with aspirations, but he was steady and calm. Caliendo was quieter, either because he wanted to think, or he took longer to figure things out. He let Leggiero do the talking, and seemed content for it to be that way. Belotti was the wild card. He fidgeted with things—his empty espresso cup, a napkin that he folded and unfolded repeatedly, and he smoked one cigarette after another as if he were responsible for exhausting the supply. As a trio, they seemed to be close, each of them knowing their place in whatever scheme they were working on, and yet they also seemed willing to welcome this Corsican stranger into their midst. They'd taken him as he was, and that was all he needed.

Before long Vince Caliendo asked Nicky what he was doing in Hollywood.

"Had to get out of New York," Nicky said.

"Cops?"

"Sure. Cops and a whole bunch of other stuff that can stay right back in New York."

"You got connections here?"

"Some."

"Anyone known, anyone made?"

"No one reliable. This is new territory for me."

Leggiero smiled. "We all start somewhere, eh?"

"Sure, but I don't plan on stayin' anywhere long. Bottom of the ladder ain't for people like me."

"I like you, kid," Leggiero said. "You got balls. Maybe we can give you a helping hand." He lit a cigarette and leaned back in the chair. "You drive?"

"Sure."

"You got a license?"

Nicky shook his head. "Never needed one."

"Here you're gonna need one," Leggiero explained. "There's a system here. There's a way things are done. Might sound crazy, but that don't change it. We got pickups and deliveries, you know? Sometimes those deliveries go places where you wouldn't expect them to go, and you got to color inside the lines, if you know what I mean."

Nicky said he understood. He bluffed it, and he knew he was bluffing. As long as no one saw through it, all would be well.

"Anyways, we can get you a loaner for the meantime. Cops out here figure we all look the same anyways, so we might as well take advantage of that."

Leggiero stood and the others followed suit.

"You can be here Friday morning?" Leggiero asked.

"Yeah, no problem," Nicky said.

"Be here at ten o'clock," he said. "Friday morning, ten o' clock, and we'll have some work for you."

"I'll be here."

An hour later Nicky was back at the hotel room. Lucia and Frankie were already there.

"How did it go?" Nicky asked.

"Looks hopeful," Lucia explained. "We're going back to see him again on Friday morning."

"Hey, this is good news. You're on the road, eh? This is the start of something big, right?"

"Well, we'll see," Lucia said.

Nicky grinned. "You gotta be positive. You have to get a positive attitude about this stuff. That's how things happen. You gotta do the work, but you gotta decide what you want first and just keep on going until you get it."

"I will do my best," Lucia said. "And you . . . how was your day?"

"Looks like I got some work, too," Nicky said. "I got a meet on Friday as well."

"And what's the work?" Lucia asked.

"Well, kinda like you, I don't really know until I get there," he said, and gave no further explanation.

Later he took Frankie aside.

"I got an in," Nicky explained. "Deliveries, pickups, that kind of thing. I'm not asking what, and maybe I don't wanna know. Not a word to Lucia, okay? She wants it all straight and simple and life ain't like that, especially when you're starting out from nowhere."

"I understand," Frankie said.

"We'll see how it goes," Nicky added, "and maybe there'll be an opening for you. For now, you just take care of her. She wants auditions, and she'll get 'em. I just need someone I trust to keep an eye on her."

"Not a problem, Nicky. I can do that."

"You're a good man, Frankie. You're a good friend. Things is gonna work well for us here. I can feel it."

Nicky went to speak to Lucia.

Frankie stood by the door and watched them. He was the man in the middle. Secrets from Lucia, secrets from Nicky, and he'd given a vow of silence to both.

He did not like the situation at all, and yet he could see no immediate way to change it.

TWENTY

RKO was a film company born out of a strange alliance between a Jewish-Russian émigré called David Sarnoff and Joseph P. Kennedy Sr., onetime bootlegger, anti-Semite, lover of Gloria Swanson and father of nine. Kennedy led a life both charmed and cursed, and—even in the late 1920s—he was no stranger to the motion picture industry.

At the helm of both Film Booking Offices of America and the Keith-Albee-Orpheum Theaters Corporation, Kennedy merged the two to form Radio-Keith-Orpheum. His eight million dollar buyout offer for the Pantages theater chain was refused by its owner. That same owner found himself on trial and was ultimately convicted for the rape of a seventeen-year-old Vaudeville dancer called Eunice Pringle. The *Los Angeles Examiner*, owned by William Randolph Hearst, a close confederate of Kennedy's, heavily biased the reportage against Pantages. The trial broke Alex Pantages financially. The Pantages Theater chain went to Kennedy for three and a half million dollars. In 1931, on appeal, the rape charge brought by Eunice Pringle was dismissed. Pantages, right to the moment of his all-too-early death in February of 1936, protested his innocence, stating time and again that Kennedy had set him up.

During the First World War, Kennedy had been assistant general manager of a Bethlehem Steel shipyard in Boston. It was here that he established a lifelong friendship with Franklin D. Roosevelt, then secretary of the navy. Forewarned by Roosevelt that Prohibition was about to be repealed, Kennedy accompanied Roosevelt's son, James, to Scotland. They secured rights to distribute in America. The money never stopped flowing, and a great deal of it was diverted into a presidential campaign.

As of May 1938, Joe Kennedy was serving as the forty-fourth United States ambassador to the United Kingdom under Franklin D. Roosevelt, but Kennedy still held his territory in Hollywood. RKO was his company. He'd fought to create it, fought to keep it through the Depression, and he knew all too well how much money there was to be made.

A young David O. Selznick, almost single-handedly responsible for reviving RKO's fortunes in the early '30s, had jumped ship to work for his father-in-law at MGM. But one of Selznick's final recommendations as head of production was that an RKO contract he'd drawn up for a Broadway hoofer called Fred Astaire be honored. Despite the Astaire screen-test memo that read *Can't sing, can't act, balding, can dance a little*, RKO took Selznick's advice. In a movie called *Flying Down to Rio* they gave Astaire fifth billing after a dancer called Ginger Rogers. *Variety* magazine loved Astaire; the rest was history.

RKO prospered. They made popular movies at a time when American audiences couldn't get enough of them. As a company, it grew rapidly, gave employment to a huge number of people, one of whom was Morris Budny. As with all things, there was a food chain. If Morris Budny held any position in the food chain of RKO, it was way, way down that line. Budny was an accountant. For the right money he would cook books better than the Hollywood Roosevelt head chef seared a tenderloin.

Ironically, he had taken care of some minor tax matters for Jack Dragna's brother and consigliere, Tom. Tom Dragna had become a naturalized US citizen and needed to present the myth of legitimacy.

Hollywood was a wheel of many spokes, all spokes running to the same hub. Had Lucia Mariani known that she was dealing with a man who'd assisted the Dragnas, the very mafiosi with whom her brother was now trying to secure employment, she would not have believed it.

Coincidence was rarely just that.

Whatever his position, Morris Budny did know people. One of those people was James Halliday, deputy to the assistant casting director, Musical Comedy Division, RKO Pictures. It was Halliday who kept an appointment with Lucia Mariani and Frankie Madden that subsequent Friday morning, and Halliday saw something in Lucia that was quite different from that which his lecherous colleague, Morris Budny, had seen.

Frankie Madden had done all he could to prepare Lucia for seeing Budny a second time. Saying nothing to Nicky had been tougher than he'd imagined, especially when Nicky had taken him aside and asked if everything was okay with his sister, if something had happened at the audition.

"She seems different," Nicky had said.

"Everything was good," Frankie lied, and was surprised at how easily the lie left his lips.

Friday morning the three of them had breakfast together. Nicky started talking about finding a real place to live.

"We can't live in a freakin' hotel like hobos forever," he said.

"We need money," Lucia replied.

"I can take care of money. The money is my problem for the moment," Nicky said.

"You found real work, then?" she asked, her tone one of suspicion.

"Some. Maybe. I'll find out today."

"Doing what?"

"Driving. There's a lot of driving work around."

"A taxicab?" Lucia asked.

Nicky laughed. "No, not a taxicab. You see me drivin' a cab, Frankie?"

Frankie shook his head. Said nothing.

"So what kind of driving?" Lucia asked.

"Driving me crazy with the questions, that's what," Nicky said, and would say nothing more.

Frankie watched the exchange between them. He'd been there at the Roosevelt. He'd seen Lucia deal with Budny, how swiftly she'd masked her true emotional feelings and turned the situation to her advantage. Though Nicky may never have seen it and Lucia may have utterly denied it, the Mariani siblings had a great deal in common. Beneath their very different facades, they possessed the same blood and the same assured self-interest.

They left the hotel together, went their separate ways.

"You gonna be okay?" Frankie asked Lucia.

"I'm going to be fine," she said, and it seemed sincere.

Tommy was there at reception, and he showed them up to the suite.

On the way, Frankie asked Tommy's name.

"O'Bannon," he said. "As Irish as they come. And you?"

"Frankie Madden."

Tommy looked askance at him. "Not one of Owney's lot, are you?"

"Who?"

"Owen . . . they call him Owney Madden. Hell's Kitchen mob. Gangster from New York. George Raft . . . you know George Raft, the actor?"

"I know who he is," Lucia interjected. "Plays real tough guys."

"Well, he's pretty tough in real life," Tommy said. "Used to be Owney's driver."

Frankie shook his head. "Never heard of any o' them."

"Well, you and he havin' the same name might provoke some interesting assumptions around here," Tommy said.

Frankie wanted to know what he meant, but Lucia said, "Not even George Raft? "*Scarface*, *Limehouse Blues*, *Dancers in the Dark* . . . you've heard of those, right?"

"What's the deal here, lady?" Tommy asked Lucia, accentuating his Irish accent. "You an' up-an'-comin' movie starlet and your man here ain't got a clue?"

Lucia smiled. "He is not my man, and he has plenty of clues, just not about the movies."

The elevator slowed and stopped. The door opened and Tommy led the way.

Budny was all smiles and pleasantries. He welcomed Lucia and Frankie, even tipped Tommy, and when he showed his guests through to the spacious ante room, a man rose from a chair at the small writing desk and walked forward to meet them.

"James Halliday," the man said. "RKO Pictures."

Lucia took his hand. "Lucia Mariani," she said, "and this is my friend Frank Madden."

Frankie shook hands with Halliday. This man was not in the same league as Budny. Halliday was a class act—immaculately dressed, polite, respectful, well spoken. Frankie had the impression of a man who did not need to assert his importance; he was just self-assured and confident in who he was and what he was doing.

"So, I understand you have an interest in taking some auditions," Halliday said, indicating chairs near the center of the room. Lucia and Frankie sat down and Halliday returned to the writing desk.

Budny tried his best to disappear. He found another chair and moved it to the side of the room as if to exclude himself from the proceedings.

"I am very interested in the possibility of some auditions, yes," Lucia said.

"I am sure that can be arranged," he said. "You're Italian-American?"

"Corsican," she said. "Technically, that makes me French."

"Technically?"

"We have a long and complex history, Mr. Halliday. Whether or not you consider yourself Italian, French, or Corsican depends not only on heritage, but also how much of a nationalist you are."

"And what do you consider yourself, Miss Mariani?"

"I am an actress, Mr. Halliday. I can be whatever the role demands of me."

Halliday laughed. "Well, that is certainly a great deal more interesting an answer than I usually get from young ladies seeking auditions and screen tests."

Lucia smiled beautifully. "I can assure you I am not a usual young lady."

Halliday laughed again. "Oh my," he said. "Well, we should definitely have you come down to Culver City and take some headshots. I'll have a look at the audition calendar, and we can see what's on the roster for later in the year."

"Culver City?" Lucia asked.

"It's just our backlots. It's called Forty Acres. It's less than ten miles from here. If you've seen any of our pictures recently you'll recognize some of the sets built down there, I'm sure."

"Well, of course. I'd be very happy to come to Culver City.

Frankie watched her. She was reserved, almost demure in her manner, but beneath that elegant facade, he knew she would be just a riot of excitement. This was why she'd come to Hollywood. This was where her whole life had been taking her, and now she was being given the chance she'd always wanted.

"Monday," Halliday said. "Come over on Monday. Morris can give you directions. In fact, organize a car, would you, Morris?"

"Yes, yes, of course," Morris said, all too eagerly.

"Shall we say eleven o'clock?"

"Yes, that would be perfect," Lucia replied.

"Well, good, that's settled, then, Miss Mariani."

Halliday rose. Lucia rose, too, and they shook hands.

Budny walked Halliday to the door, shared a few discreet words, and then he returned to Lucia and Frankie.

Budny seemed agitated. "I've done what I said. I hope we can forget all about this unpleasant misunderstanding now." He sat down, and for a moment he looked very small and insignificant despite the grandeur of the room.

"I think it was a little more than an unpleasant misunderstanding, wouldn't you, Mr. Budny?" Frankie said.

"I'm sorry. I really am." He hesitated again, seemingly unsure of whether he should say something or not. "Your name is Madden?" he asked.

"It is."

"You're not related to . . ."

"Owney?"

"Yes," Budny said. "Yes, that's him."

Frankie leaned close. "I'm not so sure it's any of your business who I might or might not be related to, Mr. Budny."

Budny's face paled. "No, no, of course not. None of my business."

"However, you kept your agreement, and that's to be acknowledged."

"So, to Monday," Budny said, a sense of relief now evident in his voice.

"We'll be here at ten in the morning," Frankie said. "And like Mr. Halliday said, you should have a car for us."

"There'll be a car, of course. Absolutely. Without a doubt."

Lucia didn't say anything during the entire exchange. When she looked at Budny there was something in her eyes that was almost devoid of emotion. She didn't say a word to the man, merely pinned him to his seat with that glare, then looked away dismissively.

She stood near the door until Frankie opened it for her.

As soon as the door was closed the cool detachment disappeared. She could barely contain her excitement. The girl blew hot and cold. She could look a man in the eye with a killer's glare, and then a minute later she was as thrilled as a five-year-old on Christmas Eve.

"Culver City," she said. "We're going to Culver City," and then as they neared the elevator she grabbed Frankie's arm as if to anchor herself to the earth.

Lucia was unpredictable, impassioned, headstrong even, but beneath that there seemed to be a measured strength, a sense of balance, even a streak of cruelty that she managed to effortlessly hide.

The more time he spent with her, the more she confounded him. The more she confounded him, the more time he wanted to spend with her.

Frankie did not doubt how easy it would be to fall hopelessly in love with Lucia Mariani.

Easy and dangerous in equal parts.

TWENTY-ONE

"It's a simple collection routine," Tony Legs said.

"We call it the Candy Run," Paulie said. "Candy from babies, you know?"

"We got half a dozen or more places, gotta make some phone calls on the way, see if other joints need pickups, but it's a straightforward business."

Tony Legs tossed the car keys to Nicky and indicated the rear of the restaurant. "Out back," he said. "Maroon DeSoto. Drive it around front for us."

Lenny Falcone opened the door into the alleyway behind the Al Fresco. Nicky walked down toward the street, saw the car, got in and started the engine. His father had taught him to drive when he was a little kid, roped wooden blocks to the pedals so he could reach them. What would he have thought now had he known he was driving for the Dragna crew in Hollywood? Nicky smiled to himself.

At the front of the building Tony Legs, Paulie, and Vince were smoking, laughing together, taking their time while Nicky sat with the engine idling against the curb. There was a ladder, and there he was, right at the very bottom. However, he'd found the ladder. That was the main thing. Nicky watched the trio on the sidewalk and he knew it wouldn't be long before he'd be telling men like this to go get smokes, to bring the car around, to *Spare me the details, just take care of it, okay?*

If there was something he and Lucia had in common it was the desire to reach the top, to find the limelight. Perhaps the primary difference between them was that Nicky did not care how it happened, just as long as it did.

The trio got in the car, Vince up front in the passenger seat. He opened the glove box, and inside were a couple of pistols.

Nicky felt a rush in his lower gut.

"You ever use one of these?" Vince asked.

"Sure," Nicky said. In truth, the closest he'd ever got was his father's shotgun. He'd used it once, back when he was twelve or thirteen. The kick had put him on his back, and he and his father had laughed like hyenas.

"Ain't gonna kill no one," Vince said. "Use 'em when someone needs shakin' up a little, that's all. Sometimes these assholes think they can keep Mr. Dragna waiting, and Mr. Dragna ain't so fond of that."

Paulie leaned forward from the backseat. "He says the only person who should keep you waitin' is a woman. Says bein' late is a woman's purgatory."

"A woman's what?" Tony Legs said.

"A woman's purgatory," Paulie said. "Like something she can do and she don't get into trouble for it."

Both Vince and Tony Legs laughed.

"You're a dumbass motherfucker, Paulie," Vince said. "The word is *prerogative*. Jeez, where the hell did you go to freakin' school?"

Paulie didn't seem offended by their laughter. "School? Me? What the hell would I go to school for?"

Tony Legs nodded. "The man has a point there. He really has a point."

"Which way?" Nicky asked.

"Up here on Sunset, then head for Vine," Paulie said. "I'll show you."

"Get a map," Vince said. "Learn the place like a cabdriver. You need to know your way around. You ever drive Mr. Dragna home, you don't wanna be askin' which direction to take, right?"

To Nicky it was just a maze of streets and boulevards. The whole of San-Nicolao would have dropped between two or three blocks. He followed Paulie's directions, turned left onto North Cahuenga Boulevard, and wound up down a side street behind a bakery and coffee store.

Vince and Paulie went into the building. Tony Legs and Nicky stayed in the car.

No more than five minutes and the two returned with a paper bag. The bag went in the glove box with the pistols and Vince told Nicky to head back the way they'd come.

So it went—five, six different places, each time two of them would get out, returning minutes later with a bag or an envelope. Soon the glove box wouldn't close, and Paulie took the guns out, put them in a bag and tucked them under the passenger seat.

By noon they'd reached Seward at the end of La Mirada.

"Couple more places, and then we'll get some lunch," Tony Legs said, as Nicky turned left and headed up toward Fountain.

Nicky needed to use the bathroom, but he didn't want to mention it.

"You should come in this time," Paulie said. "This guy's an asshole. Fucking Turkish or something, but a real asshole."

"Armenian," Vince said. "He's an Armenian asshole."

"Turkish, Armenian, whatever the fuck. It don't matter," Paulie said.

"You are such an ignorant motherfucker," Vince said.

"What the hell, Vincent? On Wednesday we get Italian history, today we're doin' world freakin' geography. What the hell is the matter with you?"

"Here," Tony Legs said to Nicky. "Take a right here and pull up on the corner."

Nicky slowed down and stopped in front of a diner. Paulie reached beneath the seat and took out the guns. He tucked one inside his jacket, handed the second to Vince.

"You should come in," Paulie said to Nicky. "Tony can stay in the car."

According to Vince, the Armenian's name was Grigor Zakarian. The restaurant was called Tavush – named, apparently, after the province of his birth.

Zakarian was five foot nothing, maybe two hundred pounds, as wide as he was tall. He wore a stained A-shirt, and his arms were hairier than a coconut. He greeted the arrival of Dragna's three men with, "What the hell is this now? What you people fuckin' want from me now?" His accent was thick and guttural, but whatever he might have lacked in diction he made up for in attitude. It was very clear that the trio were unwelcome guests.

"You owe and you owe and you keep on owing," Paulie said.

"And I pay and pay and keep on paying," Zakarian said. "How can I pay more when I don't have it?"

"Don't wanna know what you do and don't have, Mr. Zakarian," Vince said. He and Paulie started walking. Zakarian backed up to the counter, then went through to the kitchen in the rear. Vince and Paulie followed him. Nicky followed Vince and Paulie. A young woman was at one of the stoves. She disappeared quickly.

"No wonder you don't make any freakin' money," Paulie said. "This place is filthy. This place is a goddamned pigsty."

"Why you say this to me, Paulie? Why you be so rude?" Zakarian said.

Paulie feigned shock. "What did you say?"

"There's no need to be rude," Zakarian said. "I'm not rude with you. I don't say these bad things to you."

Paulie approached Zakarian menacingly.

"What you gonna do, Paulie? You gonna hurt me?"

Paulie pulled the gun from the waistband of his pants and brandished it.

"What the hell?" Zakarian said, evidently shocked. "You bringin' guns now? What is going on here, Vincent?"

"Put the gun away, Paulie," Vince said.

Nicky wondered where the girl had disappeared to.

"I've had enough of this, Vince," Paulie said. "Every week it's the same bullshit story. You pay us, Grigor. That's the rules. That's the way it works."

"And if I don't have money, you have to wait. I always pay. Even sometimes I pay more because I am late, but I always pay. That's the rules."

Paulie was incensed. Later Nicky reckoned that Paulie had gone in there with a view to upsetting Zakarian. All he knew was that Vince was telling him to *Calm the fuck down, Paulie,* but Paulie wasn't listening.

Paulie grabbed the little guy by the hair and hit his head on the corner of a metal countertop.

There was blood immediately.

"Vincent!" Zakarian shouted. "Tell him to stop this crazy—"

Zakarian didn't finish the sentence. Paulie pushed him down to the ground and kicked him hard in the chest.

"Paulie!" Vince shouted.

Paulie's blood was up. He had the gun out, was sticking it in Zakarian's face.

"You Turkish Russian whatever-the-fuck-you-are motherfucker! You gotta pay, okay? That's the way this fuckin' works! You gotta pay Mr. Dragna, you asshole!"

"I'm gonna pay, Paulie," Zakarian pleaded. "I'm gonna pay, okay? Always I pay." He looked up at Vince, who was now standing behind Paulie. "Don't I pay, huh? I always pay, don't I, Vincent?"

Vince nodded. "Get him up off the goddamned floor, Paulie. What the hell are you thinking?"

Nicky hadn't said a word; didn't have a word to say. Paulie had a wild streak, and he sure as hell wasn't going to get in the firing line.

Paulie backed off. Zakarian picked himself up off the kitchen floor. He was winded, breathing heavily, and his head was bleeding from where Paulie had bashed him against the stove.

"What the hell?" Zakarian said. "What is wrong with you? You crazy in the head. I thought we were friends, eh? I thought we were good American buddies—"

Paulie started laughing. From the sound of that laugh, it seemed he'd not had enough.

"Good American buddies? Is that what we are? You're a fuckin' Turkish fucking midget and I work for Jack Dragna, and you better come up with the fuckin' money, Grigor, or I'm gonna come back here and kill you."

"I am Armenian," Zakarian said, "and if you kill me, then my brother will come find you and send your fuckin' balls to your mother in a fuckin' candy box—"

"Grigor, no—" Vince started, but it was too late.

The rage filled Paulie's eyes. He still had the gun in his hand, and he brought that gun down dead center on Zakarian's skull.

Zakarian dropped, and as he fell his head collided once again with the edge of the stove. He hit the ground awkwardly, his arms beneath his body, and he did not move.

"Jesus Christ!" Vince said. He shoved Paulie aside, tried to lift Zakarian.

"Get the fuck over here!" he hollered at Nicky, and Nicky came running.

Paulie backed away, a smug self-satisfied grin on his face.

Vince and Nicky managed to get Zakarian into a sitting position, but he was a heavy guy.

There was blood streaming from his nose, from his left ear, and there was a wide gash across the right side of his head. The blood soaked into his A-shirt, into Nicky's shirt cuffs, onto his pants.

Zakarian's eyes flickered open and they were nothing but whites. He moaned deliriously, and then Vince was telling Paulie to help, to get Zakarian off the ground.

"Hospital," Vince said. "We're taking him to the fuckin' hospital, okay? Not a fuckin' word, Paulie! That's what we're doing."

"You gotta be fuckin' kiddin' me," Paulie said. "Let the asshole bleed to death."

Vince swung out and slapped Paulie right in the face.

"Get him up, Paulie! Now!"

Paulie was stunned for a second, and then he snapped to. He took Zakarian's legs, and the three of them managed to maneuver the man out of the kitchen, through the diner, and into the street.

Tony Leggiero was out of the car. "What the—"

"Open the back door!" Vince shouted.

Tony Legs did as he was told.

Zakarian was seated as best he could, still mumbling something, his eyes rolling back.

"Get back in there and clear the fuckin' place up, Paulie!"

Paulie hesitated for a split second, and then he turned and hurried back into the diner.

"North Vermont," Vince told Tony Legs. "Get going!"

Tony Legs drove, Vince in the passenger seat, Nicky in the back holding Zakarian upright as best he could.

Hollywood Hospital was less than ten minutes. Tony Legs pulled up in the ambulance bay, stopped the car, and then Vince and Nicky got Zakarian out of the back and carried him up toward the doors.

"Down," Vince said.

Nicky was baffled.

"On the fuckin' sidewalk, kid. Put him down on the fucking sidewalk."

Nicky let him down. Zakarian moaned painfully.

People were looking. Nicky saw people in white coats hurrying out toward the bay from the triage unit.

Vince was running back to the car. Nicky went after him. Tony Legs was away and down the street before they even had time to close the doors.

"Fuckin' Paulie, son of a bitch," Vince said. "We gotta do something about him. We gotta sort him out."

"It'll be taken care of," Tony Legs said.

The car hurtled down North Vermont.

Nicky looked at the blood on his hands, his cuffs, the blood that had soaked into the front of his pants.

For a moment he felt sick. He breathed deeply. He focused on something else. He didn't like what he was feeling, and yet he knew he couldn't show it. The farther they got from the restaurant, the more he managed to gather his senses. This was it. This was what he'd walked into, and he'd done it with his eyes open.

He wondered whether it was too late to turn back. More importantly, if he did, where would he go?

Once more he looked at the blood on his hands, and he closed his eyes.

He'd made a decision, and if there was anything his father had instilled in him it was the need to honor your decisions.

This was where he became a man. He had no choice. Sick though he was, he understood that he really had no choice.

TWENTY-TWO

Saturday morning, June 11th—working out of Central Division on the corner of First and Hill—Detective Louis Hayes took the call about Grigor Zakarian. Hayes had taken the weekend shift out of boredom. Sitting alone in a one-bedroom apartment, listening to the radio, going to the grocery store and doing all he could to stay off the liquor was not the best way to spend a weekend. Hollywood Hospital was less than five miles, and there was little else happening. At least this was something to occupy his attention.

He drove down there, chatted with a pretty nurse, took his time finding the ward where they were holding Zakarian. It was protocol, much the same as a gunshot wound. If someone came in looking like they'd gone a half dozen rounds with Baby Arizmendi, then it was routine to call the cops and get some questions answered.

Within three minutes of the interview's commencement, it was evident that Grigor Zakarian had nothing to say to this kid cop, Louis Hayes. Within those same three minutes Louis Hayes knew that here was another example of an all-too-frequent rollover by Dragna's bagmen. This was prime Dragna territory, a small privately owned diner in the neighborhood, some poor schmuck paying through the nose just to keep the place from being burned to the ground by the very people he was paying.

Zakarian was in bad shape. He had two busted ribs, a cracked collarbone, and his skull was fractured. There'd been some minor internal bleeding, but the doctors had fixed him up.

Zakarian would live to see another day, and whoever had done this would sure as hell be back to collect their outstanding payment.

"How much are we talking?" Hayes asked. "Twenty, thirty bucks? And for that, they do this to you?"

"I don't know what you say," Zakarian said. "I fall down the fuckin' stairs, okay?"

"You must have one hell of a stairwell, my friend."

"I'm not your friend."

"Well, I don't see no one else visiting you, Grigor, so maybe we should become friends. I could bring some flowers and candies next time I visit."

Zakarian smiled. He understood the game.

"So, you gonna help me out here, or you gonna let these assholes keep taking your money and breaking your face?"

"I don't know what you mean," Zakarian said. "I am having accidents, that's all."

"Who was it this time? That's same crowd of Italian punks that I keep hearing about? Leggiero, Belotti, and the other one?"

"I don't know anyone like these names."

"Sure you don't," Hayes said. There was nothing happening here. That was the magic of the protection racket: its sheer simplicity.

Hayes got up from the chair, ready to leave, and then he hesitated.

"You just don't get it, do you, Grigor?"

"Get what?"

"The way this works. These guys are gonna keep comin' back and comin' back until they've taken everything you've got. Is that why you came to America, so you could work yourself to death filling someone else's pockets?"

Zakarian just looked at Hayes.

"Is this the life you wanted? Is this really the American Dream you came looking for?"

Again Zakarian was speechless.

"Ah, what the hell," Hayes said, his anger and frustration evident in his tone. He put his hat on and wished Grigor Zakarian a speedy recovery.

"Mind those stairs, eh?"

Zakarian frowned.

"The ones you fell down. Jeez, I guess you banged your head so hard you lost your memory."

Back at Central, Hayes looked up the Dragna trio he kept hearing about. He'd written their names down, started keeping a record in a journal. Paul Belotti, Vincent Caliendo, and Antony Leggiero. They were punks, nothing more nor less, but punks became hoods became killers became psychos. Like Mickey Cohen. There was a man who could've been a good boxer. Fighting Patsy Farr back in 1930, even Chalky Wright in '33, he'd shown promise, but as with so many other fighters, he was lazy. A boxer was an athlete, and that was less a job and more a lifestyle. You wanted your name in lights, you had to work hard at it. Damned hard. As for this trio of bagmen, their names surfacing ever more frequently in his patch, it would only be a matter of time before someone got hurt an awful lot worse than Grigor Zakarian. One day someone was going to die, and then those boys would graduate from Little League and get a price on their heads. What were they, half a dozen years younger than Hayes himself, and already this was their life? It was a tragedy, pure and simple.

Hayes took mug shots of the three Italian boys and drove over to Tavush. It was still open, albeit empty, despite the hospitalization of its owner. He stepped inside, called out, and a young woman came through from the back.

"Hello, miss," Hayes said.

The girl nodded an acknowledgment. She was young, late teens, perhaps early twenties, fair-haired, pretty in a fragile way.

"I am Detective Hayes, Central PD. You are?"

"You have ID?" the girl asked, her tone suspicious.

Hayes produced it. She took it, looked at it closely, looked up at Hayes.

"You don't believe me?" he asked.

The girl returned Hayes's ID. She didn't respond to his question.

"So, who are you?"

"Milena Saroyan."

"And you are related to Mr. Zakarian?"

"I am his niece."

"And were you present when Mr. Zakarian was assaulted?"

The girl hesitated. "I am busy," she said. She turned and walked back through to the kitchen.

Hayes followed her.

Milena busied herself cleaning the hot plate. Hayes took the photos from his jacket pocket and laid them out on the table that centered the kitchen.

"These three," Hayes said. "These were the guys who came here?" Hayes indicated the photos of Leggiero, Caliendo, and Belotti.

The girl appeared uncertain. She was afraid, no doubt about it, and Hayes backed off.

"So Grigor must be your mother's brother?"

"Yes, that is right."

"And how long have you been in America?"

"I was born here," Milena said.

Hayes smiled. "You have some coffee on the stove?"

"Yes, I do. You want some?"

"Yes, please. That would be great."

"Cream and sugar?"

"No, just as it is."

Milena fetched coffee for Hayes. Hayes sat on the edge of the steel table against the wall by the door.

"It's a nice place you got here," he said.

"It's okay."

"You cook everything?"

"I do, yes. Sometimes Grigor cooks, too, but only special things."

The tension seemed to ease a little. Hayes drank his coffee, and when the girl stopped cleaning the plate and poured herself a cup, he felt it was right to ask her again.

"So do these guys come down here regularly?"

Milena hesitated. "Every month."

"And your uncle pays them."

"Of course."

"Why of course?"

Milena laughed nervously. "You know why."

Hayes nodded. "I do, yes."

"So why do you ask a question that you know the answer to?"

Hayes shrugged. "Keep you talking, I guess."

"Look, I can't help you. You should not have come here."

"You can help me, Milena. And your uncle. Eventually it all makes a difference. Will you just look at the pictures again?"

Milena smiled. It was the first time. She had a very pretty smile and Hayes told her so.

Milena seemed momentarily off guard, as if she was unfamiliar with compliments.

"Okay," she yielded. "Show me the pictures."

Hayes laid them out on the table.

"This one and this one," she said, indicating Belotti and Caliendo. "This one," she said, indicating Leggiero, "was not here. But there was another one aside from these two, and that one there may have been outside in the car. I don't know."

"So there were four of them?"

"Yes."

"And which one hurt your uncle?"

Milena looked at Hayes, and Hayes could see right through that expression.

"I can assure you—"

She smiled resignedly and shook her head. "No, you can't, Detective Hayes. You can't assure me of anything."

"But if we don't start somewhere, then we'll never get anyplace. These are just punks. You don't have to be afraid of them."

"They hurt my uncle. They put him in the hospital."

She was right. They were just punks, but they were nasty punks, and they could go on hurting both Zakarian and his niece.

"I promise you," Hayes said. "I promise you that if you can help me, if you can just show me which one hurt your uncle, then I will move heaven and earth to get him arrested and put away."

Milena looked at Hayes. Her gaze was searching. She was trusting him, and he knew it.

She took a deep breath, and then without even looking at the photos again she said, "This one," and pointed at Paulie Belotti.

"Not a good face," Hayes said. "Looks like an asshole."

Milena tried to laugh, but couldn't. Her uncle had been badly hurt, and seeing the face of the man who did it was a painful reminder.

"You've not been up to visit him, have you?" Hayes asked.

"No."

"You want me to take you?"

Milena seemed uncertain. She shook her head.

"Really, it's fine. I'd like to take you. I think it's the least I can do."

"That is very nice of you," she said.

"What can I say?" Hayes said. "I'm a nice guy."

On the way she asked what happened to his hand.

"It's a terrible story," Hayes said. "When I was a boy we lived in the woods north of Virginia. We used to have to sleep in the trees so the bears didn't get us. However, living in the trees makes you prone to attack by these huge eagles, and this one night . . ."

Hayes glanced sideways. The look of bemusement on the girl's face was priceless.

"I'm teasing you," he said.

Milena laughed, but Hayes didn't think she got the joke. Her mind was elsewhere, preoccupied with her uncle and whether or not her willingness to help Hayes had merely served to endanger them further.

She didn't ask about his fingers again, and Hayes didn't venture another explanation.

Zakarian's first question when Hayes and Milena appeared beside his bed was for his niece.

"You didn't tell him anything, did you?"

"I am actually in the room as well, Grigor," Hayes said. "And no, she didn't tell me anything that I didn't already know."

Zakarian frowned. "Which means that you tell him something—"

"Uncle, I didn't—"

"Grigor, that's enough," Hayes said. "The girl is traumatized. Can't you see that?"

"Ha! Traumatized? I am traumatized—"

Hayes raised his hand and Zakarian fell silent.

"I brought her up here to visit with you. You are family, for Christ's sake. Be fucking nice to each other, okay?"

"You don't use language like that in front of my niece," Zakarian said.

"Better than having to watch you get beat up by a bunch of Italian punks," Hayes replied.

Zakarian didn't respond.

"So, what game we playing here?" Hayes asked. "Let's do nothing to help the cops. Is that what we're playing?"

"You don't understand—"

"If there's one thing I do understand, Grigor, it's that these punks are working for Jack Dragna, and Jack Dragna can only continue in business as long as people like you do nothing to help us nail him."

Zakarian seemed unimpressed. "You think I can do something? You think one guy like me is gonna do anything to hurt someone like Jack Dragna?"

"So at least you know who he is."

"Everyone knows who Jack Dragna is," Zakarian replied. "You think we're stupid?"

"I don't think you're stupid. I think maybe you're not so brave."

"Go to hell."

"Only if I'm taking a bunch of these thieves and killers with me, Grigor. Only if I make sure that Jack Dragna gets there before me."

"I'm not the man you want," Zakarian said. "You're looking for someone who can help you get to Jack Dragna, you're looking in the wrong place. I'm going to get out of here, go back to my restaurant, and keep my head down."

"And what about Milena?"

Zakarian frowned. "What about her?"

"You think that if you don't pay up they won't resort to hurting her, too?"

"I will pay up."

"You didn't this last time. Otherwise you wouldn't be here."

Zakarian was quiet for a time. He looked at Hayes, at his niece, back to Hayes, and then asked, "What the hell do you want from me?"

"I want you to pay them, Grigor. I want you to get a message to them, tell them you have their money and that they should come and get it. I want you to make them feel welcome, tell them to use your place like their own, feed them, give them coffee, whatever they want, and tell them it's on the house."

"How can I do that?" Zakarian asked. "I don't even make enough money to—"

"They won't take it, Grigor," Hayes said. "Pride won't let them. They'll pay you."

"And why I do this?"

"So you can help me get them, that's why. I need to know who they are, what they're doing. I need to know who they report to. I need to know who else they are taking money from, and then I can build a case that will put them in jail. You can help me better than anyone I can think of right now, and this is important. What has happened to you isn't right, but until I have something solid and reliable as far as evidence is concerned, I can't do anything to fix it."

"I understand that, but what's here for me?"

"What, aside from civic duty, a sense of right, your community spirit, a belief that you should treat the country where you've made your home as something of value and importance?"

Zakarian looked at Hayes like he'd pissed in the soup.

"Your protection money will be paid for you," Hayes said. "And we will keep an eye on you and Milena, and if our surveillance of these characters results in conviction for a crime that has a reward, then you'll get the reward."

"How much?"

"How much what?"

"How much reward money?"

"Depends on the crime... and if there is a reward."

"Like a murder."

Hayes frowned.

"What are you asking me, Grigor?"

Grigor paused. He looked at Milena, and the expression on his face was anxious.

Turning back to Hayes, he seemed reconciled to something.

"I am asking how much reward there would be for information about a murder, Detective Hayes."

"A murder that has already happened. Is that what you're saying?"

Zakarian nodded. "Yes," he said. "A murder that has already happened."

TWENTY-THREE

The fact that Nicky Mariani came home in clothes other than those in which he'd left did not go unnoticed by Frankie.

If Lucia noticed, she did not comment on it.

Nicky's mood that Friday evening, a mood that seemed to continue throughout the weekend, was also noticeably different. He seemed agitated. That wasn't right, but it was the best way to describe his inability to settle, like someone had wired him up to the light switch and his nerves were on fire.

This was not the only thing that preoccupied Frankie's mind as Morris Budny's paid-for limo drove them out to the Culver City backlot on Monday morning.

Nicky had left early, and Lucia was too excited to stay still. He was not able to have a conversation with her.

They didn't see Budny at the Roosevelt, but Tommy O'Bannon had been told to expect them and he directed them toward a waiting car.

The drive was short. Lucia talked incessantly, but Frankie was asking himself how this had all been so easy. Okay, so maybe Budny did think she was the granddaughter of some West Coast Mafia big shot, and maybe he was worried that Frankie was in fact related to Owney Madden, but these people had money and contacts. A couple of phone calls, a question or two in the right ear, and whatever pretense Frankie and Lucia might have concocted would fall apart. In a city of so many people pretending to be someone else, surely finding out who someone really was wouldn't have been so difficult?

Maybe Halliday owed Budny, and Halliday was repaying a debt. Take care of some poor starry-eyed girl, show her around a backlot, get some photos taken, and we're quits.

Maybe this was just the way things were done out here. This was not Clonegal. Hell, it wasn't even Dublin. This was Hollywood, Los Angeles, and what did some poor dumb bogger from County Carlow know about the way such people worked? Nothing, that's what.

Frankie decided it would do no good to think about it. Until there were real answers, questions would serve no purpose but to frustrate him.

Halliday was in a meeting. He'd sent down a girl called Kathleen Riley. She was Halliday's deputy assistant something-or-other, and she asked them if they would like a tour.

"Absolutely," Lucia said, and she grabbed Frankie's arm as if to tether herself to the earth.

Kathleen Riley was dark-haired, pale-skinned, carried an Irish name, and Frankie wanted to ask her where she was from, where her family roots were grown, but he kept his mouth shut. This was Lucia's day, and he didn't want to distract her from it with small talk about home.

"We got a whole universe of stars down here, Miss Mariani," Kathleen said. "Katharine Hepburn, Bette Davis, Allan Lane. We had Cary Grant down here making *Toast of New York* with Eddie Arnold and Frances Farmer last year. We've got him on a seven-year contract. George O'Brien is here regularly. Jimmy Stewart just made *Vivacious Lady* which came out last month with Ginger Rogers and Beulah Bondi."

They kept on walking, crossed a parking lot and turned the corner.

There was some sort of restaurant to their right. The doors were open, and a long forest-green canopy shielded the tables and chairs below from the bright morning sun.

People sat with tall drinks and cups of coffee while young men with slick hair and white tunic tops brought plates of bagels and suchlike from the kitchen.

"Let me introduce you to someone," Kathleen said, indicating a pretty young woman seated with two other men.

Frankie hung back, let Kathleen take Lucia.

"Miss Mariani, this is Miss Lucille Ball."

The woman who extended her hand was just beautiful. She was as Hollywood as any girl Lucia had seen in any of her magazines. The brightest blue eyes and the most stunning red hair, and when she spoke she seemed genuinely pleased to meet Lucia.

"A pleasure," Lucia said.

"Well, sweetie, the pleasure is all mine," Lucille replied, and in her voice Lucia heard New York. It reminded her of where she'd come from only a short while before, but at that moment it seemed like distant history.

"Lucille is in a picture with Doug Fairbanks called *Having Wonderful Time*."

"Douglas Fairbanks," Lucia said, hardly believing her ears.

"Lucille was a model, weren't you?"

"Out of absolutely nowhere," Lucille said. "I did a few little things on Broadway, but I am so thrilled and honored to be here. It is all so exciting. Are you going to be working on a picture here, too, Miss Mariani?"

"I hope so," Lucia said. "I really do hope so."

"Well, I wish you all the success in the world, darling."

"Thank you. That is really kind of you."

"She's taken a few small roles for us," Kathleen explained as they walked away, "but I have a feeling she's going to be a big star. You know, sometimes you get a hunch about someone and I have a hunch about her. She has something very special."

They paused at another table. "This is Mr. Cecil Kellaway," Kathleen said, introducing Lucia once more to a man in his late forties. He had the kindest eyes, and when Kathleen said his name, he rose and smiled with such warmth.

"Cecil is working with Joan Fontaine and Derrick De Marney in *Blond Cheat*."

Kellaway shook hands with Lucia. "Welcome to Culver City," he said graciously.

"We're taking a little tour," Kathleen said.

"Enjoy," Kellaway said, smiling. "We have our own little magical kingdom here."

And then Kathleen and Lucia were past the tables and chairs and walking toward a line of offices that were attached to a vast hangar. Frankie joined them.

"We're going to get you some makeup and hair work, and then James—Mr. Halliday—wants you to get some shots taken."

Kathleen turned to Frankie. "Mr. Madden, right?"

"That's right, yes," he replied.

"I'll show you some more of the lot while Lucia is being pampered."

Frankie didn't care to be shown much of anything at Culver City, but the girl was pleasant and it was perhaps preferable to sitting and watching Lucia getting her face painted.

Kathleen took Lucia to one of the offices and returned a few minutes later.

"So Mr. Halliday tells me you're Lucia's agent," Kathleen said.

Frankie smiled, taken aback. "I don't know about that, miss."

"You have to start somewhere, Mr. Madden. Hollywood is all set to become the center of the universe, believe me. Miss Mariani is a very pretty girl, and if she can sing and act, then the world will be hers for as long as she can hold on to it."

"I take care of her, I guess. Take her places, keep an eye on her."

"Then you're her agent, fair and square."

The girl talked a lot, almost as much as Lucia, and Frankie feigned interest in the business of RKO Pictures and its myriad stars. Kathleen rolled out names like a telephone book, and by the time she'd finished Frankie reckoned there were more people at Culver City than in County Carlow itself.

She told Frankie to have some coffee or iced tea or whatever he liked at the restaurant. She would make sure Lucia was returned to him as soon as they were done with her.

"How does this all work, then?" Frankie asked her.

Kathleen frowned.

"This picture business. Lucia getting herself in one of these motion picture films?"

"It's very simple, Mr. Madden. People are photogenic or they're not. Some people can look wonderful in the flesh, but put them on film and they look as plain as Jane. It goes the other way as well, of course. Someone who is really not remarkable at all just lights up a movie screen. They'll have taken some photographs of Lucia, they'll perhaps have given her a screen test, have her read some lines. If it all looks and sounds good, then she'll be considered for some auditions, and then she may find herself actually contracted to RKO Pictures."

"It's that simple?"

"It can be, yes. There are some people who work for years and never get a break, but sometimes the stars align." Kathleen smiled at her own pun.

"And Mr. Halliday? He's not around?"

"Mr. Halliday is just ever so busy, that's all. Don't worry. He won't have forgotten about her, and I am sure he will see you both before you leave."

Frankie and Kathleen Riley parted company. He'd never gotten around to asking her where she came from.

As for the restaurant, it seemed that everything was free of charge. Frankie took a turkey and white cheddar sandwich and a cup of coffee. He sat at one of the small tables beneath the green canopy and caught snatches of conversations as people came and went.

"I tell you now, I couldn't move for juicers, grips, cutters, showgirls with legs to their necks..."

"... needs to come across with the money—"

"I'll tell you now, the way this goes never ceases to amaze me, Gerry. The amount of crap you have to listen to from these people—"

Frankie didn't intend to listen, but most of these people talked like they wanted the world to hear every word.

No more than ten minutes passed before a young woman approached him. She was a little taller than Lucia, her hair blond, her eyes a striking green. Her complexion was fair, and she wore the boldest red lipstick.

"Hello," she said.

Frankie rose, returned the greeting.

"I hope you don't think I'm being too forward, but I wondered if you were here for auditions," she said.

Frankie smiled. "No. Just accompanying someone."

The girl seemed awkward, ill at ease. "It's all a little bit intimidating, isn't it?"

"Frank Madden," Frankie said, and extended his hand.

The girl laughed nervously. "Oh, I'm so sorry," she said, momentarily embarrassed. "Veronica Moore."

They shook hands.

"Pleased to meet you, Miss Moore," Frankie said. "Would you care to sit down?"

The girl sat down, her purse clutched tight on her lap, just a bundle of nerves and uncertainty.

"You're here for an audition?" Frankie asked.

"I am, yes. Well, sort of. Some photographs, a screen test perhaps. I am supposed to meet Mr. Halliday, but he doesn't seem to be available right now."

"James Halliday."

"You know him?" Veronica asked. Her eyes brightened, pleased to find a connection to something familiar.

"We're here for the very same reason," Frankie said.

"We?"

"I'm with someone. She is here for the same reason as you."

"Your wife?"

Frankie laughed. "Heavens, no. Her name is Lucia Mariani. She's an aspiring actress and singer. I guess you could say I am her agent."

"Her agent?"

"Yes," Frankie replied. "In the loosest sense of the word. I take care of her, make sure she gets where she needs to be."

Veronica Moore hesitated and then leaned forward expectantly. "I need an agent," she said. "I really need someone to take care of things like that. This is all a little bit scary, to be honest. I feel like I'm out of my depth already and I haven't even spoken to anyone."

"Have you not seen Miss Riley?"

"Who?"

"She works for Mr. Halliday. She's taking care of his appointments."

"I haven't seen anyone, Mr. Madden. I was just told to be here at a certain time and here I am."

"Well, Miss Riley will be back soon enough, and I'm sure we can get everything straightened out. I can see how it would be a little bit intimidating, but you really have nothing to worry about. No matter how grand people sound, no matter how imposing it all might seem, you just have to remember that they're really no different from you. People are pretty much the same wherever you go."

Veronica smiled. She seemed to relax a little. "Oh, I'm so glad we met, Mr. Madden. It really helps to feel you're not alone."

"Would you like something to drink, perhaps? Some coffee, some tea?"

"That would be lovely," she replied. "Some tea would be just lovely."

Frankie went for tea, returned and sat with her. Veronica told her a little of herself, that she'd come all the way from Philadelphia, that she'd always dreamed of being here, that she could hardly believe she'd made it, but she understood that now the work would really begin. She talked quickly, nervously, and yet Frankie saw in her the same light of hope that Lucia carried. He wondered how many thousands, how many tens or hundreds of thousands of girls the world over saw themselves up on a silver screen and just dreamed of stardom. Was it really so different from wanting to fight for a living? Perhaps not. The need to be known, to be recognized, to be special, to be remembered. Perhaps everyone possessed such a need; it was simply that some worked harder to bury it than others.

Frankie and Veronica Moore were there for close to an hour, and then Miss Riley once again appeared.

Frankie rose to greet her, and he escorted Miss Moore out of the restaurant and into the sunshine.

"This," he said, introducing the young woman, "is Veronica Moore. She was asked to be here to see Mr. Halliday."

Miss Riley smiled, shook hands with Veronica. "Yes, of course. We've been expecting you."

Even as the words left her mouth Lucia appeared with James Halliday.

"Miss Moore," Kathleen Riley told Halliday.

"Yes, of course. I hope you haven't been too inconvenienced, Miss Moore. We've just had the busiest morning."

Veronica Moore smiled. "No, not at all. Mr. Madden here has been taking care of me."

Frankie shook Halliday's hand.

"I'm so sorry I wasn't here to greet you both," Halliday said, addressing both Frankie and Lucia. "It's been quite a time, though. We've had some headshots done, a little screen test, a few words of a song, and it all looks really very good, I must say."

Frankie looked at Lucia. She seemed more alive and energized than he'd ever seen her.

Veronica Moore extended her hand toward Lucia. "You must be Miss Mariani," she said. "Your manager here has been helping me settle my nerves. It's all a little daunting, isn't it?"

Lucia hesitated. She glanced at Frankie. Despite her evident excitement there was a flash of something in her eyes. Jealousy?

"A pleasure," Lucia said, masking whatever she might have felt. Perhaps it was nothing more than having her limelight dimmed by the presence of another bright young thing.

"Cut to the chase," Halliday said, effortlessly dispelling whatever tension might have been present. "We're casting a picture right now, and I think we might be able to squeeze Lucia into it somewhere. It won't be a speaking part, just a walk-on or a chorus line or something, but everyone has to start somewhere, don't they? I'll need you to come back tomorrow morning, say about nine o'clock?"

"Yes, of course," Lucia said, smiling like her head was full of sunshine.

"There's just a few things I'd like to get straight, Mr. Halliday," Frankie said.

Lucia opened her mouth to speak, but Frankie glanced at her. Lucia understood Frankie's desire to address his own questions. She stepped away and engaged Veronica Moore and Kathleen Riley in conversation.

"Business," Halliday said.

"Yes," Frankie said. "Just so I have a grasp of what's going on here."

"Ask away, Mr. Madden. What do you want to know?"

"Tell me something, Mr. Halliday... What kind of game are you people playing here? How does this work? I spoke to your Miss Riley there, and she said nothing much at all that made any sense."

Halliday seemed baffled. "I'm not sure what you mean, Mr. Madden."

"Well, let's just say that your friend Mr. Budny owed me a favor. He speaks to you, you come to the Roosevelt and see Lucia. Next thing I know she's down here and you wanna see if she can get in one of your pictures there. What's the deal with that?"

Halliday smiled, shook his head. "I'm sorry... I still don't know what you're asking me, Mr. Madden."

"Well, where I come from, sir, there ain't no such thing as a free sandwich, if you know what I mean. Seems all a little bit too convenient and whatever. Your girl there said that there's people who work all their lives and never get a chance to be in a motion picture film, and yet here we are, you met Lucia on Friday and you're all set to make her a star."

Halliday laughed, but it was out of genuine surprise.

"I think we're a little ahead of ourselves, Mr. Madden. This is a business, like any other. Luck has a great deal to do with it, but sometimes it's just a matter of knowing someone who knows someone else. I'm a casting director. I'm always on the lookout for new faces, fresh talent, someone with something a little special. Morris... Mr. Budny happened to mention that you and he were acquaintances, that I might be interested in meeting Miss Mariani, and that's all there is to it. Just one of those things, really. Nothing sinister at all."

"And if you want to have her work here?"

"Then we'll draw up a standard contract and you can take it away for legal perusal. Kathleen tells me you're acting as Miss Mariani's manager—"

"Yes, let's say that I am."

"Well, all the simpler then. You and I will agree on the basic terms, you take the contract away, sign it, get it notarized, and we're all done."

"And what's happening tomorrow at nine exactly?"

"That's when we're holding the final auditions. But, like I said, we have only walk-ons and very small parts to cast. If she's chosen, and that's a *big* if, and she does well, then she'll be put on a preferred list for future auditions."

Despite his immediate suspicions, Frankie liked Halliday's manner. He seemed genuine and sincere.

"Okay, then," Frankie said. "We'll be here at nine tomorrow."

"Just one question, Mr. Madden... You're new to this business, right?"

Frankie smiled. "It's that obvious, is it?"

"I started somewhere too, as did Morris Budny, as does everyone. Just a word of advice. Never let them know that you don't know. Act like you understand everything and ask questions elsewhere. There's a lot of crooks in this business, and if they think you're naive or ignorant, they'll take advantage of you."

"Appreciated, Mr. Halliday."

"Some of us are still gentlemen, but we're a dying breed, Mr. Madden, a dying breed."

Frankie extended his hand. They shook.

"Thank you for your help, Mr. Halliday, and we'll see you in the morning."

Halliday had arranged a car to take them back to the Roosevelt, and from there they took a cab home.

Once en route, Lucia asked about the girl.

"What about her?"

"She seemed awfully friendly."

"Did she, now?"

"Yes, she did. And she gave me her phone number and address. She said that if you wanted to represent her, then she would be very grateful."

"Well, she was just there for the same reason as you. She was alone and a little nervous, that was all. She talked an awful lot." Frankie smiled. "Hell, she talked even more than you."

"So you're my agent now," Lucia said matter-of-factly, "and maybe you'll be representing other people as well."

"Maybe so, Lucia, maybe so. Let's take it one day at a time, eh?"

Beyond that they didn't speak. Seemed Lucia had made a very rapid transition from starstruck to shell-shocked.

Frankie was grateful for the quiet. He needed time to think. He'd gone from wanted terrorist to illegal immigrant to Hollywood manager in little more than six months, and he'd not chosen any of them.

TWENTY-FOUR

The simple truth was that Paulie Belotti had crossed the line.

The incident with Grigor Zakarian was not the first of its kind, and Momo Adamo, Jack Dragna's underboss, had always had reservations about him. He was okay with Tony Legs and Vince Caliendo, thought they were stand-up guys, but he didn't much care for the company they kept. Tony and his buddy Caliendo needed to keep Paulie Belotti under control. This was the message from Momo Adamo.

Nicky had left the hotel early on Monday. He was out and away before Lucia and Frankie had even woken. He figured that showing keen was a good sign, and he was up at Tony Legs's place by eight.

Tony Legs was asleep. Nicky sat and waited in the kitchen while a girl with bare feet and a bare ass and nothing covering her up but a man's shirt traipsed around the joint like she didn't care who saw her. Her nonchalant attitude was an all-too-clear indication of the kind of people with whom he was now acquainted. The rules were different here, and those were perhaps rules Lucia would never appreciate nor understand. Sometimes there was only one way to get something done, and you either stepped up or stayed home.

Tony Legs came down just before nine, said he needed to shower and shave and then they'd get going.

"We got some business today," he told Nicky, and then he grabbed the girl and kissed her and said, "Donna, sweetheart, make some freakin' coffee already."

The girl just smiled, said nothing, and went about the business of making coffee. She continued to make no attempt to hide the fact that she was three seconds from naked.

When coffee was ready Tony Legs came and sat with Nicky in the kitchen.

He said, "Nicky boy, we got ourselves a situation." He drew out the word—*sit-choo-ayshun*—and he shook his head like this was a grave matter.

"Paulie is a dumbass. He's a hothead, you know? He gets excited.

He's got a short fuse and it don't seem to take nothin' at all to get it lit."

Nicky said nothing.

"Mr. Adamo is upset. He doesn't like the attention. We got to talk to Paulie, get him to see sense."

Nicky, knowing what little he did of Paulie, didn't figure him for the talking sort.

"Now, seeing as how this is all new territory for you, we don't have a problem if you wanna stay out of it."

Still Nicky said nothing. He knew what was coming, and though there was a sense of deep unease in the pit of his stomach, he also knew that there was no way he could back down. Unpleasant and unpredictable things sometimes happened in this business—just as Paulie himself had demonstrated with the Armenian—and if you wanted to reap the rewards of this business, you just had to take them in your stride.

"I understand," Nicky said.

"So you don't wanna bail?"

"I'm good," Nicky said, doing his utmost to hide his true feelings.

They were going to tell Paulie Belotti to straighten himself out, and if he made a noise or behaved like an asshole, then they would give him a beating. Nicky felt sure of it.

"You're a good kid," Tony Legs said. "You keep it all buttoned down, you know? You got a cold shadow."

"So when do we see him?"

"Today. We can't wait. He keeps on upsetting people then it'll be out of our hands, and we wouldn't want that. We brought him in, so we're responsible for him. Maybe we'll take a drive up into the hills, you know? Change of scenery."

Tony shook his head and sighed. "I like the guy. I really do. We grew up together in this racket, but he is a crazy son of a bitch sometimes, and you don't need that kind of aggravation. There was no need to hurt that Armenian guy. Okay, so he had an attitude, but he's always had an attitude. He pays every time, sometimes late, but he still pays. You put a guy in hospital, you're just delaying the next payment. It ain't rocket science. Anyways, Momo says Paulie needs to understand the game, or he can't play no more."

Donna came back into the kitchen. She was dressed, all set to leave.

"You want me to give you a ride home, sweetheart?" Tony Legs asked.

Donna shook her head. "'S okay, baby. I'm gonna take a walk up the block and see my girlfriend." She crossed the room. Tony Legs grabbed her around the waist and pulled her close.

"Say hello to my buddy," Tony Legs said. "This is Little Nicky. He ain't French and he ain't Italian, but he's something in between."

Donna smiled, and there was trouble in that expression. She was a beautiful girl, no doubt about it, but there was something about her that Nicky didn't like. There was a coolness in those blue eyes, an edge of cruelty beneath the mischievous smile.

"Like me. I ain't all good and I ain't all bad, just somewheres in between." She held out her hand. "Pleased to meet you, Little Nicky."

"Donna," Nicky said, really wishing he could be introduced with some other name, something more fitting, something more serious.

"He's like Kid Napoleon," Tony said, as if reading Nicky's thoughts. "That's what we should call you, you know? Kid Napoleon."

"Yeah," Nicky said. "Kid Napoleon . . . like Billy the Kid, right?"

"You got a six-shooter?" Donna said.

Nicky laughed. There it was, the sass and attitude.

"No, but I do," Tony said. "Now scram, sweetheart, before you both get in trouble."

Tony Legs got up from the chair and walked Donna to the door of the apartment. They exchanged words and then she was gone.

Nicky needed to get himself a girl. Maybe Donna had a friend. Maybe she'd tell her friends about Kid Napoleon and then his girl would know Tony's girl, and things would be set up even better.

"We go fetch Vince," Tony Legs said, interrupting Nicky's train of thought. "We'll talk in the car. Then we go get Paulie."

The businesslike attitude shared by Tony Legs and Vince was something of a surprise to Nicky. Sure, they said it was all business, that this was nothing personal, but it *was* personal. There was no escaping it. Paulie was their friend. They had known him forever. The truth was simple: Loyalty rested first and foremost with the business, and that was all there was to it.

"So, what are you planning for Paulie?" Nicky asked, feigning indifference.

Tony Legs waved the question away. "Just got to make him see sense, you know? He just needs to understand that he can't go on making noise. That's all there is to it."

"Maybe we tell him we gotta take someone up into the hills," Vince said. "Tell him we got someone in the trunk. We go for a drive, we dig a hole, we get talking. We tell him that if he don't sort himself out then he's gonna find himself in a hole just like that. We gotta do something that'll shake him up, scare him a little, you know?"

They picked Paulie up a half hour later. Paulie didn't think it was anything but a regular day.

"We got some business," Vince told him. Tony Legs was driving, Nicky up front, Vince and Paulie in the back.

"We got a stiff in the trunk," Tony Legs explained.

Paulie looked like someone had pulled a gun on him. "Serious?"

Vince laughed. "No, we're just fucking with you, Paulie. Jeez. You think I'd say something like that for a joke?"

"Who is it?"

"Does it matter?" Tony Legs asked.

"Sure it matters. I'm gonna get rid of a stiff, I wanna know who it is I'm getting rid of."

"There's a guy did used to run a book for Momo. He ripped off some money. Big money. More than ten gees. Bomp whacked him. We gotta take him up into the hills and bury him or something."

"Or something?"

Vince shrugged. "Maybe we chop him up and throw him all over the place. I haven't decided yet."

"Okay," Paulie said.

Nicky listened to them talking. It was like listening to them ordering a sandwich, hailing a cab, asking for another round of beers. Were they really like this, or were they just wiseguys, bluffing and bullshitting each other? Nicky let them talk. He ventured nothing. He knew he couldn't change the course of events now, and he knew there was no way of backing out.

It didn't take long to find a secluded grove of trees. Tony pulled the car over and he and Nicky got out.

Vince fetched the shovels from the trunk without letting Paulie see there was no stiff in there.

Paulie didn't think twice. He just took the shovel and started walking around, pacing out an area of ground, kicking stones away. The sun was high, the day was warming up, and he wanted to get the thing done before it became too hot to work.

Nicky took the second shovel. He started hefting dirt with Paulie.

Vince and Tony had a smoke and talked about nothing specific.

Halfway done, they swapped over.

"I wanna go look at this guy," Paulie suddenly said, and started walking toward the car.

Nicky acted fast, almost instinctual. "Don't," he said.

Tony and Vince stopped digging.

"He stinks. Really stinks. You open that and we got a thousand flies to deal with."

"How long's he been dead?" Paulie asked.

"Long enough," Tony Legs replied. "You don't even wanna see him until you absolutely got to."

Paulie opened the rear door of the car and sat sideways. Nicky opened the front door and did the same.

"Makes a change from working for a living," Paulie joked.

"Like my sister keeps tellin' me, if I'd just been a little bit smarter I coulda gotten a proper job."

Vince and Tony went on digging. They were sharing words that neither Nicky nor Paulie could hear.

Vince said they'd dug enough after another ten minutes. He'd already removed his hat and jacket, but now took off his tie and rolled up his sleeves. Nicky could see the patches of sweat beneath his arms.

Tony and Vince got out of the hole. They stood looking down into it without saying much. There was agitation in Tony's expression. He chained smokes one after the other.

"So, we gonna bury this chump or what?" Paulie asked.

"In a little while," Vince said. "Just gonna rest a minute."

Nicky got up and walked toward the others. Paulie followed on after him. The four of them stood around the hole and looked down. It was a good four feet deep, long enough for a body. Paulie looked up at Vince, at Tony, each of them stood there leaning on shovels, each of them smoking.

Nicky didn't understand why they weren't talking to Paulie, why they weren't explaining the real reason for being up there in the hills.

Tony Legs took the shovel from Vince and dug it into the pile of dirt that sat beside the hole. His own he held on to, leaning on it as he spoke.

Paulie lit a cigarette. "Wish there was a beer. Hellacious thirsty, I am." He looked away toward the trees, the backdrop of the valley beyond, and Tony Legs took the shovel from Vince and walked toward him.

The sun was behind Tony Legs, and he was nothing more than a silhouette.

Paulie shielded his eyes from the glare.

"Paulie," Vince said. "We gotta have a talk."

Paulie smiled. "Talk? Talk about what?"

"About the thing that happened with the Armenian."

"What thing?"

"You know what thing, Paulie. Don't play dumb."

Nicky glanced at Paulie. The bluff and bravado was as resolute as ever.

"It isn't just about the Armenian," Tony said. "It's about your attitude."

Nicky looked sideways and then down at the hole. He didn't feel good. He didn't feel good at all.

Vince started around the hole toward Paulie. He was nonchalant, unhurried. There was nothing about his manner that gave Paulie any cause for concern.

"The thing is," Tony went on. "Mr. Adamo ain't much one for attention. He doesn't like the kind of attention these stunts attract. You understand what I'm saying?"

Paulie shrugged his shoulders. Vince was now beside him. "Mr. Adamo got something to say to me, he should fucking well say it."

Vince put his hand on Paulie's shoulder. "Now, that's exactly the thing we're talkin' about," he said. "This thing you got. This attitude, Paulie. It's not necessary, you know?"

Nicky stepped out of the glare of the sun. He could see Vince and Tony. Their expressions had changed. Something else was happening here and Nicky did not like it.

"What the hell are you guys talking about?" Paulie asked.

"Until you're a chief you're an Indian," Vince said. "You're an Indian, Paulie. You're right here with me and Tony and Nicky, but you seem to got some kinda idea that you're the big boss of the hot sauce or something. That's not the way it works. We work for Mr. Adamo. Mr. Adamo works for Mr. Dragna. Mr. Dragna, well, he answers to whoever he answers to in the Commission. There's a ladder, my friend, and you is way down at the bottom of it with us poor schmucks here. That's what you don't seem to get, my friend, and that's what's gettin' you in trouble."

The facade shifted for just a moment. A flash of anxiety found its way into Paulie's expression. "You tellin' me I'm in trouble?"

Nicky felt a little sick. There was a tightness in his chest. He looked at the shovel in Tony's hands.

"If you're in trouble, you're the one who made it," Vince said. "No one else."

"So what the hell are we doin' here?" Paulie asked.

Nicky could hear the edge of anxiety in Paulie's voice. The man was unsettled, edging toward afraid, and he had no practiced wisecrack to dispel the tension.

"So, we gonna bury this fuckin' stiff or what?" Paulie asked. He took a step toward the car.

Vince put his hand on Paulie's shoulder.

Nicky understood then, understood precisely what he'd hoped was not the case.

"There ain't no stiff in the trunk, Paulie," Vince said.

Paulie tried to shrug away Vince's hand, but Vince gripped his upper arm.

Vince leaned closer. "You got to understand something, Paulie. It ain't difficult. It ain't complicated. You can't go around doin' the things you're doin' and badmouthin' people and causin' trouble and not have it catch up with you. Everyone gotta take responsibility for who they are and what they do."

"What the hell are you talkin' about, Vince?" Paulie asked.

Nicky took a step backward. He felt like he was going to be sick. His knees were weak, his hands sweating, and his shirt collar felt like a noose. This was not what he'd expected, not what he'd expected at all.

They weren't just going to hurt Paulie. That hole had been dug for a purpose.

"Let go of me, Vincent," Paulie said. "So maybe I shoot my mouth off, maybe I get a little riled by some fat Armenian fuck trying to weasel his way out of paying Mr. Adamo, but I ain't no snitch, right? I ain't done anythin' so bad. I get the message, okay? I get the freakin' message—"

Paulie never finished what he was saying.

With a swift shove, Vince sent Paulie into the hole. Paulie landed awkwardly on his knees. He reached up immediately and got his hands on the edge of the hole, but Vince kicked his hands back.

Paulie yowled in pain. He looked up at Vince, at Tony. In his eyes was nothing short of panic.

"Jesus Christ almighty, Vince!" Paulie hollered. "What the hell are you doing?"

Nicky knew then, knew without doubt. They were going to kill Paulie Belotti. That had been the intention all along. His knees were barely able to hold him upright.

Once again Paulie tried to clamber out of the hole, but Vince lunged forward and pushed him down.

"No!" Paulie screamed. "You can't do this!"

Paulie looked at Nicky. The terror was there, the abject and indefinable terror. He knew what was going to happen, and he knew there was nothing he could say to change the outcome.

Nicky took a step back. He wanted to turn, to run, to escape this nightmare, but he barely made it three feet before he found himself unable to move, rooted to the spot.

"Enough of this," Tony Legs said, and in that same moment he swung that shovel over his head and brought it down like an ax.

Tony's aim was wide by a foot, and the edge of the shovel caught Paulie's shoulder.

For a split second it was as if nothing had happened, and then a wide scarlet crescent opened up over Paulie's back and he screamed like a banshee.

Paulie's face was a mixture of agony and confusion. Whatever motivation he'd previously lacked was gone. He came roaring up out of the hole and started toward Tony Legs.

Tony Legs was taken by surprise. He took an involuntary step backward, and he was undone. The back of his right foot caught a rock and he went over.

Before he could even think about what to do, Paulie was over him.

Vince ran sideways, grabbed the second shovel, came from the other side with a view to hitting Paulie again.

Paulie saw him, ducked the sweep of the shovel, and lunged toward Vince. Vince lost his balance and went sideways to his knees. His first thought was to get away from Paulie, who seemed ready to tear them all limb from limb. Threatened with the end of his life, he seemed twice as large, twice as fast, twice as strong.

"What the fuck—" he started screaming, and Nicky was aware of how loud Paulie's voice seemed in that moment. In that dry and almost airless heat it would carry a hundred miles and everyone in Hollywood would know that Paulie Belotti was being murdered by his friends.

Vince had let go of the shovel, and Paulie was trying to grab it.

Everything moved so fast. It spun out of control like some surreal nightmare. Paulie kept on hollering and bleeding, hollering and bleeding. He was shouting that he would kill them all, every one of them.

Later, when Paulie was still and quiet, Nicky Mariani would again be surprised by his response to the situation. It was not so much the speed with which he snatched the shovel from the ground, nor the ease with which he hefted it in his hand, but the measured and calculated precision with which he brought it down dead center onto Paulie's head.

The sound was not what he expected, a dull *pop* like a faraway gunshot, and Paulie dropped to his knees.

Tony Legs was still all over the place, still trying to get to his feet. Vince was on his knees, leaning back with this expression on his face like the end of the world had happened.

Paulie Belotti was on his knees, too, the edge of the shovel still embedded in his skull, and when Nicky yanked the shovel back and loosed it, Paulie just fell face-forward and started bleeding into the dirt.

"What the fuck," Tony Legs said.

Vince got up and stood over Paulie's body.

Nicky stood for a second. He let the shovel slip from his hands. He looked at Vince, then back at Paulie, lying silent and motionless on the ground.

There had been a tornado of noise and confusion, a scene of utter madness, and then all of a sudden there was nothing but silence.

The blood spooled out of Paulie's head and soaked into the dry dirt.

"Jesus Christ al-fucking-mighty," Vince said.

Nicky stood stock-still for a second more, and then he turned, staggered three or four steps and started heaving and retching.

Tony Legs stepped back and sat on the pile of dirt.

Vince walked back to the car and sat in the backseat.

There was nothing but the sound of birds for a while.

Nicky was on his knees then. His throat burned, his eyes stung with tears, and he could barely find the strength to breathe.

After a while he just turned and sat down on the ground. He noticed a spray of blood on the cuff of his shirt and he retched again. It was nothing but a sharp bolt of pain in his chest.

He looked back at Vince, at Tony, and then once more to the dead body of Paulie Belotti.

"What the fuck?" Vince was saying. "What the fuck?"

"We gotta get him buried," Tony said. "Help me get him in the hole."

Nicky watched without a word as they hefted Paulie Belotti off the ground and dropped him into the grave he himself had helped to dig.

The pair of them took the shovels and started filling it in. Vince stopped after a moment and said, "We need to turn him over. Ain't right that he gets buried facedown."

"You turn him over if you're so worried about it," Tony said. "What do you think's gonna happen? He's gonna come back like a werewolf or a vampire or somethin' and bite you?"

Vince paid no mind to the quip. He got down in the hole, a foot each side of Paulie's torso, and he tried to turn Paulie over. The body was too heavy, the position too awkward, and Nicky watched him struggle for a little while before he felt he had to help.

They got Paulie turned over. He stared at Nicky, his expression now less horrified than disbelieving.

Vince leaned down and closed Paulie's eyes.

"You did good, kid," Tony Legs said.

Nicky didn't say anything, merely climbed out, took the shovel from Tony, and started work.

"That was a freakin' mess," Vince said. "Jesus, I did not expect that."

Vince pitched in and helped Nicky. It took a while, but eventually they were done. The three of them walked back and forth over the grave until the dirt was as flat as they could get it.

"How come the dirt is flat when we got Paulie under there and yet he takes up a whole bunch of room?" Vince asked, and then he lit a cigarette.

Neither Tony nor Nicky had an answer for him.

Nicky scattered some brush and dry leaves around the place, walked back and checked to see if it looked okay. It was as good as they'd get it.

They walked back to the car in silence.

Tony Legs drove back to his apartment, stopping once en route to make a call and tell whoever that the thing with Paulie was fixed. When he got back into the car he seemed glum.

"I'm gonna miss the cheapskate," he said. "You know, in all the time I known him he never once offered to buy a drink or pay for a meal. You always had to ask him, and ask him twice."

"Yeah, he was a cheapskate bastard," Vince agreed.

Tony mentioned again that Nicky had done good that morning,

that had he not been there then things may have turned out very differently.

"You really are Kid Napoleon," Tony said. "Like we got our own Little Caesar, right? You got balls, kid. You really have."

Nicky didn't say anything, couldn't say anything. If this had indeed been a proving ground, then he had proven himself. Perhaps that was all that mattered. And there was something else. He and Frankie were now bonded in blood. He could never speak of it, but he now understood.

Nicky just sat back and closed his eyes. He tried to breathe without gagging. He tried not to picture the blood as it had pooled around Paulie's head. He tried not to think of coyotes dragging him piecemeal out of the ground before the week was out, of his bones being scattered far and wide, of his skull bleaching in the sunlight.

He felt everything and nothing. His chest hurt. He was afraid, even terrified. He had reacted, done the only thing he could think of doing under the circumstances. Had he not killed Paulie, then Paulie would have . . . Well, who the hell knew what would have happened?

He wanted to laugh; he wanted to cry. He wanted to have never gotten in the car with Vince and Tony. He thought about what Lucia might say, what his mother and father would say, but he could not imagine their words. The world had just exploded in his face, and there was nothing he could do about it.

Paulie was dead. Nicky had hit him in the head with a shovel and killed him.

He had done what he'd done, and there was no going back.

TWENTY-FIVE

Milena Saroyan opened the rear door of the restaurant and let Louis Hayes in. The place had been closed over the weekend, and wouldn't open again until Grigor felt better. He'd been released from the hospital, but he was suffering acute pains on the left-hand side of his face. The doctor had told him it was to be expected, that he should keep the painkillers to a minimum, that if he was still having trouble in a week he should come back.

Hayes was bringing photos, mug shots of all the characters he knew in Dragna's crew. Somewhere among them were the three who had beaten up Grigor Zakarian, but now Hayes was interested in something a great deal more serious.

The week running up to Christmas Day of the previous year had been characteristically busy. Even crooks took a little time off for Yuletide, and they had quotas to meet and targets to achieve before Santa showed. In and among the routine Central traffic—the vice busts, the bookies, the protection circuit, the drunks and dealers and dopers and deadheads—there was a girl. Okay, so she was a chippie, but she was young for the game. No more than eighteen or nineteen by the look of her, she turned out to be sixteen years old. She was tiny, maybe five two or three, weighed in at ninety pounds after a good dinner, and someone had cut her from neck to navel. Whatever had been done to her had been done in a wild fit of rage. The cops on the scene couldn't fathom the kind of hatred and anger that would provoke such an act. The younger of the two uniforms, a greenhorn by the name of Robert Beck, tried to convey what he had seen to his wife. She said it made her feel sick, that he shouldn't talk of such things at the dinner table. Beck said that such things were facts of life, dinner table or not. *Not any regular life,* she'd replied, and Beck could not disagree.

The killing hit the headlines. It was Christmas, after all. Hooker or not, there was something horrifying and tragic and desperately sad about the whole business. Her name was Sandra Mayweather and her picture said it all. She looked like the child that she was. The backstory was all too familiar. She'd come from someplace, some Bohunk, East Jesus nowheresville that seemed to be the breeding ground for Hollywood hopefuls. Just one more aspiring actress, desperate to believe their talent would shine, hopelessly unaware that pretty faces—likes shoes, like clutch purses—passed in and out of fashion on a whim. Eloquent and emotive monologues—even if the girl was capable of such a thing—counted for nothing when faced with bat-wing eyelashes or a retroussé nose.

Sandra Mayweather was one of the unlucky ones. Right out of school in Paint Lick, Kentucky, she'd gotten enough money saved to get a bus to Los Angeles. She got off that bus in a summer-print dress, flat shoes, and a suitcase no bigger than a bread box. Stars in her eyes, her heart filled to bursting with some lifelong dream of seeing her name in lights, and then she hit the sidewalks. She had neither the smarts of Lucia Mariani, nor the protection of Frankie Madden, and whatever money she'd brought with her was gone inside a week. She looked and sounded exactly as she was, a small-town beauty pageant runner-up, and Hollywood ate her up and spat out the bones before the month was done.

How Sandy Mayweather went from hopeful actress to cheap hotel hooker was textbook, safe to say that her last trick was a killer and he killed her good. Hayes wound up with the case three days before Christmas because he had no wife, no kids, and he needed the overtime pay. The case was a bust before it even opened. No one saw anything, no one heard anything, and even those who Hayes knew had seen and heard something just lied and lied some more even when he got angry and unpleasant. If there was one place in the world where *It has nothing to do with me* was exemplified better than anywhere else, it was here.

By New Year, Sandy Mayweather was just another statistic. Her body was shipped back to Paint Lick, her folks buried her along with her Hollywood dreams, and that was the end of that.

The death of Sandy Mayweather haunted Detective Louis Hayes. Hayes was a realist, always had been, hoped he always would be. Empathy, sympathy, compassion and *feelings* were not part of the job. They stopped you getting the job done, and that was a fact. Nevertheless, there was something about Sandy that was special. Why, he could never have explained. Maybe it was how she looked, what had been done to her, the room in which she'd been found. Maybe it was simply that it was Christmas. Whatever the reason, she seemed to represent all of the lost and forgotten ones, the ones that fell through the seams and cracks and were never heard of again.

And so, when her name came from the lips of Grigor Zakarian, it meant more to Hayes than any other name he could have uttered.

"That girl. Sandra something. The young one at Christmastime. I know who killed her."

That was all he had to say. Hayes knew precisely who he meant, and he was all ears.

The first question he asked of Zakarian was who, the second was how did he know.

"I need to know how much money," was Zakarian's predictable reply.

Sandy Mayweather's folks, probably pooling everything they could, had scratched together five hundred bucks. It was a lot of money for them, but when Hayes said *Five hundred bucks* Zakarian looked utterly unimpressed.

"Five hundred bucks? To give you her killer? I need a lot more than that."

"There isn't any more. Five hundred bucks. That comes from her folks back in Kentucky. They're poor farmers. They didn't have much to begin with, and now they don't even have a daughter. If you have a heart, then you take the five hundred bucks and tell me what you know."

"You have it here?"

"What?"

"The money."

Hayes looked at Zakarian in dismay. "What the hell are you talking about?"

"Do you have this five hundred dollars?"

"No, of course I don't have the five hundred dollars, Grigor. What the hell do you think I'm gonna do? Walk around with five hundred dollars in my pocket in case someone tells me who killed Sandra Mayweather?"

"So I tell you who killed her and you go get me the money, right?"

"Jesus, do you have any idea how this works?"

"Tell me how it works, Detective Hayes." He made himself comfortable against the stacked pillows like he was all set for a bedtime story.

"You tell me what you know. I follow it up. If, and only if, your information leads to the successful arrest and conviction of the perpetrator do you get the reward money."

Zakarian looked baffled. "I got to wait for all of that?"

"Sure you do. What do you think happens here? You tell me something, I give you the money, then we shake hands and part company?"

"I don't know," Zakarian said. "I'm no cop, am I? I own a restaurant."

"So who killed her, and how do you know?"

"How do I know? I'll tell you how I know. He said so. Right in my restaurant. Right there, sitting at the table drinking coffee, he said he done it. He has the newspaper right there in front of him and her picture is there and he says he killed her."

"And who was it?"

"I get the money for sure if you find him and I am right, yes?"

"Yes, Grigor, you get the money . . . but only if we get him."

"Same kid who did this."

"What?"

Grigor gingerly touched the side of his head. "This. What happened to me. This kid who done this to me is the same one who killed that little girl."

Hayes smiled knowingly. "You're spinning me a web here, Grigor. You're just pissed at this kid—"

Zakarian looked back at Hayes unerringly, and there was something in his eyes that Hayes had not seen before.

"You're certain?" Hayes asked.

"I might be a lot of things, Detective Hayes, but I am no liar."

"So what is the kid's name?"

"Paulie. They call him Paulie."

"And you can positively identify him from his picture?"

"Sure I can."

"And you're not just saying this because he hurt you?"

Zakarian looked back at Hayes with that same expression, an expression that required no explanation.

And that was where it had ended until Monday morning when Milena let Hayes in through the back door of Tavush.

Grigor was back in the kitchen, seated near the stove. Whatever he was eating smelled good.

"You want some *byorek*?" Zakarian asked.

"What is it?"

"Pastry and cheese."

"Sure."

Zakarian nodded at Milena, and she made up a plate for Hayes. She brought him some coffee as well.

Hayes ate, and when he was done, he took a bundle of photos out of his pocket and laid them out on the counter.

"That one," Zakarian said. "That's Paulie."

Hayes picked up the photo.

"That's the one who did this to me," Zakarian said. "And that's the one who said he killed that girl in the newspaper."

"You're sure?"

Zakarian frowned. "How many times do I say I'm sure before you know I'm sure?"

"You've said it enough times now," Hayes replied.

He looked at the young face that looked back at him. *Paul Belotti.* Had he been asked he would have said there was nothing special about this one, nothing that differentiated him from any of the other myriad thugs, hoodlums, soldiers, and button men that made up Dragna's crew, but now that he looked more closely there seemed a cruelness to this man's face that he had not previously noticed. It was nothing more than suggestion. Everyone looked innocent until you found out what they'd really done.

"So, you find him, you take him in, you beat the hell out of him until he confesses, and then I get my money."

"Something like that," Hayes said.

"How long?"

"I don't know, Grigor. I really don't know. You gotta let me do my job."

"And in the meantime, I just keep paying these guys and they come in here and drink coffee and say their bullshit things to me."

"Yes, you keep everything the same."

Zakarian looked at Milena. "You know, she works here every hour that we have, and I cannot even pay her."

"What do you want from me, Grigor?"

"I want you to help me out."

Hayes took ten bucks from his wallet and put it on the counter. "That's an advance," he said. "I will do what I can to get you some more, okay?"

Zakarian took the money and tucked it into his shirt pocket.

"And I want you to help me out," Hayes said.

"What, you don't think I am helping you already?"

"I need you to keep your eyes and ears open. These guys come in, anyone from that crew comes in, I need you to listen and tell me what they're talking about. Doesn't matter what it is, even if it sounds like nothing, I need to know, okay?"

"Okay, so now I am a snitch."

Hayes smiled. "A snitch is a bad guy who gives up other bad guys, Grigor. You're no snitch."

"Then what the hell am I?"

"You're a good citizen, that's what you are."

"I hear them talking," Milena said.

"You are not involved in this," Zakarian said sharply. "You stay out of this business."

"He's right," Hayes said. "Don't even think about it. These are bad, crazy people, and the last thing in the world you want is to get involved with them, even in this way—"

"But it's okay for me, yes?" Zakarian interjected.

Hayes looked at him and said nothing.

"I help you, you pay me and you get this guy off my back. That's all I want," Zakarian said. "I will listen and tell you what I can."

Hayes got up. He thanked Milena for the *byorek* and the coffee and left the way he'd come.

Milena slid the bolt home behind him.

Hayes stood in the back alley behind Tavush and thought about Sandy Mayweather. The kind of man who could do such a thing to a girl like that did not deserve any forgiveness. What he deserved was the full force of the law bearing down upon him. Irrespective of all liberal attitudes and pious words of forgiveness, for some people the only thing that seemed just and right was an eye for an eye.

Paulie Belotti was one such person, and Hayes was going to do everything within his power to find him.

TWENTY-SIX

The audition went better than even Halliday could have expected.

It was true, no doubt, that Lucia Mariani was a good-looking girl, but on film she came alive.

Frankie watched her smile and pout and laugh and bat her eyelids, and he wondered where the hell that kind of confidence came from. Put a camera in front of her and she was a different person. He also knew that a sense of protectiveness was not the only thing he was now feeling for her.

"We're going to have to change your name," Halliday said. "A stage name. Lucy seems obvious, but we'll need a surname as well. Any preference?"

Lucia seemed baffled.

"Politics, my dear," Halliday explained. "You may not be Italian, but you have an Italian name. Unless we're selling you as Italian, then we have a problem. Preconceptions, misconceptions, prejudices, and all the rest. It's just a great deal simpler if we make you an American."

"I have no idea," Lucia said. "I'll have to think about it."

"No time to think about it," Halliday said. "I need a name for the cast roster." He looked at Frankie. "Give her your name," he said. "Madden will do just fine. Lucy Madden. That sounds like an up-and-coming Hollywood star to me." He smiled enthusiastically and wrote down the name on a piece of paper. He told her she would be needed on set at Culver at eight in the morning, Thursday the sixteenth.

It was that simple. Lucia Mariani became Lucy Madden and she was cast in a motion picture film.

The difference between Lucy Madden and Sandy Mayweather may not have been obvious to anyone outside the business, but Lucy Madden had something that Sandy never had and would never get. Halliday saw it in a heartbeat, knew what it was called, and even Frankie—unschooled in all things cinematographic—saw it.

Lucy Madden had *star quality*, and that's all there was to it.

"Now people will think we're married," she told Frankie.

"Or that we're brother and sister."

"Oh, I think we're nothing like brother and sister, Frankie," she replied, and there was something in her smile that implied something else unspoken.

Later, as they made their way home, she told Frankie that none of this would have happened without him.

"I didn't do anything much," he said. "I just showed up, so I did."

Lucy took his arm and pulled him closer as they walked. "I love the way you talk sometimes," she said. "Some of the things you say are really charming."

"I just talk the way I talk."

"I know you do, but it makes me happy to listen to you. Anyway, I mean it... If you hadn't been with me, then who knows what would have happened in that hotel."

"Yeah, that was a situation there, no doubt about it."

"And you understand what I'm doing here... I mean, here in Hollywood. You understand what I'm trying to be."

Frankie smiled. "You can't be anything but whatever you already are," he said. "You know Oscar Wilde?"

Lucy shook her head.

"Irish writer. A brilliant man who had a great deal of trouble. Anyway, he said that you've to be yourself because everyone else is taken."

"I don't mean I'm trying to be a different person. I mean trying to be an actress. Some people would think it was just crazy to come out here to Hollywood with a dream like that."

"Ah, well, that's where I differ from everyone else," Frankie said. "If it's drowning you're after, don't torment yourself with shallow water."

Lucy laughed. "I don't even know what that means."

"Sure you do. It means that if you're gonna do something, then do it right. Don't go at it half-armed and hopeless."

Lucy came to a stop at the top of the street. They were a half block from the hotel. She let go of Frankie's arm and looked at him intently.

"What?" he asked.

"I'm just looking."

"For what?"

"Who you really are. I am looking to see if I can find out who you really are."

Frankie laughed. "Well, there's a great deal more to everyone than what you see, Lucia—"

"You have to call me Lucy now. That's my name. Lucy Madden."

"Whatever you say, Lucy."

She went on looking at Frankie, her brows knitted.

"I think you've seen enough," he said, and looked away.

"I don't think I've even seen the half of you," she replied.

"Well, you go on looking all you want, and if you find someone there that I don't know about, be sure to let me know."

"I will do." She took his arm again and they kept on walking.

"We have to find somewhere else to live," she said. "It's not right that we all stay in a hotel together, and we sure can't afford it for much longer."

"I need to find work."

"I thought you were my agent," Lucy said.

Frankie laughed. "And what the hell would I ever know about doing anything like that?"

"You've managed fine so far."

"Say whatever you like, I'll not be earning a living from some part of what you're gonna get paid."

"So what about that girl . . . the one we met at Culver City? She needs an agent too. You could represent her and take a cut of whatever she earns as well."

Frankie smiled. "You really see me as some Hollywood big-shot film agent?"

"I believe people can be whatever they want to be."

"I'm not so sure. Doesn't seem to me that an Irish bareknuckle fighter would fit in so well around here."

"Too proud, Frankie Madden?"

"Pride has nothin' to do with it. Man has to earn his own keep. Can't be a parasite on someone else's livelihood."

"Okay . . . then maybe you could get some work with Nicky," she suggested. "He seems to have made some contacts. He's off somewhere every day and I haven't heard him complain that there's no work."

They reached the steps, and Frankie hesitated before he spoke. "Truth?" he said, which was more rhetoric than a real question.

"Of course," Lucy replied.

"If it's all the same to you, I'll not be gettin' involved in whatever your brother has gotten himself involved in."

"Meaning what?"

"Meaning that his kind of people and my kind of people are very different."

Lucy assumed the same expression as she'd done when Halliday asked her to pick a name.

"You got stars in your eyes, Lucia . . . Lucy. You got stars in your eyes so bright that you're not seein' what's right there in front of you. We've been here a week, and already we've beaten up a man and blackmailed him into getting you an audition. I'm not sayin' he didn't deserve it, but it's not how I expected things to be. As for Nicky, he's up to his waist in some kind of trouble. Knowing what little I do of him, I guess he'll be up to his neck before another week is out."

Lucy seemed genuinely perplexed. "Trouble? What kind of trouble is he in?"

"Damned if I know, but he came home on Friday night in different clothes. That much I saw with my own eyes. Now, I don't know what might happen during the day that would mean changing your clothes, but I'm guessing it's not good."

Lucy was laughing. "Oh, you're so suspicious, Frankie. He spilled coffee on his pants. He told me what happened. He spilled coffee on his pants and he had to change, that was all."

"Is that what he told you?"

"Yes. It's nothing sinister. You really thought that he was involved in something bad?"

"I don't know what he was doing, but I doubt very much there was any coffee involved."

"Well, we'll ask him tonight."

"I don't think that's such a good idea," Frankie said. "Never good to corner a man with questions he might not want to answer."

"I'm going to ask him. He can't lie to me. He's my brother. He made promises, and he has to keep those promises. We're going to ask him, and that's the end of it."

"Suit yourself," Frankie said, and went up the steps to the front door of the hotel. "If things get awkward, don't say I didn't warn you."

"Well, I think you're going to be very surprised, Frankie Madden. I think you're going to find that there's a very simple and innocent explanation for all your suspicions."

"Let's hope so, eh?" Frankie said, and he held the door open for her.

She reached up and touched his cheek as she passed him. She smiled so sincerely, so artlessly, that Frankie was quite taken aback.

"I know you're only trying to look after me," she said, "but I'm more than capable of looking after myself."

Frankie thought back to the fight in New York, the way she had goaded him on, that flint in her eyes, that hardness in her spirit. He also remembered the controlled fury in the Roosevelt Hotel, the way she had suddenly turned a desperately awful situation into something that was to her advantage.

Yes, he thought, *I'm sure you are perfectly capable of looking after yourself.* For some reason he then felt a deep sense of anxiety that he could have well done without.

TWENTY-SEVEN

That Monday evening—as Detective Louis Hayes began the laborious process of locating Paulie Belotti—the trio that were responsible for Paulie's death and burial were enjoying a meal in a small Italian restaurant as guests of Joe Adamo, brother to Dragna's underboss, Momo. Notwithstanding his profession and reputation, Joe Adamo had an almost kindly face. Glasses gave him the appearance of a college professor, and he wore his dark hair slicked back. That appearances were invariably deceptive became clear when he opened his mouth, however.

It was Joe who recognized two of the three people at a nearby table.

"The kid's name is Mickey Rooney," he said. "That woman is Fay Holden. The other guy I don't know." He paused to light a thin cigar. "Hollywood people in here all the time," he went on. "I don't just mean crowd fillers and walk-ons. I mean real stars. Walter Pidgeon, Myrna Loy, Paul Muni . . . Hey, you see that movie he did? *Scarface*. You seen that, right?"

Tony Legs and Vince had seen it. Nicky didn't know anything about Paul Muni nor the movie so he kept his mouth shut.

"Great movie," Joe said. "Tony Camonte. That's the guy he plays. He's holding that Tommy gun, right, and he says 'Lookit, Johnny. You can carry it around like a baby.' You remember that scene? Laughed my ass off."

The boys laughed, Nicky too. He felt to do otherwise would be rude.

"And then he calls it a typewriter. Says he's gonna write his name all over town with it. Great movie, sure. Great freakin' movie."

The waiter brought a bottle of wine. He asked Joe if he wanted to taste it.

"Just pour the wine. It's fine. And bring some bread, huh? Gonna die of starvation here."

The waiter poured wine, brought a plate of bread, some prosciutto, olives, some oil.

Like the other Italians Nicky had met, Joe Adamo talked a lot and didn't stop even when his mouth was full.

"So, Tony Legs here tells me you done good, kid," he said to Nicky. "That thing. That business you took care of. Said you handled yourself real well."

Nicky nodded deferentially. He understood who Dragna was, Momo, too, and he knew that making friends with these people was as good as writing your own paycheck.

"You giving this kid some runaround money?" Joe asked Tony Legs.

"Given him some, Mr. Adamo, sure."

Joe dug into his pocket and took out a roll of fifties. He peeled off a couple, folded them in half and slid them across the table to Nicky.

"Father fuckin' Christmastime, kid. Get yourself a suit, some new shoes, whatever you need."

"That is very good of you, Mr. Adamo," Nicky said. "I really appreciate that."

Joe reached out and gripped Nicky's forearm. "Tony here tells me you do what's asked of you, keep your mouth shut, show some initiative. More like you we can use."

"Whatever you need, Mr. Adamo."

Joe laughed. "That tells me right there that you ain't no Italian. Italian kids got nothing but backchat and wisecracks, but what the hell, eh? These are times of progress and change, right? This is America. We gotta move forward or we're standing still."

Nicky drank some wine and took a piece of bread. He dipped it in the oil.

"So this business with the Armenian guy," Joe went on. "What the hell, eh? This kind of thing... I mean I understand, of course. This kind of thing happens, but there's a time and place, right? Right?"

Tony Legs and Vince agreed, though it seemed obvious to Nicky that Joe Adamo wasn't looking for agreement. His questions weren't even rhetorical; he just wanted to hear people agreeing with him.

"So there's gonna be some changes around here. There's some new business, some new districts, some new overheads to meet, and you three are gonna be needed to keep this all on track and running smooth. Details, who does what, all that kind of thing can wait, but for now I just need you to understand that me and Momo are overseeing all of this for Mr. Dragna. If I say it, then it's Mr. Dragna saying it, you understand?"

"We understand," Vince said.

"Good, so let's eat." Joe looked at Nicky. "And you, drink some more wine already."

Nicky refilled his glass.

"What do they call you? Little Nicky, right?"

"That's what they call me."

Joe shook his head. "I don't like it. It's like a schoolyard name. What else you got?"

"Kid Napoleon," Tony Legs said. "Like Little Caesar, you know? He comes from the same freakin' place as Napoléon."

Joe started laughing. "Well, make sure he doesn't get into any fights with any fuckin' Russians, eh?"

The table broke up.

Nicky wasn't sure what happened then. Perhaps the Holden woman had given Joe a disapproving look, but suddenly he turned on her.

"What?" he said, his tone challenging and aggressive. "It's a freakin' restaurant, lady. We have as much right to be here as you and your punk kid. And yes, I know who you are, and you may be all Hollywood, but this is our city and you people go to work every day 'cause we say so. Now mind your own damned business."

Nicky had not seen what provoked Joe Adamo's outburst, but within a minute the Holden woman, the Rooney kid and their companion had gathered their things and were leaving the restaurant. There were other diners, but they seemed to pay no mind. Perhaps they knew well enough to say nothing.

The waiter approached tentatively. "Have you had a moment to look at the menu, sir? Shall I perhaps tell you our specials?"

Joe waved a piece of bread in the waiter's direction. "Bring some more bread. Get us some veal, some pasta with garlic and olive oil, and some fish. White fish is what we need."

The order went in to the kitchen, and once again Nicky observed that these people assumed a position and held it. There was an unspoken hierarchy. They said what they wanted to say. They anticipated no opposition. If that was the way it was done, then so be it. This kind of thing he could understand and appreciate. A roll of money in your pocket, a disregard for the importance with which others viewed themselves, an expectation that others would just fall into line and follow your orders. Joe Adamo considered himself the most important man in the room, and if anyone disagreed they could go to hell.

Dinner complete, Adamo took Nicky aside. He put his arm around

Nicky's shoulder. The man was drunk, but Nicky didn't doubt he meant every word.

"You got a spark, kid," he said. "I see it. I had the same. I came up from nothing, too. Me and my brother turned this place on its head. We kicked everyone's asses to get here, but we got here. You ain't never gonna be family, you know? You can't be. You ain't from the same place as us, but that doesn't mean you can't get a piece of something. This is the future. This is how it is. We work with the Irishers, the Jews, whoever. Business is business. Don't care where the money comes from. It all spends the same, right?"

Nicky could feel the fifty-dollar bills burning a hole in his pocket. If money was a drug, then that was an addiction he would happily take on.

"You do things right, Kid Napoleon, and things will go right for you," Adamo said, and he gripped the back of Nicky's neck and squeezed it. It was an avuncular gesture, and Nicky felt that within that small moment he had somehow been understood and accepted more than had ever occurred at home, in New York, anyplace else. He felt like he belonged here, right here in Hollywood, and for a very different reason from Lucia. Hollywood was swollen with money, and there could be no more important reason for being here than that.

Adamo went outside. His driver opened the passenger door of a Ford convertible and Adamo got in. Nicky watched the car disappear.

"Looks like you got yourself a friend for life," Vince said, once they'd returned to their table.

"Never know how long that's gonna be in this business," Tony Legs said. "Just ask Paulie."

They stayed a little longer, finished the bottle of wine, and went their separate ways with an agreement to meet at noon the following day in the foyer of the Knickerbocker.

Nicky was back at the hotel by ten, found Lucia and Frankie in good spirits.

"I got a job!" Lucia told him, more excited than he'd ever seen her. "I did my audition today and I start work on Thursday!"

Nicky was thrilled. He wanted to see his sister happy. He had made a promise to their parents that he would get her to Hollywood, and here she was.

"And my name is now Lucy Madden," Lucia said.

"What?" Nicky looked at Frankie, horrified.

Frankie laughed. "Sure, we went up to City Hall and got married."

"It's a stage name," Lucia said. "I have to have a stage name and that's what was decided."

Nicky nodded slowly. "Looks like we're all getting new names, eh?"

"What do you mean?"

"The guys I work with, they call me Kid Napoleon."

Lucia seemed puzzled. "Why do they call you that? I mean, I get the Napoleon thing, but why—" She stopped talking. She looked at Frankie. Frankie shook his head. *Not now*, that gesture said. *Let's not do this now.*

"Why would you need a name like that, Nicky?" she asked. Seemed she had her mind set on walking that road and Frankie was not going to dissuade her.

"No reason. It's not important, Lucia—"

"It's important to me, Nicky," she said.

Lucia crossed the room and sat down. There was an edge to her voice. Suddenly they were no longer celebrating the success of her audition.

Frankie stood near the window. He felt as if he really didn't belong. Brothers and sisters always fought and always would. He knew that from personal experience.

"Leave it alone, Lucia. We were talking about your movie thing. It's great news, okay? I am really happy for you. What we're talking about now doesn't matter at all."

Nicky got up and started toward the bathroom.

Lucia intercepted him, looked him right in the eye.

"Tell me about these people," she said. "Tell me what you're doing. This work you're doing, Nicky . . . what kind of work is it?"

Nicky frowned, aggravated now that this had turned into some kind of interrogation.

"Nicky, seriously . . . I want to know what you're involved in—"

"I gave my word," he said. "I gave my word that I would get you to Hollywood, and you're right here, okay? Does it matter how I did that? What happened back in New York is history. We don't ask questions. We don't talk about it. Sometimes you just do whatever has to be done, and once it's done you don't think about the cost. Don't be naive, Lucia. Wise up, okay?"

"Wise up?" Lucia echoed. "You're telling me to wise up?"

Nicky took a deep breath. From Frankie's vantage point it appeared that Nicky was on the boil. He wanted to tell Lucia to back down, that this was neither the time nor the place, but he knew his words would be meaningless. In her own way she was as stubborn and ruthless as her brother. That had been nowhere more evident than back at the Roosevelt with Morris Budny. Perhaps they were both capable of using the other as a stepping-stone.

"I know what you're doing," Lucia said.

"Oh, you do? Is that so?"

"Yes, it is, Nicky, and I want you to stop. I want you to do something honest and legal, something that I don't have to read about in the papers."

"Honest and legal. What makes you think I'm doing something that's not honest and legal?"

"Because I know you too well, Nicky. I know what you want, and I know that you'll do whatever you have to do to get it—"

"I did what you wanted, remember? I did what I had to do for you."

"I know you did, Nicky, and I owe you everything, but we're here now, it's done, and we can start over—"

"Okay," he said coldly. "I understand. So we do whatever needs to be done to help you, and to hell with me, right? To hell with Nicky and whatever Nicky wants—"

"That's not what I'm saying—"

"No? Well, there's a fucking surprise, because that's exactly what I just heard."

"You're getting angry," she said, her tone softer. "I don't want to get into a fight, okay? I just want you to know that I love you and I want you to be happy, and I owe you everything for getting me to Hollywood, but I don't want you to get into trouble."

"I will do what I have to do, just like you, little sister," Nicky said, and there was no respite in his manner. He had been challenged, and he wasn't going to let it lie.

"So, what are you telling me?" Lucia asked. "You're telling me that you're just going to go on seeing these people who call you this stupid name, that you're going to carry on being involved—"

"You wanna see something?" Nicky asked. "I'll show you something, Lucia."

He took the two fifty-dollar bills from his pocket and held them in front of her face.

Her eyes widened.

Nicky held the money close to her face. "Smell that," he said, and there was a cruel glint in his eyes. "Smell that. That's what got you here. Nothing else. Not your fucking talent or how pretty you are or anything else. I made the money to get us here, and I will make the money to keep us here."

Frankie could feel the tension pulsing between them. He wondered if Nicky had ever struck his sister. He thought to say something to defuse the situation, but felt that any word would merely aggravate the disagreement further.

"Is that what this is about, Nicky? The money? You just want money and it doesn't matter what you have to do to get it?"

Nicky didn't respond.

"Where did you get this money?" Lucia said. "Where did so much money come from? You just have a hundred dollars in your pocket . . . just like it was nothing—"

Nicky sneered. "A hundred dollars, five hundred, a thousand . . . This is nothing compared to what's out there, and we can all have as much as we want."

"As long as you are prepared to break the law and hurt people and steal—"

"You don't understand anything," Nicky snapped.

"I understand enough. I don't know what you're doing, but you have to stop it, Nicky. What would Papa say?"

"Papa? What would Papa say? You think I'm stupid, Lucia? You think I don't understand what girls like you have to do to get into the movies?"

Lucia hesitated for just a second, and then she slapped her brother's face with such force that the shock was as great as the pain.

Nicky raised his fist, and Frankie was there in a heartbeat.

That fist remained clenched and just inches from Lucia's face. She did not flinch. They stared at each other like wild beasts separated by an invisible cage. Neither hatred nor loathing, what passed between them was an intense defiance. Neither one would back down or yield.

Nicky turned and looked at Frankie. "I kept my promise," he said coldly. "This crazy bitch is your problem now."

Without a further word, without even looking back, Nicky stormed out of the hotel room and slammed the door behind him.

Lucia didn't move until the sound of his footsteps had vanished into silence.

She snatched a vase from the small table by the window and hurled it against the wall.

TWENTY-EIGHT

Late on Wednesday afternoon Louis Hayes received a call at Central.

It was Milena Saroyan.

"You need to come talk to Grigor," she said. Her voice sounded strained.

"What's happened?" Hayes asked.

"You just need to come," she said, and she hung up the phone.

Hayes took a pool car and drove over to Tavush. The front door was locked, the sign read *Closed*, and Hayes started to get worried.

Shielding his eyes against the reflection from the sun, Hayes peered through the glass into the dim interior of the restaurant. It wasn't even five and the place was shut up. Something was wrong. He knew that before he even saw Milena waving at him from behind the countertop. She was pointing to the side of the building, motioning for Hayes to walk around back.

Hayes went as directed, down the side of the adjacent building and along an alleyway at the rear.

Milena was waiting for him in the back doorway of the restaurant.

Even before he reached her he could see the bruises and swelling on her face.

"What the hell—" he started, but Milena shook her head, waved him inside, pushed the door shut with her foot.

Hayes looked at the girl. She was distressed, her eyes red from crying, her face swollen on the right side, but it was only when she stepped through into the kitchen that Hayes saw the extent of her injuries.

Her hands. Milena's hands had been burned.

"Show me," Hayes said.

Milena looked up at him. She instinctively held her hands away from him, tried to hide them behind her back.

"Show me, Milena," he said.

Milena hesitated, and then she complied.

She held out her hands as if ashamed.

The palms were red and weeping, the skin burned away, the tips of her fingers blistered.

"Christ almighty, Milena. You need to get to the hospital," Hayes said. "I'm taking you now."

"No," she said. "No hospital."

"This is not a matter for discussion, Milena. I am taking you to the hospital now."

"But Grigor—"

"Where is he?"

Milena glanced upstairs toward the apartment above the restaurant.

Hayes stepped past her and went on up.

He found Grigor slumped in a chair, his face bruised, his lip cut and bloody, a wide gash over his right ear.

"Jesus, what the hell happened, Grigor?" Hayes asked.

Hayes turned as Milena entered the room.

"You called him," Zakarian said. "I told you not to call him."

"Of course she called me, Grigor. What the hell do you think this is? What happened here? Who did this?"

"I cannot help you, Detective Hayes," Zakarian said. "We are done now. All finished. I don't want reward. You do whatever you like and keep us out of this. This is not why we come to America."

"Who, Grigor?" Hayes asked, his tone insistent. "Who did this?"

"Who does not matter. What happens does not matter. I am finished, okay?"

"He asked them," Milena said.

"Enough, girl," Zakarian interjected. "You bring enough trouble by calling him. You tell him nothing."

Milena stepped forward. "He asked them about this one that killed the girl."

"Belotti?" Hayes asked.

"Yes, the one who came last time and hurt him."

"Some of them came here?"

Zakarian leaned up awkwardly. He was evidently in a considerable amount of pain. "You say nothing more, Milena. I tell you now. You say nothing more. You can do nothing but it is worse for us."

"How can it be worse?" Hayes asked. "Have you looked in the mirror, Grigor? Have you seen Milena's hands? We need to get you both to the hospital—"

"No. No hospital."

"You don't have a choice, my friend," Hayes said. "You don't get her hands treated they'll get infected. She won't be cooking anything in your damned restaurant then, will she?"

"You can't do this."

"You'd be very surprised at what I can and can't do, Grigor."

"Those boys came," Milena said. "Three of them. They came to eat, and they were just talking. Grigor asked about Paulie. Why wasn't he with them?"

Hayes turned and looked at Zakarian. "I asked you to listen, Grigor, not interrogate them."

"They got angry," Milena said. "They wanted to know why he was asking about this Belotti. What was he thinking? Was Grigor going to try to get his revenge on him?"

"They were crazy," Zakarian said. "They started laughing at me. Then they got nasty. They started hitting me again. I ran to the kitchen. They came after me. Then they saw Milena."

Zakarian fell silent. He looked at Milena. His eyes filled with tears.

"One of them grabbed her. She pushed him. He got really mad. He pushed her back and she fell against the stove. That's when she burned her hands."

"They told me it was a warning," Milena said. "And then they beat Grigor some more, and they were shouting at him, telling him that if he talked to anyone, if he asked any questions about Paulie they would kill us both."

"One of them was called Napoleon," Zakarian said.

"Napoleon?" Hayes asked.

"That's what he said. He said that if we didn't keep our mouths shut and stop asking questions then they would take us for a drive in the hills and Napoleon would kill us."

"And did they say who this Napoleon was?"

"He was with them. He didn't say anything. He was here the other time when Paulie hurt Grigor," Milena said.

"Okay," Hayes said. "Okay, okay. Hospital. That's where we're going. All three of us. Emergency room. No arguments, no discussion, nothing. We're going to get you fixed up and that's all there is to it."

"But you—" Zakarian started.

Hayes turned and silenced him with a look. "Get up out of the chair, Grigor. Get your coat. I am taking you both to the hospital."

Milena was seen first. Her hands were cleaned, treated with iodine, and bandaged. The burns were relatively superficial, but sufficient to give her considerable pain. It would be a week or more before she'd be able to use her hands to cook or clean or anything else.

Hayes sat with Milena in the waiting area while the ER attendants dealt with Grigor.

"This is a terrible business," he said, "and I feel completely responsible for dragging you into it."

"This is America, no?" Milena asked.

"This is one part of it. A bad part. A part you wouldn't have encountered had it not been for me."

Milena smiled as best she could. It was an expression of weary resignation. "We already had these people in our lives, Detective Hayes. They were already threatening us and taking our money before you showed up. My uncle should not have asked any questions, but he wants the reward money. He is so desperate to escape this situation and he doesn't know what to do."

"I put him in that situation," Hayes said, "and you, too. I'm sorry for this."

"I think perhaps this would have happened anyway."

"You're being very philosophical about this, Milena. You're a very courageous young woman."

Milena laughed, but there was no joy in that sound. "Perhaps we have not had such an easy life, but there are many people who do not have an easy life. I lost my parents, and now I live with my uncle. He brought me here to America to give us both a better life. He is a good man, but he cannot fight these people by himself."

"I am trying to help," Hayes said.

"I know, Detective, but you're also alone, like us. We're fighting to keep our restaurant open. We have very little money. I don't even know how we'll pay for our medical care today."

Milena breathed deeply, as if she was fighting back a wave of grief.

Hayes put his hand on her arm. "You don't have to pay for your medical care, Milena," he said. "That's already taken care of."

Milena looked up at Hayes. Her eyes brimmed with tears. "Why are you helping us?"

"I'm trying to help everyone," he said, "but you can't help them all at once."

"You're a good man, too, Detective Hayes," Milena said.

Hayes didn't respond.

Milena fell silent. She leaned back in the chair, rested her hands on her lap, and closed her eyes.

Hayes sat there with her, and though he felt something, he could not have described it. He could imagine how it was to have a child, to care for someone, to think of their welfare in the same moment as your own. Beneath that was his own anger, his frustration, his hatred of the people who had done this. Belotti may not have been present this time, but he was involved. Caliendo, Leggiero, and now someone who called himself Napoleon.

This was a bad business, just as he'd told Milena. What he hadn't told her was how bad, how wretched, how degraded and evil these people really were.

Watching the girl then, those few minutes before the nurse came and told him that Zakarian was ready to leave, Hayes swore to himself that he would find whoever had done this and make them pay.

No matter what they said at the academy, in the department, in the briefings, it was not *just* business. Sometimes these things encompassed real people, people who did not deserve to be dragged down into the sewers of this city, and then it became personal.

Very personal indeed.

TWENTY-NINE

By nine fifteen on Thursday morning it was obvious that Eve Lansing was not going to show. Why was unimportant; she was just a no-show. James Halliday had a problem and he needed a girl to solve it. It was three lines—*Can I take your hat, sir?*, *Yes, sir, right through there at the bar,* and *Oh, I'd say about ten minutes.*

It was Frankie who came forward with a solution, and Halliday was impressed.

"Have Lucy take Miss Lansing's line," Frankie suggested. "They're close enough in size. They won't need to change her outfit. And the other girl that was here before, Miss Moore. We have her address and phone number. We could send a car to fetch her, and she could take Lucy's part."

Costumes got Lucy into the hatcheck girl outfit; a car went for Veronica Moore; fitting and makeup was done by half past ten.

Frankie watched as people went about their business. Halliday made a point of approaching Frankie and acknowledging his quick thinking.

"Maybe this business suits you more than you think," he said, and then smiled and took his leave as Lucy came toward them.

Lucy was flustered, overcome by a wave of nausea and nerves. Whatever confidence and self-assurance she might have possessed at the audition seemed to be a distant memory.

Frankie put his arms around her shoulder and guided her away from the attention of others present.

"What's happening?"

Lucy looked at him, eyes wide, almost as if she were in shock, and she took a couple of deep breaths.

"I feel dizzy," she said, her voice a whisper. "Really dizzy and sick."

Frankie smiled reassuringly. "Just nerves," he said. "Like the moment before a fight starts. It'll be fine, believe me. You just do what you do best."

"I don't think I can. I think I'm going to make a mess of it."

"You think these people feel any different?" Frankie asked. "You think it was any easier for them? Everyone feels the same way, Lucy. Everyone gets nervous when they do something for the first time. You're going to do great. I know you can do it. They'll love you."

She inhaled deeply, exhaled again. "Not so good, Frankie."

"Breathe," he said. "Just keep breathing. Get out there, think of everything you've done to get here. Think of how proud your mother and father would be if they could see you now. Think of how happy they'd be to know you're on the way to realizing your dreams."

That seemed to be the magic bullet for Lucy. She straightened up, smiled, took another deep breath, and stepped forward. She was steady on her feet. She was going to be fine. She was going to knock them dead.

"Thank you," she said. "I don't know what I did to deserve you, but I'm glad I did it."

For a moment their eyes met and they did not look away. They did not smile. They did not utter a word.

The air snapped between them.

"Lucy Madden!" someone shouted. "Do we have a Lucy Madden on set?"

Lucy reached out and touched Frankie's arm, and then she turned and walked toward the set.

Two takes, simply because the director wanted a particular smile—*That's lovely, but can we get it a little more playful . . . a touch more coquettish, okay?*—and Lucy Madden was dispatched to the set office.

Veronica Moore fulfilled her role as well, and afterward was effusive in her gratitude.

"It was nothing at all," Frankie told her. "Just seemed like a good idea, you know?"

"Well, I can't thank you enough, Mr. Madden . . . and you, too, Miss Madden. I am really pleased that I met you both."

Frankie accompanied them both to the credits department and was asked for his agency details.

"Erin," he said after a moment's thought. "The Erin Star Agency."

Paperwork was produced, employment terms were signed and witnessed right there and then. Both Lucy Madden and Veronica Moore were ably represented by their theatrical agent, Mr. Frank Madden. Lucy was lit up like a firework. Her moment of nerves was as distant as the moon. She was a real honest-to-God contract player for RKO.

Veronica Moore had to leave for another appointment, but Frankie and Lucy stayed for the rest of the day. They watched numerous scenes lit and filmed, and much to Frankie's surprise, he actually enjoyed the experience. People addressed him politely, asked him his business, and when he said he was there representing two of the actresses, he was granted a degree of respect that was altogether unfamiliar. This was a world of its own devising, it possessed its own rules and protocol, and Frankie Madden believed that this was actually a world within which he could find a place.

As if to confirm that very thought, a messenger came looking for him to deliver an envelope. Within it was a message from Kathleen Riley. It was brief and to the point. An actress called Jean Walker had just been signed by RKO and required an agent. Would Mr. Madden be interested in speaking with her? Frankie didn't mention it to Lucy, told her that the message from Miss Riley concerned the delivery of contracts. He didn't wish to dim or detract from the limelight within which Lucy was bathed. However, he had every intention of speaking with Miss Jean Walker, and he would discuss it with Lucy a little later. Perhaps—once again—here was a path that he'd not chosen, but more a path that had chosen him.

That evening, Frankie and his newfound starlet-to-be, Miss Lucy Madden, took dinner in a restaurant near the hotel. The food wasn't so great, but it was cheap, and Frankie knew that money would wind up on the conversational agenda before too long. Lucy had earned twelve dollars that day, and—significant though it was—it would not last long. However—also inevitably—the conversation turned to Nicky.

"He'll come back," Lucy said, and there was a forced certainty in her voice that suggested she didn't believe what she was saying. Nicky would rather cut his own throat than apologize or recant. He was proud, and pride so often became irrational defiance. If anyone extended an olive branch, it would have to be Lucy, and Frankie told her so.

Lucy was quite for a moment, and then she said, "I know. He is so stubborn."

Frankie smiled.

"What?"

"Nothing," he said.

"Tell me, Frankie."

"You're cut from the same cloth, you pair."

"Meaning what?" She set down her knife and fork as if preparing herself for a confrontation.

"That however stubborn he might be, you could be judged the same way."

Lucy frowned. "I am not stubborn."

"Maybe stubborn is the wrong word," Frankie said. "You have a fierce belief in your own rightness." He leaned back in his chair. He smiled. He wanted to appear as relaxed as possible.

"And what's wrong with that? How would anyone ever achieve anything if they didn't feel that way?"

"Self-assurance and believing you're right aren't the same thing."

"All of a sudden you're the philosopher."

Frankie nodded sagely. "I am indeed."

"I don't agree with you."

"I know you don't. I could have told you that right at the start."

"Oh, so what you're saying is that if I don't agree with you then I'm stubborn?"

"No, I'm saying that if you don't also look at it from the other person's point of view then you'll never win a fight."

"Is this some of your boxing philosophy?"

Still Lucy was tense, even aggressive. She was being challenged, and Frankie knew all too well that very soon it would become less a matter of debate and more a matter of who could win.

He stayed right where he was, continued with the same easy tone of voice. "Maybe it is. Winning a fight isn't just about hitting harder than the other guy. It's also about seeing what your opponent is going to do before he does it, and not getting in the way."

"I don't think Nicky and I are opponents," Lucia said. She had that flash in her eyes; the spoiled girl who always got her own way.

"I wouldn't be so sure. Two days and he's made no attempt to contact you, and you're sitting here telling me how this isn't going to resolve unless he backs down. I don't know him anywhere near as well as you, and I know that's never going to happen."

"You seem determined to spoil one of the best days of my life."

"You were the one who brought it up."

"So, let's not talk about it anymore. Let's drink champagne and be famous."

"You drink all the champagne you want, Lucy. If I drink anything, it'll be an Irish whiskey. As for being famous—"

"I know. I know," she interjected. "Let me keep a little of my dream before you drown it, okay?"

Frankie smiled. He could not defend himself against her. She was foolish, naive, beautiful, elegant, single-minded to the point of being blinkered; she was driven and motivated, and yet beneath the femininity and grace there was a core of toughness and emotional strength that belied all outward appearances. Frankie wondered whether Lucia would make a far worse enemy than her brother. That question aside, he had no intention of finding out.

Lucy drank champagne, and when they walked back to the hotel, she held on to Frankie for fear of losing her balance.

The feeling of her arm through his, of her momentary dependence upon him—not only physically, but emotionally—was something he could get used to very easily. He knew that, and he knew how dangerous it was to again feel that way. For now, for the foreseeable future, perhaps forever, he had lost his own dream. He knew that he'd never stand on the canvas and hoist a belt above his head. Nothing so simple as choosing another identity would make the past disappear. What had he expected? How had he believed that there would ever be another outcome? Whatever name he chose, as soon as that name was in lights, as soon as the world saw who he was, there would be people from New York asking after his whereabouts, and once they found him, it would be only a matter of time before they learned his real identity and from where he'd come.

The past was gone. Let it die right where he'd left it. This was what he now had, a future very different from the one he'd imagined, and he had to make a decision to go with it, or strike out on his own and see what he could create alone.

History would find him unless he divorced himself from it entirely.

"Frankie?" Lucy slurred.

Frankie slowed up. They were a minute's walk from the hotel.

"Do you believe in me?"

"Believe in you about what, Lucy?"

"Do you believe that I can be a star? Here, in Hollywood? Do you think I can be a movie star?"

"Sure. Why the hell not? It happens to people, so why not to you?"

Lucy looked up at Frankie. She reached out her hands and placed her palms flat on each side of his face.

He started laughing, took her wrists and tried to put some distance between them.

"No," she said. "Don't. Just look at me, Frankie . . . Look me in the eye and tell me that I am going to be a star."

Frankie smiled. She really was a great deal drunker than he'd thought.

"If you need me to tell you that," he said, "then . . . well, you know that I don't need to tell you that. You know that you can, and that's all you need."

Lucy lost her balance and Frankie grabbed her beneath the arms. He held her steady until she regained her footing.

"I think you should lie down a while, get your head back on straight, you know?"

"Thank you for helping me today . . . for being there. I don't know what I would have done without you."

"You'd have done just fine," he said. "That's what you'd have done."

Frankie started walking her toward the hotel, but once again she stopped and turned to face him.

This time she reached up and put her hands on his shoulders. She moved quickly, far quicker than Frankie had anticipated or expected, and she kissed him hard on the mouth.

Frankie—eyes wide, almost losing balance himself—was so taken aback that he could not speak.

She pulled away, took one look at his expression, and started laughing.

Frankie started to say something, but she pressed her finger to his lips.

"Ssshhh," she said, and she started laughing again.

It was then that she lost it completely, and Frankie anticipated her falling before her knees even buckled. He caught her, held her up, got her arm around the back of his neck, his own arm beneath her shoulders. She weighed next to nothing, and he helped her up the stairs to the hotel room with no difficulty. There was no one there to see them, no one who could have said a disparaging word, and Frankie was grateful for that.

He got Lucy into the room, got her coat and shoes off, and then carried her through to the bed. He laid her on her side just in case she was sick, and he sat on the edge of the mattress. She was out cold before her head even touched the pillow, and he knew that the kiss had been nothing more than the foolish and spontaneous reaction of a drunken girl. He doubted whether she would even remember it in the morning.

Frankie felt hollow inside. He did not know what he was doing. He did not know where he was headed, if there was even a destination to be reached. One thing was certain, that he could not leave her now. With Nicky gone, with no one here to keep an eye on her, the Morris Budnys of this world would devour this girl complete and leave nothing but a shadow of who she'd once been.

Frankie got up and walked to the door. He would check on her every half an hour, make sure she was okay. She just needed to sleep off the drink and get herself straight again.

He paused at the door and looked back at her.

Daniel McCabe and Lucia Mariani. That's who they really were, and they would never be anyone or anything else. No matter the disguise, what lay beneath the facade would never change.

Frankie knew all of this was an illusion, a fantasy, perhaps some strange Saharan oasis that promised ever-unreachable horizons.

For Lucy's sake, he hoped not.

Frankie closed the door quietly and went to his own bed. He did not undress. He merely lay down, stared at the ceiling, and wondered how long it would be before his own dark history found him.

THIRTY

By Saturday morning, Louis Hayes was pretty much convinced that Paulie Belotti had skipped town.

He'd been after the guy for five days. Every which way he turned he was greeted with laconic shrugs, vacant expressions, disinterest and dismissal. Even his CIs and stoolies were coming up with nothing. Paulie Belotti had gone ghost, and that was all there was to it.

Hayes did consider the possibility that he was dead, but that seemed unlikely. He maintained that doubt until a chance comment in an unrelated interview sparked his interest.

Friday night had seen the usual haul of bums and drunks and dopers. The tank was full, and Hayes and a colleague were processing them out one by one, if only to unstink the joint. Central basement got to smelling like roadkill on a hot weekend, and it was one of those *Someone's gotta do it and there ain't no one else* assignments that were the bane of duty cops.

One guy stood out from the rest. His name was Simon Close. His clothes were smart. Take away the scuffs and wine stains, the bruised face and the swollen knuckles, and he could have passed for an uptown character. He was more nervous than a dog crapping razor blades. Hayes guessed he'd never been pulled in before. According to the arrest notes, Close had been dragged out of a street fight. He'd screamed self-defense, hollered up a storm about how some hooker had robbed him blind, taken his wristwatch, a gold pen, an ivory comb that he'd been given by his dead grandmother. The guy was a real handful until they closed the cell door, and then he went quiet. Three in the morning he was sat on the floor, knees up to his chin, head down, the expression on his face one of utter despair.

It was after ten by the time Hayes sat him down in the office and took his name and address. He explained that they weren't going to charge him, that he was being cautioned, that he needed to keep his fists in his pockets and his feet off the street.

"What's the deal with you anyway?" Hayes asked. "What are you doing fighting in the street?"

"Someone stole my money and my watch and a pen and a comb," Close said. His tone was one of indignation, his accent undeniably English.

"Your money and your watch and a pen and a comb," Hayes said.

"You don't have to be condescending, Detective," Close said.

"You don't have to be in the drunk tank, Mr. Close."

Close looked sheepish for moment, and he lowered his eyes.

"So, what the hell happened?" Hayes asked. "You really aren't our usual type of Friday-night guest."

"I was accosted on the street by a prostitute."

"She accosted you?"

"They always accost you, Detective. That's their stock-in-trade."

"So you weren't out looking for a hooker?"

Close looked like Hayes had badmouthed his mother. "God almighty, no!"

"Okay, calm down. It was just in the notes here that you were arguing with a hooker and it got physical. Tricks . . . customers, men usually only argue with hookers about a price."

"She was trying to pick my pockets. She got very close and she was trying to pick my pockets, and I tried to get her to stop and she accused me of doing something inappropriate, and this big man came over and started pushing me around."

"Her pimp, right?"

"I guess so. He didn't have a business card."

Hayes smiled. "So what happened then?"

"I pushed back."

"Not such a good idea, I'm guessing."

"No."

"The big guy clobbered you and they took your stuff anyway, right?"

"Right, right, that's exactly what I've been saying, but no one wants to hear it."

"Lucky you got me, then," Hayes said. "I'm a regular Saint Jude, Patron Saint of Desperate Cases and Lost Causes."

"That's the second time I've heard that."

"What?"

"A reference to Saint Jude."

"Is that so?"

"Yes. Last night I heard it from another table in a restaurant.

Didn't seem like the sort of conversation I'd want anyone to know I was overhearing."

Hayes was intrigued. "How so?"

Close hesitated. He looked at Hayes, saw the glint of interest in his eyes. "That caution you mentioned—"

Hayes laughed. "All of a sudden we got ourselves a lawyer. What are you telling me here, Mr. Close? You telling me that if I don't caution you then you're gonna tell me about a conversation you overheard last night?"

"Yes, Detective Hayes. That's what I'm saying."

"Okay, so what makes you think I have even the slightest interest in your Saint Jude conversation?"

"Because I think these people were talking about someone who got killed."

Hayes didn't say anything for a good five seconds.

"Where were you?" was the question that broke the silence.

"Musso and Frank's Grill up on—"

"I know where it is," Hayes said. "And you overheard a conversation that led you to believe that someone had been killed. That's what you're telling me?"

Close nodded in the affirmative.

"Okay," Hayes said. "You got yourself a deal. You tell me everything you can about this conversation, and I'll let you go without a caution."

"I have your word on that?"

"You have my word."

"There was someone called Kid Napoleon—"

"Kid Napoleon?" Hayes asked, unable to conceal his surprise.

"That's right. That's what they said, anyway. They said that someone called Kid Napoleon had taken care of someone else. They didn't say the person's name, but they said that he was up in the hills and that the only things likely to find him were buzzards."

"And what makes you think that this conversation was even a real thing, you know? It could have been two guys just bullshitting each other." Hayes reached for his coffee, took a sip.

"Because one of the guys was Joe Adamo."

Hayes near-choked. He had to turn sideways and cough into the trashcan so as not to spray Close with coffee.

When he had regained his composure he asked Close if he'd just said Joe Adamo's name.

"Yes, Joe Adamo. He said that someone called Kid Napoleon had taken care of some guy in the hills."

"Okay, fine, good . . . That I understand. The thing I don't understand is how you know who Joe Adamo is."

"Because of my brother-in-law."

"And he is?"

"A bail bondsman. He tells me all the stories, you know? There isn't anyone he doesn't know, nothing he doesn't know about. He's got radios that pick up on KGPL at seventeen twelve kilohertz—"

"Best you don't tell me that kind of thing, Mr. Close. Even though we know it happens, it's not something we wanna hear about, if you get my drift."

Close didn't reply.

"So, there was nothing that anyone said to suggest who had been taken care of?"

"No, nothing at all. I got the idea that they all knew who they were talking about. Evidently it was someone who had upset them."

"Evidently."

"So, I can go now?"

"A couple more questions," Hayes said. "What is it that you do, Mr. Close?"

"My job? I'm a voice coach, Detective. I train actors and actresses to speak properly, to master dialects and accents."

"And you're English?"

"Yes, I am."

"And you're married to an American, hence the brother-in-law with the illegal radio receivers. Or is he married to your sister?"

"I *was* married to an American. An actress. She disappeared a while ago with a twenty-five-year-old Errol Flynn lookalike."

"I'm sorry to hear that, Mr. Close."

Close smiled. "I wouldn't be, Detective Hayes. I'm certainly not."

"And is it a habit of yours to get drunk and argue with hookers in the street?"

"Not at all, no. If you want to know, I was celebrating."

"Might I ask what you were celebrating?"

"I just got a big job, a big movie shoot. Going to be working with Maureen O'Hara and Cedric Hardwicke. Even better than that, I am going to be teaching Charles Laughton how to talk like the Hunchback of Notre Dame."

"Well, I guess that's reason enough to celebrate."

Close got up and took a moment to survey the state of his clothes.

"This is shameful," he said. "I'm really very ashamed. I really am."

"Well, I'm sorry you lost your money and your watch and a pen and a comb."

"Well, I hope some good comes of it, Detective Hayes. Maybe you'll find out who this Kid Napoleon is and who wound up in the hills."

Hayes showed Mr. Close out of the building and went back to his desk. He wrote down Adamo's name and *Kid* before the *Napoleon* he'd already jotted on his scratch pad. It was like *Little Caesar*, that movie with Edward G. Robinson, except in the wonderful world of the talkies the guns weren't loaded and the blood was ketchup.

Joe Adamo and his brother, Momo, were the real deal, no doubt about it, and if someone had been taken care of then it had to have been authorized by Dragna himself.

What he would give for a line into Dragna's world. That was the thought at the forefront of Louis Hayes's mind as he went for a fresh cup of coffee. And if Dragna was now using a hitter other than Frank Bompensiero and Jimmy Fratianno, then maybe there were things going on that Hayes really should know everything about.

He had to find Paulie Belotti, for sure, but maybe while he was looking for Belotti he could look for this so-called Kid Napoleon, too.

THIRTY-ONE

First came the Carthaginians, then the Greeks, the Etruscans, and the Holy Roman Empire. Then came the Vandals, the Byzantines, the Lombards, the Saracens, the Genoese, and all the while swords clashed and the blood flowed and men died both for what they sought and what they hoped to defend.

Corsica, mountain of the sea, was drenched in blood. It took blood to build an empire, blood of enemies, traitors, sometimes friends.

Nicky understood this. He had no doubt that Napoleon understood it, too.

Kid Napoleon. It was a name possessive of inherent legendary status, a name of which to be proud.

These things that had happened—the killing of Paulie Belotti, the injuries inflicted on Zakarian and his niece, even though the latter had been more accidental than intentional, even the way the Adamos seemed to have welcomed him into their ranks—seemed to be dictated by destiny.

Nicky Mariani had come to America to *be* somebody. What he was, what he was now becoming, was perhaps not what he'd planned, but he *was* becoming somebody. That was the important thing. That was the thing to remember, to hold on to, especially in those brief moments when he doubted himself. There was money here. There was wealth and notoriety and endless possibilities for the future. Los Angeles was no Ajaccio or Bastia, but it was still an empire. There were kings and kingmakers, court advisers, crown princes, cavaliers, and valiant knights. There were battles to be fought for territory and title, for money, for power, and—as with all wars—there were both victors and vanquished.

Perhaps he had wrestled with his conscience, but it had not been a difficult battle.

Nicky Mariani had no doubt on whose side he wished to be when the bullets stopped. Now it was neither a matter of right or wrong; nor was it a question of morals nor ethics; it was a question of survival. If Lucia did not wish to look at the truth, then she could stay in that wretched hotel and suffer. Nicky loved his sister more than life itself, but sometimes even lives had to be sacrificed for a cause. This desperate need to forever be right, to have the last word, these prima donna performances—well, he'd had about as much as he could take. After all he had done to get her to America, to support her, protect her, bring her to Hollywood, and this was how she repaid him? Maybe that was just Lucia; maybe it was all women. Nicky didn't care; it was just a distraction from the business at hand. The very last thing he needed was someone—sister or not—telling him what he could and could not do with his life. He had seen the roll of money in Joe Adamo's hand; he had seen the ease with which he peeled off fifties, then another twenty for dinner, another five for the maître d', as if the greatest trouble he had with money was taking it out of his pocket. That was what Nicky wanted, and he understood what had to be done to get it.

The fight with Lucia was now a week behind him. Nicky had stayed in a different hotel, all the while looking for a place of his own. He'd found a house on South Coronado, a smart place, big rooms, even had a yard. The real estate people had told him how good the neighbors were, how close it was to Westlake Park; Nicky was more interested in the size of the basement, how many cars could be parked outside. The deposit was two hundred bucks, rental was a hundred and eight bucks each calendar month, and he paid for his own utilities and waste disposal.

On the morning of Tuesday the 14th of June, Nicky received word that the South Coronado place was available. Eighty bucks remained from the money Joe Adamo had given him. He borrowed the rest from Vince Caliendo and Tony Legs. That very same evening he sat on the floor in the empty house. He felt like a regular citizen. For a while he couldn't stop laughing, and then he realized that not only did he have no furniture, he also had no bed, nowhere to hang his clothes, nothing. He realized how much of a chump he was and started laughing again. Then he went out to find a liquor store.

The following morning Vince and Tony Legs arrived with coffee and pastries and instructions from Joe Adamo. They sat on the floor together and talked about the trouble they could cause.

"There's another family," Tony Legs explained. "They work for Mr. Dragna, unofficially, kind of unofficially . . . It's complicated. Boss is called Giordano. Sal Giordano. Anyway, there was an agreement that Giordano and a few of his boys would look after some bars and clubs and some movie theaters, you know. Turns out they have been looking after a little too much, if you get my drift."

"Skimming more than their piece off the top, shortchanging Mr. Dragna," Vince said.

"So we gotta fix it," Tony went on. "We gotta make an example of this, you see. Gotta make it clear that you don't rip us off, and if you do rip us off then we are going to find out and make things very unpleasant."

Nicky just listened. He didn't have any questions; it all seemed straightforward enough.

"So, there's a few places we gotta check on, ask some people what happened, how much they paid, who they gave it to. We gotta make a list of names, and then we gotta make some house calls."

"We don't gotta take care o' them like we took care of Paulie, but we gotta deliver a message," Vince added.

"Mr. Adamo says this month alone we're short maybe three, four grand. Whatever we collect, we keep ten percent, split it equal. If there's anything we pick up on the side, then we keep that, too."

"Like a bonus," Vince said, smiling. "A productivity bonus, right?"

The three of them finished breakfast and left. The first place they visited was a club up on West Third near Columbia. It was an old-time spit and sawdust joint, long wooden bar, worn-out leather stools, frequented—even at eleven in the morning—by regulars who were as much furniture as the furniture. The owner was a guy called Mitchell King, long time ago Californian oil worker who busted his legs in a drilling accident. Company paid him off and he bought a bar. The profits he didn't gamble he quickly drank, possibly to help ease the pain of losing so much on the tracks, and he was hocked up to his neck to various bookies, loan sharks, and liquor suppliers.

If Nicky needed any confirmation regarding the decision he'd made, listening to King bitch and whine about his lot in life was good enough. The man had next to nothing, and from the sound of him it was heading downhill to nothing at all.

"So you paid on time?" Vince asked him.

"When did I ever not pay on time?" King asked.

"How much?"

"Last month, sixty bucks. Same as always."

"And who'd you give it to?"

"Same guy as always."

"What's his name?" Tony Legs asked.

"Danza. Mr. Danza. That's how he introduces himself, and that's what I call him."

"He come alone?"

"Nope."

"How many of them?"

"Two, sometimes three. They drink a load of booze, sometimes they want a sandwich and I gotta make it for them."

"The other names?"

"Who the hell knows?" King replied. "I never spoke to no one but Mr. Danza."

"Okay," Tony Legs said. "And you gonna pay again end of this month, right? We don't got a problem here?"

"Like I said already, when did I not pay, huh? Answer me that. When didn't I pay?"

Tony raised his hands. "I'm not sayin' you didn't. I'm just makin' sure that there ain't no problem here."

King laughed, but it was cold and humorless. "Oh no," he said. He held up his hands as if showing them the bar, the shitty paint job, the worn-out tables and chairs, the cracked window on the right side of the door. "Last thing we got here is any kind of problem."

The next place was no more than three or four blocks north. The owner was out, but the barkeep knew Tony Legs, called him by his first name.

"Sure, just as regular as clockwork. Bobby Danza and his buddies show up on the first. We pay them; off they go."

"You know who is with him?" Tony asked.

"Guy called Sergio Azarro. They call him Zazzy. Another guy called Marco. Don't know his family name."

Tony Legs and the barkeep shook hands. The barkeep didn't ask questions or voice any complaints.

So it went for much of the day. Similar places, similar questions, always the same three names—Roberto "Bobby" Danza, Sergio "Zazzy" Azarro, and Marco Angiletta.

Nicky, Vince, and Tony Legs made a stop at a diner over near Cotton, and were playing the fool with the waitress when a handful of cops came in from Central. One of them was plainclothes, seemed to be all eyes and ears in their direction.

"Asshole," Tony Legs said.

"You know this one?" Vince asked.

"No, can't say I do, but that doesn't make him any less of an asshole. They're all assholes to a man."

Had they taken the time to ask, they'd have learned it was Louis Hayes. He was there collecting lunch—egg and cheese, shaved ham, extra pickle.

The trio were back on the sidewalks for the afternoon, comparing amounts paid to amounts collected. It looked like Giordano's boys were skimming maybe a hundred fifty, two hundred bucks a week off the top. According to Bobby and his friends, people had not been paying on time. According to the people, it was clear they had. The question was whether Sal Giordano knew about this little racket, or whether the collectors had used their own initiative. If it was Sal, then Sal was finished. If Sal knew nothing, then he'd walk but his boys would maybe wind up keeping company with Paulie Belotti in the Hollywood Hills.

Nicky listened to the banter, the wisecracks about what would happen to who and how much it would hurt.

"Schmucks," Tony Legs said. "For a handful of bucks, a ten here, a twenty there, I just don't get it. A man makes an agreement, he keeps the agreement. A man says he'll do so-and-so, then he better do so-and-so and nothing else. Right, Nicky?"

"Man's word is all he's got," Nicky replied.

"On the nail right there," Tony said.

Nicky wondered where this would go. Would they be making another pickup, taking some other wiseguy into the hills so he could dig his own grave? Seemed that loyalty was everything here. Break your word and it was all over and done with; there were no second chances. How that made him feel he wasn't sure. All he could think of was the way Paulie Belotti's head had sounded when the shovel hit him, and yet the whole thing seemed like some long-distant dream, maybe nothing more than a story someone had told him. Whatever happened, he would be as much a part of it as Tony Legs and Vince Caliendo. In effect, he'd killed Paulie and taken his place in this little trio. He belonged, and he wanted to belong, but it still gave him pause for thought every time the business of violence and murder was raised.

Just after six, Tony Legs made a call to Joe Adamo. He explained the situation, listened carefully, and was given some information.

"We gotta go pick up Bomp," Tony told the others.

"I told you about him before," Vince said to Nicky. "Frank Bompensiero. Everyone calls him Bomp, but you don't call him that unless he says it's okay, okay?"

"Sure."

"He's San Diego," Tony Legs said. "He's only three or four down from God as far as you're concerned. Don't bullshit him. Don't even wisecrack unless he's in a mood for it. Keep your mouth shut until he asks you your business, you understand?"

"Yeah," Nicky said. "I got it."

"Anyway, he's up here on some other business, and Joe says we go get him and then pick up these Giordano clowns. Joe says he wants 'em taken to the warehouse."

Vince laughed, but it was hollow and cruel-sounding. "Oh boy, they is fucked."

Frank Bompensiero was eating in a restaurant owned by some guy with an interest in the Brooklyn Dodgers. Word was that the Dodgers were looking to move to Los Angeles, that maybe there was money for a stadium. It wasn't going to happen anytime soon, but *great oaks from small acorns* was a motto for a reason.

Tony Legs went into the place, was out within two or three minutes.

They waited in the car at the end of the street, and when Bomp came out the door, Vince got in back with Nicky.

Tony Legs got out and opened the passenger door for Bomp.

Bompensiero's hair was thin and he smelled of bay rum. His suit must have cost fifty bucks. He didn't say much at first, merely glanced back at Vince and nodded an acknowledgment. Once they were moving he looked back again.

"Who are you?" he asked Nicky.

Tony Legs said, "That's Kid Napoleon."

Bomp laughed.

"Nicky Mariani," Nicky said.

"You call yourself Kid Napoleon?" Bomp asked.

"I don't call myself anything, Mr. Bompensiero," Nicky replied. "These guys call me whatever they want."

"Call me Bomp. Everyone calls me Bomp whether I fuckin' like it or not." He laughed again, and was still laughing when they stopped at the lights.

"So, what's the deal here?" Bomp said. "We got some of Sal's people on the take or what?"

"Seems that way," Tony Legs replied. "Don't know if they're in it for themselves, or they're doing it on Sal Giordano's say-so."

"Nah, won't be Sal. Sal is okay. Jack wouldn't have had him take on these collections if he wasn't solid. I think we're gonna find that these boys are doin' it all by themselves."

"Gonna find out soon enough," Vince said.

Bomp glanced back again. "You're the Caliendo kid, right?"

"Yes, I am."

"Knew your pa. Good man. Worked with him in San Diego, coupla other places. He got pinched, right?"

"He did, yes."

"Bad business. How long he got?"

"I don't see him coming out for a while yet," Vince said. "Unless he escapes."

"Where there's a will there's a way," Bomp said. "I'll send him up a parcel or somethin'."

"He'd appreciate that," Vince said.

"So, where these monkeys at, then?" Bomp asked Tony Legs.

"They hang out at a bar called Mister Sam's."

"I know it," Bomp said.

No one spoke for a little while, and then Bomp shifted sideways and looked at Nicky.

"I know your name from some place," he said. "You're the one who whacked Paulie Belotti, right? Heard you took his head off with a fuckin' shovel."

"Maybe that was an exaggeration," Nicky said. "Wasn't quite like that."

"Let it go," Bomp said. "Don't deny it. Let 'em think you chopped Paulie's head off with a shovel. People ain't scared of what you did. They're scared of what they think you did."

"I'll remember that," Nicky said, and he meant it.

Mister Sam's was more upmarket than most of the places they'd seen that day. There were rugs on the dark wooden floor, and there were booths in back with leather seats and table lamps. Whatever they were serving up for dinner smelled good, and Nicky was aware of how hungry he was.

Bomp knew the barkeep. The barkeep knew Angiletta, Azarro, and Danza. They had private dining rooms in back, and the trio had taken one. They had some girls back there, all legs, no smarts, and Bomp told the barkeep that he was going to go back there and have some words. Bomp slid a ten across the counter.

Nicky, Vince, and Tony Legs went with Bomp. There were three men, and Bomp didn't want some bullshit standoff. Most instances, Bomp's reputation was enough, but every once in a while there was unnecessary foolishness.

"Nice joint," Tony Legs commented as they walked through. "Maybe I bring my girl here sometime."

Zazzy was the first to get up when Bomp came through the door.

"Oh fuck," he said, and then he realized he'd screwed up before the conversation even started.

Bomp smiled. "Oh fuck, exactly."

Marco Angiletta was a big man, easily six foot and two fifty. He looked to Zazzy for some kind of explanation.

"I am Mr. Bompensiero," Bomp said. "Maybe you've heard of me."

Bobby Danza—wiry, hard eyes, hair flat to his scalp, a nasty scar down the right side of his nose—opened his mouth. From his expression, it looked like he was all set to start lying.

"Only thing that comes out of your mouth, my friend, is a polite request for these pretty ladies to leave as quickly and quietly as possible," Bomp said.

"Hey, you can't just—" Angiletta started, to which Bomp said, "But I can, you see? I can do whatever the fuck I like, buddy boy. Now ask the girls to leave and lets us guys have a little meeting, okay?"

The girls, insufficiently bright to take the initiative, waited for instructions.

"Go," Bobby Danza told them. "Go. Get out of here."

The girls went, understanding that whatever cash they'd hoped to receive before the evening was out was now a matter of history.

Vince caught the attention of the last girl to leave. "You were never here," he whispered. She opened her mouth to respond. "Just nod," he said. Her eyes widened fearfully, she nodded as instructed, and Vince closed the door behind her.

Bomp took a chair from against the wall and sat on it backward. He rested his forearms on the back, his chin down, and he waited.

No one moved.

"Sit, sit, sit," he said eventually.

Angiletta, Azarro, and Danza sat. They looked uncomfortable but not guilty. Perhaps they were merely well practiced at hiding it.

"The question I have is simple," Bomp said. "It's just a yes or no answer."

He paused, seemingly for no reason other than affect.

"Do we understand each other?"

Bomp looked at each of the three in turn.

Nicky watched their eyes. Only Bobby Danza met Bomp's gaze, and the expression on his face was one of disdain and superiority.

Nicky felt his blood rise. He felt like hurting Bobby Danza, if for no other reason than to see that expression wither and disappear.

"Okay . . . so here's the question, boys. And remember, the more you think about the answer, the less likely it is that you're telling the truth, and I want you to know that the truth is all I am after." Bomp got up. "So, here we go. Was Sal Giordano aware of your little skim operation on the collections, or was this something you cooked up alone?"

There was silence for just a heartbeat, and then Bobby Danza said, "What the fuck are you talking about, Bomp?"

Bomp smiled. "Did I say you could call me that? Are we friends now? Is that what you think?" He reached forward and took a fork off the table. He raised it and inspected the tines.

"He didn't mean anything by it, Mr. Bompensiero," Azarro said. "Everyone knows who you are. Everyone knows your name."

"Sure they do, and my name is Mr. Bompensiero, just exactly how you said it."

"He's right," Danza said. "I didn't mean anything disrespectful."

"It's of no concern," Bomp said. "And to be honest, the only disrespectful thing is to lie to me. In fact, you can call me a horse's ass, but just don't lie to me."

"No one is lying," Angiletta said. "I don't know what this skim operation is. I have no idea what you're talking about."

"Is that so?"

"Yeah, sure. We collect up the money for Sally . . . Mr. Giordano. We package it up, and then it gets delivered."

"And you all deliver it, or just one of you?"

There was a moment's hesitation.

"We all—" Bobby Danza said, but both Azarro and Angiletta said, "Bobby takes it."

"So now we have a different kind of thing," Bomp said.

"I don't always take the money," Danza said. "You guys have taken the money before."

Neither Azarro nor Angiletta responded. Looking sideways at Danza, the expressions on both their faces could not have been more telling.

"Seems like you've dug a hole, my friend," Bomp said. "If I was you I'd say nothing right now."

"But this is bull—"

Bomp raised his finger to his lips and Danza fell silent. He then indicated Angiletta. "Up," he said. "Come here."

Angiletta did as he was asked.

Bomp squared up to him, looked him straight on, said, "Answer me truthfully. Do you know anything about money being skimmed off the top of the collections?"

"Not a goddamned thing," Angiletta said. His tone and body language seemed unequivocal.

Bomp asked the same question of Azarro and got the same response.

"You stay here," he told them. "Finish your dinner, whatever you want. We are gonna take a ride with your friend here and get this straightened out."

Danza was unable to speak. He knew he was done for, whichever way it went.

"You're driving," he told Vince. To Tony Legs he said, "You stay here, and make sure these assholes don't call anyone or go anyplace for at least half an hour." He turned to Nicky. "You bring him out to the car."

Bomp tossed the fork onto the table and followed after Vince.

Nicky walked around to where Bobby Danza was seated and told him to get up.

Danza got up. He looked like a man en route to the gallows. He glanced back at his two friends, and they each looked away.

Then he looked at Nicky.

"Don't fucking look at me," Nicky said, and the voice that came from his own lips sounded like that of a very different man.

THIRTY-TWO

Since the fight and Nicky's departure, Frankie and Lucy had done nothing but spend time together. If she remembered kissing him, she didn't speak of it, and there'd been nothing in her manner to suggest that it was anything but a drunken, impulsive moment, forgotten as soon as it occurred. It had been only a few days, but at once it felt like both an hour and a thousand years. They had gone to auditions, photo shoots, voice lessons, even looked for a house or an apartment they could rent, and all of it conducted as if they were a couple.

One afternoon they took lunch at Musso & Frank's on Hollywood Boulevard. Lucy said she wanted to meet some stars like Fred MacMurray, but there didn't seem to be anyone there.

At the bar they got talking to a writer called Fitzgerald. He was dressed in a tweed three-piece and a high collar despite the temperature outside. His hair was thick, center-parted, and his manner was that of someone quite out of place and unsure of where to go. Maybe he was simply drunk, but he seemed more than happy to listen to Lucy's excited chatter.

From Frankie's perspective, the guy seemed a little weatherworn and cynical about the whole deal.

"I wrote a few things," Fitzgerald said. "Always hoped they'd be adapted, but the best I got was a stage show and a silent movie that no one's seen, and something back in 1922 that everyone's forgotten about. Sometimes it's all so hideously depressing, but you just carry on, you know?"

"Are you working on a new book now?" Lucy asked him.

Fitzgerald waved the barkeep over, asked for another gin rickey.

"Something for you, miss?" the barkeep asked.

"Just a club soda," Lucia said. "Thank you."

"*The Last Tycoon*," Fitzgerald went on. "That's what it's called." He laughed dryly. "Wretched thing... Should have been finished long ago, but it's hard to give a damn when no one else does."

"You can't think like that," Lucy said, and to Frankie she sounded so desperately naive and innocent. Perhaps there was some advantage to believing things were better than they were, though he had yet to see what that advantage might be.

Smiling, Fitzgerald said, "I'm past forty, my dear. I had a heart attack in Schwab's. I have recurring tuberculosis and I drink far too much. I want the world to love me and they think I'm a hack." He reached out and touched her hand. "Your beauty is unashamed, as is your spirit. Don't let a lousy drunk like me quell your ardor or dim your flames."

The barkeep brought their drinks.

Fitzgerald downed the contents of his glass in no time, and then he slid off the barstool. "And now I must go," he said.

He kissed Lucy's hand, shook Frankie's, almost lost his balance as he maneuvered his way out into the street, and then he was gone.

A red-coated waiter told them a booth was ready. Frankie took a steak, Lucy a salad. Frankie spent much of the meal listening to Lucy's ever-shifting viewpoint about her brother. He did not have the heart to tell her, but he was tiring of it. As far as he could see, they were just as stubborn as one another. Frankie wanted no part of it. But he couldn't leave. Not only would she then be alone, but he would be alone, too. Try as he might, he couldn't escape the clutches of his own heart. Lucia Mariani, Lucy Madden, whatever name she gave herself, had cornered him. There was no way out.

Throughout the past few days he'd sensed a change in her. She grabbed his arm when they crossed the street, even held his hand sometimes, looked at him just a little too long and made him feel as if he should turn away. He never did. If she did not feel the tension between them, then she came from some other world, some other universe. Nights, he would lie awake hearing nothing but the sound of his own breathing, and he would think of her in the next room, no more than ten feet away, and he would ache inside. Hell was being unable to hold something you could reach.

But Frankie said nothing, and Lucy did nothing to encourage him. It was a stalemate, and he was too unsure of his own thoughts to break it.

Before they left Musso's Lucy used the restroom. Standing at the bar, Frankie picked up an old newspaper that had been left behind. He absentmindedly turned the pages, seeing nothing until a headline caught his eye. *Ireland Votes*. That was all it said. Two words. The article went on to explain that Ireland was in the throes of a general election. The piece suggested that de Valera would maintain power, that he might even secure the first majority in the history of the state.

It was neither de Valera nor the political situation back in Ireland that provoked the reaction in Frankie; it was the simple fact that he had been unaware of it. His home was three and a half thousand miles away. His mother, his sisters, his crazy drunken father, and people were going to the polls to determine the course of history. Whether it was de Valera or Cosgrave, Fianna Fáil or Fine Gael, whether the sun shone or the rain poured didn't matter. What mattered was that he had left it all behind and could never go back. A moment of blind unthinking madness and he had banished himself from his own future.

And Lucy knew nothing, not of his past, his real name, what had happened that terrible night in November of the previous year. And then there was the matter of his being found. *Meadow of the Foreigner*. A debt owed, a debt that would one day require repayment. Frankie set the paper aside. He closed his eyes and leaned his head back against the wall. He felt a wave of emotion building in his chest, his throat, and he wanted to get outside, to be alone, to be away from all of this.

He was a fool. He was a dreamer. Here he was, desperately holding on to the vain notion that Lucy Madden could love him for who he was when he wasn't even being true to himself, let alone to her.

Should he tell her, just so as not to carry this burden alone? She was no priest, and no forgiveness could ever be given, but saying something would at least give some degree of relief. Or would it? Would it just drive her away, perhaps forever? Was his true punishment to be truly alone for the rest of his life?

"Hey."

Frankie opened his eyes.

Lucy stood looking at him, a bemused expression on her face.

"Hey," Frankie said.

"Tired?"

"A little."

Frankie got up and opened the door for her. Out on the street she once again took his arm, and they walked in the direction of the hotel.

"I think they'll give me the part, you know? I really do."

Frankie hesitated.

Lucy stopped right there on the sidewalk. "What's up, Frankie?"

Frankie smiled. "Nothing."

"You don't think I know you well enough not to know when you're gone?"

He laughed. "It's okay. I just read something in the paper. It was nothing important, just a political thing back home—"

"And it made you homesick."

"It did, yes."

Lucy started walking again, pulled Frankie even closer, a gesture of empathy perhaps, and she said, "I think about home too. I try not to, but I can't help it."

Frankie didn't respond.

"Talk to me," she said.

"What's there to say?"

"Anything. Just don't be silent. Tell me about your home. Tell me about your parents. Do you have brothers and sisters?"

"I have sisters," he said, immediately guarded.

"How many?"

"Three of them."

"And brothers?"

"No, no brothers."

"And what does your father do?"

"He drinks."

"Oh," she said.

"Oh, indeed."

"Don't you want to write to them, tell them what you're doing? Tell them about me, about Hollywood, about how you're now the director of a theatrical agency?"

Frankie laughed; Lucy laughed with him.

"I live in a hotel with a girl who's taken my surname but isn't my wife. I have about four dollars left in the world. I have no job, no prospects, nothing at all."

"You have me," she said.

"I have you? Is that what I have, is it?"

Lucy let go of Frankie's arm and took his hand. Frankie responded by taking her hand from his.

"You can't be actin' this way, Lucy. It's not right."

She frowned. "What do you mean?"

"Don't play that game. You know what I mean."

"Well, you may think I know, but you'd be wrong there—"

Frankie shook his head. "I'm serious."

Lucy hesitated.

"I'll say it and be damned," Frankie said. "You can't be givin' a man a hope. You can't spend all this time with someone—"

"I know."

Frankie looked at Lucy.

"I know," she repeated, "and I'm sorry. I don't know what to tell you. I don't know what to think. Nicky's gone, and I know that you—" She stopped midsentence.

"You know that I what?"

"Nothing," Lucy said. "I don't know anything."

Neither of them spoke until they had once again reached the hotel.

Frankie stepped past her. He went through the front door and on up to the room. Lucy took her time, but she came through the door to find him standing by the window looking down into the street.

"We have to make some decisions," he said.

"Okay."

"We have to decide where to live, if we're going to live in the same place, and we have to decide what kind of relationship we have. I can't go on living like this. I can't go on much longer without earning some money. This theatrical agent nonsense is just that. It's nonsense. I don't know anything about this business, and I don't think I want to know anything about this business. This is not my life. This is not who I am, Lucy . . . Lucia . . . Jesus, I don't even know what to call you."

"You used to call me Miss Lucia. You used to stand on the street and wait for Nicky because you were too scared to come upstairs."

Frankie laughed reflexively. "Scared?"

"You were scared of me, Frankie Madden. Big old Irish fighting champion, kill a man with his bare hands, and you were scared of a little girl like me."

"To hell with you, woman. You're talking foolish now."

"Am I?"

"Sure you are. Scared of you? Why in God's name would I be scared of you?"

"Because men are always scared of women. Women can make men do anything they want."

"Is that so? Well, I knew you were a dreamer, girl, but I didn't realize you were completely mad. You've hidden it well, but the truth is out. You're a mad one, and a seriously mad one, at that."

"You don't believe that I can make you do anything?"

Frankie sat down at the writing table. "Enough now," he said.

Lucy crossed the room and stood no more than six feet from Frankie.

"Kiss me," she said.

Frankie looked up at her and started laughing. "I'm gonna have to punch you in a minute. Quiet down now, will you?"

"Kiss me now or never kiss me again."

Frankie was still laughing, though beneath that was a sense of aggravation. It wasn't right for her to tease him in this way. She must know how he felt about her. Wasn't that a thing? Woman's intuition? There were moments when he knew his feelings were painted large as life on his face, and if she couldn't see that then there had to be something very wrong.

"I'm serious," she said, and she took a step closer. "I'm going to count to five... One..."

"I'm serious, too, Lucia. This isn't right. You can't ask me to do that. It's not right to tease a man this way—"

"...Two... Three..."

She smiled at him, and he felt his heart hammer in his chest.

"Right now, whatever you're doing. Whatever game you're playing. This isn't the way to treat someone who..." Frankie's voice trailed away. He felt awkward, uncomfortable, cornered.

"This isn't the way to treat someone who... what, Frankie?" she asked.

"This has to end," he said.

"What has to end?"

"This crazy way of going on. I can't stay here in this hotel with you. I can't move into an apartment with you. I can't keep on pretending that this is the life I want. I don't belong here. I belong back home in Ireland with my family—"

"So go," Lucy said. "Get enough money together for a boat ticket and go back to Ireland."

Frankie sighed. "It's not as easy as that."

Lucy didn't push it. She looked at Frankie and shook her head resignedly. "Well, if you can't go and you can't stay, then you're in more trouble than I thought."

"That'd be right enough."

Lucy smiled. "There you go again, your strange expressions that make me laugh."

"Laugh all you want," Frankie said. "I'll not be changing the way I talk for you. And that foolish business earlier, about how girls can make men do whatever they want... What the hell was that about?"

"That was just about getting you to kiss me."

"And why on earth would you want me to do that?"

"Do I need a reason?"

"Of course you need a reason. You don't just kiss people for no reason."

"You're not just *people*, Frankie. And I can kiss you for no reason. I did before and you didn't seem to mind."

Frankie smiled. "Oh, you remember that, do you? I thought you were drunk."

"Oh, I was, but I remember everything," she said. "I also remember how good it felt."

Frankie didn't speak.

"You don't have anything to say?"

He shook his head. "I don't know what to say. I don't know if you're telling me the truth or you're still teasing me."

"Have I been teasing you?" Lucy asked. She took another step forward.

"You're treading on dangerous ground," Frankie said.

"I don't do anything unless I mean to," she replied.

Frankie got up, ostensibly to move away from her, but once out of the chair he stood still. Watching her was like being hypnotized by a cobra.

"I know how you feel about me, Frankie Madden . . . and I'm flattered. Of course I am. I mean, what girl wouldn't be? You're smart and funny and handsome and strong, and you have this way of saying serious things that make me laugh so much. And you're so worried about feeling the way you do, and so concerned not to make a fool of yourself, that you've been completely blind to a very simple fact."

She moved even closer, and there was a faint Mona Lisa smile on her lips.

There wasn't a single word in Frankie's mind.

"You want to know what that very simple fact is?"

Frankie found his voice somewhere. "Y-yes," he said. "Sure . . . go ahead and tell me."

"That I feel exactly the same way."

Frankie lost his voice again.

"Believe it or not, I love you," she said. "And I want you to love me back."

She was up against him then, and Frankie couldn't move a muscle.

"So, are you going to do as I say or not?" she whispered.

Frankie put his arms around her and pulled her close. The emotion he felt was extraordinary... like coming home, like finding the answer to a question he'd believed would never be answered, like knowing that somehow, some way, it would all come out right in the end.

Lucy Madden... Lucia Mariani... whatever she might call herself, had permitted him an escape route from his fears, and for that he owed her the world.

For the first time since that night in November of the previous year, he felt as if he had a right to exist.

He was a man, a human being, a real person, and there was no way in the world to describe it.

"So do as I told you," Lucy whispered.

Frankie said nothing. He just kissed her.

THIRTY-THREE

They stopped en route just once. Bomp told Vince to pull over by a phone booth. He was gone no more than three or four minutes, didn't say who he'd called or why.

The warehouse, as Bomp called it, was not so much a warehouse as an aircraft hangar. It was out toward the hills themselves, back down a winding road that was bordered on each side by a high wire fence. The odd streetlight cast a sodium yellow glow, and the feeling of unsettling desolation was merely contributed to by Bobby Danza's plaintive excuses.

There's been a misunderstanding. It's not how it looks. Okay, so maybe my math was a little off... Math has never been a strong point for me...

Nicky sat in the back with Danza.

Bomp was up in the passenger seat, and after ten minutes or so he just turned and pinned Bobby Danza with a dead-eyed look.

"Usually it's a man's mouth that breaks his nose, Bobby," he said. "If I were you, I wouldn't say another fuckin' word, okay? You're only makin' it worse. The more you bitch and whine, the more I wanna hurt you."

Bomp told Vince where to pull over, and from there they walked fifty, maybe a hundred yards. The entrance to the warehouse was through a bank of trees and hidden from view, and it was only once inside that Nicky grasped the sheer size of the place.

It had to have been owned by a film company, or maybe leased by them for storage. The place was stacked to the rafters with stage props, lighting rigs, shipping containers, and costume racks. Back in the shadows was a complete carousel, the faces of the horses peering out of the shadows. It was eerie and unsettling, and—considering their reason for being there—the atmosphere seemed altogether appropriate.

Up at the far end, farthest from the door through which they had entered, was an open space for loading and unloading. Chairs were stacked to the right, and Bomp told Nicky to set out five of them, one for Bobby Danza, four facing it.

He told Danza to sit on the floor until otherwise instructed. He again reminded him to keep his mouth shut.

Bomp had been here before, perhaps many times. Probably those painted horses had heard the pleadings and promises of many men. Nicky and Vince didn't speak. They just did as Bomp requested, asked no questions, didn't even look at Bobby Danza.

From a packing crate to the right, Bomp hauled out a cardboard box. In it were glasses, a bottle of Scotch. He set out four glasses, half-filled them, offered cigarettes and a drink to everyone, Danza included. Danza took the Scotch and drank it down, his hand shaking as he did so.

"Fuckin' heathen," Bomp said. "That's twenty-year-old Scotch. You're s'posed to sip the damned stuff."

Danza didn't reply.

Bomp took the glass from Danza and moved away. Vince and Nicky went with him.

"Jesus, you try and be decent to a guy, even though he's a thieving son of a bitch, and he just goes on being disrespectful."

Nicky did not much care for Scotch, had planned to down it in one and get it over with. He was glad then that he'd waited.

"Bought that Scotch in Vegas," Bomp said, and then he started laughing. "Scariest fuckin' flight I ever took in my life. Comin' out of there on this tiny prop plane, and the wind is going crazy, turbulence you know, and this plane is swinging left and right, and even the girl up there, the stewardess, she is white like a freakin' ghost, looks like she's gonna piss herself—"

The sound of someone down near the door halted Bomp midsentence.

"Here we are," he said, and he left Vince and Nicky and walked down the length of the warehouse.

Bomp returned with a heavy-set man, shorter by a head, spectacles with thick rims, an unlit cigar in his mouth.

"Sal . . . Mr. Giordano—" Bobby Danza said, and he started up off the floor.

"Stay right the fuck where you are," Sal Giordano said. His tone was somewhere between anger and disgust. "You'll get a chance to speak when I tell you."

Bomp introduced Vince and Nicky to Sal Giordano.

"You the crazy bastard who whacked Paulie Belotti with a shovel, right? I heard about that. Jesus, you kids are dangerous. Nothin' classy as like shootin' the son of a bitch, maybe put a rope around his neck . . . No, you go whack him with a shovel. Heard you damn near cut his head right off of his shoulders."

Nicky wanted to say that it didn't happen like that; he wanted to explain that it was reflexive, instinctual, that it had not been a matter of viciousness or cruelty. It had been business, nothing more. He merely shook Sal Giordano's hand, said it was a pleasure to meet him. He remembered what Bomp had said: *People ain't scared of what you did. They're scared of what they think you did.*

"So you pair went out and asked some questions, right?" Giordano asked Vince.

"Yes, Mr. Giordano. Three of us. Tony Leggiero is back with Angiletta and Azarro. Doesn't seem like they knew anything about it."

"Who are you?" Giordano asked Vince.

"Vincent Caliendo, Mr. Giordano."

"Caliendo . . . is that—"

"Yeah, that's right," Bomp said. "Gino Caliendo's boy."

"Good man, he was. Shame what happened. He up in San Quentin, right?"

"Yes, sir," Vince replied.

Sal Giordano smiled. "Sir," he said. "Call me Sal, kid. Your family is good people." He turned to Nicky. "Anyway, to business. You go get Bobby. Have him sit in the chair."

Nicky fetched Bobby. Bobby was quiet and compliant. Nicky sat him down, and the four of them sat facing him, Vince and Nicky at each end, Bomp and Sal Giordano in the middle. Where it had come from Nicky did not know, but beneath Bomp's chair was a small canvas bag.

"I knew your father," Sal said to Bobby. "Not the sharpest guy in the world, but he had a good heart. I was sorry to hear he passed away, but those are the breaks, right? Everything has its liabilities. And you, it seems, have become a liability to me."

Bobby Danza looked like a man with no past or future. This was it. This was the moment. Say the right thing, and he had the slimmest of all chances. One word wrong, and he was dead.

"I didn't mean no disrespect, Sal," Bobby said. "I made some mistakes, okay? I'll admit that much right here and now—"

"Hell, that's real gracious of you, Bobby," Sal said, making no attempt to disguise the sarcastic tone to his voice.

"What I meant to say . . ."

"What you mean to say and what you actually say sure as hell need to be the same thing right now," Sal explained. He spoke slowly and succinctly, as if dealing with a petulant child that was trying his patience. "The simple truth is that you skimmed off the top. You went around with your friends, you collected my money, and then you were very careful to count it all up and deliver it to me, but you delivered short—"

"But, Sal, it wasn't like—"

"Don't interrupt me, Bobby. Really, there's not a great deal that aggravates me more than being interrupted." Sal paused to see if Bobby was planning on aggravating him some more, but Bobby seemed to have gotten the message.

"So, as I was saying, you delivered short, and there's not a great deal you can say that's gonna change that fact."

Danza looked set to piss himself.

"I need to know if these other two were involved, Bobby," Sal said. "Just tell me the truth."

Danza took on an expression of resignation. He shook his head. "No, Sal."

"You can call me Mr. Giordano, Bobby. My friends call me Sal, and you stopped being a friend just about the same moment you decided it was a good idea to steal from me."

"I'm sorry, Mr. Giordano. I really am sorry. I promise you it'll never happen again—"

"You don't need to make any such promise, Bobby. I *know* it's never gonna happen again."

However frightened Bobby Danza had looked, he doubled it up.

"Mr. Giordano," he said, and his voice was plaintive and desperate.

Giordano raised his hand. "I have to say one thing for you, Bobby. You didn't deny it. I'll give you that much. Maybe you do have a little of your father in you. Maybe the thieving streak came from your mother. I don't know, and I guess we never will."

"No, Mr. Giordano . . . please . . ."

"One other question . . . you got any of this money left, or did you spend it all?"

"I got it," Bobby said, all of a sudden a light at the end of the dark tunnel he'd been walking down. "I got it all. In my apartment. I can go get it for you now. I can go get it right away."

"That's okay. We can take care of it."

Sal Giordano seemed satisfied. He started up out of his chair.

"Mr. Giordano, please . . . please don't—"

Giordano was on his feet. He looked down at Bobby Danza and

slowly shook his head. "Please don't what, Bobby? 'Please don't kill me, Mr. Giordano'? Is that what you were gonna say?" Giordano smiled, almost paternally. "Don't worry, Bobby. I'm not gonna kill you. I stopped killing people a long time ago."

The relief on Bobby Danza's face was immediate and profound. Just as immediately that relief was wiped clean off his features when Giordano added, "Delegation, Bobby. That's what it's all about. Good business depends upon the ability to delegate. Nowadays I get other people to do the killing for me."

Bomp started laughing, and he, too, got up.

Bobby Danza started pleading with Sal Giordano, then with Bomp. Bomp backhanded Bobby and sent him sprawling sideways off the chair. Bobby scuttled back to the wall and sat there with his arms around his calves. He looked like a whipped dog.

Bomp and Giordano shared a few words out of earshot of Nicky and Vince. The two men laughed about something, and then they shook hands. Bomp walked Giordano to the door at the far end of the warehouse, returned within a minute, and told Bobby to sit in the chair again.

Bobby did as he was told. Now it was no longer a matter of not getting whacked. It was a matter of getting it done quick and painless. The man, for all his faults, was no longer pretending there was any other outcome. Understandably, he didn't want a slow and painful end.

As if in echo of his worst fears, Bomp said, "We're gonna hurt you some, Bobby. Not a great deal, but we are gonna hurt you. You deserve to get hurt because you are a thievin', lyin' son of a bitch."

Bomp leaned down and picked up the canvas bag. From it he took a length of rope. He gave it to Nicky, and Nicky tied Bobby to the chair. Nicky could feel his pulse racing. This was something disturbingly exhilarating. He was feeling something he'd never felt before, not even when he'd hit Paulie with the shovel and watched him go down. This was a different emotion. This was no longer business, no longer matter-of-fact.

From the same bag, Bomp took a hammer, a pair of bolt cutters, and a straight razor.

"In Rome, where I'm from, there's something called *La Bocca della Verità*," he said. "It means 'mouth of truth.' It's a legend, you know, but there's this face carved out of stone, like the face of an old man or something, and the legend goes that if you put your hand in his mouth and you've been lying, then he'll bite it off. Now, you've been lying, so we're gonna do our own *bocca della verità*, but we're only gonna cut your fingers off, okay?"

Bomp handed the bolt cutters to Vince.

"Fuck, no," Bobby said.

"Fuck, yeah," Bomp replied. "Left hand pinkie."

Vince got up, seemed hesitant. He stood near Bobby, and Bobby looked up at him, tears in his eyes, his arms pulling against the ropes that held him to the chair.

Vince grabbed Bobby's left hand and got the pinkie between the blades of the cutter.

"Oh Jesus no, no... Don't fuckin' do it. Please don't—"

Nicky watched as Vince gritted his teeth and just closed those blades down on Bobby's finger. The finger came away clean as anything, and Bobby screamed like the world was coming to an end.

Blood oozed from the stump and soaked into his pants.

Nicky was surprised at how little blood there actually was. There was a reflexive moment of disgust, even a hint of nausea, but it passed so quickly as to be of no concern.

Bobby was pale and sweating. Vince didn't look so good either.

"Makin' you sick, kid?" Bomp asked him.

"I'm good," Vince said, but Nicky knew he was putting on a face.

"You get used to it," Bomp said, but Vince's expression suggested that getting used to it was one of the very last things he wished to do.

"Take another one," Bomp said. "His thumb. Take the son of a bitch's thumb."

The thumb was tougher, the bone thicker, and it took a good two goes before it came away.

Vince looked almost as rough as Bobby Danza, and when Bobby managed to wrench his hand up and the blood jettisoned from where his thumb had once been, Vince set the bolt cutters down and walked to the far wall.

Nicky could hear Vince doing his best to hide the fact that he was retching, and Bomp just kept telling Bobby to *Quiet the hell down, will you?*

"Maybe Mr. Danza has had enough," Bomp said. "I think he got the message."

Nicky had been watching, thinking, calculating. He wanted to make a statement. He wanted to make his presence felt. If the killing of Paulie Belotti had brought him to the attention of the Adamos, then maybe he needed to do something even bolder to let Jack Dragna know he'd arrived.

"Maybe he's had enough," Nicky said, "but maybe his friends haven't." He turned to Bomp. "We got an old saying in Corsica. Watch out for those who are stealing nothing. Maybe they're planning to steal everything."

Bomp smiled. "I like that. That makes sense to me. So what message you wanna send?"

Nicky got up and walked to the chair where Bobby Danza sat writhing and sobbing. He stood there for a moment, aware of his own breathing, the sweat on his skin beneath his clothes. He was aware of Vince, still there by the wall, still struggling with what he'd done.

He knew what he had to do. He understood that here they spoke a different language, and he needed to get fluent, and fast.

He picked up the bolt cutters, got the blades around Bobby's left ear and just cut it off.

"Jesus, kid," Bomp said.

Bobby hollered blue murder, and Nicky backhanded him. Bobby's head snapped back awkwardly. Blood ran down the side of his head and soaked into the collars of both his jacket and shirt.

Bomp got up and looked at the mess that was Bobby Danza. "Okay, enough now," he said. "Now we just finish it."

Nicky could feel his heart thundering. His scalp itched. His muscles jumped involuntarily. He didn't know why, didn't question it, but he just wanted to hurt Bobby Danza. He thought about how mad he was at Lucia, about how much he loved her, how much he missed her, about who would back down first and make an effort to resolve the disagreement.

He turned to see Bomp approaching with the hammer. For a moment Bomp just stood there weighing the thing in his hand, and then he held it out toward Nicky. Nicky didn't think. Nicky didn't hesitate. Nicky just took the hammer and brought it down on Bobby Danza's head.

The sheer force of the blow cracked Bobby's skull. The head of the hammer was lodged, and Nicky had to wrench it free. He hit Bobby again, yet again, and blood sprayed back and hit his face, his shirt, his pants.

Vince made no attempt to hide his revulsion, whereas Bomp just stepped around, put his hand on Nicky's shoulder and said, "That'll do it, kid. We gotta clear this mess up, you know?"

Nicky dropped his arm, and the hammer slid from his grip. It hit the floor with a dull thud, and there was silence in the warehouse.

The painted horses looked on.

For the first time since he'd left Corsica, Nicky Mariani felt as if he had a right to exist.

He was a man, a human being, a real person, and there was no way in the world to describe it.

THIRTY-FOUR

Change happened, and fast, not only for Frankie Madden and the Marianis, but for the world.

Whether he chose to acknowledge it or not, de Valera's success in the Irish general election of June, 1938, was one of many events that tore at Frankie Madden's mind.

Home, wherever it was, remained indelibly imprinted in the geography of the heart.

Caught between self-interest, individual desire, and familial loyalties, Frankie was pulled back and forth as if in some relentless tug-of-war. His emotions strayed wildly, and he saw no respite or easy solution.

Perhaps it was the same for Lucy, her life illuminated by the lights of Hollywood, but with the estrangement of her brother so close on the heels of her departure from Corsica, it was perhaps true that the gravitation she and Frankie felt, their need to not let go of each other, was somehow born out of a profound fear of loneliness.

Neither could return home, but for very different reasons.

Even though Lucy could not bring herself to contact her brother, she nevertheless knew where he was. She had employed a private eye to find him within weeks of their fight. She knew of the South Coronado house, but that was all she knew. She had not told Frankie, and nor would she tell him. She loved Frankie, but he was not family.

The Erin Star Agency was at the heart of everything, however. That seemed to be an anchor for both Frankie and Lucy, irrespective of what might be happening elsewhere.

Perhaps nothing more than the Irish in him, the effortless charm for which he became known, Frankie learned very quickly that ingratiating himself into the favors of casting directors was not unlike dealing with a small and somewhat pampered child.

His manner of speech differentiated him from the dozens of hopeful agents that haunted the back lots and studio cafeterias; people met Frankie Madden once and they remembered him. An assistant casting director, arriving a good fifteen minutes late for an appointment, apologized profusely, only to hear Frankie say, *I'm only after gettin' in myself.*

Without the faintest clue as to what Frankie meant, the casting director asked for clarification. This led to a half-hour conversation about the similarities between colloquial expressions in Ireland and over in Boston. The casting director's parents had been first-generation immigrants out of Poland, settled not fifty miles from Boston, and from that point forward he always came to Frankie first when he had openings.

Frankie, finding his feet, always on the lookout for roles for which Lucy might audition, had a natural flair for dealing with people, and—as with most every other business—getting on in Hollywood was all about getting on with people.

Lucy possessed a natural organizational skill, a sense of innate order in the way she managed the affairs of the agency. Soon it became relatively commonplace to receive requests for representation based on word-of-mouth referral. The books started to fill up with young actors and actresses, each of them driven by the same passion that Lucy herself knew all too well. Alongside the bright and the beautiful came the jobbing extras, the crowd fillers, those who never sought the limelight but just wanted sufficient work to keep themselves off the unemployment lines.

In August of 1938, close to securing a real house from where they could also work, Frankie and Lucy found themselves coping with a demand that stretched not only their resources, but their seeming capabilities. It related to two books, the first being *The Wizard of Oz*, the second being *Gone with the Wind*. MGM had acquired the rights in the previous February, and word had it that both projects would be substantial. The *Gone with the Wind* producer, David O. Selznick spent a hundred thousand dollars auditioning close to one and a half thousand unknowns for the Scarlett O'Hara character, though many believed this was nothing more than a very wise marketing ploy. He went on to screen-test Diana Barrymore, Paulette Goddard, Susan Hayward, Lana Turner, and a host of others before naming Norma Shearer. Mere weeks before principal photography began, the final decision was again changed and a relatively unknown English actress called Vivien Leigh was afforded the much sought-after role. Both Selznick's picture and Mervyn LeRoy's *Oz* production were at the forefront of Hollywood's collective consciousness, and the Erin

Star Agency, among many others, experienced the highest demand for personnel.

It was during this time that Frankie and Lucy really began to get a grasp of the gargantuan machine that was Hollywood. The quantity of reality that was devoted to creating a fantasy was its own spectacular irony, and though at first Frankie Madden felt so far out of his depth that his head spun, he quickly grasped several key factors that made everything so much easier to understand and navigate. Here, in Tinseltown, everything was about ego. Even those who could not have been less important wanted to feel important. If you made people feel important they remembered you. If you remembered names, then people felt obliged to remember yours. A brief handwritten note and—in the case of a woman, a bouquet of flowers, in the case of a man, a bottle of good Irish whiskey—was more likely to get you a face-to-face with a casting director than any amount of phone calls. Treat them all as if they are three or four times more important than their actual pay grade and you could make more friends than Disney.

Frankie Madden found a niche for himself. He was hardworking, persistent without being aggravating, and he was easy to like. That was the crux of all of it. As the last vestiges of summer vacated Hollywood for other climes, it seemed to Frankie and Lucy that all they had to do was what they were already doing, and everything would be fine.

However, in September of 1938, as Frankie Madden and Lucia Mariani moved into a small house on Santa Ynez Street between Sunset and the freeway, the world beyond the American mainland was inching ever nearer to cataclysm.

Unbeknownst to them, Hollywood—ever a world of its own—was fighting its own demons. In July, the Justice Department had instigated proceedings against eight major picture studios for violations of the anti-monopoly laws. Senator Sullivan had made a statement in front of the House Committee on Un-American Activities that Hollywood was becoming nothing more than a breeding ground for communist propaganda. It seemed to Frankie that whatever spells might be woven here, they were nothing but shadows and silhouettes through which the harsh light of reality could effortlessly penetrate.

Perhaps there was no greater testament to that than this ever-increasing threat of a European war.

Most of the newspapers were sidelining the subject for other more mundane matters, and those who did make comment were selling an optimistic message. Europe was another world, and Hollywood was far too engrossed in creating its own.

Neville Chamberlain held talks with the German führer. He returned triumphant, holding aloft the "peace in our time" letter, which—he assured the British people—was as good a guarantee against war as had ever been obtained.

Mussolini began the process of expelling all Jews who had entered Italy after 1918. French troops headed for the Maginot Line as tensions mounted in Czechoslovakia. The Sudeten Germans held mass rallies calling for unity with Germany. In blatant and seemingly unstoppable outbursts of anti-Semitism, firebomb attacks swept across Vienna, and on the night of November 9th more than seven thousand Jewish shops in Germany were looted and hundreds of synagogues were burned down. Fearing that the German insurers of Jewish businesses would go bankrupt, the National Socialist party announced that any claim made by a Jew would be retrieved and given back to the insurer. Glass alone accounted for millions of marks of damage, to which Göring responded, "They should have killed more Jews and broken less glass."

Still, the real prospect of war did not reach America.

Frankie Madden watched the world teeter ever closer to the brink of international conflict. He felt it was inevitable, and his heart was torn as he knew that Ireland would be dragged into it whether it cared to be or not.

Through the early months of 1939, he and Lucy worked ceaselessly, ever increasing the number of people they represented, Frankie always on the lookout for something that would get Lucy on the screen.

Such an opportunity arrived in the early summer of 1939, when MGM announced the production of *Broadway Melody of 1940*.

Frankie and Lucy were in the kitchen. Breakfast was done and they were taking time to catch up on ongoing business.

Frankie mentioned the Broadway picture, told Lucy she should follow up on it.

"We have Lynne Carver on our books. She has a role, and they're looking for more singers and dancers," he said. "I can get Lynne to take you over there, and I'm sure they'll give you a screen test."

"You really think it's a good idea," Lucy said.

Frankie seemed baffled. "It's going to be a good picture. Fred

Astaire, Eleanor Powell, music by Cole Porter. Astaire's only just left RKO. He hasn't done anything for MGM for years—"

Lucy smiled.

"What?"

"Listen to you."

"Listen to me, what?"

"You really do sound like a proper Hollywood theatrical agent."

Frankie walked from the sink and sat down at the table facing Lucy. "What do you mean, do I think it's a good idea? You don't want to do a screen test?"

"I don't know, Frankie. I'm not so sure I'm really good enough."

Frankie reached out and took her hand. "No one's good enough. That's the thing. It's all make-believe anyway. If you don't think you're good enough, just pretend you are."

"You can get me a screen test?"

"Absolutely. I'll get a car to take you and Lynne up there. It'll be fine."

Ultimately, Lucy Madden's brief and almost-unnoticed appearance as an extra in the Astaire film did more to dampen her enthusiasm rather than encourage it. Frankie said nothing, but the weeks became months and Lucy seemed less and less concerned with work for herself. It seemed that every opportunity Frankie presented was met with a reason why such a thing was either impractical, not the right time, or unsuitable. They concentrated on the agency, and the drive and determination to make it succeed was considerable. Each focusing on their individual strengths—Frankie meeting people, talking his way into the offices of producers and casting directors, Lucy managing the existing clientele, soliciting referrals, dealing with all the many vital behind-the-scenes administrative functions that kept the business running smoothly.

There was no doubt about it, Frankie Madden and Lucy Mariani worked very well together, and their industry reaped benefits, both in reputation and financial returns. The Erin Star Agency was small, a modest operation, but it attracted a roster of quality artistes and loyal clients. Frankie, despite the extinguishing of his life's passion, was happy. He could have used that word, and he would have meant it. He believed he had somehow been given a third chance, perhaps deservedly, perhaps not, but he was determined not to waste it.

And then the fall came, and the world changed so very much. Whatever optimism might have been harbored concerning the unlikelihood of war was dashed into pieces when the Polish invasion began on the first of September. Within eight days the Nazi blitzkrieg brought German troops to the gates of Warsaw. Sixty thousand dead, more than three quarters of a million in captivity, and Russia and Germany divided the country between them.

Britain and France established the Allied opposition, swiftly followed by Canada, Australia, and New Zealand. The vicious cancer of war was entrenched in the very substance of mainland Europe, now virulent and pandemic.

Frankie read of these events as they occurred, trying his best to understand the consequences for Ireland. De Valera declared Ireland's neutrality. The northerners, despite British rule, were exempt from conscription. It had been the same in the 14–18 war. Perhaps the English feared another uprising. Training and arming many thousands of Irish nationals would prove beneficial in the short-term, but once the war was over those men would still be trained and armed. Perhaps their thoughts would turn to another war somewhat closer to home.

Echoing Woodrow Wilson in 1914, Roosevelt proclaimed the neutrality of the United States. How long he believed he could remain an isolationist he did not say, but it seemed that the Americans could not deny their vast resources to the war effort for long.

In the first days of November, just three weeks after rejecting Hitler's supposed mediation plea between Britain and Germany, Roosevelt signed the Neutrality Bill and authorized the sale of arms to the Allies.

Hitler understood not only the potential military might of the United States, but also the influence its vast propaganda machine could bring to bear upon the hearts and minds of enemy territories. By the summer of 1940, with conquests both in the East and the West, continental Europe was closed to American films.

Film studio executives were advised by Congress to concern themselves with cinematic inspirations other than the war.

Frankie Madden and Lucy Mariani turned their attentions even more diligently to their work. They each possessed deeply felt anxieties—Frankie for his family in Ireland, Lucy for hers in Corsica—but the real anxiety, had they faced facts, was that there was nothing at all they could do to change what was happening.

The world was at war, and—even in their darkest dreams—they could never have imagined how long it would continue and how many lives would be lost.

THIRTY-FIVE

Nicky, for all his bluff and bravado, was still a man alone. He did not belong, and he knew it. His pride and arrogance prevented him from making any move toward reconciliation with his sister, but he ached to hear her voice. They had spent their childhood and teenage years in a country so different from America. Had there been other familiarities around him, perhaps the degree to which he missed her would not have been so great. But he was a stranger in a strange land and could not escape the feeling that to be without Lucia was to be without half his life.

Still Nicky was quite as industrious as his sister, but in a very different way.

Whereas there were a million Hollywood hopefuls crowding the corridors of casting-agency offices, finding their way onto film sets in the hope they'd be noticed, tracking the whereabouts of those who'd already accrued film credits in the hope that they'd be seen and remembered, the ranks of wannabe hoodlums and underworld big shots was equally abundant.

Nicky needed to get more attention from people who mattered. People like Joe Adamo, Mickey Cohen and – most important of all – Jack Dragna.

How he accomplished that was a story in itself.

Scarcity was the word on everyone's lips. Even though the European conflict was many thousands of miles away, it had not been so long since Americans had been engaged in the Great War of 14–18. A quarter of a million wounded, more than a hundred thousand dead, and though the privations suffered by the United States were nothing in comparison to those experienced by the Europeans, it was nevertheless a matter of great concern. War was war, and war meant shortages. Nicky's own parents had been in their twenties during the Great War. They had told him stories of the horrors that became all too commonplace, the atrocities perpetrated, the catastrophic consequences of trench warfare. *As if the whole world had gone crazy*, his father had said. It preyed upon Nicky's mind;

he thought of them often, wondered if there was any way to bring them to the United States. If not that, then perhaps there might be a way to send money to them.

For now, limited as he was—both in influence and contacts—Nicky had to focus on establishing himself as a player within his own world. Certainly within the confines of Nicky's direct influence, the killing of Bobby Danza had established him as the head of that small self-styled gang. He and Caliendo, Tony Legs, the recent addition of Tony's cousin, Maurizio "Mo" Vianelli, gave them a group of four, always together, always into something, forever looking for something better.

Something better landed in Nicky's lap just a handful of weeks after the German invasion of Poland.

Understanding something of supply and demand, an inveterate gambler by the name of Johnny Grafton—in the hole for close to two grand—offered up an opportunity that, at first sight, seemed like a whole bundle of nothing.

Grafton, a meat wholesaler, doing everything he could to avoid the inevitable discussion regarding his debt to one of Dragna's bookies, was finally cornered in a bar on Highland. It was Tony Legs and Mo Vianelli that got him, and when he started jabbering about truckloads of beef coming out of the Midwest, Tony had sense enough to set up a meeting between Grafton and Nicky.

The rendezvous was a diner off of North La Brea.

Grafton, heavy-set, not so bright, was clutching at straws. He took home less than twenty dollars a week. Sure, he and his family dined on the best cuts of prime rib and tenderloin you could get in LA, but it was rare to find a bookie who'd take an IOU written on a hanger steak. How Johnny Grafton had dug himself in a hole that was two grand deep was an all-too-familiar story—accumulators that didn't accumulate, double-or-nothings that gave up the latter not the former—and now here he was, sat across a table from Nicky Mariani, wondering whether he would lose his teeth, his fingers, or his life.

Nicky was patient. He listened to the pleas for time and patience. He wasn't interested. What he was interested in was a truckload of meat.

"Tell me about the meat, Johnny," Nicky said, and then he sat back and waited.

"The meat?"

"You said something to Tony about meat. You work at the wholesalers, right?"

"We cut and pack it. We store it. Tons of the stuff. It comes in from the Midwest in these huge trucks. Tons of beef. Best quality in the city."

"And it goes where?"

"You know, everywhere . . . supermarkets, restaurants, anyplace people buy meat."

"How much is a truck of meat worth . . . not when it comes in, but when it's cut, packed, and sold out?"

"A whole truckload?"

"Yes, Johnny . . . a whole truckload."

"Well, hell, there's gotta be forty sides in there. That's maybe two fifty, three hundred pounds. Half of that is ground. The other is gonna be your steaks, your rib roasts, your prime, all that stuff."

"How much, Johnny?"

"What we talkin' here . . . maybe twenty, twenty-five cents a pound coming in, mark it up, selling it in short weights . . . I guess you're lookin' at something in the region of three and a half grand a truck, maybe four."

Nicky turned and looked at Tony Legs. Tony Legs smiled.

"Hey, wait a minute here," Johnny said. "No one said anything about a truckload of meat, now."

Nicky leaned forward and closed his hand over Johnny's. Johnny instinctively tried to withdraw, but Nicky gripped the man's wrist and held his hand to the table.

"We got two grand here, Johnny," Nicky said. "I don't owe it. You do. You know what they say about debts like that?"

Johnny Grafton shook his head.

"Hole that deep, you either climb out fast or lie still and get buried."

"Oh man—"

"Oh man, nothing," Nicky interjected. "A couple trucks of meat and we can call it quits."

"A couple? What the hell are you talking about, a couple? That's three and half, maybe four grand of meat just in one truck. I only owe two grand."

"You wanna sell the meat for us as well? Is that how you want to do it?"

Johnny looked at Tony Legs. Tony looked back without expression. Johnny Grafton was seeking sympathy in entirely the wrong place.

"So," Nicky said. "Let's talk cows, my friend. Let's talk all about this prime rib and tenderloin we're gonna be enjoying."

Three weeks later the first heist ran as smooth as a Swiss watch. Just for the hell of it, even though both Tony Legs and Vince Caliendo warned him off, Nicky went on the job. He carried a gun, he ran that truck down, and he hauled the driver out of the cab and knocked him to the ground. Mo Vianelli was there, a couple of other heavy hitters on loan from another crew, and that truck was diverted to a disused warehouse way on the other side of town. The driver went with them, and even though no real physical harm was done to the man, he came away shaken and stunned by the whole experience. The performance he gave for the police certainly convinced them that he was not in collusion with the stick-up crew. He was also sufficiently traumatized to remember nothing about the men who'd assaulted him, stolen his truck, and then left him tied up in the warehouse. To all intents and purposes, it was a solid heist. No clues, no names, no descriptions, and no idea where ten thousand pounds of cow had disappeared to.

Nicky, however, knew exactly where it disappeared to. That meat went into every Dragna-owned or -managed club, restaurant, diner, and bar in Hollywood. Some of it wound up in Long Beach, Anaheim, Santa Monica, and Pomona. Rumor had it that Jack Dragna even sent thirty pounds of prime rib to George Raft, the iconic Hollywood hard case, onetime driver for Owney Madden, a man who could lend a great deal more than mere imagination to the roles he played in the screen.

If that first heist didn't get Dragna's attention, the second one did.

Johnny Grafton wasn't to know, but the second truck that was diverted and robbed was carrying a cargo that did not appear on any manifest or bill of lading. Buried inside one of the beef carcasses was a sack of money. All told, that canvas sack held a little more than thirty grand, proceeds from another robbery that had taken place four months earlier. That robbery, the Federal Bank in Riverside, had gone unsolved and unreported. No one knew who'd pulled the job, no one knew who'd hidden the money inside a cow carcass, though some careful investigation by a couple of detectives on Dragna's payroll identified one Harold Fenman, employee of the meat-packing company, a colleague of Johnny Grafton, but—far more importantly—brother-in-law to a known bank robber called Thomas Allen Jackson, now serving an eight-to-ten for an entirely different matter.

Nicky Mariani could have kept that money, but Nicky knew the real value of that thirty grand was far more than thirty grand. He sent word—politely, respectfully—for an audience with Jack Dragna, and that audience was granted.

Nicky arrived at a small restaurant and was shown through to a room in the back behind the kitchen. Despite the inauspiciousness of the surroundings, the meeting itself was of great significance to Nicky. From what he understood, most of his contemporaries had never even seen Dragna, let alone received an audience.

Jack Dragna was the same age as Nicky's father, forty-nine years old, but he looked a good deal older. There was an ordinariness in his features that belied the cruelness in his eyes. Dragna was born in a town called Corleone in Palermo, Sicily, and though it seemed he'd tried to disguise his roots, Nicky could hear his past as clear as anything.

"Mariani," Dragna said, and waved Nicky toward him.

Nicky walked, in his hand a canvas bag filled with money.

"So, I hear you have something for me. Is that right?"

Nicky nodded in affirmation. "Yes, sir, Mr. Dragna."

Nicky held out the bag. Dragna nodded to a man standing at the side of the room that Nicky hadn't even noticed. The man came forward, took the bag, looked inside, and then delivered it to Dragna.

Dragna set the bag aside, indicated that Nicky should join him at the table.

"This is a hard business," Dragna said. "This is a business of contradictions. We are involved in vice, corruption, blackmail, extortion, robbery, even murder . . . and yet we expect to trust one another, to be trusted in return."

Nicky listened, said nothing.

Dragna smiled. "Some would say that you were a fool. Some would say that here was an opportunity to make a little something for yourself. A man can know many things, but it is a rare man who knows everything. I don't know that I would ever have heard of this had you not brought it to me."

Nicky stayed silent.

"So tell me, kid . . . Why tell me, why bring me this tribute?"

Nicky frowned. "Because this is your territory. Your city. I work for you, Mr. Dragna. A man who steals from the hand that feeds him does not deserve to eat."

Dragna smiled, turned to look at the man who'd delivered the money. "You hear this? Can you believe this?"

Nicky held Dragna's gaze. He felt afraid, but also excited. He needed to make an impression; he needed Dragna to know who he was and afford him some authority, something beyond the nickel-and-dime foot soldier work that others of his age and experience were limited to.

"You are not Italian," Dragna said.

"I am Corsican, Mr. Dragna."

"Which means that you were Italian a long time ago."

Nicky visibly flinched.

Dragna laughed, gripped Nicky's hands and held them. "I see you have the defiance I expected!"

Nicky smiled. Again, he said nothing.

"So, tell me where this money came from."

Nicky gave the precise details of how it had been obtained and said that he was at Dragna's disposal for any further action required.

Dragna then asked about him, when he'd arrived in America, how he'd traveled from Corsica. Nicky gave only so much information as was asked of him, knew his place, ventured nothing to make himself better regarded. He did not mention Lucia, and he said nothing of the events in New York.

"Being an outsider can be a good thing or a bad thing," Dragna said. "Maybe you can be of use to us. If America goes to war, then we become a problem. We are all immigrants, but now we are immigrants from a military foe. Will we be extradited or interned, who knows?" Dragna leaned forward. "But war is full of opportunity and potential. No matter where or when, no matter who is fighting, war creates a need that cannot be easily satisfied. Food, clothing, liquor, luxuries. Legitimate business will be denied us. But you? You can prove your French origin with genuine documentation, right?"

"Yes, Mr. Dragna, I can."

Dragna smiled. "Then we shall see what can be done, young man. You made a good decision to come to me with this." Dragna patted the bag of money on the table. "This is nothing compared to what you can make by working for me. You saw that without being told, and that has been noted."

"Thank you, sir. But for me it was not a question of whether I should bring the money. The money is yours by right, and I could not see it any other way."

Dragna smiled. "Kid Napoleon, right?"

"I have been called that," Nicky said.

"Then that is who you are. Kid Napoleon. Go now. I will send word through Joe Adamo. We will get something organized for you."

Nicky rose, thanked Dragna again, and walked to the door.

"It's going to be a good war for you," was Dragna's parting shot. "Mark my words, Kid... It's gonna be a good war for you."

THIRTY-SIX

Frankie Madden could not deny what he observed.

There were moments when Lucy was elsewhere, at least in her thoughts, and he knew those thoughts were for her brother.

Lucy, if not by law, was still as good as his wife. Frankie loved her—unconditionally, he told himself—but he saw the shadow that followed her, and it concerned him. He did not doubt that he was loved in return, and the months that had elapsed since that night in June of 1938 had been the happiest of his life. In many ways, the realization of something he'd believed to be nothing more than wishful thinking had served to alleviate his own sense of loss. Losing his home, his family, losing the chance to ever again fight competitively, had created a vacuum within him. That vacuum had been all but satiated by Lucy. He wanted for no one else, and he was committed to her happiness. He knew all too well that this would mean the inevitable reconciliation between brother and sister, and that—in so very many ways—concerned him greatly.

Frankie believed that Nicky knew precisely what was happening with his sister. Irrespective of ego and arrogance, he was neither stupid nor uncaring. He would be keeping track of her, if not directly, then through his contacts. Frankie was not blind. Even from his own limited experience, he saw that Hollywood was riddled with corruption. He knew of Jack Dragna, the Adamo brothers, the influence they possessed through the unions, and he felt sure that Nicky Mariani had done whatever was necessary to ingratiate himself into that world, into the business of corrupt money.

For that was the driving force of Hollywood, and anyone who said otherwise was both blinkered and naive. Hollywood was money. The studios were about money. Those who sat behind mahogany desks, those who drank cocktails and dressed for dinner, who feigned culture and sophistication and an endless appreciation for the arts, were some of the most ruthless and uncompromising people Frankie had ever met. If a star made money, they stayed a star. Once the money stopped, that star was cast aside and another younger, hungrier personality stepped forward from the wings. Look behind that hungry face and there was a line of a thousand more, and a thousand beyond that.

In truth, despite the success the agency was now enjoying, Hollywood scared Frankie Madden. It duped people into believing they wanted—*needed*—to be someone else, and then it bulldozed them into the costume.

For Lucy, movie roles had been few and far between, but he had noticed something in her. He believed the hunger had returned, and though he did not question her, though he did not ask her what was going on, he could see that she was beginning to once more want the very thing for which she'd journeyed to Hollywood. As yet, even a year from that first appearance, the parts offered had not promised overnight stardom. Hat-check girl, cocktail waitress, nightclub singer, gangster's moll #2. Lucy took them, and she was paid well, but—surprising to Frankie, if not to Lucy—the greater part of their income came from the Erin Star Agency. By Christmas of 1940 there were more than thirty-five aspiring starlets and silver-screen heartthrobs on their books. They'd also acquired a reliable reputation for ghost singers, the unacknowledged songbirds that provided the voices for the less musically gifted screen stars.

The percentage that the Maddens earned from myriad walk-ons, bit parts, crowd fillers, and stand-ins mounted up, and after six months of official trading their accountant informed them that it would be smart to rent an office, hire a permanent secretary, put up a shingle, and call themselves directors.

Achieving what they did had been work. There was no doubt about it. In some instances, it was Lucy's beauty and enthusiasm that had created opportunities for growth, but in others it was Frankie's persistence and willingness to keep talking until someone listened.

Coincidentally, it was news of a writer's death that opened an unseen door for both Frankie Madden and Lucy Mariani. In December of 1940, just a few weeks after Roosevelt's reelection, Frankie noticed a photograph and an obituary in the *LA Times*. He was waiting for Lucy in the kitchen.

"Sweetheart," he called out. "Take a look at this."

Lucy, reading over his shoulder, said, "Oh my God, it's him . . . from Musso's that day."

"F. Scott Fitzgerald," Frankie said. "And look who owned the building where he lived . . ."

"Harry Culver," she said. "I've met him on the backlots."

"He was young. Just forty-four."

"Tragic," Lucy said.

Frankie mentioned the death of Fitzgerald to a young up-and-coming actor called Ronald Reagan. Reagan would appear as Custer in an Errol Flynn picture called *Santa Fe Trail*, which was due for release after Christmas.

"No service call-up for him, then," Reagan had said.

"You think the USA will go to war?" Frankie asked.

"I have no doubt. And if we do, then it's people like us who have to set an example, wouldn't you say? People who are known, people the public recognize."

"I'm Irish," Frankie explained. "I'm not welcome at this party."

Reagan had gripped Frankie's shoulder. "Hell, you better get yourselves set up for a lot of work, then. They won't stop making movies, and talent is gonna be as rare as hen's teeth."

Later, Frankie told Lucy about his conversation with the actor.

"You think he's right?" she asked. "You think America will go in with Europe?"

"I don't know," he said. "But what that feller said made a lot of sense. They start conscripting all the actors, then we're going to have to get a lot more people on our books."

"James Stewart was up at Culver the other day," she said. "He just appeared in something called *The Philadelphia Story*. Did you know he was a pilot?"

Frankie shook his head.

"Apparently so. Even flies back to see his folks in Pennsylvania. You know him and Cary Grant, I think Henry Fonda and Robert Taylor, too, have all invested in a pilot training school for the air force. You remember we met his agent a few weeks ago, Leland Hayward?"

"Yes... represents Fred Astaire and Karloff, right?"

"That's him. He started it off, the flying school thing. More and more people are talking about it. I think it's inevitable, to be honest."

More than food for thought, it spurred Frankie on to establish himself and the agency even further. He approached it as he had always approached things. Once he'd decided, he made a commitment, and there was next to nothing that could divert his energies.

For Lucy, it made her aware of the fragility and unpredictability of all things. She asked herself what she wanted—what she *really* wanted—and found that her dreams had not changed so much after all.

She again started to look for work, and when she saw an opportunity she went at it with a greater degree of dedication than Frankie had previously seen.

In July of 1941, *Sergeant York* was released to much acclaim, not only for Warner but for its star, Gary Cooper. The Erin Star Agency had fourteen on-set personnel. Partly due to her direct connection to RKO, Lucy had been able to secure contracts between June and October of the previous year for an entirely different film. RKO's studio president had signed a contract with a young actor and theater director called Orson Welles. Welles, then merely twenty-five years of age, set out to make a movie adaptation of Conrad's *Heart of Darkness*, but was then drawn to the stylized biography of the press baron, William Randolph Hearst. The resultant film, *Citizen Kane*, provoked scathing comments from Hollywood's queens of gossip, Hedda Hopper and Louella Parsons, the latter being a Hearst employee. Those who sought attention were as well served by notoriety as anything else, and for the Maddens' agency to have provided so many people for two such notable productions did them no harm at all.

Notwithstanding the fact that their lives had irreversibly and unrecognizably changed within three short years, they were nevertheless in for a greater surprise.

Events that transpired in the latter part of 1941—both personally and politically—turned their world upside down.

On a personal level, Frankie Madden was just as responsible as Lucy for the catalyst that would bring Nicky Mariani back into their lives in the most unexpected way possible. In hindsight, perhaps it could have been prevented, but due to its nature, it was ultimately inevitable.

A chain of events, yet to change the direction of their lives, began with a chance meeting between Frankie Madden and a man called Freddie Fleck. Fleck was a New Yorker, an assistant director and production manager, and for some reason he took a shine to Frankie.

"You remind me of some of those wild characters back in New York," he said. It was a pre-premiere drinks party downtown. Frankie was there alone, making conversation, mingling, trying to get a good word in about the agency to those who mattered.

"Irish immigrants, all troublemakers, fighters, drinkers to a man,"

Fleck went on. "Great stories, let me say. Every one of them had enough stories for a whole host of films."

Fleck had worked with Howard Hughes, King Vidor, and Garson Kanin. He'd directed Jean Harlow, Joel McCrea, and a young comic actress called Lucille Ball in *That's Right—You're Wrong* back in 1939. Frankie mentioned that he'd met Lucille Ball back at the Culver City lot in June of 1938, and that appeared to cement the friendship between Frankie and Freddie Fleck.

"Working on a project called *The Magnificent Ambersons* with Orson Welles now," Fleck told Frankie.

Frankie's inquiry led to the discovery that a teenage actress was needed, or at least an actress that could carry a teenage role.

"It's an important role. Welles is a firebrand. Everyone is interested in what he's doing. Anyone who snags a good part in a Welles production is going to find the work rolling in after that."

Frankie told him about Lucy, said that she was a very gifted up-and-coming actress on the agency's books.

"Bring her over," Freddie said. "Of course, everything is Orson's—screenplay, production, direction—but Rufus Le Maire and Bobby Palmer are both working on casting, and I think Art Willy's doing the New York stuff, and I know all of them. Bring your girl over and we'll give her a screen test, at least."

And so it was. Frankie spoke to Lucy, and though he'd expected that same self-doubt that she'd manifested before, this time there was nothing.

"Yes," she said. "I really want to go. I don't care if I don't get it. I just want to start again and make this happen."

They went over to RKO's Gower Street studios. It was early November 1941, and the Amberson mansion was already close to completion. The set itself was a breathtaking marvel of engineering and construction, built like a real house but with walls that could be lowered, raised, or rolled back to permit continuous takes. The camera could move from one room to the next as if passing through solid brick.

Though Welles himself was a mere twenty-six years old, just four years older than Frankie, he possessed a charismatic presence that defied description. He was more than six foot tall, broad in the shoulders, and his dark eyes were brooding and intense. When he spoke, his voice was commanding and direct.

"Who are you and what are you doing here?" was the first question that left Welles's lips as Frankie and Lucy came around a corner with Freddie Fleck.

Freddie smiled. "Orson, you are such a bulldog. Stop it. Have some manners, goddammit."

Welles paused, looked at Freddie as if deliberating his response, and then his face relaxed into a welcoming smile.

"This," Freddie said, "is Lucy Madden. She is here to screen-test for the Lucy Baxter role."

"Ah," Welles said. He paused for a moment, looking Lucy up and down. He drew a smile circle in the air. "Turn, turn," he said.

Lucy did as she was asked.

Welles came a little closer, held out his hand. Lucy took it.

"Look up toward the ceiling," Welles said. "Now look at me... now look at Freddie."

Welles released Lucy's hand. "Yes... interesting. An interesting look, Freddie."

Lucy smiled graciously. "It's a real honor to meet you, Mr. Welles."

Welles seemed not to hear her, but turned to Frankie and said, "And you are?"

"Her agent, Frankie Madden."

Welles nodded sagely. "Good. Business." He looked back at Lucy again, reached up suddenly and put his hands on Lucy's neck. He held her head straight and then turned it left, right, tilted her chin upward and moved her head to observe her profile.

"Yes, yes, yes," Welles said, to no one but himself, and then looked at Freddie and said, "Get the test done. I want to see it today."

With that he turned and started away.

"Thank you for your time, Mr. Welles," Frankie called after him, but Welles neither turned back nor made any indication of acknowledgment.

"That's Orson," Freddie said. "Sometimes abrasive, sometimes hilarious, sometimes a complete monster, but always a genius."

The test was done. At first it was simply a matter of Lucy walking back and forth in front of a white background. Then she was asked to smile, to look away, to suddenly turn and stare at the camera. She was given a single sheet of paper, upon which was typed a nursery rhyme. She was asked to recite it, to recite it a second time more slowly, then to read it in different emotions—angry, scared, elated.

Frankie watched from the sidelines and willed Lucy to be brilliant. Whatever nerves she might have experienced were nowhere to be seen, and Freddie Fleck seemed thrilled by the whole occasion.

"This is something special," he told Frankie while Lucy was back in makeup. "Your young lady has something, I tell you. She really does have something."

Later, Lucy asked Frankie if anything had been said, if he'd given any kind of indication of how he felt about the test.

"He was more than happy," Frankie told her, but he said nothing more. He didn't know how fragile her renewed enthusiasm might be, and he did not wish to add to the pressure she was already placing upon herself.

Three days later Lucy Madden got a callback.

At first she couldn't believe it, but Frankie read the message three times and it finally sank in.

"It's great news," he said. "It's really wonderful."

"This could be it, Frankie!" she exclaimed. She hugged him, kissed him again and again. She was laughing, almost beside herself with excitement. "I can hardly believe it! I can't even imagine what it would be like to work with someone like Orson Welles."

"Well, I guess you're going to find out soon enough," Frankie said.

"Do you think so?" she asked. She was like a child at Christmas. She looked fit to burst. "Do you really think so, Frankie? Do you think it could actually happen?"

"It's what you want, Lucy. It's why we came here to Los Angeles . . . Hell, it's why you came to America! Of course it could happen."

"Oh, it's just too good to be true," she shouted, and she kissed Frankie again.

They returned to Gower Street and Lucy did a second test, this time with a male actor reading through lines with her. "You maintain a fixed smile, you hide your emotions," Freddie told her before she went on. "This young man, this George, is trying to get you to show him something, to tell him how you feel, but you will have none of it. He leaves, you remain stoic, but once he is gone you're lost. Your eyes fill with tears . . ."

Lucy followed his instructions to the letter. She was captivating, no doubt about it, and Frankie watched her spellbound.

Though it made him uncomfortable, he suspected that the emotion she hid and then displayed had something to do with the loss of Nicky.

The young man with whom she'd read the lines was very encouraging. He complimented Lucy, said he really hoped she'd get the part as he felt they could work well together.

"Tim Holt," Freddie told them when the young man had left.

"He's already been cast. His word will count for something. Not a great deal, but something."

On Tuesday, December second, Freddie Fleck sent a telegram to Frankie and Lucy.

Orson decides today. Wishing you the best. It's looking very good indeed.

Lucy was beside herself with anticipation. She could barely hold herself together.

"Just imagine," she said. "Just imagine if I got it. How incredible would that be? Working with Orson Welles . . ."

"I'm trying not to be too optimistic," Frankie said, "But I think the screen test you did was amazing. I really do. Honestly, I think you have as good a chance as anyone for this."

"Did Mr. Fleck tell you who else was being tested?"

Frankie shook his head. "They don't talk about it. Seems to be an unwritten rule."

"Oh, I can't believe it!" Lucy went on, pacing back and forth between the sink and the kitchen table. "I can't believe that I might actually get this. It would mean so much. I mean, this is a huge picture. It has a big budget, right?"

"More than three quarters of a million dollars."

"Three quarters of a million dollars," she echoed, as if such a sum was beyond belief.

Frankie had never seen her so enthused and excited. He understood that such things were utterly unpredictable, that there was no way to divine the direction that casting would go. He'd had enough experience to realize that whatever you expected, the unexpected always seem to happen. A different viewpoint, a producer who took a particular shine to an actor or actress, and then there was the whole business of payoffs, backhanders, favors owed, debts called in, nepotism and the "casting couch."

In that moment Frankie could do nothing but be carried along on a wave of hope and optimism. He prayed that Lucy would get the part, and that was all he could do.

THIRTY-SEVEN

On Wednesday, November 6, 1940, Detective Louis Hayes was shot in the leg by a man called Jimmy "Five Aces" Marsolino. Jimmy was no made man, no high-life gangster; he was a drunk and a card cheat.

It was a day after Roosevelt's return to the White House, said return—according to some—assisted markedly by his assurances that the United States would not go to war against the Axis.

Regardless, the seeming inevitability of war had no bearing on the Hayes shooting. True, there were some who would have argued that Los Angeles was a war zone, but the weapons drawn were all American-made, as were the bullets, one of which entered Hayes's right thigh approximately eight inches above the knee. Despite skimming the bone, it was a through-and-through, it's .38 caliber leaving an exit wound the size of a golf ball.

Five months prior to the shooting, almost two years to the day since he'd visited Grigor Zakarian at Hollywood Hospital, Hayes had made detective first class. The promotion, it seemed, had not improved his detection skills. He had made no progress on finding Paulie Belotti, nor this mythical Kid Napoleon. Additionally—aside from Zakarian's assurance that he'd heard Belotti admit to her murder—the actual circumstances of Sandy Mayweather's death were still as much a mystery to him as when he'd first stepped through that motel room door and seen her unzipped for the world.

The previous three years had been a roller-coaster ride for the LAPD. Good cops had turned out to be not so good, and the stink of corruption had wafted all the way down from the mayoral office to the sidewalks themselves. Mayor Frank L. Shaw, perhaps Dragna's only real challenger for King of Los Angeles, had been recalled back in September of '38. Replacing him was former Superior Court Judge Fletcher Bowron. It was Bowron to whom the Citizens Independent Vice Investigation Committee had appealed, charging Shaw's administration with funding election campaigns with the profits from brothels, bookies, and slot machines. Despite the ultimate failure of CIVIC's suit, Bowron heard them. Elected to mayor on a fusion ticket, Bowron promised a *new broom* policy. Acting Police Chief David Davidson was replaced by Arthur C. Hohmann, chosen not by Bowron but by the Police Commission. Bowron and Hohmann promised a new LAPD and a new city, free from the graft and vice and corruption of the past. All precincts, Central particularly, were charged with routing out the insidious virus of organized crime. The mission, though well intentioned, was a pipe dream, and every man from captain on down said as much. Those selfsame captains, the commanders above them, even the deputy chief, were undoubtedly possessed of the same viewpoint, but defeatism was not an acceptable party line. And when it came to the Los Angeles crime family, it was men such as Detective First Class Louis Hayes who appreciated that the primary obstacle in tackling *organized* crime was its fundamental disorganization. There was a *capo di tutti capi*, there were underbosses, consiglieres, *caporegimes*, but the people with whom Hayes crossed paths, the men who populated the cells, interrogation rooms, and bail offices were merely soldiers. There were hundreds, if not thousands, and they routinely understood less of the organization than Hayes and his colleagues.

Aside from any real grasp of the network that existed in Los Angeles, the previous police administration had been so profoundly corrupt, its operations so embedded and entrenched within the very woof and warp of the criminal fraternity, that the gangs took no notice of threatened police action. If the police said they were going to rout out organized crime, it was merely lip service to a lapdog press.

The circumstances of Hayes's shooting were not themselves particularly noteworthy. There was no high-speed car chase, no frenetic on-foot pursuit; there was merely a drunken standoff outside a bar on South Olive, each man possessed of an opinion and a sidearm to back it up.

Hayes was babysitting a greenhorn called Victor Lewis. Lewis, hopeful detective, was full of questions, so much so that Hayes's patience was wearing thin. They had been in the office all morning, most of the afternoon, and Hayes took the call simply to change the scenery. By the time they reached South Olive, Hayes was an hour from the end of his shift.

Put a loaded firearm in the hands of a drunk and the waltz will end in tears. The shot fired was unintentional, but what was done could not be undone. Hayes had been hospitalized for two weeks, in recuperation for a further four, and though he made an excellent recovery, a noticeable limp now accompanied his inability to play the piano. At times he wondered why God—if indeed there was one—possessed such a vengeful streak and what he had done to provoke it.

The enthusiasm with which he'd returned to active duty impressed both Captain Mills and Lieutenant Fuller. Hayes was asked to consider heading up a new Vice Unit within Central. The post offered a significant bump in salary, an office, a secretary, and a driver. Hayes agreed to everything but the driver. He just didn't see himself as the chauffeured type.

Hayes's official posting was initiated on Monday, February 3, 1941. Beginning with three men, Vice Unit expanded to six within the first five months. Hayes and his crew, nicknamed St. Louis's Blues, were responsible, almost single-handedly, for more arrests than any other department in the city. Fuller was pleased with the Blues, as was Mills, and Hayes believed he was at last doing something worthwhile and constructive.

That belief did not last long. It soon became apparent that the faster they brought in arrests, the faster the slick lawyers got them out. It was all so much oil on glass, and it rankled. When Hayes heard rumor there was a betting pool in the public defenders office to see who could get a man out of Central's holding tank the fastest, Hayes knew he was treading water.

Arrest and charge fifty, a hundred, two hundred, and he was no closer to Adamo or Dragna. He began to recognize the work of Dragna's hitmen, Frank Bompensiero and Jimmy Fratianno, but eyewitnesses and those prepared to testify were as rare as snake spit.

On December 4, something changed, and that change came in the form of a young woman called Bernice Radcliffe. Both Lucy and Frankie Madden would have known Bernice as Eleanor Wilson, for it was under this stage name that she was registered at the Erin Star Agency. Bernice had been one of those to appear in a scene in *Sergeant York* and had in fact made eye contact, albeit briefly, with Gary Cooper. That role, along with many earlier such roles, had not brought her to the attention of anyone influential, least of all a casting director or producer. Ironically, she had shared a table with Gene Kelly at Van de Kamp's on the corner of Ivar and Yucca, the exact same bakery where Lucy and Frankie had stopped before their meeting with Morris Budny at the Roosevelt. How she'd come to share that table was a tale she'd told so many times that even she had wearied of it, but she kept telling like it was some sort of incantation. It was a small moment of grace and wonder that had punctuated the frustration and monotony of her life.

Bernice had been in Hollywood for the better part of two years, and her fortunes did not seem to be looking up. As was the case with so many similar girls, she'd started to supplement her income with party work. Put on your best dress, show up at some Hollywood Hills mansion, don't eat the canapés, don't drink the liquor, just look good, smile plenty, and make the guests feel like the house was forever graced with the bright and the beautiful. From there it was a short road to escort; from escort you were little but a weekend away from hooking. And when you ventured across that line, the clientele you entertained were no longer Hollywood royalty, but rather those who lived in the same zip code zones merely because they could afford it.

It was obvious that Bernice Radcliffe was no veteran of the vice scene. The night of her arrest was her third outing in such unsavory company, and with a dislocated wrist, a missing tooth, three broken fingers, and a cracked rib, it looked like it might be her last. Bernice, if nothing else, knew when she was licked. It was in that state of overwhelm and disillusionment that Louis Hayes found her at Hollywood Hospital on the morning of December 4. Sometimes it was obvious that someone was in no mood to get back on the horse.

Had Hayes gone in through the ambulance bay he would have seen a young man carrying a woman into the hospital and shouting for help, but Hayes took the front entrance. By the time Hayes reached Bernice's bedside, that young woman in question was already being attended to in a private room.

Hayes sat by the bed for a few minutes. Bernice wasn't doing so good, looked like she'd argued with the fast train to Fresno, and Hayes waited patiently until she seemed ready to speak. The doctor had okayed her for a few questions, but with the entreaty not to tire her out.

"You want to tell me what happened, Bernice?" Hayes asked her.

"I got the hell kicked out of me is what happened," Bernice replied. Her lower lip was badly swollen, the right side of her face heavily bruised, but despite her injuries Hayes could see that she was a very pretty girl. Beauty was both a blessing and a curse, it seemed. If anywhere was testament to that, it was Hollywood.

"Were you out at a party?"

"You could call it that, I guess."

"You were paid to go?"

"I'm not a hooker, okay? I don't do that. Never have, never will."

Hayes didn't argue with her. "You just tell me what happened in your own words," he said. "Take your time."

"I know some people," she said. "Sometimes they want a crowd of girls for a gig, you know? We put on our best dresses, we show up, we make the place look good. I thought it was one of those."

"And it wasn't."

"It wasn't, no."

"Where was the place?"

"I don't know . . . somewhere up West Sixth. Near Rampart, I think. I just got in the cab with a couple of other girls."

"How many girls ended up there?"

"Four, six maybe."

"And guys?"

"Maybe the same."

"And they wanted hookers?"

Bernice didn't speak for a moment. She looked away nervously, then straight ahead. She nodded in the affirmative.

"And you said no, right?"

"Right."

"And they knocked you around."

"One guy. One guy did this to me." Bernice looked up at Hayes. The expression in her eyes was one of utter hopelessness.

"Where are you from?" Hayes asked.

"Originally, Ohio."

"Cleveland?"

She tried to smile and struggled. "Why does everyone immediately assume we're from Cleveland or Cincinnati?"

"Because . . . hell, I don't know. I just said Cleveland because I did five years there."

"I'm from a nowhere place called Columbus Grove."

"So why d'you come to Hollywood?"

Bernice frowned. "Er, because . . . well, because it's Hollywood." She shook her head. "You are a detective, right?"

Hayes smiled. "Dumb question. Just trying to make conversation, that's all."

"Trying to put me at ease?"

"Yeah, I guess."

"I'm in hospital. I don't have medical insurance. I got a cracked rib, three broken fingers, my tooth is missing . . ." Her voice trailed off and she started to cry.

"You're an actress, singer, dancer . . . what?" Hayes asked, eager to get the interview back on track.

"Right now I'm going home," Bernice replied. "Fast as they release me."

"You've been here how long?"

"Two years."

"Any work?"

"Bit parts, walk-ons, the usual kind of nothing."

"You had enough?"

Bernice took a handkerchief and wiped her eyes. "I had enough about a year ago, told myself to give it another year." She shook her head resignedly. "You know, I met Gene Kelly once. He told me I smiled like I had a mouthful of stars. He was a gentleman, a real sweetheart." She sighed. "Now I smile like a prizefighter."

"Your folks don't send you money?"

"My folks don't know where I am."

"How old are you?"

"Twenty-one."

"You really gonna quit and go home?"

Bernice looked at Hayes as if he hadn't understood a word she'd said.

"I'm sorry," Hayes said. "Not a good time for that question, is it?"

"So are we done, Detective?"

"I need you to try to remember where this house was," he said. "And I would really like to know the name of the guy who did this to you."

"So you can do what?"

"Arrest him. Charge him. Get him arraigned."

"Which would require identifying him or testifying or whatever else, right?"

"We'd need you to identify him, yes—"

"I'm gonna go home, Detective. I'm gonna get on a bus and go home. I'm not doing identification parades or filing complaints or anything."

"I understand, Bernice, but—"

"But nothing," Bernice interjected.

Hayes paused. He sighed audibly. "You know how many people I speak to, how many could help me but won't? I'm trying to do what I can to deal with this kind of thing, but I can't do it alone."

"You want me to feel sorry for you, Detective Hayes?"

"Sure I do, Bernice. That's exactly what I want."

Bernice leaned back against the pillow and closed her eyes. "The guy's name was Mo," she said. "That's what they called him. Mo Vianelli. He only said it once, but I remembered it because it made me think of *vanilla*."

"Mo . . . like *m-o*?"

"I guess. Short for something. That's what they called him, like I said."

"Any other names?"

Bernice opened her eyes and half smiled. "Guy called Tony Legs."

"Tony Legs."

"Yes, Tony Legs. Dumb name. He was the one who told Vianelli to get me out of the house. He was mad with him, said he was an asshole, that he didn't want anything to do with it and that he had to get me out of the house."

"And you don't remember the name of the street."

"All I know is that it was up near South Rampart. One of those Spanish street names."

"Remember the name of the cab company?"

Bernice started to shake her head and then winced. "No," she said.

"And the girls that were already in the cab . . . you recall any names?"

Bernice exhaled slowly, as if Hayes was now trying her patience. "I really don't want to talk anymore, Detective. Now you know as much as me, okay? That's all I'm gonna say."

"One other question and then I'm gone, I promise."

"Shoot."

"Who represents you, and do you ever use a stage name?"

"That's two questions."

"Give a man a break, sweetheart," Hayes said.

"Eleanor Wilson, and I am represented by the Erin Star Agency."

"How d'you spell that?"

"E-R-I-N. I think it's an Irish word. The guy that owns it is from Ireland, I think."

"And where are they based?"

"I told you one, you got two. That's enough now, okay?"

Hayes smiled. He didn't have a great deal, but he had something. Mo Vianelli. A house up near South Rampart. The Erin Star Agency—maybe legit, maybe a front for girls. He'd soon find out.

"Thank you for your time, Bernice," Hayes said, putting away his notebook. "You know, for what it's worth, I really am sorry this happened to you. It sucks. I get that. However, I don't think you should give up. The ones that make it are simply the ones that never quit."

Bernice tried to smile again and it was evidently hard work. "I appreciate the sentiment, Detective, but knowing when you're beaten isn't cowardice. It's just knowing when you're beaten."

Hayes smiled. He didn't agree with her viewpoint, could never have agreed, but he didn't challenge her. She needed to explain this any way she could. She needed to find a reason to go and make it someone else's fault. *I couldn't possibly continue because...* was the swan song of so many broken dreams.

Like playing the piano, maybe. Okay, so he'd had an accident, lost a couple of fingers, but maybe he had something to do with the accident in the first place. Maybe, sometimes, people made bad shit happen to themselves just so they'd have a reason not to persist. It was a sobering thought, and he didn't much care for it.

"You think of anything else, you call me at Central," Hayes said.

"I'll do just that, Detective," Bernice replied, and they both knew full well no such phone call would ever take place.

THIRTY-EIGHT

The morning after the second test at Gower Studios, the world seemed a different place to Lucy Madden.

She woke with a sense of anticipation, and although she knew that to feel too eager was to set herself up for a greater disappointment if she did not get the part, she could not help it. Everything was so exciting. She only had to think of it and she could feel her pulse quicken, her stomach alive with a thousand butterflies. She merely had to close her eyes for a moment and she could hear Mr. Welles's voice.

Yes . . . interesting. An interesting look, Freddie.

Get the test done. I want to see it today.

She knew she'd done well. She knew she'd projected, that her enunciation was good, that she'd responded well to the other actor. Freddie Fleck was happy with her—she could see that in his eyes, and Frankie had been even more excited than she.

"You're like a cat on hot bricks," Frankie told her on the morning of the third.

"I can't help it," Lucy said. "I just can't bear it . . . It's too . . ." She laughed at herself. "Listen to me. I'm like a little girl."

"Well, as far as I can see, you did everything that could be done. You read beautifully. I know Freddie is really enthusiastic, but these things have a way of going how they're meant to go. A director can have a viewpoint, a producer something completely different, and they can sometimes never agree. look at what happened with *Gone with the Wind*. In the end the person who makes the decision is the one who's putting their hands in their pockets and paying for it."

"I know all that, Frankie, and I understand, but can you just imagine what it would be like to get this. Everyone says that Orson is the boy wonder, the golden child. Everyone says that whatever he touches will be enormously successful. If I get this, Frankie . . . Well, if I get this, then I know I will have the career I've always wanted."

Frankie grabbed her and held her tight. "I'm just gonna hang on to you for a while so you don't explode or float away or something, okay?"

Lucy was laughing, Frankie, too, and it seemed that nothing could go wrong. It was too right. It was too perfect. It was a dream, for sure, but it looked like one of those dreams that could very easily come true.

Later that evening she was calmer. Lucy took stock of her situation, considering not only what would happen if she secured the role, but also how she would feel if it was given to another. She was not a jealous woman. She would not resent someone else's success. But, having said that, she knew from experience that she did not take failure well. It was in her Corsican blood to fight, and accepting that nothing could be done about a situation was anathema to her. If she was not chosen, then she would have to think about her future once again. She would have to decide whether the career path she'd always wished for was actually beyond her reach. There was no point in being maudlin or despondent. She had to be pragmatic. If working in the agency had taught her anything, it was that there were hundreds of wonderfully talented actors and actresses who would never get *the break*. This was show business. This was reality. This was life.

Over dinner, she asked Frankie what he thought.

"I think that there's nothing to think until we hear back from Freddie," he said. "I know it's difficult. I know it's frustrating and exciting at the same time. I don't think there's anything else you can do, and if I haven't heard anything from Freddie by the end of tomorrow I'll probably go see him. Maybe I'll leave it until the following morning, but I won't let it go. You know that, right? I want this for you just as much as you do."

"I know you do," Lucy said, and she reached out and took Frankie's hand. "I don't know that I could have done this without you. I really do love you so much."

Frankie opened his mouth to speak but was cut short by the sound of the telephone ringing in the other room.

Frankie glanced at his watch and frowned.

He looked up at Lucy. Her expression was pure expectation.

"Don't get too—"

"Answer it!" she said. "Just answer the phone, Frankie!"

She followed him out of the room and into the lounge. Frankie picked up the receiver.

"Yes," she heard him say. "Freddie . . ."

Frankie was silent. He nodded his head, and then he said, "I think you should tell her yourself, Freddie."

Frankie held out the phone to Lucy.

Lucy looked at the phone, looked at Frankie, and Frankie could not hold his expression. He broke into the widest grin she had ever seen.

Lucy screamed. "I got it? Did I get it?"

Frankie said nothing. He just stood there with the phone and the grin on his face, and Lucy damned near shrieked loud enough to deafen poor Freddie Fleck when he told her the news.

"You got it, sweetheart," Freddie said. "You broke the bank. You backed the winner. You made it to the finish line. Orson says you're his girl, no doubt about it."

"Oh my God, Freddie! Oh my God, oh my God, oh my God!" she hollered, and then she dropped the receiver and threw her arms around Frankie and squeezed the life out of him.

On the other end of the line, all Freddie Fleck could hear was Lucy's shrieking and Frankie's laughter, and he was reminded that despite all the noise and madness that was Hollywood, there were moments like these—moments of real magic—when it all made perfect sense.

THIRTY-NINE

On Thursday, December 4, Lucy Madden got sick.

That day had begun as usual—matters of business, the usual wrangles over union fees, terms of contract, all else that occupied their usual day-to-day routine.

"Some of the people they send over to straighten things out aren't so bright," Lucy commented. "They could have walked right off the set of a George Raft movie."

Frankie knew the kind of people she was talking about; he also believed that they might be employed by the very same people as Nicky. Ironically, he'd heard someone repeat a quote from Orson Welles himself—*The classy gangster is a Hollywood invention*, or words to that effect—and Frankie could not have agreed more.

Their conversation turned, of course, to *The Magnificent Ambersons* project, and how the agency would run in Lucy's absence.

"I need to talk to Freddie about rehearsals, when they're looking at principal photography," Lucy said. She could hardly believe the words that were coming from her own lips. Not only did dreams actually come true in Hollywood, but they had come true for her. "And what will you do without me?" she said.

"I'll be heartbroken and hopeless," Frankie said. "I'll probably turn to drink, spend all our money on cheap liquor and cheaper women, and you'll come back to a shell of the man I once was."

"Foolish," Lucy said. "You'll have to hire someone, of course—"

"Lucy, it won't be a problem. It's going to be fine. Whatever happens now will be a change for both of us, and we will just deal with it. If the movie is anywhere near as successful as I think it'll be, then you're going to have a very different career altogether, right? Let's just take this one step at a time. Let's not worry about a problem until there's a problem, okay?"

"You're right, of course," she said, and she reached for the coffeepot to refill their cups.

It was in that moment, even as she held the pot, that she felt herself drifting. It was the strangest sensation, almost as if she was outside her own body and watching what was happening from a distance.

The pot just slid from her fingers, and Frankie—seeing it all unfold in slow motion—could do nothing to stop it.

The pot hit Lucy's cup, the cup broke, the pot went sideways, and coffee spilled across the table and cascaded onto the kitchen floor.

The sound that escaped from Lucy's lips was as if she were being deflated. Her eyes rolled white and she sort of slumped sideways.

Frankie moved fast enough to catch her before she lost her balance completely, and he scooped her up into his arms and carried her out of the kitchen.

He laid her down on the sofa in the front, and within a matter of moments she was looking back at him as if nothing had happened.

"You all right?" he asked, visibly distressed.

"What's going on?" she asked.

"You dropped the coffeepot, sweetheart. You looked like you passed out."

She tried to sit up, and a wave of dizziness and nausea overtook her.

"Whoa," she said, and lay back down.

Frankie put a couple of cushions behind her to support her head, and he went to the kitchen for a damp cloth.

When he returned Lucy's face was varnished with a thin film of sweat. She was pale, visibly so, and Frankie felt a sense of panic rising in his chest. He remembered when Erin got sick, how they thought she might have tuberculosis, and his mind started reeling at the implications.

"Hospital," Frankie said emphatically, and grabbed the car keys.

He carried Lucy out to the car, laid her on the backseat, dropped the keys as he tried to start the ignition, feeling all the while that somehow what was happening had to be his fault.

He took the route he knew, pulled into the same ambulance bay as had been used by Tony Legs, Vince Caliendo, and Nicky Mariani when they'd delivered Grigor Zakarian. Frankie lifted Lucy out of the backseat and rushed through the doors, was immediately attended to by porters and nurses.

They had Lucy on a gurney and were asking her questions, people crowding her, a doctor indicating that she be moved into a bay where a curtain was drawn.

Frankie went after her, was steered away by a nurse who said, "Let us deal with this, sir. You take a seat over there and we'll tell you what's going on as soon as we know."

Frankie did as he was asked, his hands shaking, his mouth dry. He thought the worst, could not stop himself. As the minutes stretched out behind him he knew with everything he possessed that losing Lucy would be his punishment . . . for Bobby Durnin, for Aleksy Bodak, for the blackmail of Morris Budny, most of all for deserting his family in Ireland and pretending that the past did not exist.

The past was there, replete with guilt and myriad ghosts, and they threatened to snatch away his sanity as he waited for word of the woman he loved.

FORTY

"Forgive enough to be compassionate but not so much as to be weak. Forgive those who never expected to be forgiven. Punish those who thought they'd get away with it."

Joe Adamo leaned forward and extinguished his cigarette. He sat back and smiled at Nicky Mariani.

"A great man told me that many years ago, Nicky, and you would do well to remember it. Some talk about money, about sex, about drugs . . . but the real addiction is power. Like this great man you speak of, this Napoleon, addicted to power. Like Mussolini, Hitler, these crazy bastards in Europe. It is not the war itself. It is the power to start a war. Who knows where it will end, and who cares, eh? Men have been fighting one another for the same reasons for thousands of years, and nothing ever changes. All you can do is look at what is happening and ask yourself how you can profit."

Nicky didn't say anything. He knew two things about Joe Adamo: that he didn't trust those who broke eye contact, and he hated interruptions.

"So," Adamo continued, "you have done well. I'm happy, as is my brother, and Mr. Dragna, too. He is impressed with your honesty." Adamo smiled. "When did I ever think I'd hear myself say that, eh? The thirty grand you gave him, the heists with the meat. You made a lot of money, but you didn't forget whose territory you were working."

Adamo leaned forward and gripped Nicky's forearm reassuringly. "Rare to find someone who isn't in this business solely for themselves. Man who recognizes his position on the ladder is a man who can see how to climb it, right?"

Nicky nodded in affirmation but said nothing.

"Anyway, Mr. Dragna has been talking. There are some clubs downtown, the Venus Lounge and the Starlight. Small places, but they make good business. They are on the same block, corner of Vine and Selma, easy to be in both places at the same time. Mr. Dragna thinks maybe you can clean them up a little, get a better type of clientele in there, people with more money. He says that if you do good like you have with the collections, like you did with the meat thing, a bit of initiative, a bit of creativity, you know, then there will be more opportunities. Take Tony Legs with you, Vince Caliendo. Take your two buddies. You guys seem to work well together."

Adamo reached for another cigarette from the packet and lit it.

"However," he said, "you gotta take it easy with the crazy lifestyle. I'm hearing things, you know? I got big ears and I listen good. You got some troubles around your house, some girls got hurt, right? Tell me that you're not the kind of man who likes to hurt a girl, Nicky."

"No, Mr. Adamo. Last thing in the world I would do."

"So who is this asshole who hurts girls?"

"Cousin of Tony Legs. His name is—"

Adamo raised his hand. "I don't need to know his name. I don't *want* to know his name. He's not in this picture, okay? He doesn't go in with you on this new enterprise. You do whatever you have to do. Speak to Tony. If Tony don't like it, then that's Tony's loss. He can stay with his crazy son-of-a-bitch cousin and you can find someone else to work with. I mean, I understand the need for people to get hurt sometimes, but that's the point right there, you see? Sometimes people do dumb things and you gotta teach 'em a lesson. Hurting some poor girl, putting her in the hospital . . . that ain't right, and I don't care where you come from."

"I understand, Mr. Adamo."

Adamo smiled. "I know you do, kid, and that's why we're here talking in my house. You may not be Italian, but you're a good listener, you do as you're asked, and you know when to keep your mouth shut."

Nicky kept his mouth shut, but he smiled and nodded respectfully. He had come into the business after both Tony Legs and Vince Caliendo, but he knew there would be no problem with him being given the clubs by Mr. Dragna. Tony and Vince weren't leaders, and weren't scared to admit it. In fact, one of the problems with Tony was that he didn't stand up to people the way he should. His asshole cousin was a fine example, coming over to the house, getting drunk, harassing some poor girl and getting violent when she told him she wasn't interested. Tony had gotten him out of there before Nicky really understood what had happened. Had Nicky known, he'd have beaten the cousin all the way to Christmas and back via the scenic route. That kind of bullshit got people's attention, and attention was never good, especially around your own home.

Anyway, the girl was dropped off at Hollywood Hospital, the dust had settled, and Tony had been told not to invite his cousin anymore.

"But nothing, Tony," Nicky had told him when Tony made a face. "He's family, sure, I get that, but we got more important business going on than keeping your family happy. He doesn't come back to the house, and that's the end of the matter."

Tony backed down. Nicky had a temper, wasn't afraid to let it go, and if you got in the way there would be all sorts of damage.

Since Bobby Danza there had been other shallow graves in the Hollywood Hills, and Tony Legs didn't want to be lying to his own family about what had happened to the cousin.

The incident with the girl had been two days earlier, and now Nicky was being offered a chair at the table. Maybe not the boss's table, but certainly in the same restaurant. Memories were short in this game, and it never served to remind people of what they'd forgotten. Nicky was twenty-six years old, had close to three grand in cash hidden in various places, no shortage of girls, a slick car, and now he was going to run some clubs for Jack Dragna. Life was getting better, moving in the right direction, for sure, and he never let himself forget that.

The downside was Lucia. Nicky knew that she and Frankie lived together even though they weren't married. He knew their address. He knew about the agency, the movie jobs she took, and even though it was like a hole right through his life, he could not bring himself to end the stalemate. Finding her could not have been easier. Dragna and his people had eyes and ears everywhere. Had he wished, it would have taken nothing more than a few words to have Lucia's agency closed down. A couple of union issues, some unpaid dues, and that would have been that. But the situation with Lucia was not about proving himself superior. Nor was it about revenge. The situation with Lucia was about principles, and sometimes you had to stick to your principles no matter how much it hurt.

Nicky had kept his word, and now her life was her own. He did his best not to think about it, to look to the future, and the Venus Lounge and the Starlight were definitely on the road to somewhere better.

"So, go do your worst, kid," was Joe Adamo's parting comment.

Back at his own place he explained the deal to Vince and Tony Legs.

As he'd expected, there were no complaints from either of them about Nicky being given the job.

"It's gonna be a good deal," Vince said. "This is the start of something big for us."

Nicky agreed. Since the killing of Paulie, the three of them had been pretty much inseparable. The South Coronado house had become their den, their headquarters, and even though both Vince and Tony Legs had their own places, the parties, the business meetings, anything that mattered, took place at Nicky's house. Nicky liked it; it established him further as the lynchpin of the trio. Even Joe Adamo, when talking to Nicky about Vince and Tony Legs, had started saying *your boys*. The business with the girl, this asshole cousin, Mo Vianelli, was both a distraction and a potential liability. If the girl wound up talking to the cops, if she remembered his address, the names of those present, then they might get interested. But then again, Hollywood was drowning in wannabe actresses who hooked on the side. Some of these girls were on so many pills they struggled to remember their own name.

The day after speaking with Joe Adamo, Nicky was home. A girl had stayed over, and not for the first time. Her name was Rita Morrison. Rita was no Hollywood dreamer. She was not some country girl out of Bohunk, East Nowhere, with a pocketful of bus tickets and a head full of dreams. Rita was tall and brunette and possessive of a sassy, self-confident attitude that sold people on her before she even smiled. And when she smiled she looked like a million dollars. Rita waitressed at a place up on West Third where Nicky sometimes had breakfast, and she'd spilled a half pint of orange juice down his shirt. The look of utter horror on her face had started Nicky laughing. Rita's expression had turned to dismay, confusion, bemusement, and when she realized that Nicky was actually laughing for real, she started laughing, too. The other customers wondered what the hell was going on. The boss rushed over, apologizing profusely, said he'd pay to have the shirt cleaned. He then started berating Rita, giving her a real headache, and Nicky had interrupted him.

"Hey, mister," Nicky said. "What's the deal here? You never had an accident? Give the girl a break, would you? She didn't do it on purpose."

Nicky went home, changed his shirt, came back to a promise of free breakfast for a week. On the third morning he'd asked Rita if she wanted to come make breakfast at his place instead.

"That would mean arriving real early," she said.

"Or arriving the night before."

"What kind of girl do you think I am?" she asked coyly.

"Kind of girl who spills orange juice on people."

"One time," she said. "One time I do that and now it defines my personality?"

Nicky liked her more every time he spoke to her, and he told her so. He also told her that not only did she seem un-Californian, but she didn't seem much like a waitress.

"Arizona born and bred, and I'm a singer," she replied. "Everyone here is something else. And everyone has two names. That's Hollywood."

"So, how come you're not singing?" Nicky asked.

"Annoys the customers, especially the Carmen Miranda numbers. Fruit salad falls off my head and it just goes downhill from there."

Nicky laughed. She was smart and funny, and she looked a little like that Lamarr actress in the *Algiers* film. There was a movie theater down the block from his house and they kept showing reruns.

"Okay, so I'll be a gentleman," Nicky said. "How about dinner? Let me take you to dinner, and then we'll talk about breakfast."

"I'm free tonight," Rita said, "and I'm already kinda hungry, so don't take me anywhere swanky that serves three shrimps and a slice of avocado and calls it a proper meal, okay?"

"Okay," Nicky assured her.

Three dinners, one nightclub, a drunken late-night cab ride to find another bottle of champagne, and Rita Morrison stayed over. She also quit waitressing. When Joe had spoken of the Venus and the Starlight, Nicky had already seen an opening for Rita. If she could carry a tune, then it would give her a bump to just get out there and sing.

So that morning, Friday, December 5th, it was Rita who called out to Nicky from the front bedroom.

"Nicky, there's a guy outside your house."

"What guy?"

"You know, I think it might be Henry Fonda."

Nicky walked through from the bathroom. His hair was wet, and he had a towel around his shoulders. "What the hell is Henry Fonda doing in the front yard?"

"No, of course Henry Fonda isn't in the front yard. It's some guy. How the hell would I know what guy?"

Nicky walked to the window and looked down toward the street.

“What the hell—” he started, but he lost his words before finishing the sentence.

“Who is it?” Rita asked, but Nicky was already out of the room and heading downstairs.

“Nicky!” she called after him. “Nicky!”

She heard the front door opening. The man outside just stood there, as if uncertain of his next move.

It was that hesitation, that almost indiscernible pause, that gave her the uneasy feeling that something bad had happened.

FORTY-ONE

Lucy remembered the last time she'd been in the hospital. Seven years old, her throat inflamed and swollen, her mother stricken with worry, her father methodical and matter-of-fact. The hospital had not been like this, but rather a small rural doctor's surgery in Cervione, a little more than four miles from San-Nicolao. She'd been lying in the backseat of the car, her mother cradling her head in her lap, her father driving, her mother urging him to go faster, faster as he navigated his way around herds of sheep that seemed determined to block the road. It was four miles, but it seemed like a journey to the other side of the island.

The doctor was nice to her. His name was Casta, and he told her that if she sat still and let him look at her throat, her mouth, her ears, then he would give her some candies to take home.

Lucia sat still. Dr. Casta examined her. He told her that she had glandular fever, that it was nothing to worry about. He told her that she would feel hot and tired, and maybe she would have tummy ache, but she should not be worried. He then gave her some candies, as promised. They tasted of aniseed. She did not like them, but she didn't say anything.

On the way back home her mother fretted about how and why Lucia had gotten sick. She asked herself what she could have done, who might have exposed her to this virus, whether or not she should stay home.

"That's enough," her father said. "She is a child. Children get sick. She will be fine. I don't want to hear any more."

Lucia lay there, her mother stroking her forehead. She could feel the worry emanating from her. She wanted to tell her that she was fine, that she really didn't feel bad at all, but she liked the attention.

Now it was different. Lying on a gurney in a small consultation room in the Hollywood Hospital, she was the one who was worrying. Frankie had been with her, and then they asked him to leave. The doctor who came was not like Dr. Casta at all. He was courteous but distant. He asked her questions, seemed impatient, frustrated with the answers she gave, and he wrote things down on a sheet of paper without explaining anything at all.

Then a nurse came. She was pleasant enough, but she seemed harassed and rushed by the endless number of patients that kept arriving.

"Understaffed," she explained to Lucy. "Ironic, but the head of department is sick and I am two nurses down. I am sorry, but you're just going to have to bear with us."

For what seemed like a small eternity, Lucy lay on the gurney in a hospital gown. She was cold, though outside the day was bright and warm. She did not know what was wrong, and no one seemed able to explain anything. She didn't feel dizzy or light-headed anymore. She was just thirsty. A second nurse came back, took her blood pressure, and then asked her for a urine sample. She stood there while Lucy did it, and Lucy couldn't ever remember feeling so awkward. The nurse took the sample away, and Lucy was left alone for another hour or more.

As she lay there she tried hard not to think the worst. She was afraid, no question about it, but of what she was afraid she did not know. That she had contracted some terrible disease, that she had a tumor in her head, that she was suffering from some wasting illness that would leave her incapacitated and unable to care for herself? If that was the case, would Frankie leave her? Would Nicky abandon her? What would she do? Would she end up back in Corsica, nothing more than a burden to her parents?

Lucy told herself not to be stupid. There was nothing wrong. She was dehydrated, perhaps. She was overtired, nothing more significant than that. Both of them had been working tremendously hard during the previous weeks, and it was bound to have taken its toll.

And then another thought struck her, and the emotion that accompanied the thought was strangely terrifying.

Lucy sat up. She pulled the hospital gown around her and shuddered. She did not like what she was thinking, but once she had thought it there was nothing she could do to drive it away.

That thought and all the attendant emotions—fear, excitement, disbelief—seemed to overtake both her mind and her body.

She got up, started pacing back and forth from one wall to the next within the confines of the small consultation room. She wanted Frankie to be there. She wanted Nicky. She wanted her mother.

She turned suddenly as she heard footsteps approaching the door. She held her breath. The footsteps passed. Lucy went back to the gurney and sat down again. She lay on her back, on her side, then she got up and stood against the wall and closed her eyes. She pressed the palms of her hands flat against the cool surface behind her. She breathed deeply, tried to focus her every sense on what was happening, willing it to not be what she thought, at the same time fighting her own instincts.

She thought about Freddie Fleck, the phone call, the movie role in *The Magnificent Ambersons*. She thought about Orson Welles, the way he'd looked at her, his commanding presence, the intensity of his eyes, how he'd made her feel almost transparent.

Footsteps again, and this time she knew that someone was coming.

She sat on the edge of the gurney, and sure enough the door handle turned and the doctor came back into the room.

He held a manila folder in one hand, a sheet of paper in the other, and on his face was a smile that said everything that needed to be said before he even uttered a word.

"Miss Madden. We have your results."

Lucy swallowed. She blinked, blinked again, almost as if she was in shock.

She knew the joy and elation she'd felt only hours before were going to be swept aside by what was now coming.

"Am I—" she started.

She looked up at the ceiling. She could feel the tears already burning in her eyes. She felt the overwhelming sense of something so very important, something so profound and meaningful being torn right out of her hands, and there was nothing she could do about it.

She did not want to believe what was happening.

"Miss Madden? Are you okay?"

Lucy looked at the doctor. He seemed different, somehow softer, friendlier, less distant.

"Okay, o-okay," she said. "Tell me . . . am I sick?"

The doctor smiled. "No, you're not sick."

"Then what? What is it?"

"There's no other way to say it apart from just saying it. You are pregnant, Miss Madden. You're going to have a baby."

FORTY-TWO

Hayes looked at the wiseguy smirk on the kid's face in the mug shot book.

Maurizio Vianelli. That's who it was. Mo Vianelli.

Associate of Vincent Caliendo. Hayes knew Caliendo, not only because he was one third of the two of Dragna's bagmen that had put Grigor Zakarian in hospital, but also because of his father, Gianluigi, up in San Quentin on an eight-to-twelve for armed robbery since July of '39. But there was another connection here, for Mo Vianelli was the cousin of another of the group, Anthony Leggiero. Could he also be this 'Tony Legs' of whom Bernice Radcliffe had spoken? Leggiero had come up on a protection beef a while back. Nothing came of it, but that didn't mean it hadn't happened. These people were all connected one way or another. So-and-so knew someone who was cousin to someone else, and his brother-in-law celled with some other asshole in such-and-such a prison, and they all met up weekends for beer and bullshit conversations about how they really had Los Angeles sewn up now that Jack Dragna and Micky Cohen were getting along.

And this house where Bernice Radcliffe had taken her three strikes may very well have been South Coronado. That was the only Spanish street name that Hayes could see near that end of Rampart.

South Coronado was a long street, and even if he trawled through housing records and rental agreements there was no way of knowing what he was looking for. The property could be in anyone's name, and more than likely had no documented connection to Vianelli, Caliendo, or Leggiero. Hayes went the route of the casting agency instead. He guessed this Erin Star Agency was a front for hooker services to the weird and wonderful of Hollywood. There were many such fronts, and there was no shortage of girls on their books. Erin Star was easy enough to track down, and as soon as he found the records of directorship alarm bells started going off. The name that came up on the title was Frank Madden. Hayes was all too familiar with Owen Madden, or Owney as he was more often called. Madden—Irish heritage, English-born, brought into America by his widowed mother and a prominent member of the Gopher Gang—was Manhattan. If this Frank Madden was a relative of Owney, then was New York trying to get a line into LA? Was Frank Madden brokering a deal with Dragna for his New York bosses? If so, then there was no doubt that this Erin Star Agency was a front for something.

Three phone calls and Hayes had the home address for Frank Madden. It was up on Santa Ynez, just across the freeway. He took a drive over there early on Friday morning. The house was innocuous, but what had he expected? A sign outside, *KEEP OUT—GANGSTER BUSINESS ONLY* perhaps? Hayes drove past the property a couple of times, then parked fifty yards away. He sat for an hour, maybe a little longer, was all set to head back to the office when he saw a young man leave the house, get into a car, and drive away. Hayes followed him, no clue as to whether this was Frank Madden or not, but just curious to see where he went. The coincidence stepped beyond the bounds of coincidence. The drive took him to South Coronado, and here the young man exited the car, walked twenty yards or so, and then stood outside a house for a good three or four minutes before a man came down and greeted him.

Hayes started writing things down. License plates, house numbers, dates and times. It was neat enough for church. Bernice Radcliffe is represented by the Erin Agency; she goes to a party on South Coronado, gets herself a good kicking from Mo Vianelli; Vianelli is connected to Caliendo and Leggiero; the Erin Agency appears to be owned by someone who could very well be connected to Owney Madden. Last he'd heard, Owney Madden had had to flee New York after his suspected involvement in an unsolved murder. He'd gone to Hot Springs, Arkansas, and had opened a club called the Southern. In fact, it was the Southern where Lucky Luciano had gotten himself arrested a few years earlier. Notwithstanding his physical location, Owney could very well be managing just as much as he did back in New York.

Hayes watched the Santa Ynez man and the South Coronado man, and all the while a woman looked down at them from an upstairs window. After exchanging some words, the two of them went inside.

Hayes waited for another half hour and then headed back to Central. Checking the South Coronado address, he found the name Nicolas Mariani. Mariani had no record, no yellow sheet, and Hayes was pretty sure he'd never heard the name before. From all appearances, this Mariani guy was a newcomer, but Hollywood was as much the El Dorado for cheap hoods from New York, Chicago, and Atlantic City as it was for the likes of Bernice Radcliffe. Hollywood was swiftly becoming a graveyard not only for dreams of fame and fortune, but also moral character and human decency.

Hayes had to make a decision. If Bernice Radcliffe was unwilling to file an official complaint against Maurizio Vianelli, then Vianelli was a dead end. If this Frank Madden character was in fact a relative of Owney, then New York seemed set on sinking its claws into Los Angeles. That did not bode well for anyone's future. As of this moment, there was nothing to pursue, but the congruence of events between a routine assault and a possible connection to Owney Madden had piqued Hayes's curiosity. It was something to keep tabs on, that was for sure, and he might take a drive over to South Coronado every once in a while just to keep an eye. Likewise, the Erin Agency and the Santa Ynez address were worth monitoring if there were no other priorities.

Whether any of it would amount to a hill of beans was unknown, but if half of police work was response, the rest was prediction. There was no argument. LA was a world apart from Cleveland. The guys there were players, no question, but they were Little League in comparison to Dragna, the Adamos, and Bompensiero. Hayes figured there were more shallow graves in the Hollywood Hills than there were coyotes to dig up the bones. Out here, this was the way of things, and things didn't look like they were going to change anytime soon.

All things considered, Hayes was not unhappy about his decision to come to Hollywood. Unhappiness was having your heart set on being a pianist and then losing your fingers. His emotional state, when he took the time to get in touch with it, drifted somewhere between frustration and stubbornness, certainly as far as his work was concerned. His personal life was another matter. He had a girl. More accurately, he *maybe* had a girl. She was neither singer nor actress; she was not a wannabe fashion model who'd hitched hopeful and hungry all the way from Poughkeepsie; she was not the usual arm candy that came five-for-a-dollar in the old-time speakeasies and juke joints down Sunset, Wilshire, and Melrose. No, this girl was anything but Hollywood. She was out of San Francisco, had a college certificate and a taste for European literature; she would listen to Russian classical alongside Fletcher Henderson and the Austin High Gang. Better than that, she had opinions. Opinions about everything. Her name was Carole Delaney, and their meeting had been fortuitous. Just as Hayes did not believe in coincidences when it came to the likes of Bernice Radcliffe, Nicolas Mariani, and this Frank Madden character, so he did not believe in coincidences in his personal life. Hayes was neither a fatalist nor a man of religious persuasion, but he did believe that there was something beyond the immediately tangible and perceivable world around him. Sometimes things just happened, and you had to accept that there was nothing you could do to control them.

It had been a couple of months earlier. He'd been downtown on a solicitation bust, chasing a lead that could have been something but rapidly turned into nothing. More often than not, tip-offs were based on hearsay and rumor, possessed the substance of smoke rings, and when you went after them they vanished faster than flies. Hayes was done for the day. He'd stopped at a store to get cigarettes. It had been late, maybe eleven, eleven thirty, and a woman in a cocktail dress was trying to get directions to a cabstand from the checkout guy.

"Problem here?" he asked.

The woman looked sideways at Hayes like he was just some other schmuck. She didn't respond to his question.

She asked the guy again, but the guy was Chinese. He knew prices, how to make change, but very little about cabstands.

Hayes asked again if there was something he could do to help.

The woman didn't reply.

"You know I can arrest you right here and now," he said.

The woman glanced back at him, her brows knitted.

"Statute fourteen, section five, subsection three, Harassment of Orientals While Under the Influence. This is a particularly serious violation because of the cocktail-dress clause." Hayes did the whole thing deadpan, even produced his badge.

"What the hell?" the woman said.

"I mean it, lady. You can't stand there looking as good as that, trying to make yourself understood by someone who doesn't even know his own name in English, and expect to get away with it."

"Are you really a cop?"

"I'm not just any cop," Hayes said. "I am a detective, first class, and my reputation has been built on busting shady dames like you for exactly this kind of thing."

The woman started laughing.

The Chinese guy was even more confused.

"I'm gonna have to take you in," Hayes said, "unless you can give me one good reason why you're out here late at night, on your own, giving this poor guy a headache about cabstands."

The woman turned to face Hayes. She really was pretty, and there was something about her that said right off the bat that she was no Hollywood hostess.

"I got ditched, okay?" she said.

"What did you do? You give him as hard a time as you're giving this guy?"

"You really are a comedian, aren't you?" she said. "Maybe you should get yourself one of those half-hour Friday-night slots at a club down Sunset. Get this stuff out of your system before you go to work, you know?"

"I'm off-duty."

"Then enjoy your time off, Detective First Class." She turned back to the Chinese guy.

"I'll take you home," Hayes said.

"Sorry?"

"It's late, you're alone, and even though I have no doubt you're more than capable of taking care of yourself, I'd actually much prefer it if you would let me take you home."

The woman smiled knowingly. "This is a line, right?"

Hayes shrugged. "What do you think? It's working, right?"

"No," she said matter-of-factly. "It isn't working at all."

Hayes put on a dejected face. "Oh well, can't kill a guy for trying."

"You really are a cop?" she asked.

"Sure I am," Hayes said. "You saw my badge."

"You can get those anyplace. Two bucks."

"Really? Shucks, I paid three for mine."

The woman laughed again.

"Detective, and yes, first class. Louis Hayes, Central Vice Unit."

"Carole Delaney," the woman said.

Hayes extended his hand. "Pleased to meet you."

They shook. The Chinese guy now seemed to understand that whatever was happening had nothing to do with him.

"So, you really want to give me a ride home?"

"Sure I do. I was a Boy Scout, lady. Gotta do one good deed a day. Otherwise I'll go to hell."

And so Hayes had driven her home, and en route they'd laughed some more, and she had told him she was out here from San

Francisco, working on a research project for the mayor's office cultural department.

"It's propaganda," she explained. "The war, you know? I majored in film studies, did history as a minor. They're putting together a team of people who can liaise between the War Department and the movie studios. If we get into this, and that seems pretty inevitable, they already know that cinema will be a powerful propaganda tool, not only for recruitment, but also for civic morale."

"You really are an academic," Hayes said, and then he caught himself. "Hell, that didn't come out the way it was intended."

Carole laughed. "And how was it intended, Detective Hayes?"

"I meant . . . well, you know, in this line of work the kind of girl who's out on her own at night in a cocktail dress is—" Hayes paused. "That isn't going to sound any better."

"You're in a hole. Stop digging."

"I will."

"Up here on the left past this stoplight," Carole said. "I live in those apartments."

Hayes waited at the light, then pulled over and switched off the engine. He got out, walked around, opened the door for her.

"First-class gentleman as well, I see," she said.

"You say that now, but wait until the citation arrives. Statute fourteen, section five, subsection three. Harassment of—"

"I got it, Detective Hayes."

"Of course, there is a way to get me to overlook such a serious and flagrant violation of the law."

"And what would that be, Detective? Don't tell me you want to take me to dinner or dancing or something, right?"

Hayes frowned. "Hell no. I was gonna ask you to come over and clean my house."

Carole smiled. "Yes," she said. "I'll go to dinner with you. I've been here three weeks and you're the first person I've met who doesn't qualify as misogynist, condescending, or just plain dumb."

And that had been that. Hayes had yet to find out exactly why she'd been dumped and deserted in a cocktail dress, and they were now at a point where it didn't seem to matter. Carole Delaney was a very smart lady, and Hayes didn't know whether to pinch himself or start going to church.

Four times he'd taken her out, and four times it had been really good. They made each other laugh, and they didn't run out of things to discuss. She was interested in his work, and he was fascinated with how Hollywood was going to put together a sales pitch for the war.

Next date was the following evening, Saturday the sixth, and sooner or later he was going to wind up at her place, or she was going to wind up at his, and then it would become something a great deal more significant.

That was what he wanted. He couldn't deny it, and he was trying so hard not to jinx it by trying too hard. If he wound up with someone like Carole Delaney, then he was a man more blessed than he'd believed.

For now, just until he saw Carole again, he would keep his head in the game, and that game was doing his job the best way he knew how.

Hayes looked over his notes about Bernice Radcliffe, Frank Madden, Nicolas Mariani and the South Coronado property, the other bits and pieces he'd picked up, and then filed them in a dossier all their own. There was something going on there. What, he did not know, and though there was nothing specific to investigate as yet, he sensed that there would be.

Given time, people always showed their true colors, and he believed that Frank Madden and Nicolas Mariani were colored very wrong indeed.

FORTY-THREE

Nicky Mariani could not conceal his surprise when he opened the door to Frankie Madden. His immediate thought was for Lucia, that something bad had happened, that she was sick, injured perhaps.

"Frankie Madden," he said. "What the hell are you doing here?"

"Hey, Nicky," Frankie said. "I . . . well, I—"

"Come in . . . Come in, man," Nicky said, and stepped aside.

Frankie went into the house, stood in the narrow hallway until Nicky had closed the door. Nicky then showed him through to the kitchen, and Frankie took a seat at the table.

"I came here to tell you something important," Frankie said. "Something about Lucia."

"And she couldn't come visit herself?"

"No," Frankie said. "Not right now."

Nicky sat down, his expression one of immediate concern. "Something's happened? She's sick, right?"

"No, Nicky, she's not sick. Not exactly, anyway."

"So what, then? What's happened?"

Frankie hesitated, perhaps still experiencing shock himself. He glanced toward the sound of someone coming down the stairs. Rita appeared, seemed uncertain as to whether she should head back the way she came.

"Make some coffee, sweetheart," Nicky said.

Rita didn't say a word in response. She gave Frankie a somewhat throwaway smile and crossed the room to the kitchen.

"So what's happened?" Nicky asked. "Why are you here, Frankie?"

"Lucia . . . Hell, Nicky, there's no easy way to tell you. Lucia is pregnant."

There was silence between them. It was the first time Frankie had actually said it out loud to anyone, and here he was, saying it to someone he'd hoped never to see again.

Lucy had known exactly where to find Nicky. This fact told Frankie that not only was she capable of hiding something from him, but that she would never be able to let go of Nicky. Both these issues were cause for concern, but they were not the priority right now. The priority was that he was going to be a father, that he and Lucy were going to be parents, that they would need to get married as quickly as possible, and that Nicky Mariani—irrespective of what business he was involved in, irrespective of the people with whom he was now associating—was going to once more be a part of their lives.

"Pregnant," Nicky said.

"Yes."

"And you're—"

"Yes, Nicky. I'm the father."

Nicky leaned back in the chair. He looked at the ceiling, at the floor, anywhere but directly at Frankie, and then he closed his eyes, took a deep breath, and exhaled slowly.

"You're not married," he said. It was a matter-of-fact statement, no hint of a question. Had his sister married without telling him . . . well, Frankie guessed such a thing would have been tantamount to declaration of war.

"No, we're not married . . . and that's why I'm here. Well, that's the second reason I'm here."

"You're getting married," Nicky said.

"Yes."

"When?"

"We hope tomorrow."

"Tomorrow?"

"Yes. We hoped to get a license and marry tomorrow. Apparently you can get what's called an expedited license. You have to pay more for it, of course, but it can be done, you know. And . . . and—"

"You want me to be there."

"Of course," Frankie said, and was not surprised at how easily the lie left his lips. *I don't want you there*, was what he wanted to say. *I don't want anything to do with you, because I understand what you're doing, Nicky. I understand who you're involved with and the kind of life you're living. It pains me to even see you, but I have no choice. You will be uncle to my child, and Lucia will never let me exclude you.*

Nicky rose slowly from the chair.

Frankie felt compelled to get up and face him. He did not know what was coming. Nicky had made no indication of his feelings.

"I don't know what to tell you," he said, his voice calm and measured. "I cannot tell you that I agree with what has happened . . . but it has happened. She's my kid sister, but I know you, Frankie. I feel like we grew up together, even though we've only known each other for... How long has it been? Three, four years?"

"Nearly four years," Frankie said. "We met in March of thirty-eight."

"But we went our separate ways in June, Frankie. I will never forget it. A stupid disagreement, a fight about nothing, and I haven't seen my sister in three and a half years." Nicky shook his head. "You have any idea how that feels, Frankie?"

Frankie said nothing. He thought of Erin, of Brenda and Deirdre. He thought of Clonegal and all that had happened to bring him to America. Most of all, he thought of Lucy, how they would be married, how they'd raise a child together, how his wife-to-be didn't even know his real name.

Was Nicky so much worse than he? Were they both not equally guilty of living a lie?

"It's been tough, Frankie. It's been really tough."

Frankie looked at this stranger before him. Nicky had changed; there was no doubt. He seemed sincere. The words communicated something with which Frankie could empathize, and yet he could not shake off the feeling that Nicky would lie to the pope if it would be to his advantage.

"We are going to be family," Nicky said. "You understand that, Frankie? You and I are going to be family."

Nicky smiled, and then he held his arms wide.

Frankie hesitated for just a second, but he did not believe that Nicky noticed.

They hugged, and Nicky held him tight, and he said, "You are a good man, Frankie, and even though this is all happening in the wrong way, I still believe it's right. I know you love my sister, and I know you will make a good husband."

Frankie didn't speak.

Nicky let him go, and then gripped his hand firmly.

"My parents should know. They should be here. This is not how my sister should be getting married, and she should not be marrying for this reason, but we cannot change reality, can we? Sometimes we are dealt a hand and we can do nothing but accept it." Nicky smiled. "Seems fate decided to throw us together, Frankie, and we never had reason to complain about that, did we?"

"No, Nicky," Frankie replied, and again the lie came so effortlessly.

"So, we go see her, yes?"

"Yes," Frankie said. "We go see her."

They went in separate cars. Nicky gave Rita money. He told her she could stay, take a cab home, whatever she wished.

Frankie led, Nicky followed, and they drove over to Santa Ynez. Pulling up and standing there on the sidewalk near the house, Nicky said, "This city kills me. We were so close all this time, and yet we could have been a million miles away. How does this happen in a place? How is it that people live so close to one another and yet no one connects?"

"I don't know," Frankie said. Was he surprised at Nicky's question? Not at all, because Nicky was all about Nicky. Lucia was in the wrong, as far as he was concerned, and nothing would change that viewpoint.

Before Nicky reached the door, Lucy opened it. For just a moment she and Nicky stood looking at each other, and then—without a word—they embraced. Frankie had the distinct feeling that his presence was unnecessary, but as he tried to pass Lucy, she grabbed his hand and pulled him close. There were tears in her eyes, in Nicky's, too, and she whispered, "The family is back together again."

"I am so sorry," Nicky said, and he gripped Frankie's arm and held on to him.

"It was my fault," Lucy said. "All of this was my fault."

"No, it was me. I was stubborn," Nicky replied, and Frankie knew both of them were saying these things solely to elicit a contradiction from the other.

"But it doesn't matter now," Nicky said. "None of it matters. We are back together, and that's the only important thing now."

Nicky let go of them both and stepped back. He looked her up and down, grinning from ear to ear. "You're going to be a mom," he said. "I'm going to be an uncle. This is amazing. This is just wonderful!"

Lucy started crying, and everything about her communicated a sense of relief. "I was so desperately afraid, Nicky," she said. "I was so afraid you would be ashamed of me and hate me—"

"Ashamed of you?" he echoed. "Hate you? How could you ever think something like that?"

"Because of what happened. Because of the fight we had. Because me and Frankie aren't married."

"No one need ever know," Nicky said. "You get married. We get a license and you get married, and then in a month or two we can tell people that you're going to have a baby. And we must get word to Mother and Father. We have to tell them."

"No," Lucy said. "If we tell them they will want us to go home, and I don't want to go home, Nicky. I want to stay here. I have work, you know? I can continue to work for several months yet, and then we'll—"

"We're standing in the street," Frankie said. "Let's go inside at least, eh?"

Lucy laughed. "Yes... Come in, Nicky... Come into the house."

The three of them went in, and Lucy busied herself with making coffee in the kitchen. Frankie and Nicky sat at the table, and while Nicky exchanged words with his sister, Frankie took note of Nicky's suit, his shirt and tie, the wristwatch, the gold cuff links. There was money, and a good deal of it. He did not doubt the source of that money, and he felt an all-too-familiar sense of unease overtake his thoughts.

"It's a shame we can't wait a week or two, you know," Frankie said. "I have just taken on two clubs. Nice places. Gonna make them a lot smarter, but they're pretty slick already. Up on Vine and Selma. We could've had a wedding party there."

"Well, we could always have a party later," Lucy said. "I just feel like we need to get married right away. That's the right thing to do."

"We could just do the City Hall thing, make it official," Nicky said, "and then later we could do a proper church service and have a reception and a real party, and—"

"We're going to keep it low-key," Frankie interjected, "considering the circumstances."

Nicky did not protest. "I understand completely."

"But we want you to be there for the marriage itself," Lucy said. "You have to be there, of course."

Nicky smiled, looked at Frankie, and Frankie knew exactly what was in his mind.

"Someone has to give her away, Nicky," Frankie said. "Of course I would ask you to be my best man, but you can't do both."

"Sure I can," Nicky said. "We can do whatever we like."

"Exactly," Lucy said, caught in the spirit of the moment. "We can do whatever the hell we like."

"So let's go now," Nicky said. "Let me take you to City Hall and I'll pay for this license that Frankie was talking about—"

"You don't need to do that, Nicky—" Frankie started.

"Let him do it, Frankie," Lucy said. "It's okay for him to help if he wants to."

"I'm going to give you both all the help you need," Nicky said. "You want money, no problem. You want to find a bigger house, no problem. Anything you want, you just ask." He turned to look at Frankie. "Okay, brother-in-law?"

Frankie nodded. He tried so hard to smile sincerely. And then he just sat back and watched Lucy and Nicky laughing together. It was clear—perhaps more so then than ever—that here was a bond that could never be broken. Three years of resentment and bitterness had been swept away in a second. Their differences were more than forgotten; it was as if they'd never existed in the first place.

On the surface, Lucy was happy, happier than he'd seen her in a long time. What Nicky did not see, and what no one but Frankie and Lucy knew, was the profound internal conflict that she was now experiencing. She had been given her greatest wish, and within hours that wish was all but snatched away. They had spoken of what she would decide—whether to pursue the role she'd been given, or whether she should step down gracefully. The doctor at the hospital had said she was slightly anemic, that she should take things easy, that all was well but it was early days and she had to be careful. Frankie did not know what Lucy would decide, and he knew that trying to influence that decision was the worst thing he could do.

If she took the role, she would have to tell Freddie that she was pregnant. Notwithstanding the fact that the picture company—intent on precluding any association with something so scandalous as a young, pregnant unmarried star-to-be—might very well refuse to take her on now, it would be unprofessional and disrespectful to withhold the truth from Freddie Fleck. If Freddie knew, Orson Welles would know, and even if he considered that Lucy was the only person to take the role, his decision would mean nothing against the wishes of the producers.

For now Lucy hid the storm of emotions she was experiencing admirably. Ironically, she perhaps gave the most convincing performance of her short career. Her fear that Nicky would be angry had proven unfounded. Beyond that, there was something that would tie them together with even greater force. A bloodline that could not be ignored or questioned, and if these people were anything like the Irish, then this would mean the world.

As the room was filled with laughter, with reminiscences, with plans for the future, Frankie Madden was torn in half. He loved Lucy, loved her as much as any man could love a woman. He was proud and excited at the prospect of being a father, and though he knew his own family could never be part of it, he felt somehow reconciled to this. It was a burden, but it did not weigh so heavy on his heart.

The weight on his heart came from Nicolas Mariani, and though Frankie had never been one to make decisions based on gut feeling or intuition, there was something altogether menacing and sinister about this reunion.

Something his father used to say came to mind. An old Irish proverb. *May misfortune follow you the rest of your days, but never catch up.*

Frankie Madden hoped with everything he possessed that misfortune had not at last found him with a plan to punish him for his sins.

FORTY-FOUR

The conversation happened that evening.

Frankie did not raise the subject. He waited patiently for Lucy to broach it.

"I've been thinking," she said.

Once again they were in the kitchen, seated across from each other at the table.

"About the best thing to do."

Frankie nodded, remained silent.

"The doctor at the hospital said that I was anemic, you know? Just a little, but that it was important to rest, to make sure I walked and got some sunshine."

Lucy looked down at her dinner plate. She had barely touched her food. "And to eat more than I do," she added with a wry smile.

"Lucy—" Frankie started, but Lucy raised her hand.

"I know what you're going to say, Frankie. I know I'm only one month pregnant, that there will be time, that the work won't be too stressful, but there's something you don't know."

She looked up at him.

"Something that even Nicky doesn't know."

Frankie didn't say a word.

"Before Nicky... before Nicky was born... our mother..." She shook her head and sighed audibly. There was some deep well of sadness in that sound. Frankie believed he knew what she was going to say.

"Before Nicky was born... well, my mother lost two babies. She lost two children, and both within the first few weeks of the pregnancy."

Frankie nodded slowly. He smiled sympathetically, reached out his hand to hold hers. "Just because your mother—"

"You're not a woman, and you don't have to carry our child," she said. "It breaks my heart, Frankie..." She looked up at him, and her eyes were filled with tears. "It really breaks my heart, Frankie, but when it comes to family you have to make sacrifices."

"But I honestly believe that—"

"I've made a decision and I believe it's the right one. Maybe nothing would happen. Maybe everything would be fine. But what if something did happen . . . ? What if the work was too demanding and I lost the baby . . . ? What then? Can you imagine carrying that around with you for the rest of your life? That you had a choice, and you made the wrong one and someone died."

Frankie knew exactly how that felt. He knew it twice over. He did not utter a word.

"I know this is our child, Frankie, but I'm the one who's pregnant, and so it must be my decision."

Frankie saw that flash in her eyes, the very same defiance that her brother possessed. Willful to the point of stubbornness, hard headed and immovable. It was that same intractability that had kept her from her brother, and now she was exercising it in her concerns for the unborn child. Frankie could see her viewpoint, but he didn't agree with it. He suspected there was yet another unspoken agenda concerning her career. If she didn't try, she couldn't fail. That same ghost haunted the air between them, and there was a sense of familiarity in the atmosphere.

"I understand," Frankie said, "and I respect your decision utterly. I'll speak to Freddie in the morning and let him know that you're no longer available for the film."

"Thank you," Lucy said, and then she rose from the table and went upstairs.

After a moment or two Frankie walked out into the hallway and stood at the bottom of the stairs

He could hear her up there, the unmistakable sound of crying, subdued and intermittent.

Frankie felt redundant, incapable of thinking the right thought or saying the right word.

He returned to the kitchen, started clearing away the plates and cutlery.

They did not speak of it again that evening, and when Frankie lay beside her in the bed it was a few moments before her breathing relaxed and she was asleep.

Frankie lay awake for some time. He thought about the following day, about the weeks and months to come, about the baby and how much would change.

As if dealing with Lucy's ever-shifting emotions was not enough, Frankie also knew he would have to contend with Nicky. Nicky

– once given Lucia's blessing – would work his way back into their lives, and Frankie knew there was nothing he could do to stop it.

Soon enough, Nicky confirmed Frankie's fears. Concerning the wedding itself, Frankie knew that whatever he might have wanted was not even going to be discussed, let alone considered. Citing the tradition that the bride and groom should not see each other on the evening before their marriage, Nicky spirited Lucy away to a hotel. Frankie spent the night alone, and even though he was no drinker, he drank anyway.

On the morning of Saturday, December 6th, two men arrived at the Santa Ynez house. They had to beat on the door to wake Frankie, and when he opened up they came right on in as if they owned the place.

"You're the guy who's marryin' Nicky's kid sister, right?" the first one said.

"Yes, I am," Frankie replied. "And who the hell are you?"

The man grinned and extended his hand. "Tony," he said. "Tony Legs. And this deadbeat here is Vince. We've come to get you straightened out."

"Straightened out?"

"Sobered, showered, shaved, suited and slick, my friend."

"It's okay," Frankie said, not for a second fooled by the friendly manner and evident enthusiasm. These guys were hoods, no doubt about it. Nicky's association with these people was the precise reason for the estrangement of the Marianis, and yet here they were—on the doorstep, in the house—telling Frankie how they were going to get everything arranged for the wedding. "I really don't need any help. Don't get me wrong, I appreciate it, but everything is under control—"

Tony Legs laughed. "Nothing is ever under control, my friend. Best laid plans an' all that. We're gonna help you out. Get you a good suit. We got the cars arranged and someone to take pictures an' everything."

"Really, you don't need to do any of this—"

"We ain't doin' nothin'," Vince said. "This is all Nicky. His kid sister's gettin' married. He only got one sister and he's gonna do right by her. Of course he is. Would be an insult to not let him do that much at least, wouldn't you say? I mean, if it was your kid sister that was gettin' married—"

Frankie raised his hands as if conceding defeat. "I understand," he said, not because he agreed, but because he knew that this would only get worse if he fought it.

Vince made himself at home in the kitchen, put coffee on the stove, helped himself to Danish pastries. Frankie went upstairs and took a shower. He shaved, got dressed, and then stood looking at himself in the mirror. He asked himself if he was going to let this happen, understanding that he really had no choice. If he wanted Lucia Mariani as his wife, then he took the whole package. Perhaps, had there not been a child, he might have had second thoughts, but responsibility alone forced his hand. His love for Lucy was challenged by her loyalty to her brother, and Frankie was right there in the middle. He could not have one without the other.

It was in that moment, faced by his own reflection, that he started to understand.

The child that he'd once been—forever full of philosophical questions, seeing the sky and asking what might lie behind it—had believed that there was a balance to all things. If not, then life did not make sense. Irrespective of the poetic lines employed, men had been saying the same thing for thousands of years. Reap what you sow. Lie down with dogs, you'll rise with fleas. The right hand giveth, the left hand taketh away. He had done wrong. It was not a matter of stealing coins from church, telling lies, taking the Lord's name in vain. It was a matter of killing people. Two men. Two innocent men. Dress it up any which way you could, it was still murder, intentional or otherwise. Did he deserve to be rewarded with someone such as Lucia Mariani? Perhaps, yes. Could that ever be unconditional? It seemed not. This was his penance, his test, his amends. Marry the girl; raise a family; keep them all honest and fair and straight despite the brother. Maybe God had in fact given him this test, and if he succeeded then there was some small hope of salvation for his eternal soul. He was Catholic-born, Catholic-raised, and he could never escape the church.

And so it was. He made his decision. It was all or nothing, and he chose it all.

Frankie Madden closed his eyes, took a deep breath, and went downstairs to speak with Nicky's friends.

FORTY-FIVE

When war finally came to American shores, it came like a hurricane.

The fire that rained on Pearl Harbor was a fire of unbelievable and epic proportions, as if hell itself had somehow been unleashed from the sky.

Within seven hours, attacks were carried out in Hawaii, the Philippines, on Guam and Wake Island, and against the British Imperial outposts of Malaya, Singapore, and Hong Kong.

The Japanese Imperial Navy launched two waves of fighters and bombers from six aircraft carriers. The US Fleet possessed eight battleships. Not one escaped without damage. Four were sunk, along with three cruisers, three destroyers, an anti-aircraft training ship, and a minelayer. The Japanese lost sixty-four men and twenty-nine aircraft. The Americans lost a hundred and eighty-eight planes, two and a half thousand men, and a further eleven hundred were wounded.

This was the news to which Mr. and Mrs. Frank Madden awoke on the first day of their honeymoon.

Frankie stood looking from the window of the Hotel Indio. Lucy was still asleep. The previous day had been a whirlwind, one moment blurring into the next, from the appearance of Nicky's friends to the final goodbyes. Everything from the license itself, which Frankie felt certain had been expedited with bribes, to the post-ceremony meal, the flowers, the photographs, the gifts, and the cars had been *taken care of* with an endless stream of ten- and twenty-dollar bills. And then they were in Palm Springs, a luxurious resort hotel more than a hundred miles from home, ferried here in a limousine by a uniformed chauffeur.

Lucy had been wide-eyed and speechless much of the time. She reveled in the attention. If she perceived anything amiss in the way her wedding day had been overtaken by Nicky and his friends, then she neither showed it nor uttered a word of protest. Frankie did not have the time nor the inclination to bring it to her attention. He rode with it, somewhat lost for words when he took a moment to think about what was *really* happening. He was marrying Lucia Mariani. He was marrying a girl he'd met in New York more than three and a half years earlier, a girl he'd never imagined would be his wife. Beyond all that, this girl was carrying his child.

Had he ever really believed that this would happen, that this could ever come true?

Frankie looked away from the window and back toward the still-sleeping form of his wife, and he closed his eyes and said a prayer. It grieved him that Erin and his sisters did not know, that his own family were oblivious to what was happening. Again, this was part of the test. He had to tell himself that. It was the only way to reconcile the conflicting emotions that raged in his mind and in his heart.

Lucy woke minutes later. Her first thought was to wish her new husband a good morning, her second was for breakfast.

"I'm famished," she said. "Absolutely famished."

Once Lucy dressed, they went down together.

The restaurant was almost full, but near silent. Faces were long, people looking at their untouched plates, intermittent comments ignored or acknowledged with monosyllables.

"What's happened?" Lucy whispered. "It's like a wake in here."

Frankie waved over the maître d', requested a table. As they were shown the way, Frankie asked why everyone was so quiet.

"You've not heard, sir?" the maître d' asked.

Frankie's lack of response was sufficient an answer.

"The Japanese, sir. There has been an attack against the American Fleet in Hawaii . . . about two hours ago, sir. Reports are varied, but it seems that we've suffered serious losses, both from the Fleet itself and many deaths. We believe that more than a thousand men have been killed."

The color had disappeared from Lucy's face. "Oh my God . . ." she said.

"Then we're at war," Frankie said matter-of-factly.

"There's been no statement from Mr. Roosevelt yet, sir, but we expect one very soon."

"And if we declare war on Japan, then their allies will declare war on us."

"Yes, sir. I think it's only a matter of time before we're sending our boys to Europe."

"You really think it will come to that?" Lucy asked. "I mean, it's thousands of miles away . . . Surely it can't go on much longer."

The maître d' indicated a table in the window. "Please," he said. "Let me take your breakfast order."

Frankie was satisfied with coffee and toast, whereas Lucy's appetite didn't appear to have been inhibited by news of the Japanese aggression.

Frankie watched her eat. He tried not to think of home, of those he knew in the south, but he couldn't help himself. He remembered de Valera's declaration of neutrality back in 1939, but he doubted such a thing would stop those who wanted to fight. They were Irish, after all, and they rarely waited for an invitation. With America drawn into this conflict, it was now a war for the whole world. He understood little of the politics, of this Adolf Hitler and his National Socialist party. Nevertheless, from his own brief and dramatic experiences in Ireland, he understood that when it came to territory and political convictions a ruthless lack of mercy started to color the thoughts of men. To prove themselves right, even when terribly wrong, there was little that some men would not do. Frankie could not deny that he was afraid—for himself, his wife, his unborn child—not only because he was once again involved with Nicky Mariani, but because the world complete seemed to have lost its mind.

"Are you really not hungry?" Lucy asked, interrupting his train of thought.

"I'm fine," Frankie said.

"You're upset by this news, aren't you? I am, too, of course I am, but I think this will all be over before they start sending Americans to fight. And besides, even if they did start sending them, it wouldn't apply to you or Nicky, would it?"

"No," Frankie said, and then another thought crossed his mind. Exemption from conscription on grounds of nationality would require documentary proof. He had documents, the very same documents with which he'd gained access to the United States, but they were forgeries. Sure, they had sufficed for the previous day's formalities, a cursory glance from a bribed city official, but for the purpose of exemption from military service? In such a situation the authorities would be particularly resolute and focused, especially when faced with the prospect of those intent on evading conscription. Replacement documents would be possible, but it would cost a considerable amount of money, and how would he find someone to undertake such a thing? Once again, Nicky Mariani. And to give Nicky such an inside view of his personal circumstances, to risk the possibility that questions might be asked about his whereabouts and activities before he arrived in the States . . . that would be too great a risk. No, he could not give Nicky any greater influence or information.

"Come back," Lucy said. "You've gone again, Frankie. Your wife is here and she wants to talk to you."

Frankie smiled. He leaned forward and took her hand. "I'm sorry," he said. "It's just all so much to take in. I couldn't be happier, Lucy. I really could not be happier in myself, but I worry about these things. I think the war will escalate, and I can't imagine what will have to happen to make it end."

"But it is there, Frankie, and we are here. All three of us. Until it reaches our doorstep it has nothing to do with us. We're starting a family, and as soon as our baby is old enough to be looked after I have to get back to work. I want a child. I am so excited about being a mother, but I still have my dreams. I want . . . I *need* to do that, too, Frankie, and if that's going to happen, then I'm going to need all the help I can get."

Frankie saw the same distant moment in her eyes. She did not want to know about the war, just as she did not want to know the truth about Nicky. They were together again, and that was all that mattered.

And if it had been Deirdre or Erin, what then?? If one of his sisters had been involved in some criminal enterprise, would he disown them? No, he did not believe he would.

Emotions, loyalties, obligations, promises made, they all came to the fore, and Frankie could see no way out but to move forward. This was now his family, and his family was all that mattered.

"You're right," Frankie said. "It's going to be okay. We're going to be fine. The war will end soon enough, and I doubt there will be any significant American involvement."

Lucy hesitated. She looked out the window, and then she turned back to Frankie. "Are you worried about Nicky?"

"Worried about Nicky? How d'you mean?"

"I can see it, Frankie. I'm not blind. I know you don't like him."

"I like him," Frankie said. "Of course I do . . . but I am not sure I like the friends he chooses."

"He's headstrong and impulsive, I know that," Lucy said. "He can be arrogant and stubborn, too, but I don't think he's bad. I think he's just—" She looked away again.

"Just what?"

"He's trying to make his mark, Frankie, like all of us. Isn't that what we're all doing? We're trying to make our mark, trying to achieve something, and I know you can't fight anymore, and I understand how difficult that must be, even more so now considering the decision I've had to make—"

Frankie was shaking his head before she finished talking.

"Okay," she said, "maybe I don't understand how difficult it must be because I never understood the need to do that in the first place."

"Are we having our first husband-and-wife argument?"

"We're just talking about Nicky."

"Nicky is your brother. He's the only brother you've got, and if we were talking about one of my sisters, then I would be saying exactly the same thing. We forgive too much when it comes to people we love, Lucy. Nicky is a good man, but I think he's taken the wrong direction. Maybe you don't want to look at it, but it's right there, Lucy. I know how easy it is to see only what you want to see."

"I haven't spoken to him in more than three years," she said, "and I needed him to be there for when we got married, okay? I need him to know that we're having a baby. He's going to be your child's uncle whether you like it or not."

"I know, I know, and I'm not trying to drive him away. I'm just being careful—"

"You think he's going to take over our lives the way he took over our wedding? Is that what you're afraid of?" Lucy smiled knowingly. "I know Nicky better than anyone in the world. Nicky's still the little boy he always was, and he'll never change. Yes, he can be a troublemaker and sometimes he can be spiteful, but he's not naturally bad. I don't believe anyone is naturally bad. We've all done things that we shouldn't have done. We've all done things we regret. Does that mean we should be punished forever?"

"No, of course not," Frankie said, all too aware of the fact that he had married this girl under an assumed name. Even though she'd been present when Bodak was killed in New York, she was completely ignorant of his history in Ireland. Daniel Francis McCabe was as much a ghost as Bobby Durnin and Frankie's namesake, Johnny Madden. And then there were those who had smuggled him into America, the fact that one day someone might appear with the words *I come from the Meadow of the Foreigner*. The truth was inescapable: More than both the Marianis together, he was guilty of hiding from reality.

"He's not going to take over our lives, Frankie," Lucy said. "He's excited. His sister got married. Nicky's spontaneous and generous, but he's also inconsistent and fickle. He'll be like a child at Christmas for a few days, and then we won't see him for a month. He'll show up for a first birthday, he'll spoil our child terribly, and then he'll vanish again. Don't worry about Nicky, okay? I can take care of him."

Frankie did not believe that, though he said nothing. Frankie did not believe anyone could control what Nicky did or did not do, least of all Nicky himself.

Frankie was now Lucy's husband, for better or worse, until death parted them. Lucy had taken him at face value, knowing nothing of Ireland. She had not hidden her brother from him; she had not lied her way into this marriage.

Once again—as if an echo of the past—it was Frankie Madden who was guilty of the greater crimes.

"Yes," Frankie said. "I know you can." He smiled and took Lucy's hand. "It's going to be fine. It really is."

FORTY-SIX

The Russians had pushed the Nazis back from the Crimea, but the winter war raged on without sign of respite.

US troops had landed in Ireland in January, much to de Valera's consternation. He said such an action violated his country's neutrality. Those troops, however, were not withdrawn.

From the West Coast of the States, a hundred thousand Japanese had been evacuated. Churchill and Roosevelt met in Washington. Jack Benny and Carole Lombard did their utmost to satirize the insanity of what was happening in Europe in *To Be or Not to Be,* but the brutal reality of a world at war could not be ignored.

The United States Army had established a Cinema Services Section. Capra had signed up. Darryl F. Zanuck, 20th Century's head of production, had resigned and was now serving as a colonel in the Signal Corps.

Frankie Madden worked hard. Lucy worked alongside him until her doctor urged her to rest. The Erin Star Agency sent extras and walk-ons to the sets of *Casablanca*, De Mille's *Reap the Wild Wind* and, ironically, *The Magnificent Ambersons*. Lucy did not speak of it in personal terms. She had never asked what Freddie Fleck had said when Frankie had told him she would not be able to take the role. That part had gone to Anne Baxter, and Lucy didn't say a thing about it.

The business was prosperous and financially sound. The war, it seemed, created an even greater demand for escapism and fantasy, and movie production did not slow as expected. Frankie routinely proved himself more than capable of holding his own in Hollywood. He was known, he was respected, and he was successful. Oftentimes he found himself in restaurants alongside Humphrey Bogart, Edward G. Robinson, and Barbara Stanwyck. He shared a cab with Johnny Weissmuller, met James Cagney when the agency provided a host of dancers for *Yankee Doodle Dandy,* and on one occasion received a half dozen bottles of champagne from Busby Berkeley's casting director for advising him on extras for *The Gang's All Here*.

It seemed like a lifetime since that morning in the Hotel Indio in Palm Springs. For the Maddens, soon to be a family, the world had changed in so very many ways. However, with each passing week, America was becoming as much a part of the conflict as the remaining allies. The world was truly at war.

And then, on Saturday, July 18, 1942, Lucy went into labor.

To some extent, Lucy had been right about Nicky. From their return home after the Palm Springs honeymoon to her admission at Hollywood Hospital that July morning, they had seen Nicky merely half a dozen times. When the refurbished Venus Lounge had opened in the previous May, Nicky had held an impromptu party for Lucy. By that time she was into her third trimester. Her pregnancy was pronounced and visible, despite her petite frame. It seemed that new clothes lasted no more than a week or two before they became uncomfortable.

In truth, it was not a party for the Maddens; it was merely a means by which Nicky could show them how successful he had become. It was a gathering of thieves and crooks, an entourage of court jesters and drunken knaves for the self-proclaimed King of Hollywood. Frankie had heard of Jack Dragna, and though Dragna himself did not make an appearance, he was introduced to a man called Joe Adamo, another one called Momo. To Frankie they appeared arrogant, as if entirely used to getting precisely what they wanted. Momo, specifically—heavy-set, his eyes cold and dismissive—gave off an aura of hostility and menace. These were the very people he'd feared. These were the people who would see Nicky Mariani dead or in jail.

Nicky and his friends became increasingly drunk and vociferous. Frankie and Lucy sat at a table to the side of the dance floor, waiting only for the moment they could leave without appearing rude or ungrateful. And leave they did, hailing a cab at the corner of Selma and heading straight home.

Unbeknownst to Frankie and Lucy, unbeknownst to anyone at the Venus that night, the comings and goings were observed and noted by Detective Louis Hayes of Central Vice.

FORTY-SEVEN

Hayes himself could not go to war. With missing fingers and the limp he acquired from the Marsolino standoff on South Olive, he was medically ineligible. Old Jimmy "Five Aces" was ineligible, too, having been caught once again with that fifth ace secreted somewhere about his person. Whoever did the catching also stabbed Jimmy through the heart. One knife, one puncture wound, one dead cardsharp. Italian he may have been, as patriotic as the next man, but while his brother, Salvatore, lost his life on the beachhead at Salerno as the Allies retrieved Italy from the clutches of the Third Reich, Jimmy gasped his last breath in a garbage-strewn alleyway near the Famous Five and Ten Café on South Main. Hayes had looked over the investigation notes for that case. It was evident that no one really gave a damn about Jimmy, and cared even less for who might have killed him.

As for Nicolas Mariani, Frank Madden, and the new Mrs. Lucy Madden, Hayes had learned little of great consequence. The Erin Star Agency seemed legitimate enough. There had been nothing to confirm or deny any relationship between Frank Madden and Owney Madden. Mariani himself was established at both the Venus and the Starlight. Both clubs were owned by mailbox companies, those companies co-owned by some other outfit, that outfit a front for something else. Aside from violating the 1934 Securities and Exchange Act, there was little to warrant a surveillance authorization. It was common knowledge that drug-trafficking, bank robberies, murders, loansharking, extortion, and prostitution were organized at these places, all of it under the aegis of Dragna and the Adamo brothers. Actually investigating such activities or taking any preventative measures was a totally different matter, however. Dragna's Los Angeles influence and authority stretched from Ventura to San Clemente, as far east as San Bernardino and Palm Springs, but—as with all such setups—proving that either Dragna himself or his underbosses and consiglieres benefited from any illegalities was nigh on impossible.

Discovering the connection between Nicky Mariani and the new Mrs. Madden had been straightforward enough, but a closer look into their past revealed the fact that they were not Italian, but Corsican. Knowing little of Corsica, Hayes made a brief perusal of its history and learned that this was the birthplace of Napoléon, Emperor of France. It seemed too coincidental to Hayes. He very clearly recalled the conversation with Simon Close in June of 1938, the mention of an overheard conversation in Musso & Frank's about a certain *Kid Napoleon* and someone who'd been taken care of in the Hollywood Hills. Had Mariani and the others killed Belotti? If so, why? It was another world of unanswered questions, the kind of questions that only found answers when some sorry sap was hauled in on a murder beef and gave up his compadres to get a better deal.

It was Hayes's undying interest in all things Dragna that kept him alert for the activities and associations of Nicolas Mariani. He knew that one day he would get Mariani in a chair, and there would be a yellow sheet between them. On that day he would ask him about *Kid Napoleon* and Paulie Belotti, and see if the arrogant smirk disappeared from his mean Corsican face. Meantime, the routine drug busts, brothel raids, armed robberies and killings would have to keep Central Vice occupied.

July of 1942, and Louis Hayes took a weekend away from the craziness. He and Carole Delaney had taken a weekend trip down the coast. It had cost him a week's pay, but he'd booked two nights at a hotel in Newport Beach, a concert at the Balboa Pavilion, late-night dancing, a speedboat ride out into the Pacific to see the flying fish, and maybe, just maybe, if the mood was right, he would finally produce the ring he'd been carrying around for more than a month and ask her to marry him.

The prospect scared him more than any standoff with Jimmy Marsolino. He was thirty-two years old, and since the break-up seven years ago that had precipitated his move to LA, Carole had been his first serious girlfriend. There had been dates, sure, but Hayes had known from the get-go that nothing long-term would ever come of them.

Carole was different. Carole was a keeper. So much so that a rejection of his proposal would be the death knell for the relationship. He couldn't have her say no and then carry on like nothing had happened. It was Vegas or bust.

On the drive down they talked of work.

"They'll need a great deal more pro-US propaganda now," she told Hayes. "Jimmy Stewart is already flying. We had him do that radio thing with Orson Welles, Edward G. Robinson, and a few others just after Pearl Harbor, and then that *Winning Your Wings* film as well. That aired in May, and we've got maybe a hundred thousand recruits already. They're pouring the coals on the USO, too, and I'm going to be involved in that. Cagney's in, and they'll get a load more on board. To be honest, I couldn't be busier. And I have to say that all the reservations I had about coming out here were completely unfounded. It's a great city, and I love the work I'm doing."

"Necessary work," Hayes said.

"Sure, but no more necessary than what you're doing."

"I don't have a big thing on my exemption, Carole," Hayes said. "I'm not in a funk about not going to war. And I don't feel guilty or that I've somehow avoided my responsibility. I'm a little more realistic than that."

"I know you don't feel bad about it, baby," she said, "but I worry about you sometimes."

"Why are you worried about me?"

"Because people can be assholes."

Hayes laughed. "Sure they can. What does that have to do with anything?"

"People say things. They make judgments. They give their opinion without taking the time to find out all the information. I hear it at work. So-and-so is a coward. So-and-so is trying to find some way to make sure he isn't called up. I mean, I know everyone has to register, but they have this lottery thing and the only way to make sure you're not called up is to be exempt. Rumor is that voluntary enlistment will finish at the end of the year, and that Roosevelt wants nine million men in the army by the end of next year."

"I still don't see what that has to do with me," Hayes said. "I'm a cop. I've been a cop for nearly twelve years. I have a finger and a half missing from my left hand, I got shot in the leg and I stump around the place like Quasimodo, and I don't think anyone is gonna suspect that I cut my own fingers off or shot myself in the leg to get out of military service."

"You do not stump around the place like Quasimodo," Carole said, laughing.

"Ygor, then. Like in *Son of Frankenstein*."

"Okay, sure. Ygor, then. I can see that. Except that Bela Lugosi is way more handsome."

"I gotta say that as girlfriends go, you're pretty harsh, you know?"

"You've had better girlfriends, have you, Detective Hayes?"

"All of them. Every one. You're pretty much the worst I ever had."

"Is that so?"

"Yep."

"Figure you must have booked two rooms for tonight, then, because you sure as hell ain't sleepin' in the same bed as me, mister."

With each wisecrack that left her lips Hayes grew ever more certain that here he'd lucked out. This girl was *the* girl. She understood the cop thing. She understood the late nights, the extra shifts. She understood the swings in temperament, and she just rode with it. They were way past the *I love you... And I love you too* stage; they had stayed over at each other's respective houses more times than Hayes could recall. There had been late nights, lie-ins, days doing nothing but enjoying each other's company, drive-in movies, dinners out, and all of this for the past nine months. Nine months didn't seem that big a deal, but they had clicked, no question, and Hayes had seen nothing in her manner or behavior to indicate she was any less enthusiastic about the relationship than himself.

But was it too soon? Guys at work had courted for three, four years. Would he just kill the simple joy of what was going on between them by throwing this into the mix? Maybe the last thing in the world she wanted was a husband. There was no way to tell what was going on in her mind, and the only way to find out was to ask her.

Louis Hayes and Carole Delaney arrived at the Hurley Bell, a mock-Tudor inn built to look like some ancient hotel in England.

Carole got out of the car and took off her sunglasses.

"We're staying here?" she asked.

"Sure," Hayes said. "Why, don't you like it?"

She grinned like a kid on Christmas Day. "It's absolutely beautiful, Louis," and then she turned and looked at him, held his gaze for just a little too long, her expression as implacable as Mona Lisa. There was a question in that moment, a question that went unasked and unanswered. Guys took girls to special places for special reasons. That was the truth, and Carole Delaney knew it.

Car parked, luggage ferried to a gorgeous room, their things unpacked, they stood together at the window and looked out towards the bay. The sky was clear and bright, the sun was warm but not overbearing, and Louis Hayes knew there was no such thing as a perfect time and that there'd never be a better time than that moment.

The box weighed heavy in his pocket, the ring within all set to burn its way out of the box, through the fabric, and drop to the floor.

"Let's take a walk," he said.

"Sure," Carole replied, and he took her hand and headed for the door.

FORTY-EIGHT

It seemed that with each passing day the heat grew more oppressive. Unlike home, where the breeze would find you around every corner, Los Angeles was like hell.

Doing her best to forget what had happened with the Welles film, Lucy threw herself into the agency work with even greater determination and commitment. Notwithstanding the relentless demands on her time and energy, she could not help but be affected by the steady stream of young actresses that walked through the doors of the Erin Star Agency. She saw them head off to Gower Street, to Culver City, to Goldwyn Mayer, and RKO. She watched as Frankie chatted with them, wondering if he was attracted to them more than he was to her, feeling an insidious sense of envy overtaking her thoughts. She forced herself to push such considerations away. People responded to her differently, even people she knew. Whereas a stroll down the street for lunch used to draw admiring glances and complimentary smiles, she now felt almost invisible. Men could see that not only was committed to some other man, but she was as unavailable as it was possible to be. It was utter craziness on her part, and she knew it. She had no more wish to be swept off her feet by some stranger than she had a wish to walk on the moon. That was not the point. There was a gulf between possibility and impossibility. That was the point. A wealth of possibilities were now impossible, and that did not only relate to her career. She had changed; she had become someone else; she knew it, and the world knew it too.

Despite all of this, Lucy knew her emotions were being dictated by her ever-changing physiology. The doctor had told her to expect wild shifts in temperament and mood. Apparently such things were commonplace during pregnancy. She knew it was all foolish. She knew Frankie loved her, was devoted to her, and the way he fussed over her, making sure she ate, that she never dehydrated, that she slept, was evidence enough that he wanted this child perhaps even more than she herself did.

Beyond all of this, there were the moments of guilt. The pangs of

What might have happened if...? when she thought about the role she'd turned down, the doors it might have opened, the opportunities that may have been presented. It was all pointless. She knew that. She could no more afford to waste her thoughts and energies on such things than she could turn back time itself. But she was a dreamer, a fantasist—always had been, even as a little girl—and it was so hard to forget the things she had wished into reality, to see that reality right there in her hands and then to have it snatched away.

She knew that Frankie understood, but they never spoke if it. To speak of it would only have made it worse. She struggled in silence, and she made the best of it.

Some nights, unable to settle, she would lie awake and be plagued with dark and terrible notions. What would have happened if she'd aborted the child in those first few heart-wrenching weeks? What if she'd never married Frankie? What would happen if she lost the baby? Would she be given another chance, another shot at stardom?

Sometimes she wondered if she shouldn't just flee back to Corsica and hide her shame from the world forever.

Sometimes she wanted to drink, just to blur the edges of reality, but she could not. To knowingly do anything that would jeopardize the well-being of the child would have been a mortal sin.

In truth, she did not do anything more than think such things. She neither spoke of them nor acted upon them, and she dealt with each new day as if it were her first, making the best of it, wearing a brave face, a braver smile, doing all she could to give Frankie no indication of the thoughts and emotions she was hiding.

The child would bring happiness. The child would bring she and Frankie even closer. She had sacrificed her career for this, and she prayed that it would be worth it. Whether it would be worth it she could not know until the child arrived, and once that happened there would be no going back. She would be a mother, and being a mother was a life and a world and a universe all its own.

Every once in a while she just held on to Frankie. At first he would ask her if she was okay. Now he didn't ask anymore. Now he understood that she just needed to be reminded that he really was there, that he wasn't going anyplace, that he was solid and permanent and committed to what was happening.

As if able to perceive her innermost fears, he would whisper, "Everything is good, Lucy. I am here. Always here. Not going anywhere. We're a family now, and that's the most important thing in the world."

She heard, she understood, but she had yet to believe.

She knew that for the rest of her life she would always look back and wonder what would have happened had the road taken a different direction.

FORTY-NINE

Frankie Madden had never been so scared in his life. Perhaps scared was the wrong word. He could not describe how he felt. He could hear his wife in the maternity room. It sounded as if her arms were being torn out of their sockets. The impulse to rush in there was overwhelming. The insistence by the maternity staff that he stay in the waiting area, that his presence in the delivery room would only make their work more difficult, was equally pressing. He was caught in the middle, pacing up and down, wondering how much longer, how much longer.

A little before three o'clock Nicky arrived. If it was possible, and it evidently was, his manner of dress was even more ostentatious. The suit he wore was two-tone silk, a deep blue that turned to dark brown depending upon the light. His shoes were rich burgundy cordovan wingtips.

"What's happening?"

"She's in there," Frankie said. "Been in there nearly three hours."

Nicky smiled. "Tough, huh?"

"Nightmare."

"Come, sit down," Nicky said, indicating chairs to the side of the room. "You want some coffee or anything, maybe something stronger?"

"I'm okay," Frankie said. "I just wanna know if everything is fine in there."

Nicky sat beside him, put his hand on Frankie's shoulder. "Of course it's fine. Hell, they've been doing this for years, for decades, and girls have been doing it since the beginning of time. It's gonna be okay, Frankie. There ain't nothin' to be worried about."

"I know, I know . . . but you can't help—"

"I understand," Nicky said. "So, you got any names figured out?"

"If it's a boy, Joseph. Joseph Saveriu Madden."

Nicky's eyes widened. He looked taken aback. "Serious?"

"Your father's name, right? Saveriu."

"That's a hell of a thing, Frankie. Jeez, I don't even know what to say about that. I am really touched, you know? That really has—" Nicky turned away, and for the first time since Frankie had known him, the bluff, overconfident facade dropped away.

Nicky turned back and there were tears in his eyes.

"I don't know what to tell you, Frankie. You have no idea how happy my father will be."

"And if it's a girl we were going to call her after your mother, but then—" Frankie smiled. "But then we figured Amandina Madden was a little... well, you know..."

"Too much going on there," Nicky said, laughing.

"If it's a girl, then we'll find a name and use your mother's name in the middle."

"Oh, this is something amazing," Nicky said. "Who would've thought, eh? That day we met in New York. You knocked those guys down in the street... Hell, I can't even remember their names."

"Piero Altamura and Frederico Cova."

"You got a good memory, considering how many times you got beat in the head back then."

"Not so many times. I gave as good as I got."

"Sure you did," Nicky replied. He looked sideways at Frankie. "You miss it? You miss the fighting?"

Frankie paused. It was buried deep, but that urge to wrap his hands, to pull on gloves, to get out there and fulfill an impulse with which he'd been born was still as strong as it had ever been. He had sacrificed it. He'd had no choice.

"Of course," he said, "but what's happening here is more important."

"Being a father, sure," Nicky said. "Ha! And I am gonna be an uncle!"

Frankie needed to say something. It had remained unspoken ever since Nicky had walked back into their lives, and it needed to be voiced.

"We got a family now," Frankie said. "There's not just Lucy now. There's me and there's gonna be a child, and we've got a good thing going. You know, with the casting agency and all that, and when Lucy is able to she's gonna go back to work. She wants to act, and I know she can do really well, and I want to do everything to support her."

Nicky was nodding in agreement. "Sure, Frankie, like me. I wanna do everything to support her as well... to support you and my niece, nephew, whatever, right?"

Frankie took a deep breath. He didn't know if what he was saying or what was happening in the adjacent room troubled him more, but the moment was here and he could not postpone it any longer.

"The thing is, Nicky—"

Nicky frowned. "What's going on? What you tryin' to say?"

"I need to talk to you man-to-man. I need to tell you what's going on in my mind. I mean, it's great to have you here. It means a lot to me, and Lucy would be devastated if you weren't part of this—"

"Her name is Lucia. Her name is Lucia, not Lucy."

Frankie was all too aware of the mounting tension between them. He had known all along that this would not be an easy conversation. This would fly right into the teeth of Nicky's egotism and self-importance. Push him the wrong way and he became resolute and immovable, unable to see sense, unable to maintain any kind of rational dialogue.

"Spit it out, Frank," Nicky said, his tone harder, a little more aggressive.

"The truth," Frankie said, "is that you have gotten yourself involved with some tough people. I know who was there at the club back in May. I know who the Adamo brothers are, and I know they work for Jack Dragna—"

"Well, we can stop this right here and now," Nicky interjected. "I come down to your place of work and tell you who you should and should not associate with? Is that what I do? No, I fuckin' don't, and you got no right to tell me how I live my life. What gives you that kind of authority, huh? You think that because you're married to my sister, because you are gonna have a kid with her, you can dictate to me what I can and can't do? Sure as hell it might work that way wherever the hell you come from, but it don't work that way with me."

Frankie knew he'd have to backpedal; that was the only way to avoid an impasse.

"You're right," Frankie said. He leaned forward, his elbows on his knees, his head down. "That all came out wrong, Nicky, and you're absolutely right." He turned and looked at his brother-in-law. "I have no right to tell you anything. I get it. I'm sorry, okay? It's just that I made a decision not to fight anymore, and that decision was because of Lucia. I want to be the best husband and the best father I can be, and hauling around derelict basement and disused parking lots trying to knock the sense out of someone for a hundred bucks . . . well, that didn't seem like the best thing to do for either of them—"

"You're asking me to keep my work and my personal separate," Nicky said. "Is that what you're saying? That maybe I got some connections that ain't so . . . well, let's just say that they ain't the kind of guys you'd have over for dinner. Maybe a little rough around the edges. You want me to keep these guys on their side of the fence, right?"

Frankie sat up, looked Nicky directly in the eye. "Exactly," he said. "It's for Lucia, for the kid. I don't give a damn what you do or who you do it with. None of my business. It's just . . . well, like you said, there's—"

Nicky raised his hand. "You said all you needed to say. I understand. You're an honorable man, Frankie, and I respect that. You have my word that my business will not become part of your life."

Nicky extended his hand, and they shook.

It was a halfway measure. It was a compromise. What Frankie wanted to hear was that Nicky himself would not be a part of their life, but that was too much to ask. Lucy would not let that happen. He also understood that Nicky was a smart guy. He had seen Frankie's olive branch and taken it. He did not want a standoff. Perhaps there was some small doubt there, an uncertainty of the decision Lucia might make if forced to choose between her brother and her husband.

"So, all is good, my friend," Nicky said, and he reached out to grip Frankie's shoulder.

"All is good," Frankie replied.

"So we wait," Nicky said.

"We wait."

Whatever else they might have said in the subsequent hour was meaningless and unimportant. Frankie paced; Nicky watched him. Nicky then started pacing himself. The girl Frankie had seen at the South Coronado house showed up. Frankie didn't remember her name until reminded. Rita Morrison. Frankie said he wasn't hungry, but Nicky still sent Rita out for sandwiches.

By the time she returned, neither of them had a thought for sandwiches or anything else.

At 4:18 that afternoon, Lucy Madden gave birth to a son. He weighed in at seven pounds and nine ounces.

The maternity nurse fetched Frankie from the waiting area. Frankie looked at her, looked back at Nicky, looked back at the nurse.

"Go, go, go!" Nicky said, laughing.

Frankie nearly knocked the poor woman down as he rushed through the door.

Lying there, her dark hair pulled back from her forehead, her face florid, her features both energized and exhausted, Lucy looked beautiful. She smiled at Frankie, reached out her left hand toward him, and he stepped around the side of the bed and looked down at her.

The baby in her arms was the most beautiful thing he'd ever seen.

"This is Joseph," Lucy said, her voice cracking with emotion. "Your son."

Frankie's eyes filled with tears. He reached out his hand and stroked the baby's forehead. The baby moved its tiny arm, its mouth opened and closed, and Frankie was utterly speechless.

Lucy looked down at her son. "Joseph . . . this is your daddy. He's a crazy Irishman, but I love him so much. He used to be a fighter, but the only thing he'll fight for now is to make us happy."

Frankie sat down on the edge of the bed.

He leaned forward and kissed his wife. "I love you so much," he whispered.

"I love you, too."

Lucy looked up then at the sound of the door, and she smiled so wide.

"Nicky!" she exclaimed.

"Got room in here for an uncle?"

Lucy did not see it, but just for a moment Frankie clenched his fists.

Nicky was there at the side of the bed, leaning down to kiss his sister on the forehead, and then he looked at the baby and said, "Oh man, he is beautiful . . . so fucking beautiful—"

"Nicky," Lucy said.

"I'm sorry," Nicky said. "It's just incredible though, isn't it? You're a mom, and Frankie here is a dad, and we got ourselves a real honest-to-God family."

"And you're Uncle Nicky now," Lucy said. "So when he's broke and needs some quarters, he's gonna come asking for you, okay?"

"Fine by me," Nicky said. "Kid's gonna get spoiled something terrible. And you wanna know something else? You wanna know something incredible? I'll tell you now, no word of a lie . . . Joseph here has got the same birthday as Napoléon V. I studied it. I looked it all up. No such thing as coincidence, right? It's an omen."

Nicky reached out and gripped Frankie's arm. "Your son here... gonna shake the world, eh? He's gonna shake the world, Frankie Madden... You wait and see."

"Sure he is," Frankie said, and he looked at his wife and his son and felt as if a shadow had been cast across his life.

This moment, the greatest moment of his existence, could not be enjoyed for simply what it was.

This was his penalty, how he would make amends for the sins of the past.

He wondered then if the debt he owed would ever be repaid.

FIFTY

That night, lying awake in the luxurious bed at the Hurley Bell, Louis Hayes cursed himself for not asking the question.

The ideal moment had presented itself more than once that evening, but he'd hesitated, and the moment had passed.

If Carole had been aware of what was going on, she gave no indication. They'd had a great evening, a wonderful dinner, listened to music at the Balboa, walked back along the harbor as the sun set, the hubbub of voices from the seafront restaurants and bars, the sound of boats coming in from the Pacific, and just for a while it really felt as if Los Angeles and the war and all else was so very far behind them.

And yet he had still not asked her.

Hayes knew it was cowardice. He knew it was simply his own fear of rejection. Anxiety was born out of questions that had no immediate or predictable answers, and here the wrong answer would take from him the only thing that really made him happy. Without Carole, there was Jack Dragna and Joe Adamo and Micky Cohen and the rest of the lowlifes and bottom-feeders that populated the dark underbelly of his city. Without Carole, there was his own apartment—functional, uncluttered, a little cramped, no better or worse than a room in any of a dozen city hotels.

Hayes turned and looked at the clock on the nightstand. It was a little after two, and he just wanted to sleep. He was not prone to insomnia, certainly not as a routine occurrence, but tonight he was angry with himself. If he did not ask, she could not say no. That was the simplicity of it. However, if he didn't run the race, he couldn't win.

"Lou?"

Hayes closed his eyes.

"Louis . . . I know you're awake, so stop pretending you're asleep."

Carole switched the lamp on. She hauled the pillow out from beneath her head and put it behind her as she sat up.

"Hey," she said. "Wake the hell up."

Louis rolled over and looked up at her.

"Sit up and talk to me," she said.

"You were asleep," he replied. "I'm sorry I woke you."

"I wasn't asleep. Not properly. I can just feel you all restless and agitated, and I want to know what's wrong."

Hayes turned over, leaned up on his elbow. "Nothing's wrong," he said.

"Well, something's not right."

"I just have a lot on my mind, Carole."

"Work stuff?"

"Yes, work stuff. Ongoing cases."

Carole slid out of bed and padded toward the bathroom. She put the light on, filled a glass with water from the sink, and then stood in the doorway for a moment. Hayes could see the silhouette of her body through the sheer nightdress.

"You want some?" she asked.

"Sure," he said.

Carole switched off the bathroom light and came back to bed. Hayes sat up and took the glass.

"So, what's happening?" she asked.

"The war, I guess," Hayes said. "Two situations, as far as we can see. Times of conflict there's always a surge in the black market. People get nervous and stockpile things. And the other thing is this lottery draft thing is being ramped up. Estimates are that one in five will be called up, not one in nine like it is now. LA's problem is that we've got so many immigrants. All of a sudden you got a problem of Italians being a threat to national security. They've got some detained in war relocation camps under the Alien and Sedition Act—"

Carole was frowning at Hayes.

"What?" he said.

"That's what's keeping you awake?"

"Well, what we're predicting is that they won't draft the Italian-Americans, and all we're gonna be left with in LA is gangsters. City's gonna be taken over by Dragna's mob while all the good citizens are over there taking Italy back from the Nazis. Kinda ironic, don't you think?"

"You are so full of crap, Louis Hayes."

"What?"

"That is not what you're worried about. That is not what is keeping you awake."

"And you know this because?"

"Because I know you, Louis. I know all about what goes on in that pea brain of yours."

"Pea brain?"

"Yeah, pea brain. That's what men have. Some of them it's a little smaller, but never bigger than a pea."

"You sound like one of those dreadful women's rights people. What are they calling themselves... feminists? Giving you people the vote was just lunacy."

"You think so?"

"I *know* so, lady."

Carole dipped her fingers in Hayes's glass of water and flicked them at his face.

"So childish," he said. He started laughing, couldn't help himself.

"Be that as it may, Detective... now you have to tell me the truth."

"The truth," he said matter-of-factly, "is not only a relative concept; it is wholly subjective."

"Mmm," Carole said. "So now we're using some sort of philosophy-based evasion strategy, are we?"

"Evasion strategy? What are you talking about?"

"We're talking about you being all preoccupied and distant, something troubling you, something on your mind, and then lying to me with some nonsense about how Los Angeles is going to be populated by nothing but Italian-American immigrant gangsters and black marketeers."

Hayes was smiling. "You really are annoyingly sure of yourself sometimes, aren't you?"

"Absolutely," Carole replied. "Give us the vote and Lord knows what's going to happen. We're going to start thinking for ourselves, having opinions, saying things out loud even when we're not asked. It's just a wretched, wretched mess, and there's every indication it will only get worse."

Hayes took a deep breath and sighed. "There has been something on my mind," he said.

"You don't say?"

"No, seriously, Carole... there has been something important on my mind, and it's not something I want to talk about right now."

"Well, we're talking about it, Louis, so that bird has flown."

Hayes turned away and sat up. He sat on the edge of the bed, his back to Carole.

She shifted over, put her hand on his shoulder. "Hey," she said. "What is it, sweetheart? Are you sick or something?"

Hayes shook his head. "No, not sick. Not exactly."

"Look at me," she said. She moved over and sat beside him, held his hand. "Tell me what's going on."

"Sick... kind of," he said. "But just with worry, you know? I've just been really worried about something, and it's something I've created and I've just kind of made it up out of thin air, and it wasn't something that even needed to exist, but here it is."

"That doesn't make any sense at all unless I know what you're talking about," Carole said.

Hayes didn't respond. He went to move, and Carole grabbed his arm.

"No," she said. "We're talking about this, Louis. If this is what I think it is, then you just need to say it."

He turned and looked at her. He smiled. "I don't think you could guess what this is about, Carole."

"Try me," she said.

"We... well, you know, we have..." Hayes sighed again, tried to smile but struggled with it.

"We have what?" Carole prompted.

"We've been seeing a lot of each other," he said.

"Good observation," she replied. "That must be some of those famous LAPD hotshot detective skills at work right there."

Hayes frowned. "Carole, seriously..."

"Carole, seriously what, Louis? Jeez, anyone'd think this was some comedy of manners. Say what you want to say, Louis, for Christ's sake. I'm all grown-up. You think I can't deal with it? If you tell me you're gonna break up with me, then do it. I'll wallop you, but at least it's done and I can get over it."

"No, Carole... it's nothing like that."

Carole just looked at him, looked right *through* him.

Hayes cleared his throat, took a deep breath, and said, "This is difficult, and I don't want to make a mistake."

Carole held his hand. "Most problems in life are solved with twenty seconds of bravery."

"Do you know what I'm going to say?"

"I have an idea... but I can't say it for you."

"I'm not asking you to say it for me... I just wondered whether you had—"

"You're irritating me now, Louis. If you don't say what's on your mind I'm gonna break up with you."

Hayes paused, took a breath. "Carole... I love you. I love being with you. These past months have meant the world to me, and I don't want it to ever change. But I can't go on just hoping that we'll stay together. That's not how I am. That's not the kind of person I am. And so—"

Hayes got up, crossed the room to the wardrobe, and reached his hand inside.

Carole just watched him without uttering a word.

Hayes's expression turned rapidly from expectation to anxiety.

"It's in the drawer in your nightstand," Carole said matter-of-factly.

"What is?"

"What you're looking for, Louis. You took it out of your jacket and put it in the nightstand."

Hayes withdrew his hand from where he'd been searching the pockets of his clothes.

He stood there looking at her, and then he shook his head. "You are unbelievable," he said quietly. "You put me through all of this and you knew what was going on all the time."

"For about two weeks, Louis. You aren't exactly difficult to read."

"So you know what I'm going to ask you?"

"Sure I do, but that doesn't mean you don't get to ask me."

Hayes walked back to the nightstand. He took the box from the drawer and opened it.

He sat beside her, took the ring out, and looked at her.

"Carole . . . will you marry me?"

She shook her head slowly. "Not until you do it properly, Louis."

"What?"

"Do it properly. Down on one knee like my valiant knight."

Hayes didn't argue. He got down on one knee. He held out the ring.

"Carole—"

"Yes, Louis Hayes. I will marry you."

Hayes looked shocked. "Seriously?"

"No, I'm kidding. What the hell d'you think? Jeez, almighty. Men. What the hell is wrong with you people?"

"Pea brains," Hayes said.

"Hell yes, I forgot. And no, I am not kidding, Louis. I will marry you."

Hayes got up off his knee. He sat beside her. His heart was pounding, his mouth was dry, and his hands were sweaty.

"Are you going to go back to being a normal human being again now?" Carole asked.

"As fast as I can," Louis said, and he put his arm around her shoulder and pulled her close.

"Love you, Louis," she whispered.

"Love you more," he replied.

"Don't start," she said.

Hayes smiled, pulled her closer. "Yes, Mrs. Hayes."

FIFTY-ONE

A sailor with a walking cane, probably more drunk then he'd ever been in his life, weaved back and forth between cars gridlocked along Hollywood and Vine. He kissed every girl he saw. Those who resisted his drunken advances got kissed anyway.

Open-tops spilled people out onto the road, the seats and running boards quickly taken by others, all of them singing, laughing, cheering, waving newspapers above their heads, the banner headline shouting *PEACE!*

The road and the sidewalk were carpeted with ticker tape, and still the ticker tape kept falling. Horns blared, a soldier with a bugle tried to play jazz riffs but they sounded like strangled versions of "Echo Taps" and "Reveille." He gave up and climbed a streetlight, his overseas hat perched sideways on his head.

Past Lloyds and Chapeaux De Mode the drunken sailor went—on past a movie theater showing Greer Garson and Gregory Peck in *The Valley of Decision*, the title board announcing *Latest War News* right beneath the movie title—until he just stopped right in the middle of the street and started singing. What he sang no one knew or cared. Overloaded cars inched past him, girls throwing their arms around his neck, guys handing him bottles from which he swigged heartily.

The war was over. August 14, 1945, Truman's announcement sending people from offices, stores, and homes in their thousands, and it seemed that everything capable of making a sound was employed in one great roar of celebration that would more than likely have been heard in San Francisco. Car horns, whistles, sirens, trumpets, bugles, a trio of saxophonists in zoot suits playing "Chattanooga Choo Choo" outside the First Federal Savings. Three soldiers, their caps reversed, were linked arm in arm and danced out of step and out of time like drunken marionettes. The one in the middle stumbled and brought the trio down in a heap on the sidewalk, and they couldn't get up for laughing.

Nicky Mariani and his friends came down from the Venus Lounge. Louis Hayes drove as far as Fountain and could get no farther; he parked, walked to Sunset and stood there wide-eyed as a sea of people surged down every street and boulevard. He had never seen or experienced anything like it in his life.

Frank and Lucy Madden, their son, Joe, in Lucy's arms, looked down from their office window at the throngs of people, and for a little while everything else became unimportant.

Not a word was spoken of Hiroshima, of Nagasaki, of the whirlwind of hell they'd unleashed to bring the Japanese to their knees. Memories of the Jewish ghetto slaughters and the concentration camps would be eternal, and the sheer disbelief at how fifty-five million people could have lost their lives would pose questions never to be answered, but today, tomorrow, next week, and for the months leading up to Christmas, there was nothing but profound joy on everyone's faces.

By the time the end of hostilities finally arrived, Joseph Madden had celebrated his first three birthdays.

Louis Hayes had married Carole Delaney in his hometown of Pittsburgh on September 8, 1943. It was the same day the Italians signed an armistice with the Allies. Hayes's father told Carole exactly how her new husband had lost his fingers and thus his dream of playing the piano. Hayes's mother was beside herself. Her only child had not gone to war, and now he was married to a smart and beautiful girl, the pair of them still young enough to give her some grandchildren. For that day and several subsequent days, honeymooning in Wildwood, south of Atlantic City, Louis Hayes had forgotten about the war in Europe, even forgotten about Dragna, Cohen, and the Adamo brothers. It was a rare and special time, and there was no question in his mind that marrying Carole Delaney was the smartest thing he'd ever done.

Nicky Mariani had risen in the ranks of the Dragna family. No one ever spoke of his true nationality and heritage. Nicky now managed more than a dozen clubs and bars, and already his influence and reputation as Kid Napoleon was taken seriously. With Vince Caliendo, Tony Legs, Bomp, Jimmy Frat, and a host of others, Nicky had seen so many things change. With the indictment of Capone's people in March of '43, the charges brought against them for extorting two and a half million dollars out of the Cinema Technicians Union, it was ever more real to people that organized crime had its claws sunk deep into Hollywood. But people were fatigued with bad news. They wanted Hollywood to give them back the magic, and when the *Motion Picture Herald* polled their readers in May and found a unanimous wish for no more war films, only films that would distract and entertain, Hollywood listened. Clarence Brown gave them an eleven-year-old Liz Taylor in *National Velvet*, and Capra delivered *Arsenic and Old Lace* with Cary Grant and Priscilla Lane. Chaplin had a daughter, Kirk Douglas had a son, and Olivia de Havilland won a landmark Supreme Court ruling that changed the way studio players' contracts would be written forever.

Nicky had never been conscripted; nor had his name ever appeared in any lottery list or mandatory call-up register. The war was someone else's, and he did everything he could to keep it that way. Nevertheless, it did not stop him celebrating the Allied invasion of Italy and the capture of Palermo. He too had raised a glass when Mussolini and Clara Petacci were hung by their heels from a gas station facade in the Piazzale Loreto in Milan. However, it was only he and Lucy who kept themselves informed of what was happening at home. When twelve thousand German troops had arrived on Corsica in July of 1943, Lucy had to beg her brother not to leave immediately. She knew that he would very likely never return. She told him to be patient, that things would change rapidly. She was right in her estimation of the situation. The uprising began within a month. The French I Corps landed by submarine near Piana on the northwest coast. Alongside Corsican partisans and both the Italian 44th and 20th Infantry divisions they engaged the Sturmbrigade Reichsführer SS and the 90th Panzergrenadier Division. The Italian 12th Parachute came from Sardinia, retreating through Corsica toward Bastia. The Free French 4th Moroccan Mountain Division landed in Ajaccio, and during the night of October third, the Germans knew they could not hold the island, and the last units were evacuated to northern Italy.

Lucy was desperate for word of their parents, but she knew that obtaining such would be impossible for days, if not weeks. She, too, had to be patient, convincing herself that they were okay, that they had survived.

Through the last year of the war news came of the turning tide. Montgomery in El Alamein, the German surrender in Stalingrad, the routing of Rommel's Afrika Korps in the Kasserine Pass, the Kursk tank battle, the Normandy invasion, the liberation of Paris, finally the suicide of Adolf Hitler and the surrender in Rheims. It was only in the Pacific that America remained at war, her troops suffering the last desperate acts of the Japanese in their efforts to bring down the might of the capitalist United States.

With the launch of the *Enola Gay* and the dropping of Fat Man on Nagasaki, it was all over. Hirohito surrendered, MacArthur received a Japanese delegation on the *Missouri*, and the Russians invaded Manchuria.

It was only then that word came from Corsica. Saveriu and Amandina Mariani were alive and well. The profundity of Lucy's relief was matched only by the depth of loss she felt in not seeing her parents.

It seemed that her life, perhaps that of Frankie's, too, was a chain of emotional battles, one after the other with no respite in between. At least she was reassured with the news of her parents, whereas Frankie had no such news and could not even unburden the pressure he felt by discussing it with his wife.

The temptation to make some inquiries after his own family, to make some phone calls, send some telegrams, was nearly overwhelming, but he knew that opening such a door could close every other door around him.

He wrestled with his conscience, with his indecision, with his guilt.

In truth, there were moments when he believed he would lose the fight.

FIFTY-TWO

The months leading up to Christmas were hectic for all concerned. Hollywood could not contain itself. Any and all financial limitations on the movie studios, whether internally or externally imposed, were lifted. People wanted to go out. They wanted to enjoy themselves. They wanted to be reminded of all the reasons they went to war in the first place.

The bars and clubs were rammed with returning GIs. Hookers couldn't move for clients. Seeing an opportunity, Dragna's prostitution rings went into a recruitment overdrive, prices skyrocketed, and a sideline of crude, cheaply made pornographic films started realizing an additional and substantial income for those involved.

Ironically and inadvertently, it was one such low-budget sex movie that finally closed the circle for Louis Hayes. A makeshift hotel room set, a handful of arrests, and Hayes found himself questioning a young woman by the name of Dolores Rayburn, eighteen years old, not three months out of Texas. It was an uncanny reprisal of the Bernice Radcliffe story. Mo Vianelli had put Bernice in the hospital four years earlier, and given Hayes the link between Nicky Mariani and Frank Madden. Bernice had been unwilling to testify, and as far as Hayes knew she had in fact gone back to Columbus Grove, Ohio, to find some other life. Hayes really hoped that she'd found some happiness there.

Dolores Rayburn had come to Hollywood to find fame and fortune just as soon as she'd turned eighteen. She hailed from Dallas, the same as Peggy Larue Satterlee, one of the girls who'd gained such notoriety in the Errol Flynn rape case. Hell, Dolores had thought, if Peggy Satterlee can get herself screwed on Flynn's yacht, then so can I.

Just like Lucia Mariani, Dolores had quickly realized that small-town beauty pageant queens were a dime a dozen in Hollywood. If you wanted to get attention, you had to have that something extra. The attention she wound up with was not what she'd expected. It was not Errol Flynn, Cary Grant, nor Robert Walker who dedicated their unflagging attention to Dolores Rayburn, but the officers of Central Vice, chief among them Louis Hayes when he learned that Dolores's representation was catered for by none other than the Erin Star Agency.

Hayes's visit to their offices and his first official introduction to Frank and Lucy Madden took place on Monday, December 17th. Dolores had been arrested the previous Friday evening, held overnight, released on bail on Saturday afternoon. She—along with a camera operator, a director, and a sound engineer—had been charged with various violations of the Obscenity Act. Hayes knew she was a minor player in a much grander game, and he had no personal motivation to see her unduly punished. Hayes was not even interested in the men who'd been arrested alongside her, save for whatever information they could give him regarding the funding, organization, production, and dissemination of the final movies. The farther he went up that ladder, the closer he would get to someone significant.

Hayes's sole interest in the Maddens was their relationship with Nicolas Mariani, though he had no intention of alerting either Frank or Lucy to this fact. His interview on that Monday morning was merely to establish whether Dolores Rayburn's most recent work had been secured by their agency. He knew the answer to that question before he even arrived, but still he wanted to meet them in person and see what else he could glean.

The Erin Star Agency was somewhat different from the myriad casting agencies in downtown Hollywood. Situated near the corner of South Lucas and Maryland, it occupied a suite of offices on the second floor of a smart, well-kept building. Hayes had called ahead and secured an appointment. According to the receptionist, both Frank and Lucy Madden were in.

Hayes was buzzed up from the street, found himself in an internal hallway that was floor-to-ceiling boxes. The receptionist—a pretty girl who introduced herself as Edie—greeted Hayes and asked him to follow her.

"We've just moved," she explained. "Second time in a year. Now the war's over everyone's coming back to Hollywood, and everyone wants the same work."

At the end of the hallway was a waiting area with two low leather sofas and a coffee table.

"Can I get you something? Coffee, tea, club soda perhaps?" Edie asked.

"I'm good," Hayes said, and took a seat.

The table was piled high with stacks of magazines—*Movie Stars*, *Silver Screen*, and *Motion Picture*.

Edie told Hayes that someone would be out to see him very shortly, and returned to her business. The phone rang incessantly, Edie responding with precisely the same greeting, making appointments, advising those without headshots to secure the services of two or three recommended photographers, and Hayes listened to all of it with a slight sense of wonder. He understood the Hollywood thing, and he appreciated the drive that some possessed for fame and fortune, but he did not *get* it. Being in the limelight, being twelve feet high on a drive-in movie screen, never being able to go any place without people asking dumb questions and wanting autographs was something to which he had never aspired.

"Detective Hayes?"

Hayes looked up, saw a young and very attractive woman smiling down at him. Her hair was dark and full, tied back with a simple barrette. Her manner of dress was simple but sophisticated.

Lucy Madden smiled, extended her hand. "Lucy Madden," she said. "Please come through."

Hayes got up, shook her hand, followed her into her office, which—just like the hallway—was stacked with unpacked boxes and heaps of files on the floor.

Lucy navigated her way between the obstacles and took a seat at the desk.

Hayes sat facing her and took out a notepad and a photograph.

"We have just moved," Lucy explained.

"Your receptionist told me," Hayes replied.

"Did she offer you some coffee, some water perhaps?"

"I'm fine," Hayes said.

"So, you have some questions about someone we represent?"

Hayes smiled. He leaned forward and passed the photograph to Lucy.

Lucy took the picture. "I'm sorry," she said. "I think we number around two or three hundred clients now. Half of those are walk-ons and extras, and we've met them perhaps once. I have a good memory for faces, but not that many."

"That's okay," Hayes replied. "I understand completely. That girl in the picture goes by the name of Dolores Rayburn. She was arrested in a hotel room on Friday night—"

Hayes stopped midsentence, turned as the door opened behind him.

He rose from the chair.

"Don't get up on my account," Frankie Madden said.

"Mr. Madden, I presume," Hayes said, aware of exactly who the man was but not wishing to suggest he had any previous experience with either of the Maddens.

"That's right," Frankie said. He shook hands with Hayes.

Madden was fractionally shorter than Hayes. He possessed a solidity and strength in his physical shape that suggested more than enough capability to look after himself. His handshake was firm and confident. He held Hayes's gaze unerringly, and Hayes got the impression of a man who was afraid of very little, if of anything at all.

"Detective Hayes was just telling that one of our clients . . . I presume she is one of our clients, otherwise there'd be no reason for you to be here—"

"Yes," Hayes said. "She's one of yours."

"Well, this young woman—"

"Dolores Rayburn."

"Dolores Rayburn . . . was arrested on Friday night."

Frankie picked up the photograph. "We have a lot of clients—"

"Mrs. Madden told me. I appreciate that it would be impossible to remember them all."

"And can you tell us why she was arrested, Detective?" Frankie asked.

"Violations of the Obscenity Act," Hayes said. "She and several others were making a pornographic movie."

"Oh," Lucy said. "How unpleasant."

"Indeed," Hayes replied.

"And you think—"

"I don't think anything, Mr. Madden," Hayes said, preempting Frankie's question. "I am here on a routine inquiry. Background checks, the usual thing. I don't have any reason to suspect that you were complicit in securing this work for Miss Rayburn, but I have to knock doors and ask questions. My inquiry relates more to any information you might have about the people who engage in this sort of thing . . . whether you are aware of anyone talking to your clients, whether any of your clients have been approached."

Lucy turned and looked up at Frankie. She was shaking her head as she looked back. "I haven't heard anything. None of the girls have ever said anything to me about such a thing."

"Same here," Frankie said.

Hayes looked at Frankie. "You're Irish," he said.

"I am, yes."

"First generation if the accent is anything to go by."

"I am."

"How long have you been here?"

"In Hollywood?"

"In the United States."

Frankie frowned. "And this is—"

"Idle curiosity. Nothing more than that."

"I came here in the early part of 1938."

"And you're not Italian, are you, Mrs. Madden?"

"I am Corsican."

Hayes nodded. "Which is France, right?"

Lucy smiled patiently. "No, Detective. Corsica is just Corsica."

"And you have been here how long?"

"Also since the early part of 1938."

"Surely you didn't come alone?" Hayes asked.

"No. I came with my older brother."

"And he works with you?"

"No. He has his own business."

"And what business would that be?"

Lucy glanced at Frankie and shifted in her chair.

"I'm sorry, Detective," Frankie said. "I'm not sure what my wife's brother has to do with any of this."

"It doesn't," Hayes replied. "I'm Pittsburgh via Cleveland. My father's history is Scottish from way back when, as far as I can work out. Where people come from and what they do is just my naturally inquisitive nature. I guess it comes from the line of work."

"Of course," Frankie said. "So is there anything else?"

"Just one other question," Hayes said. "Madden. You're not related to Owney—"

"No, sir, I am not."

"You know who I mean, right?"

"Owen Madden. New York gangster, right? Only thing I know about him is that our very own Hollywood gangster, George Raft, used to drive for him. I've been asked that a lot, Detective, but no, I am not related to Owen Madden or any other Maddens you might have heard of. Not the sort of company I keep, if you know what I mean."

Hayes smiled. "I know exactly what you mean, Mr. Madden."

"So is there anything we have to do regarding what happened to this girl?" Lucy asked.

"If you didn't give her the work and knew nothing about it, then no," Hayes said. "Like I said, this is just routine. Sadly, this kind of thing is happening more and more. It seems to be controlled and organized from the same two or three sources, so we're doing our best to work back toward those people. The irony is that the victims of this kind of exploitation are the ones who wind up in the cells, not the Jack Dragnas and Micky Cohens of this world."

"I've heard of these people," Frankie said.

"Most everyone has heard of them," Hayes said, "and you want to keep it that way, and nothing more. Don't see them, don't talk to them, and don't have anything to do with anyone who knows them." Hayes paused for effect. "Right, Mrs. Madden?"

"Er, yes . . . of course."

"Just from the viewpoint that casting agencies, production companies, any outfit that is connected to the movie industry is a magnet for these lowlifes. Lot of money in Hollywood, and a lot of people prepared to do pretty much anything to get it."

"We'll keep that in mind," Frankie said.

Hayes got up as if to leave, and then he hesitated. "You don't happen to remember a girl called Bernice Radcliffe, do you?" he asked. "Her stage name was Eleanor Wilson. Hailed from Columbus Grove, Ohio. Got herself into some trouble with a man called Maurizio Vianelli back near Christmas of 1941."

"Was she one of ours?" Lucy asked.

"She may well have been, yes."

"Well, she either was or she wasn't," Frankie said, "and the fact that you're asking about her makes me think you know that already."

"It's a long time ago," Hayes said. "I meet a lot of people, just like you, and I can't remember every detail of every case. I just wondered if the name rang a bell."

"Not with me," Lucy said.

"Can't say I've heard of her either," Frankie added.

"Guess we're done, then," Hayes said. "Thank you for your time." He glanced around the office. "I guess you've got a lot of work to do, so I appreciate your seeing me."

Frankie came from around the desk and showed Hayes to the door. They shook hands.

"Edie will see you out, Detective," Frankie said.

Hayes turned back and smiled. "Good day, Mrs. Madden."

"Good day."

Frankie closed the door after Hayes and waited a few moments. Once he heard the exchange of words outside, he turned back to Lucy.

"This has something to do with Nicky," Frankie said. "I'm telling you now, Lucy, this has something to do with your brother."

FIFTY-THREE

Louis Hayes had been married for two and a half years, and the pressure and expectation of children had been looming for some time. Carole had moved out of her original department, war propaganda no longer required, and taken a full-time position in the Cultural Archive and Preservation Department of the mayor's office. She was happy enough, but the ache of motherhood haunted her. He could see it in the way she looked at other mothers, the little kids in tow, the momentary pauses in the baby clothes section of a department store. She said nothing. That was not her way.

In the Madden house, now an elegant, sprawling bungalow in the Hollywood Hills, Frank and Lucy coped with the ever-increasing demand for actors and actresses, singers, dancers, crowd fillers, and extras. They had branched out into behind-the-scenes crew members, representing everything from grips to lighting technicians, set designers to choreographers. Almost all the financial and administrative functions were now covered by their accountant and an office manager. Aside from that, Lucy had a receptionist and a PA. Frankie, less housebound than Lucy, still attended all the significant meetings, met with casting directors, oversaw the processing of new clients, and covered all the bases that Lucy could not cover due to her maternal commitments.

It seemed that Hollywood wished to do nothing but forget the horrors of war, and money flooded in from pictures like *The Bells of St. Mary's, Leave Her to Heaven,* and *Anchors Aweigh*. Lucy's connection to RKO kept her in the loop as far as new projects were concerned, and the studio's connection to Disney for the forthcoming *Song of the South* opened up a whole new raft of possibilities for animators, colorists, and voice-over actors. RKO's chief, Charles Koerner, was in discussion with Frank Capra about a script called *The Greatest Gift.* It had been rattling around in various incarnations since Cary Grant's agent had seen it back in '44. RKO had worked up three versions, but Grant chose instead to film *The Bishop's Wife*. Capra bought the rights, changed the title to *It's a Wonderful Life*, and preproduction had already begun both in Culver City and at the RKO movie ranch in Encino. Max Rée's original three-block sets for *Cimarron* were revamped to create a town called Bedford Falls. Jimmy Stewart and Donna Reed signed up for the lead roles. Erin Star was one of three agencies asked to provide townsfolk and extras for the production, and provide them they did. They supplied actors for *The Best Years of Our Lives*, singers and showgirls for *Blue Skies*, and for *The Yearling* they sent animal wranglers and carpenters down to the Juniper Prairie Wilderness in Florida.

Joe Madden was nearing four years of age, and he was a fighter like his father. Frankie called him Champ, and they tussled and wrestled constantly. For his mother, Joe possessed a different aspect. The little boy's eyes were constantly wide with wonder, and from his lips came an endless stream of questions. The speed with which his mind leaped from one topic to another, how he managed to throw himself so wholeheartedly into games and adventures and make-believe, was a joy to behold.

There were days that seemed to spin out forever, others that vanished in a heartbeat, and Joe grew so quickly. From one week to the next he seemed to advance more than was possible, talking to her about things he did at preschool, friends he'd made, coming home with paint in his hair and glue on his clothes, clutching in his hands a picture he'd made from dry macaroni and sequins and bits of felt fabric that were supposed to represent his mom and dad.

"But I have to go, Mommy! There are things to do!" was his response most Saturday mornings when he realized there was no preschool. So she and Frankie would take him out to the beach, to the circus, to the movie theater, anywhere to keep him looking and listening and talking.

Joe Madden fought sleep. He was a lit firework, a dynamo, and little ball of energy and sunshine that lit up the room and drew everyone present into the whirlwind of his imagination.

"I am a muksiteer!" he would shout, waving a wooden sword. "I am the king of the world!" And then he would roar at the top of his voice and chase Frankie around the house, up and down the stairs, in and out of bedrooms and bathrooms until Frankie collapsed on the floor and Joe was all over him, a whirlwind of arms and legs and laughter.

Lucy was exhausted just watching them.

And whatever Lucy might have imagined about motherhood, it was so very much more. Having a child was like being given a chance to experience your own childhood a second time. It was a rediscovery of everything that made the world surprising and exciting. It was a fresh look at all that was meaningful and significant. Most of all, it was a true revelation for her to realize how much she loved Frankie and the child they had brought into the world.

And yet the ache was still there. Despite everything she had, she knew it would never be enough. Lucy was desperate to return to the screen, even if she had to start all over by taking up some of the auditions she routinely arranged for others. She was twenty-eight years old, and she knew that establishing herself as an actress in her own right was becoming less and less realistic as the years passed. She spoke of it to Frankie, of course. Frankie was as sympathetic and understanding as he could be, but both their lives had moved in a direction they could never have anticipated. They ran a successful business. They made a lot of money. They wanted for nothing, at least in a materialistic sense. For months, Frankie had suggested that Lucy hire a live-in nanny for Joe, but Lucy was torn between her maternal responsibility and her desire for something that being a mother, a wife, a daughter, a sister, none of these things could ever deliver.

"These are really important years for him," she said. "Another six months, another year maybe, then okay, but until he's at least four I really think he needs us around as much as possible."

One afternoon was perhaps more telling than any other single event at that time. Don Siegel came in to see the Maddens with a script called *The Verdict*. It was his first feature, and already Warner had given him Sydney Greenstreet and Peter Lorre. Lucy knew Siegel from a short drama film he'd made in October of the previous year. Siegel had taken home an Academy Award for Best Short Subject, and Warner wanted to give him a shot at a full reel.

"I got a part for you," Siegel told Lucy. "Character called Lottie Rawson. You look great for it, and I can cast who I like. You helped me out on the *Star in the Night* project, and I know you're looking to get out there and do some work yourself."

Lucy asked Don Siegel if she could think it over.

"I got to get an answer soon," he told her.

Lucy prevaricated for close on a week, and then she found out that Siegel had cast Joan Lorring.

"She did Bessy Watty in *The Corn Is Green*," she told Frankie. "The girl earned herself as Academy Award nomination. I mean, seriously, if you were Don Siegel, who would you go for, me or a girl with a

Best Supporting Actress nomination? He was probably just being kind . . ."

Frankie listened to the words, but heard something else. He didn't fight her on it. There was no point. She had worked it out the way she wanted and there wouldn't be anything he could say or do to change her mind.

After the Siegel thing, Frankie knew that his wife would only ever put other people on the screen. It was a reprise of the *Ambersons*, but somehow a lesser haunting by the same ghost.

Frankie suspected other issues. Again, something akin to *If I don't try, I can't fail*. Perhaps Lucy's fear of rejection, her own reservations about her age, her concern that she would try and try again and it would all come to nothing prevented her from taking that step.

There were moments when Frankie himself felt the ghost of the past. Of course, his mind turned time and again to his sisters, Erin most of all. In April she would be twenty-three years of age. Perhaps she was married, already a mother. Of her, his other sisters, even his parents, he knew nothing and could never take the risk of trying to find out. Why no one had ever tracked him down, if not from Ireland, then certainly from New York, he did not know. To think of such a thing was to experience such a sense of dread and foreboding, and he did all he could never to bring it to mind.

As for fighting, it was like casting his mind back to some lost love, a dream from which he wished to never wake. That too was something locked securely within the part of his mind reserved for secrets and unspoken wishes.

As with so many people, Frankie and Lucy Madden seemed the perfect couple, the perfect family. Everything they possessed, they had created together. They entertained movie people; they hosted dinners, even involved themselves in local charity drives.

They didn't discuss the fact that the fringes of their world were inhabited by those solely interested in exploitation of the bright and the beautiful. They didn't speak of Bernice Radcliffe or Dolores Rayburn. Lucy thought of them, thought of them often, wondered what happened to them, whether they had rediscovered themselves, their dreams, or whether they had been silently and hungrily swallowed by the dark maw that seemed to lurk behind the glitzy facade of this town. She feared for Nicky, of what he might be involved in, whether he himself was now a part of all that made Hollywood as dangerous as it was alluring.

Rumors were heard. Production shutdowns, set strikes, murmurs of dissatisfaction with pay and working conditions for technical and support personnel were becoming ever more frequent. Behind all of them lurked the shadow of corruption and graft, an industry that should have been populated solely by the creative and the artistic now infiltrated by criminal elements, both insidious and unseen. On two or three occasions Frankie himself had been close to inflicting physical violence on the emissaries of so-called management companies, themselves nothing more than fronts for organized crime syndicates intent on sabotaging shooting schedules and holding the picture company to ransom. His fear of personal exposure was sufficient to suppress his rage and corral his fists. Fight today, lose tomorrow. That had been his mantra, and he did all he could to stay focused on the important things. Lucy, Joe, the future. He had made a life for himself in Hollywood, and the momentary satisfaction of vengeance was worth nothing compared to that. The old Sicilian adage applied: If you seek revenge, dig two graves.

Frankie Madden was a man who had somehow found a place in a world that had never invited him. A day did not go by when he did not take stock of his good fortune. He vowed never to take anything for granted. He had reconciled himself to the fact that Nicky would forever be a part of their lives, but he was a small part, and even in conversation with Lucy his name was rarely mentioned.

And then something happened. It came sideways without warning, and Frankie realized that whatever wish he might have made to be rid of Nicky forever was worth absolutely nothing at all. The bond between his wife and his brother-in-law was altogether too strong, and he did not possess the power to break it.

FIFTY-FOUR

Nicky Mariani visited the Maddens infrequently. He'd been there for the housewarming, for Joe's birthdays, a handful of times when he'd been in the neighborhood, but in the main he kept himself and his business where it belonged. Had Frankie not been on the scene, then Nicky would have made a great deal more effort to see his sister, but she was Frankie's husband—signed, sealed, delivered—and even Nicky's sense of fraternal responsibility could not circumvent her marital allegiance. There was the family you were born to and the family you created. Both were important, and often it was better not to get the two involved.

Nicky sent gifts for his nephew. He spent a good deal of money. He knew that Frankie resented it, but he didn't care. If he couldn't see the boy, he could at least do whatever he could to make his presence felt. Money was not an issue for Nicky. He was making at least a grand a week, often more. He managed the Venus and the Starlight, but there were numerous other places from which he collected. There were hookers, brothels, drugs, racketeering, protection scams, fencing, money laundering, bookmaking, all manner of discreet and indiscreet extortions going on, and wherever possible Nicky got himself a slice of the pie, however thin. Hollywood seemed to be a magnet for the best and the worst. The best, no matter how good they might have been, were still human. They possessed their vices and proclivities, and Nicky was all too eager to take advantage of those indiscretions and profit from them. If a man did not possess a penchant for teenage boys or underage girls, if he did not entertain a predilection for drugs, then there were always more than enough broke wannabe showgirls and actresses who would cry *Rape!* loud enough to be heard, falling suddenly silent and disappearing as soon as sufficient money had exchanged hands. Sometimes Nicky believed he'd fallen headlong into the horn of plenty, and it seemed to have no end.

*

In the second week of February, 1946, Frankie was inadvertently reminded of his brother-in-law. Nicky and all that his life entailed would never be too far away, it seemed.

It was Monday the eleventh, and Lucy had to get Joe to kindergarten. Most days she would walk, but the earlier part of that morning had been consumed by discussions with Frankie about the day's itinerary, where he was going, who he had to see, contracts to be drawn up and letters to be sent. She'd taken a cab. Frankie had insisted. On foot it was little more than twenty minutes, but Frankie didn't want Joe to be late.

They used the same cab company as always. The cab arrived, Lucy and Joe got in, and they headed off. Mere moments after the cab had turned the corner at the end of the street, a dark Pontiac sedan pulled away from the curb and took the same route. Frankie did not see the sedan, and Lucy was too preoccupied with getting Joe's shoelaces tied and his coat buttons fastened to pay any mind to other cars on the road. The cabdriver, however, as he took the fourth and fifth turn, did notice the sedan. He sped up. The sedan matched his speed. He slowed down. The sedan did the same. After a half mile he took a left where he would ordinarily take a right, and then went back on himself at the other end of the block. He came back onto the main street and found the sedan right there in his rearview

"Hey, lady," he said. "You know why someone might be following you?" He'd been a cabdriver long enough to know that husbands had their wives tailed, wives had their husbands tailed, and whatever you could imagine, you were sure to see it in a cab sooner or later.

Lucy smiled, frowned. "Sorry? What did you say?"

"I asked if someone was following you. Dark blue sedan back there. Been on our tail since we left your house."

Lucy looked out through the rear window, and sure enough a dark blue car was just ten or fifteen yards behind them.

"No," she said. "What makes you think we're being followed?"

"Just the way the guy is driving. Drives like a cop. Looks like there's two of them."

A momentary pang of anxiety invaded Lucy's thoughts as she once again glanced back at the car behind them.

"Just a coincidence, I'm sure," she said, but there was a nervous edge in her tone.

"Maybe, maybe not," the driver said. "Let's get your kid dropped off and then we'll see."

They were mere minutes from the kindergarten. Lucy took Joe

inside, and—as always—was thrilled to see the speed and enthusiasm with which he engaged in activities with the other children. There was certainly no shortage of self-confidence in Joe Madden, to the point that the supervisor had commented on it numerous times.

"Bright as a button," she'd said. "So much energy. A really lovely boy, and so kind to everyone, always sharing, you know? He's an absolute joy, Mrs. Madden, an absolute joy."

Lucy left Joe to his friends and headed back to the cab.

"That car pulled over when we stopped. Back there maybe thirty yards," the driver told her once she was inside. "If they're not following us, then I'm a Martian."

"Go," Lucy said. "Just go."

The driver headed away, took a right at the end of the street, and started back the way they'd come.

For a while it seemed that the sedan had not followed them, but as they drew to a halt at a stop sign, Lucy caught sight of the car.

The driver noticed it, too, called in to Dispatch and told them what was happening.

"You want the cops at your house for when we arrive?" he asked her.

"Yes," she said.

The driver told Dispatch to call the police. He gave Lucy's address.

"Your husband still home?"

"I think he will be," Lucy replied.

"What's his name and telephone number?"

Lucy gave them and the driver relayed it to his operator. "Call the husband. His name is Madden. Tell him the cops will be arriving and that his wife has been followed by two men in a dark blue sedan."

The driver left his radio handset on the passenger seat.

Lucy sat sideways, her attention never leaving the dark blue sedan, knowing that something was wrong, fearing that it had something to do with Nicky.

And then another terrible thought struck her. What if it wasn't to do with Nicky at all? What if these were people from New York, people who had finally tracked them down and were coming to ask her what she knew of the illegal fight circuits, about the unsolved murder of Aleksy Bodak?

Her pulse quickened, and she could feel her heart swelling with fear.

They were no more than three minutes from the Madden house.

The radio handset crackled into life and Lucy jumped, startled.

The driver responded with his call sign and asked if the cops had been called. "The police are there already," the dispatcher told the driver.

The driver thanked her and hung up the handset.

As they turned into the street, Lucy could see a black-and-white outside the house. Frankie was on the path. He was talking to a uniformed officer, and as the cab drew close, Lucy could see that he was angry.

Her heart sank. She did not want this to be happening.

The cab pulled over. Lucy got out and hurried toward Frankie.

The cabdriver got out as well, stood there with the car door open. He looked back along the street, and the sedan came up and pulled over no more than half a dozen houses away.

Neither the driver nor the passenger got out.

"Cops," Frankie said. "Fucking cops, Lucy! Those guys in that car down there are cops."

Lucy looked at the uniformed officer, her expression one of confusion and disbelief.

"All I can do is apologize, ma'am," the officer said. "As part of an ongoing investigation, we often keep an eye on people who might be connected to—"

"It's Nicky," Frankie said. "Nicky, goddammit!" He turned on the officer. "You're investigating her brother, right? Nicolas Mariani. That's what this is about, isn't it?"

"I am sorry, sir, but I cannot divulge any information concerning an active investigation."

"Oh, to hell with you," Frankie said. "Get off my property. Get off my property right fucking now, and take your two goons with you. Jesus Christ, what the hell is this? This is harassment."

"As I said, sir, I can only extend my apology to you and your wife for the upset this has caused—"

"How long has this been going on? How many times have you followed her? Or are you following me as well?"

"I'm sorry, sir, but—"

"But you can't give me any information about how you're harassing me and my wife, following us, Christ only knows what."

Frankie looked at Lucy. He was furious.

"Go!" he said to the policeman. "Just get the hell out of here before I do something I'll regret."

The policeman opened his mouth, perhaps to proffer another apology, but then decided against it. He walked down to the black-and-white and drove away. A moment later the sedan pulled away from the curb and followed it.

"You folks gonna be okay?" the cabdriver called up from the street.

Frankie walked down there, thanked the man, tipped him generously, and sent him on his way.

"I didn't know about this, Frankie," Lucy said as he stormed past her to the house.

Frankie stopped, turned back, and glared at her. "Your brother," he started. He closed his eyes, as if mustering all his self-control. His teeth were gritted, his fists clenched. "If your brother was here right now," he said, and then he shook his head and turned toward the house.

"Frankie," Lucy called after him.

"I don't want to hear it, Lucy," Frankie said. "I just don't want to hear it, okay?"

Lucy stood there, her mind crowded with unanswered questions, her thoughts torn between her brother and her husband, somehow feeling as if she'd been caught in a perfect storm.

In that moment, it seemed there would be no possibility of salvation.

FIFTY-FIVE

Much to Lucy's relief, Frankie did not hound her with questions about Nicky. Frankie was angry, of course, but his anger was directed toward Nicky. He knew that Lucy had no control over her brother's activities and that Nicky would always and forever be of interest to the police.

Very simply, the Maddens were caught in the crosshairs, and there was little they could do to change that.

On Valentine's Day, Frankie took Lucy to the Brown Derby. It was the seventeenth anniversary of its opening, and though seventeen years held no great significance the maître d' and the waitresses still made a fuss of it. To come from a country that had churches from the twelfth century, Frankie still marveled at the American fascination with anything older than a decade.

It was over dessert that Lucy told Frankie that they were going to be parents for a second time.

Frankie sat for a while. He could feel the air in his chest. His throat was dry, his hands steady. He looked at his wife, and though he felt nothing but joy for the prospect of another baby, he also saw in her eyes the certainty that whatever dreams she might have possessed for Hollywood were now as good as gone forever.

"Okay," he said quietly, and the word was neither an acknowledgment nor an expression of surprise. It was merely something to fill an awkward silence.

"Are you unhappy?" Lucy asked.

Frankie smiled, reached out, and took her hand. "Unhappy? No, no, not at all. Don't ever think that, sweetheart. I love that we have a family. I love that we have created this life together..."

"But?"

Frankie shook his head and smiled resignedly. "Well, we've both wound up doing something different than we planned... very different."

"You can't predict where life is going to take you," she said. "It's not possible. Try your best to go one way and you find yourself on an entirely different road."

Frankie paused. He squeezed her hand reassuringly. "And you? What do you think about it?"

Lucy laughed dismissively. "What *can* I think about it? Whatever I might think about it, it's done. We can't undo it, Frankie."

"I know, I know," he said, "but I want to know what you really think about it."

Lucy smiled. "What can I say? I love Joe with everything I possess. I love being a mother. I love that we have a family and a beautiful house and more than enough money to do what we want to do, and I am sure . . ." She glanced down at her stomach. "I am sure that I will love whoever comes along next just as much as the last one." She withdrew her hand from Frankie's and reached for the glass of water beside her plate. "However, I have to start dealing with the fact that I will never light up a movie screen."

"And I'll never put a man down on the canvas in the Olympic Auditorium," Frankie said. "I've driven past there a few times, down on Grand Avenue. Seats fifteen thousand people. All the stars go there to watch fights. Pulls at me, Lucy . . . Even now it still pulls at me and won't let go."

"We're both in the same boat," she replied.

"But the boat ain't sinking," Frankie replied.

"Always the optimist."

"Don't see any point in being negative about it. We have a good life. We have a beautiful son. We have each other."

They laughed. Frankie ordered wine. They ate the remainder of their meal and did not speak of the child, nor of their frustrated dreams, nor of what might have happened had things been different.

Later that night, as Frankie lay awake beside his sleeping wife, he thought of the ever-present shadows in the corner of his mind. Those shadows knew his real name, they knew what he had done before he escaped for America, and they would never let him be. Now he felt he could never tell the truth, not only to prevent the terrible consequences for himself, but also because he dreaded Lucy's reaction if she discovered how long he had kept the truth from her. She was willful, headstrong, passionate, and she would see it as nothing but the ultimate personal betrayal.

He slept that night, but not restfully, and when he woke he felt as if he had not slept at all.

"I telephoned Nicky," Lucy told Frankie at breakfast. "I want to tell him the news. He's going to be so excited to be an uncle for the second time. He's coming over—"

"Now?"

"In a little while."

Frankie poured himself a cup of coffee from the pot on the stove. "I'm heading out to the office," he said. He knew that if he stayed he would not be able to hold his tongue concerning the incident with the police a few days earlier.

Lucy sighed. "Will the day ever come when you and Nicky . . . ?" She let the question hang unfinished in the air between them. She knew—even before the words had left her lips—that now was not a good time. Not a good time at all. She wished she'd said nothing.

Frankie looked back at her. He didn't say anything. His response was all too clear in his expression.

"It just saddens me," she said.

"I don't know what to say, Lucy. He's your brother. You love each other and you hold your loyalties, as you should. I would be the same if he were my brother. But he's involved in bad things. I don't know what, but I just know he's involved with people that we don't want in our lives. If I let him get close, then Christ knows who will come with him."

"You can't say that, Frankie. How can you say he's involved with bad people if you have nothing to back it up?"

"Sweetheart, don't be naive. You've seen the way he dresses, the cars he drives, the jewelry, the gifts he brings for Joe. What does he do? What's his job? Where do you think all that money comes from?"

"From the clubs. He's a nightclub manager. Last time he talked to me about it he was managing at least five or six clubs."

Frankie shook his head. "A regular nightclub manager is not earning hundreds of dollars a week, Lucy. They are not *just* nightclubs. A nightclub manager does not have the cops tailing his sister and his nephew when they leave the house—"

"I don't want to talk about it," Lucy said, turning back to the stove.

"I know you don't."

She glanced back at Frankie. "Meaning what?"

Frankie smiled knowingly. "Meaning that you don't want to talk about it."

"What you are saying and what you're thinking aren't the same thing, Frankie."

Frankie set down his coffee cup and reached for his jacket. "I'm going to work. Come over after you've seen Nicky and we'll look at this contract change from yesterday."

"That's it?"

"Yes, sweetheart. That's it. We've had this discussion before, and we'll have it again. I love you. I tolerate your brother. I don't think that will ever change. It's something I have to live with, and it's a minor matter in comparison to everything that's good."

Lucy sighed audibly. "It just grieves me so that you can't be friends."

"We may not be friends," Frankie said, "but we're not enemies either. Live and let live. As long as he keeps his business away from my family, then all is well. We've already had that Hayes guy snooping around and trying to find out if we're somehow involved with Nicky, then we had this fiasco the other day, and I just don't want any more of that. I really don't."

"I don't either," Lucy replied. "But he is my brother, and I just can't shut him out."

"I know, and I don't think he'd let you even if you wanted to. You Corsicans are fierce ones, for sure."

Lucy laughed. "Not as fierce as the crazy Irish."

Frankie took her hand and kissed her. "I'll see you later. We need to get these new contracts worked out. The unions are being a nightmare."

"I'll be there," she said. "Couple of hours. I'll see Nicky, get Joe settled with the nanny, and be right over."

Frankie left, didn't look back as he reached the corner. Had he done so he would have seen a black Chrysler Crown Imperial pulling up against the curb.

Nicky Mariani emerged alone, and before he closed the car door, he paused and looked the way he'd come as if expecting someone.

Satisfied that he was not being followed, he walked on up to the Maddens' front door and rang the bell.

FIFTY-SIX

The nose of a cat will find a rat, no matter the morsels you feed it.

It was something Hayes remembered from a long-ago conversation with a fellow detective. He couldn't remember the name of the guy nor the context, but the phrase had stayed with him.

It seemed altogether fitting for what was happening within the lower ranks of the Dragna crime family, especially when it came to the activities of Nicky Mariani and his associates, Anthony Leggiero and Vincent Caliendo. Mariani, Leggiero, and Caliendo were as good as inseparable. From all appearances it seemed Dragna, through Adamo, had given managerial control not only of the Venus and the Starlight but also three or four other places to Nicky Mariani. In practice, if not on paper, Mariani had his own little empire, and the simple fact that he stayed right where he was indicated that Dragna was not unhappy with the arrangement. The clubs made money. Raids were infrequent, and Dragna's heavy hitters never seemed to be there when the cops came through the door. How much of that was blind luck and how much was from tip-offs Hayes didn't know. He was not concerned with busting the likes of Jimmy Fratianno and Frank Bompensiero for soliciting or possession; he wanted them for murder. He wanted these people to take the longest and hardest fall imaginable. Though he himself was not a proponent of the death penalty, he reckoned there were some people who deserved it.

Nicolas Mariani had stuck in his craw since the disappearance of Paulie Belotti back in 1938. He was certain that Mariani knew something of the man's whereabouts. He also knew that Mariani was wise to the inside track of extortion, protection, blackmail, illegal bookies, card games, horse racing, prostitution, and every other venture that used Dragna's clubs to launder money. For every buck that went into the tills of those places another twenty-five came out. They were legally established, they possessed the right licenses for the sale of alcohol and provision of entertainment, but all that was required was the cellars to be full of stolen liquor and they could process unlimited amounts of funds through those joints. It was a neat operation, well documented, well practiced, and enormously efficient. But there were loopholes. There were always loopholes, and those loopholes were made by men possessed of appetites greater than their loyalties. Ironic, but running a corrupt business required the allegiance of corrupt men, and there were few who could not be bought off, bribed, blackmailed, or turned when it came to a choice between their own survival and that of their employers. Honor among thieves was a myth; self-preservation was not, and Louis Hayes doubted if Nicky Mariani would prove himself any different from the other unscrupulous, self-serving lowlifes that wound up on Jack Dragna's payroll.

And so it was that an incident at a bar on North Fremont opened a door that Louis Hayes had been looking for. That door gave him access to someone he had encountered before: Maurizio Vianelli, second-generation American-Italian, first-generation scumbag.

The December '41 incident with Bernice Radcliffe had gone nowhere. Mo Vianelli may well have temporarily alienated himself from his fellow scumbags, for no other reason than such incidents brought police attention where it was definitely unwelcome, but soon enough he had ingratiated himself back into the clan. These people gravitated toward one another, and there was almost nothing that would separate them. Arrests, charges, convictions, even prison terms were all occupational hazards, and friends were always welcomed back, just as long as they'd kept their mouths shut. Betrayal was the only real sin. Those who violated *omertà*, those who broke agreements and gave up their confederates, knew that no matter how far they fled they would always be found. The one thing that matched the greed of these people was their refusal to forgive or forget.

In early December '45, a young man called Billy Resnick had gotten himself stabbed in a place called Delilah's. Billy didn't die, but he was on the critical list up at Hollywood Hospital. There was a good chance a grievous assault would become murder. Delilah's was not a Dragna club. At first it was uncertain to whom it belonged, but a little digging came up with a name Hayes had also heard before. Tommy Jackson was two hundred pounds of hamburger out of East Los Angeles. He'd thumped his way around the fringes of the illegal fight circuit, never good enough to make the grade, never poor enough to wind up brain dead or buried. He'd been allied to one of Cohen's operations, wound up fetching and carrying at some of the bigger fights at the Olympic on Grand, and rumor had it he was now a courier. Money, drugs, payoffs, backhanders, whatever was needed, Jackson was a run-go-fetcher who had sense enough not to ask questions. His lack of curiosity made him useful. It was obvious that whoever actually owned the place was using Tommy's name to obscure the connection.

Hayes went down to Delilah's to make some inquiries about the stabbing. Jackson himself was not present, and the help seemed clueless and confused.

"So who actually owns the joint?" Hayes asked a blank-faced bartender with a question-mark scar on his left cheek.

"Owns it?" the bartender said. "I have no idea, mister. I just work here."

"So who pays you?"

"Lester."

"And who might Lester be?"

The bartender frowned. "The guy who pays me. I just told you."

"And what is Lester's surname?"

"No idea. He comes down here Friday. He gives me my money. I don't see him again until the next Friday."

"He pays you in cash?"

"Sure he does. How else do you pay someone?"

Hayes smiled. "Okay, my friend. Thank you for your help."

It was then that Hayes dug a little deeper, and that's when he found Tommy Jackson's name. Next time Hayes went to Delilah's he found Tommy eating a sandwich right there at the bar.

It was a little after four, afternoon of Friday the fourteenth. Billy Resnick was still critical, had been in hospital since the previous Monday and looked to be staying there a good while longer.

"You're Tommy Jackson," Hayes said, taking an adjacent stool at the bar.

Jackson glanced sideways. "Maybe."

Hayes smiled. "You're not sure?"

Tommy shook his head. "Wiseass."

"Detective Wiseass," Hayes said, and showed his badge.

"If you're here about that bullshit on Monday, I wasn't here and I don't know anything."

"I understand that, Tommy. I expected that to be the case. However, as the owner of this place, you carry a degree of responsibility—"

"Hold up there, mister," Tommy interjected. "As the what?"

"The owner of this place." Hayes glanced back around the interior of the bar. "Your name is on the ticket, my friend. Know it or not, like it or not, you're the fall guy for this."

"Jesus Christ," Tommy said. He set down his sandwich. "That asshole. I goddamned told him not to do that."

"You got stitched, buddy. Insurance, civil claims, all on your shoulders."

"Motherfucker, son of a bitch—"

"Oh, this is nothing unusual," Hayes said. "Not the first time I've seen it, and sure it's not the last."

"Son of a bitch," Tommy repeated. He was genuinely indignant. "So what the hell're you saying, that I gotta take the fall for this bullshit?"

"Well, unless you stabbed the kid yourself, then no, you don't have to take the fall. At least not for that."

"Meaning what?"

Hayes leaned forward, looked sideways at Tommy. He played on the guy's ignorance. "Licensing law, Tommy. That's the problem. If the bar's in your name, which it is, then you are legally liable for any damages the complainant might file. If he survives, which seems pretty unlikely, then we're talking a great deal of money."

Tommy frowned. "Not from me, right?"

"Of course from you. It's your bar. You have a legal requirement to ensure that sufficient provision is made for the safety and well-being of the clientele. People come here to get a drink, to have a sandwich, not to get stabbed."

Tommy was confused. "What the hell are you talking about? You're telling me that some guy gets stabbed . . . some guy who tried to rip off Vianelli . . ." Tommy hesitated, fell silent.

Hayes feigned lack of surprise, almost as if he'd expected to hear Vianelli's name. "Did Mo put the hit on the guy, Tommy?"

Tommy laughed nervously. "I didn't say nothin'."

"Sure you did. I just heard you say it."

"Your ears are imagining things."

Hayes laughed. "I like you, Tommy. You got a sense of humor. You were a good fighter, too. I remember you when you used to fight, and then you got involved with these assholes and down it's all gone to hell. Few weeks you're gonna be looking at how to find fifty thousand bucks—"

Tommy Jackson sat up so fast the stool went over backward. "What the hell—"

"Damages. Your bar, your license, your responsibility. That poor schmuck's family is going to wind you up so tight you'll never get out. They got a lawyer already. I know him. He's good, man. Sharp as a razor. And that's fifty thou if the kid survives. If he dies . . . well, if he dies I wouldn't even like to guess what they're gonna hit you for."

"You are talkin' nonsense, man. I am not gonna get sued because some kid got stabbed in here."

Hayes eased off the stool and stood up. "Whatever you say, Tommy. You were here, you saw what happened, and you cannot walk away from this."

"I wasn't here. I didn't see what happened."

"But you *know* what happened, right?" Hayes gambled, and the momentary hesitation gave him the only answer he needed.

Tommy Jackson didn't say a word. He picked up the barstool and sat down again. He pushed the remains of his sandwich away. He looked crestfallen and defeated.

"You give me something, Tommy," Hayes said. "Give me something I can use and maybe I can make this all go away."

"Maybe?" Tommy asked. "Maybe is no damned use to me, man."

"Well, if you can tell me something real good, then I can give you a certainty."

"This is bullshit," Tommy said matter-of-factly.

"This is what happens when you swim in the deep end, my friend."

"That asshole stitched me up."

"Mo?"

"Mo Vianelli, sure. Son of a bitch. What the hell, man? What the hell is the deal here?"

"I'll tell you exactly what the deal is here, Tommy. You're a decent, hardworking guy. You're trying to make a living. It's tough. Money is short. The war's just over and everyone is doing their damnedest to keep it all together. People like Mo Vianelli just take advantage of other people. They're assholes, Tommy. Always have been, always will be. Of course he's gonna let you take the rap for this. That's the way these people work. That's why you'll go down and he'll just carry on like nothing happened."

Tommy leaned forward, his arms on the bar, his head down. He sighed audibly.

"Those are the breaks, Tommy," Hayes said. "Like I said, you swim in the deep end and—"

"I got it, man. I got it."

Hayes was silent. He gave Tommy the time to try to straighten out his thoughts.

"What's it gonna take?" Tommy eventually asked.

"You know who did it?"

"Maybe."

"We don't do maybes, do we?"

"Say I knew who did it?" Tommy asked. He sat up and looked at Hayes.

"Then everything would become a great deal simpler for you, my friend. You know how easy it would be to lose a license, an ownership certificate? Just a couple of pieces of paper, and all of a sudden Tommy Jackson has no connection whatsoever to this place."

Tommy was again silent for some minutes.

Hayes could see the tortuous route his thinking processes were taking toward the inevitable conclusion.

Finally Tommy looked at Hayes with a resigned expression. "You already know who did it," he said.

"I do?" Hayes asked.

"Sure you do. Dumbass kid owed a bunch of money to someone, and that someone ran out of patience. Kid was asked, looked the wrong way, said the wrong fucking thing . . . Hell man, I don't know what happened, but the kid got stabbed. That was all there was to it."

"Vianelli himself?" Hayes asked. "He stabbed the kid?"

Tommy didn't reply. Again his silence was sufficient affirmation.

Hayes reached out and put his hand on Tommy's shoulder. "This goes the way I want it to go, then you're never gonna hear the name Billy Resnick again."

"Resnick? Is that the kid's name?"

"It is, and I hope it's gonna be his name for a good while longer."

"You're gonna take care of this?"

"I'm gonna do everything I can, Tommy."

"It ain't comin' back to me, right?"

"Were you here when it happened?"

Tommy shook his head. "No, I wasn't."

"For real?"

"For real."

"Then I can't see how anyone can put two and two together," Hayes said. "He ain't gonna know who gave him up. First thought will be for someone who was here, so I wouldn't worry about it."

"You're sure about this?" Tommy asked, anxiety in every syllable.

Hayes nodded in the affirmative. "As sure as a man can be."

FIFTY-SEVEN

Hayes left Delilah's. He got word out to the squads that he was after Vianelli. He was picked up within two hours and taken to Central.

The attitude arrived before the man.

Hayes had Vianelli put in an interview room. He left him there to simmer for a good forty minutes.

"What the fuck is this?" was Vianelli's opening gambit.

Hayes said nothing until he was seated. Everything about him was calm and unhurried.

"What this is, Maurizio, is a bust."

Vianelli smirked arrogantly.

"I know you," he said. "You were the one who was snooping around a few years back. Trying to get me fixed up on some assault beef, right?"

"You have a good memory," Hayes said. "Her name was Bernice Radcliffe, the girl you beat the shit out of over at Nicky Mariani's place on South Coronado."

"Don't know anyone called Bernice Radcliffe. Don't know anyone called Nicky Mariani, and I ain't never been down South Coronado in my life. Can I get a cup of coffee now?"

"No, you can't get a cup of coffee, Maurizio, and Bernice Radcliffe is not the subject of this interview."

"So what the hell do you want?"

"I want a grievous assault at least, but I am really hoping for a murder." Hayes smiled. There was a hint of irony in his expression. "You shouldn't wish someone dead, should you? I mean, that's the rock and a hard place about this job sometimes. You want someone to pull through, but then if they die it means that I get to put an asshole like you in the chair."

Vianelli smiled, and then he laughed. "I'll tell you what. Why don't you go to hell?"

"If it meant finding whatever would nail you, you arrogant punk, then I would do it. But I don't need to go to hell because I got four eyewitnesses who saw you stick a knife in Billy Resnick at Delilah's on Monday evening."

A split-second smirk, and then it faded. "Bullshit. You got nothing. Besides, I don't even know anyone called Billy Resnick."

Hayes smiled. "You don't seem to know anyone. You must be a lonely guy."

"I know plenty of people, just none of these people you're talking about."

"Which people?"

"The Radcliffe girl, Nicky Mariani, this Billy Resnick."

"You got a good memory for folks you never heard of before."

"So charge me with having a good fucking memory and let me out of here."

"I've got four eyewitnesses in the bar itself. I've got a sketch artist with Billy Resnick right now—"

"Billy Resnick is too fucked up to even speak, man—"

"Is that so?" Hayes asked. "How the hell would you know that if you've never even heard of the guy?"

"I heard of him. Okay, I heard of him. Heard about what happened. He was a lowlife, man. Maybe he was a kid, but he was a gambler. He was one of them crazies who thinks he's never gonna lose even while he's losing. He owed a lot of money."

"He did, did he?"

"'S what I heard."

"Tell you what I heard, Mo. Heard he owed you a lot of money and you got pissed with him giving you the runaround, and you went over to that bar and you stuck him."

"That's bullshit. I wasn't there on Monday."

"Not what four credible eyewitnesses have stated, and not what Billy is saying. And yes, he is pretty messed up, but you didn't kill him. Right now he's coming back with a description that sounds too much like you to be anyone else. This is the big one, my friend. He makes it, you'll do an eight-to-fifteen. He doesn't, you're gone for good."

"You got nothin'," Vianelli said.

Hayes took a gamble. "I got nothing? I got you speaking to your buddy Tony Legs right afterward. From what I heard you were the big boss of the hot sauce, figured you'd killed the kid. But you didn't. Maybe that was your first mistake. After that, it was all downhill."

The smug grin was nowhere to be seen.

"You spoke to Tony Legs?"

"I didn't, no."

"But someone did."

"Maybe."

"Tony Legs ain't gonna say a thing to no one."

"Everyone says a thing, Mo, just as long as they got the right motivation. We got him on an accomplice beef. Accomplice to murder if your boy doesn't make it. Self-preservation is the best incentive you can get."

Vianelli was quiet for a time.

"I'm gonna go get you a cup of coffee now, Maurizio," Hayes said. "While I'm gone you think about this predicament you've found yourself in. You stabbed Billy Resnick. We know this without a doubt. We got four eyewitnesses and a victim account with a sketch. Hell, Billy even knows your name. You are screwed any which way you wanna look at it. I got Tony Legs begging for an out, and I don't know how tight you guys are, but I think he'll roll over on you to keep himself out of jail. It's all about looking after Number One. Always has been, always will be. You weigh up this whole thing while I'm gone, and then maybe when I get back we can talk about where we go from here."

Hayes got up and left the room. Sometimes the only advantage he had was the utter stupidity of these people. Rare exception aside, the vast majority were as dumb as fence posts. All Vianelli had to do was keep his mouth shut and Hayes could have done nothing. A law freshman could have gotten Vianelli out of there in three minutes flat, but Hayes had planted enough doubt for Vianelli's imagination to take over.

"What do you want?" was Vianelli's question when Hayes reentered the room. Everything about the man had changed. The arrogance was gone, the smirk, the bravado. All of it had disappeared. Now he wore an expression of awkward resignation and anxiety.

Hayes set down two cups of coffee. "I want Nicky Mariani."

"For what?"

"What you got, Mo?"

"I want a deal. Cast-iron, no possibility of failure. I want a deal that I get nothing on this Resnick thing, even if he dies."

Hayes smiled. "I can't do that, Mo. The kid dies, then you're gonna fry, no doubt about it. You can't sweep a murder under the carpet, my friend. That's not the way it works."

"So what the hell am I doing here?" Vianelli asked. "You can't get me a deal, then why should I give you anything?"

"I can get you a deal," Hayes replied. "I can get you a manslaughter. I could even get you a self-defense. I can get you a couple of years, maybe even six months. Most of all I can keep you alive. That's the deal here, my friend. Murder is a capital offense. There ain't no leeway on that. It's murder, then you're going to the chair. I can't make it any simpler than that."

"Ah man, this is fucked up."

"You're on the money there, my friend. Right on the money there."

Mo Vianelli sat back. He closed his eyes for a moment and shook his head. Everything about his body language indicated resignation and defeat.

"I got Bobby Danza," he said.

"And who is Bobby Danza?" Hayes asked.

"More to the point, who *was* Bobby Danza," Vianelli said. "Bobby Danza was a greedy little asshole who used to work with Marco Angiletta and Zazzy Azarro. The three of them collected money for Sal Giordano. Bobby got greedy, and he wound up in a warehouse in the hills with Frank Bomp and Nicky. Nicky broke his head to fucking pieces with a hammer."

"You were there?"

"No, I was not."

"How d'you know about this, then?"

"He told me. Vince told me. They laughed themselves stupid about it. Nicky even showed us how he did it, got a hammer from the kitchen and showed us how he hit Bobby Danza in the head."

"When did this happen?"

"Hell, I don't know. It was before the war. That much I can tell you. Maybe thirty-eight sometime. I know Nicky hadn't been here long."

Hayes didn't reply.

"So, we got a deal or what? You gonna get me off the hook on this Billy Resnick thing?"

Hayes smiled and leaned forward. "Unlike you, Maurizio, I am a man of my word. I will do what I said I would do."

Mo Vianelli picked up the coffee and drank it down. He got up, looked at Hayes with a ghost of that earlier arrogance in his eyes, and he said, "Like you said, it's all about self-preservation."

Ten minutes later Hayes was back at his desk. He sat for a while in silence, his thoughts turning on what had just happened. If he could convince Nicky Mariani that he was done for on the Bobby Danza killing, then maybe Mariani would give up Frank Bompensiero and Sal Giordano. If Bomp and Giordano were in a hole, then maybe they'd get some leverage on Dragna.

Hayes felt a rush of adrenaline, butterflies in his lower gut. This was important. This was exactly how the upper echelons were implicated and undone. You get a small fish to bait the hook for a bigger fish, and on it goes until you're in the deep end with the sharks.

Hayes went to see Lieutenant Fuller right away.

FIFTY-EIGHT

There were times when Lucy Madden did not sleep well at all, her mind agitated with images, half-forgotten memories, other things that seemed just as real as any waking reality.

There were times when she would lie beside her husband, aware of her son sleeping in a crib at the foot of the bed, aware of another child growing inside her.

There were times when she would question what she had done, what had happened to her life, how she had escaped the confines of Corsica only to find something so very different from her dreams.

She was afraid. That was the truth. Afraid for herself, what would happen to her, what would happen to Nicky, what would happen to their family. Still she'd had no direct word from their parents, and she was stricken with anxiety for the privations they must have suffered during the war. And she wondered about Frankie, his family in Ireland, why he made no visible effort to reach them, to find out if they were well, to find out if they were even still alive.

That night—Valentine's Day, 1946—was one such night.

Had she known what was actually happening with Nicky, how the events of the latter part of 1945—the stabbing of Billy Resnick, the interrogation of Mo Vianelli, the dogged determination of Detective Louis Hayes—would start to close around her brother and threaten his freedom, she would have regretted ever arguing with him. She had turned the memory of that day over and over in her mind, how she had challenged him, questioned his motives, his intentions, and how he had fled the hotel. June 1938. It was unforgettable, and—in some small way—unforgivable. Her loyalties were forever torn. Even though he would never say it directly, Nicky would never really forgive her for marrying someone so far from her own heritage. In that way he was so much like their father.

Lucy knew precisely what Nicky was doing. She knew the kind of people with whom he was now associating. She knew the *work* they did. Despite her defensive comments to Frankie, she knew Frankie was right. It was an untenable situation in so many ways, and yet she had no choice.

By blood she was inescapably connected to Nicky, and now by marriage and family she was connected to Frankie. She loved them both without reservation, but in such different ways.

And now, a second child on the way, her dreams were ever more distant and impossible. Perhaps fate had played a hand. Did she believe in such things? Did she believe in a higher power that influenced, directed, mapped out a road for each person individually? Perhaps, perhaps not.

Fear was a power she truly understood. Fear of failure. Fear of the future. Fear of the unknown. Fear of what might happen to Nicky if he continued to do what he was doing.

For a little while Lucy stood in the doorway of the bedroom. It was the early hours of the morning. Frankie slept, as did Joe. She could hear them breathing almost in unison—Frankie taking one breath for every two of Joe's. She tried to breathe in between them, to fill that moment of silence, to give herself the impression that they were all existing as one entity, one life force.

She had sacrificed her career on the altar of security and family. She knew that. Frankie had done the same, but for different reasons. She had given up her dream for her child, for her *children*, whereas Frankie had been given no choice.

He'd had to quit in order to stay alive. Now his attention was consumed, and he seemed to be accomplishing as much as she'd ever hoped he would. Money was of no concern, their home was beautiful, their son was doing so well, and yet she understood the fragility of all of it. It could all be gone in a heartbeat.

Lucy closed her eyes for a moment. She mouthed the words of some long-ago prayer that she'd recited as a child.

She committed herself to Joe, to the new baby, to her husband, but she also committed herself to doing everything she could to protect and defend her brother. In a way he was also a child, and there was no one else to take care of him.

What she had given up was now as good as gone.

She was a wife and a sister. Above all things she was a mother. These things she had, and these things had to be of such greater value, surely?

Until you had children you could never understand the power of that bond, the fact that you would do anything, the fact that the life of another meant so very much more than your own. Until you had children, you would never know true fear.

She would stand by Frankie. She would also stand by Nicky. She would do everything possible to remain resolute and strong for both of them unless the well-being of her children was threatened.

And then . . . if such a thing happened?

Such a thing could not bear a single thought, and so she did not think it.

FIFTY-NINE

Throughout the last week of December, through January, and on into the first week of February 1946 Hayes devoted his life to Nicolas Mariani.

Had Carole possessed even a single suspicious bone in her body, she would perhaps have imagined her husband was involved with another woman. What she did begin to recognize and understand was something of his obsessive nature. It did not concern her; it intrigued her. She, too, was sometimes fastidious, determined to get it right no matter what, convinced that there was a correct way to do things and that standards should never be compromised. She was committed to her work, of course, but she was more than capable of leaving her work in the office where it belonged. Louis was different. Louis brought the work home, and there were times when she sensed his agitation and restlessness, how he would get up at two or three in the morning, make his way quietly to the kitchen and sit there in darkness, a glass of milk on the table. Eventually he would return to bed and then get up again, and she would not know whether he had slept.

"You okay?" she would ask.

He would smile, tell her he was just fine, that it was merely work.

She knew it was work, but she also knew it was something beyond that.

For Louis, the facts were simple, however. They had nothing. Hayes had met with Lieutenant Fuller, even Captain Mills, and the conversation had been straight and to the point.

"So, what do we actually have?" Mills asked.

"We have a scumbag telling us that another scumbag killed a third scumbag in a warehouse in the hills a few years ago," Fuller replied.

"These scumbags have names, or do we just number them these days to save time and paperwork?"

"Maurizio Vianelli says that Nicolas Mariani killed Roberto Danza with a hammer," Hayes explained.

"And you believe that this happened?" Mills asked.

"I do."

"You seem very certain."

"I am."

Mills smiled, looked at Fuller. "He always this monosyllabic and businesslike?"

"This is a good day," Fuller said. "Today Detective Hayes is saying more than he usually says in a week."

"But he works hard," Mills said.

"No question of that, sir," Fuller replied.

"You pair can go to hell," Hayes said. "Enough with busting my balls. This is a thing, you know? We get this Mariani character, then we got a shot at Frank Bomp, Jimmy Frat, and Sal Giordano. We get those, then we are in the majors, right?"

"I got that, Louis," Mills said. "Eric agrees with me on this. There's no question that we want to chase this thing down to the ground, but you haven't got a body; you've got no eyewitnesses . . . I mean, this Vianelli character wasn't even there. He's telling us that Mariani told him about Danza, right?"

"Right. Mariani and Caliendo told Vianelli how Bobby Danza got whacked."

"Gianluigi Caliendo? I thought he was up in Quentin."

"He is. This is Caliendo's boy, Vincent."

"And this Caliendo was there . . . ? He saw the killing?"

"Yes, sir. That's what I understand."

"I sense your frustration," Mills said, stating the obvious.

"I *am* frustrated, sir. That's perhaps an understatement."

"So what do you want me to do on this?"

"I want you to get me a wiretap on Mariani's place on South Coronado. I want a tap on the phones at the Venus and the Starlight as well. I also think we need to keep an eye on Mariani's sister and brother-in-law. His name is Frankie Madden. Irish, an unknown, and there's something that doesn't feel right about him."

"Madden? Not connected to Owney Madden by any chance?"

"He says not. Anyway, the Maddens run a casting agency, but that could give us a link to escorts, hookers, Christ knows what."

"Anything else?" Mills asked.

"That'll do it for the meanwhile."

"Well, we're done, then, Detective Hayes. I can't get you any of that, and you know it."

"But—"

"Based on what?" Mills asked. "I go to a judge and tell him that Scumbag One says Scumbag Two might just have done something pretty bad to Scumbag Three and there's a reasonable chance two or three other scumbags might have been hanging around with their hands in their pockets at the same time? Come on. You know the ropes. I get that you're wound up. I get that you're frustrated. You don't think me and Lieutenant Fuller don't feel the same way? I'll tell you now, I had a case that I worked on for three years . . ." Mills shook his head. "Whatever. Unimportant. This is the beat, Louis. What do you want me to say?"

"Give me someone else," Hayes said. "Give me a uniform, even someone right out of the academy, and I'll be a two-man task force."

"All of a sudden you're a superhero, sure. You've been listening to too much *Captain Midnight* and *Dick Tracy* on the wireless."

Hayes shook his head resignedly. "So what can I get on this?"

"I can ask Lieutenant Fuller here to be very understanding of your workload. I can't give you license to run this and nothing else, but I can ask him to give you some leeway on other assignments."

"I can do that," Fuller said.

"Then you have my blessing to go chasing this Marino character."

"Mariani," Hayes said.

"Mariani. Who cares? They're all scumbags of one variety or another."

Fuller had been good to his word. There had been few other assignments, but by the time the New Year turned there was a sense of futility and demoralization undermining even Hayes's commitment to nailing Mariani. He knew that Mariani was connected to the disappearance of Paulie Belotti. He knew that Vianelli had told him the truth about Bobby Danza. However hard Hayes tried, he could find no trace of Danza. Like Paulie Belotti, he guessed that Roberto Danza was in bits and pieces in the hills someplace. The questions he asked went back and forth and wound up nowhere. The closer you got to Dragna, the more frightened people became. And you just had to mention Mickey Cohen and people blanched before your eyes.

It wasn't until the second week of February 1946 that Hayes finally got a breakthrough, and—as seemed always to be the case—it came from a most unexpected source.

Vincent Caliendo's father, holed up in San Quentin for the July '39 armed robbery, was up for parole. How Hayes learned of this was mere chance. Gianluigi Caliendo, known by all and sundry as Gino, was going to need a reference, and that reference could only come from a cop, a judge, or a state's attorney. Someone had to put their name on the line, someone had to sign the docket for the parole board. Gino Caliendo was a reformed man, a rehabilitated citizen, and he was going to color inside the lines from now on. It was all so much whitewash. Caliendo Senior would more than likely be picked up within a month for the same thing he went down for. It was in his blood, his bones, his very being; he could not be anything other than who he was. But Hayes was prepared to make a trade-off. Caliendo Senior would get him Caliendo Junior; that would give him someone inside the warehouse when Nicky Mariani killed Bobby Danza. Unless Mo Vianelli was lying through his back teeth.

On Tuesday, February 12th, Hayes had a black-and-white follow Vince Caliendo. They waited until he was alone in his car, and then they pulled him over. Predictably, Caliendo bitched at them, claimed harassment, and then they asked him to open the trunk. Hayes had given one of the uniforms an unmarked .38. The .38 was "found" in the trunk, and Caliendo was asked for his firearms license. The language got bad. Caliendo was arrested. By the time Hayes sat down opposite Caliendo, the man was hoarse from screaming obscenities at everyone within earshot.

"This is a hoax beef," Caliendo said.

"I know, Vince."

Caliendo's eyes widened.

"You put those assholes up to this?"

"I did."

"What the hell is going on here?"

"What is going on, Vince . . . rather, what *was* going on was Bobby Danza."

"Bobby who?"

"That was good, Vince. That was actually very convincing. You ever get bored of the small-time thug business, you should try out for the movies. Hell, you're in the right place."

"I have no idea what you are talking about."

"I got you, Nicky Mariani, Sal Giordano, and Frank Bompensiero in a warehouse up in the hills. I got Nicky Mariani putting a hammer in Bobby Danza's head, and I got you on accomplice to first degree."

"Go to hell. You ain't got nothin'," Caliendo sneered.

Hayes leaned back in his chair. "Don't you guys ever get tired of this bullshit? Don't you ever get exhausted with trying to remember where you weren't and who you didn't see and what you didn't hear? To listen to you someone'd think you never left the house, never made a phone call, never spoke to anyone. I thought I had a lonely life, but you guys really take the blue rosette."

Caliendo smiled. "That's me right there, Mr. Fucking Lonely. No friends, no associates, no family. I don't got nothin'."

"You've got a father, Vincent. Everyone has a father."

Caliendo didn't respond.

"Your old man went down in thirty-nine, right? He's on an eight-to-twelve for screwing up a bank job. Parole gets reviewed in—what?—about three weeks if I'm not mistaken. And if the rumor is right, I heard he was pretty sick. Heard he didn't have too much longer."

Caliendo shook his head, but Hayes saw a flash of hurt in his eyes. "Whatever you got on me has nothin' to do with my father."

"He is sick, isn't he?"

Caliendo said nothing.

"I'm gonna take your silence as a yes."

"You don't drag my father into this now. I'm telling you, buddy—"

Hayes sighed resignedly. "Sorry, *buddy*. I done the dragging. Your father's here, has been here all along."

"You're talkin' crazy, man. I don't understand what you're saying to me."

"What I am saying is that someone needs to stand up for your old man. Has to be a cop, a judge, a state's attorney. Someone has to give a reference to the parole board to say that he's gonna behave himself if they let him out of his cage. Now, you know as well as me that not only is your father *not* going to behave, sick or otherwise, but we also know that there isn't a man between here and Palm Springs that's gonna say shit to help him out. In fact, I would go so far as to say that the *wrong* word, especially from a cop, could very well ensure that your old man does the full fifteen."

Caliendo got up suddenly. His chair fell backward and hit the floor with a crash. "What the he—"

"Sit the fuck down, Vincent. Jesus, don't get so melodramatic. We're talking possible scenarios here, my friend. We're just spitballing, you know? Take it easy."

Caliendo picked up the chair and straightened it. He sat down again. He was a ball of nervous energy.

"You just need to make a decision. It's pretty simple. You gotta ask yourself what you'd want if you were in his shoes. Would you want to die in there, your last breath filled with the stink of other men, or would you want to spend your last months looking at the sky and breathing fresh air as a free man?"

Caliendo looked at Hayes unerringly. His expression was nothing but hateful.

Hayes smiled, almost paternally. "You want a cup of coffee?"

"No, I don't want a cup of goddamned coffee. I wanna know what the hell is going on here."

"Okay, you have a right to that. As we speak, I got you on an unlicensed firearms beef. With your yellow sheet, I'm guessing maybe a year, two perhaps—"

"You planted that. You know that there was no gun in my car."

"Prove it," Hayes said. "I got two uniforms. You got squat."

Caliendo shook his head. He knew he was being railroaded. He also knew there was nothing he could do about it.

"Aside from that, I am a detective. Not only am I a detective, I am a detective first class in the same stomping ground as your father. I show up to the parole board, I tell them what they want to hear, and Gino Caliendo is out within a month and back to the good life for as long as he's got left. I say the wrong thing, and he's there for another eight. They are not going to release a man like your father on compassionate grounds, believe me."

"This is fucked, man. This is a fucked-up thing you're doing. You tell us we're bad, and then you turn around and do the same goddamned thing."

"I didn't kill Bobby Danza with a hammer."

"And neither did I."

"But we both know who did, and we both know who was there."

"You want me to roll over on my friends."

"I want you to give me some guidance, Vincent. I want you to point me in the right direction. I want you to answer a few questions, that's all."

"I say anything, and I mean *anything*, and they're gonna know it was me."

"Those are the breaks, my friend. You chose the life."

Caliendo stood up and started pacing. His fists clenched and unclenched. He reached the wall, used his hands to push him back the way he'd come. He was a live wire, a cat on a burning fence.

"Oh man, this is bullshit," he said, and he walked back to the table and sat down.

"A year for you, eight for your old man, knowing all the while that you could have gotten him out before he died. Against that, a few answers to a few questions."

"You're gonna *subpoena* me, want me to testify. That's what you want, right?"

Hayes shook his head. "I want enough to convince Nicky Mariani that there is someone who will testify, that's all."

Caliendo was silent for a moment, and then realization dawned. "Hell, man, you don't even want Nicky. Jesus Christ, who is it you're really after? Frank Bomp, Joe Adamo . . . you want Dragna? Is that who you're after? You're going for Dragna?"

"All I'm interested in right now is what happened to Bobby Danza," Hayes said.

"Man, I can't tell you anything. You think I'm crazy?"

"I think you'd be crazy not to, Vince. You help me out, it all goes smoothly. Otherwise, you're screwed."

"You know what my father would do if he found out I rolled over?"

"I can guess what he'd do if he found out you had a chance to get him out eight years early and you didn't."

"You are as crooked as—"

"Fight fire with fire, Vince. That's the way it goes."

"So what are you gonna give me?"

"I'm gonna wipe any record that you were ever pulled over. I am going to lose the firearms bust. I am going to sign your father's parole reference."

"And what do you want for this?"

"I want to know when Bobby Danza took a drive into the Hollywood Hills and never came home."

Caliendo sat silent for a moment. He looked at Hayes, and then he closed his eyes and sighed deeply. When he opened his eyes again he just looked at the wall. He stayed looking at the wall for quite some time, even as he answered Hayes's questions.

"June, thirty-eight."

"The date?"

"The fifteenth."

"How are you sure?"

"Because you watch someone smash someone's head in with a hammer and you're unlikely to forget when it happened, okay?"

"And it was Nicky who killed Bobby."

Caliendo was silent.

"I'll take your silence as a *yes*."

Caliendo gave an almost-imperceptible nod of the head.

"And Sal Giordano and Frank Bompensiero were there."

Again, a simple nod of the head.

"You can tell me where it was?"

"Not a clue, man. Huge place. Carnival shit up there. Painted horses and whatever. Creepy fuckin' place."

"And what happened to Bobby after?"

"We sawed him up."

"You and Nicky?"

"And Bomp. We sawed him up into little pieces. I was sick, man. Sick as a fucking dog. Nicky thought it was great. He and Bomp kept laughing at me. It was disgusting. Most disgusting thing I ever experienced in my life."

"And what happened to him after you cut him up?"

"We scattered him all over the place. Usual thing, you know? Scatter him all around and the wildlife takes care of it."

"Apart from his head."

"Right."

"Where'd his head go?"

"I don't know."

"Bomp took it?"

"Yeah, Bomp took it. We drove back downtown and he dropped us at the Venus. He took off and Bobby's head was still in the trunk of the car."

Hayes paused for a few moments.

Caliendo turned and looked at him. There was something in his eyes, something bitter and resentful, but beneath that Hayes perceived a sense of relief, as if the confession had somehow eased the burden he'd had been carrying. For all their bluff and bravado, most of them were frightened kids. Sure, they did terrible things, but more often than not they were spurred on by others. It was a pack mentality. The true psychopaths were few and far between.

"What did Nicky kill Bobby with?"

"A hammer, like I said."

"What kind of hammer?"

Caliendo frowned. "A hammer, man. You know what a hammer is."

"Big, little, wooden handle—"

"A wooden handle, yes. Like the one for putting nails into things. A regular hardware-store hammer, you know?"

"Do you know what happened to it?"

"Bomp took it."

"Okay."

"So what now?"

"We're done for the moment, Vincent. You can go. I know you're not going to say a word about this to anyone because you'd be dead within an hour."

Vince Caliendo looked at Hayes, and there was something truly hateful in his expression.

Hayes smiled. "You go on hating me, Vince. You do that if it's gonna make you feel better. If I were you, however, I would spend your time and energy figuring out how the hell you're going to get out of this game. This is for scumbags and assholes. I think underneath all the wiseass bullshit you're a decent human being. Your father may be beyond redemption, but at least we can give him one more chance. Get him out of LA, why don't you? Take off. Disappear. I am sure he still has a whole bunch of money stashed—"

"I don't want to hear anything else you gotta say," Caliendo interjected. "If it's okay with you, I just wanna leave the building."

"I understand," Hayes said. "I'll have someone fetch your car from lockup."

SIXTY

Carole Hayes knew something was awry when her husband asked her to pick up three or four hammers from different hardware stores downtown.

It was the morning of Valentine's Day. Hayes had not forgotten what day it was. He asked her about the hammers right after breakfast and just before he produced a huge bunch of red roses.

"Hammers? You want three or four hammers?"

"That's right."

"Like a regular kind of hammer?"

"Yes, just regular hammers."

"No nails?"

"No, just the hammers. Different ones."

"Can I ask why?" She was at the stove, poured coffee for both of them.

"Best not to."

"Like this is some sort of carpentry project you've got going on," she said.

"Aw, shucks, and it was supposed to be a big old secret."

"Louis, seriously . . . that is a really bizarre thing to ask me to do first thing on Valentine's Day morning. Here's some roses . . . Oh, and by the way, I need some hammers."

"It's a work thing."

Carole raised her eyebrows. "Okay, that makes me feel slightly better than if you'd said it was a home thing."

"Could you do that for me? I know you don't have to get into the office until later."

"And you can't pick them up on the way to work because?"

"Just because," Hayes replied.

"What is going on, Louis?" Carole stood near the stove, one hand on the countertop, the other on her hip. She looked like someone expecting a lie.

"I need to do an experiment," he said. "It's pretty gross, and you really don't want to know."

"Okay, that much I understand . . . but I still don't get why I need to do it."

"I just need you to do this, Carole. Follow me to work. We'll stop on the way. We'll find a couple of places. You go in and buy the hammers, bring them out to me, and when we're done, you drive back here and I'll go to work."

"Are you up to something that you shouldn't be up to?"

"No."

"Liar."

Hayes set down his coffee cup. "Look," he said. "This is real simple. I just need you to trust me. I am doing something on a case. I need some hammers. I am not sure what kind of hammers, so I figured the best thing to do is buy three or four different ones and see which one is best."

"I understand."

"Good. Okay, so we can do this?"

She smiled. "Oh no, I didn't mean that I understand what you're doing. I meant that I understand that a straight answer is not going to be forthcoming."

"This is becoming way more complicated than it needs to be."

"The only complicated thing is why *I* need to buy the hammers."

"You don't. Actually, you don't need to buy them. I'll get them."

Carole was silent. A sardonic smile played around her lips.

"What?" Hayes asked.

"You're really not a good liar at all."

"I guess that's a plus, right?"

She laughed, and then she came and sat down facing him. "Tell me you're not being impulsive and desperate about this case."

"I am not being impulsive and desperate about this case."

"Once more," she replied, "with feeling."

"Look," he said, "I just need to do an experiment. I am going to see if I can catch someone in a lie, that's all."

"And for this you need four hammers?"

"I need one, just one, but it has to be a regular hardware-store hammer, not too big, not too small. Just a regular hammer."

"Like the one in the cupboard under the sink."

"Eh?"

"A regular hardware-store hammer, like the one under the sink."

Hayes got up, crossed to the sink and opened the door. There, in a box of assorted screwdrivers and other hand tools, was a hammer. Wooden handle, well used, it would serve the purpose admirably.

"I didn't even know we had a box of tools there."

"That's because I'm the one who uses them," Carole said. "I can fix a lamp, change a lightbulb, swap out fuses, all sorts of things."

"Yeah," Hayes said, "I was wondering who was doing all that kind of stuff around here."

"Okay, so tell me one thing," Carole said. "Tell me you're not going to hit anyone with that."

"I am not going to hit anyone with it," Hayes said.

Hayes finished breakfast. He left on time, told Carole that he might be back late, that he'd call and let her know.

She watched him from the front doorway, kept on watching until his car had disappeared at the end of the street, and then she went back inside with a sense of unease.

An hour later Hayes was leaving a butcher's shop downtown. Wrapped in several layers of paper he carried a sheep's head. He put the head in the trunk of his car and drove up toward the hills. Twenty minutes or so he took a left down a dirt track and pulled over. He took the hammer out and hit it against a few rocks, first the head, then the handle. He wedged the shaft of the hammer between two large stones, and twisted it until the wood split. Then he kicked the hammer around some more, got dirt and dead leaves into the crack. Once the hammer looked like something he'd dug up, he unwrapped the sheep's head, set it down, and then used the hammer to pulverize it. As he hit that skull again and again, bone fragments and blood and brain matter turning to paste beneath the repeated blows, he could not help but imagine what such a thing would do to a human being. It made him feel sick.

Once he was satisfied, he dropped the hammer in the dirt again, then positioned it against a tree in the direct path of the mid-morning sun. He waited until all signs of moisture had evaporated, and then he turned it over in his hands and thought about Nicky Mariani and Bobby Danza.

Hayes put the hammer in an evidence bag, folded the top, and put it in the trunk. He drove down to Central, pulled Roberto Danza's file, also those of Sal Giordano and Frank Bompensiero. For good measure he took a half dozen other random files and put them in his desk drawer. Then he called squad and told a black-and-white to pick Nicolas Mariani up. He gave the South Coronado address, the Venus, the Starlight, even the Erin Agency.

It was a little after two in the afternoon, and even though his thoughts were riddled with doubt, he knew he'd gone too far to turn back. This thing was under his skin. It would never let him be. He wanted Mariani. More than that he wanted Giordano, Bompensiero, any of these upper-echelon hitters and made men. He wanted to tear down the whole corrupt edifice and watch them stagger around and blame one another in the rubble. He wanted them to suspect everyone they knew, to feel like there was no one they could trust. He was sick of them, sick of their wiseass retorts, their manufactured alibis, their unbridled arrogance, the self-possessed certainty that they were far beyond the reach of the law. Against people like this, someone had to take a stand. He wanted to see Jack Dragna's face when he got life without parole.

It was four hours before Nicky Mariani was picked up and taken over to Central. By the time he was seated across from Hayes in the interview room it was close to seven in the evening. Whatever level of attitude and arrogance Hayes had expected, Nicky Mariani outdid himself.

"So, what's the deal here?" Mariani said. "You got me picked up on some bullshit thing, man. What gives?"

"Sit down, Nicky."

"I've had enough of sitting down. I don't want to sit down. You gotta charge me with something that means something or you gotta let me go. I know my rights—"

"I'd really appreciate it if you would take a seat, Nicky."

"You gotta—"

"We need to talk, my friend, and it's not going to be a short conversation." Hayes looked unerringly at Nicky Mariani. Evidently there was something in Hayes's expression that impinged sufficiently to create the desired effect.

Nicky sat down slowly, looked at the stack of files on the table, and then back at Hayes.

"Can I get you a cup of coffee, Nicolas?"

Nicky shook his head.

"Okay . . . well, where do we begin? I guess I need to ask you about Frank Bompensiero."

"Who?"

"Come on, really? We're gonna do this? You really think I wanna play that game?"

"What game?"

"The one where I ask you about someone that you know real well and you tell me you've never heard of them. That game."

"I can't tell you what to think," Nicky said. "You got me all figured out, who I know and who I don't. Whatever, man. That's your imagination. You go ahead and make believe whatever you like. You ask me about this guy, Frank whoever, and I tell you I don't know him."

"Sal Giordano," Hayes said. "Tony Leggiero, Vincent Caliendo, Maurizio Vianelli. Any of those names ring a bell?"

Nicky looked thoughtful for a while and then shook his head. "I think maybe I heard o' one o' them. That Leggiero guy, maybe. I can't be sure. Who are they, anyway?"

"Just a bunch of hoods and thugs you're gonna help me put away for a long, long time."

Nicky started laughing. It was spontaneous but genuine. He really was amused by Hayes's comment.

"Oh man, you really are a delusional case. *I* am gonna help you put some people away?"

"Sure you are."

"Okay. Right. I'm glad we got that figured out there, mister detective man. So, what the hell makes you think I'd wanna do anything to help someone like you?"

"Because you're a good guy, Nicky. Because this whole Kid Napoleon thing is just a front. That's what they call you, right? Kid Napoleon. You think you got your own little Corsican Mafia thing going on, right? Let me tell you now, my friend, you're a little boy in a man's game, and you're gonna help me straighten all of this out so you and your sister can get along with your lives and do something constructive and decent."

"Hey, whatever the hell you got goin' on here has nothin'—and I mean *nothin'*—to do with my sister."

"Your sister is a different story, Nicky. I'll grant you that. I got to say that you are already starting to make a mess of things for her, though. I already had to go over there and talk to her about Dolores Rayburn and Bernice Radcliffe—"

"What the hell are you talkin' about? Who the hell are these people now?"

"Bernice was the girl that Mo Vianelli busted up in your place on South Coronado. Dolores Rayburn was just some other girl that we figured was maybe connected to you, connected to people you knew. Bad business, porno-movie stuff, all the kind of stuff your people get into."

"My people? What are you talking about, *my* people?"

Hayes sighed and leaned back. "Look," he said. "I really don't want to play this game. I really don't. I've been doing this a long time. I know what I'm doing. I'm a professional. I get paid to do this shit. You get paid to do your shit. I know how it goes. I've been around the block a good few times. So, we can sidestep each other all night, or we can have a real honest-to-God conversation about the nightmare of trouble you've gotten yourself into, or we can pretend that each of us has no idea what the other is talking about. The latter is just going to postpone the inevitable, so I think we should just get the fuck on with it and stop wasting each other's time."

Nicky eyed Hayes suspiciously, and then he smiled knowingly. "You're good, man. I've been questioned a few times by a few different cops and you're good, you know? If I was in some kind of trouble then maybe you woulda got me with that line there, but I ain't in any kind of trouble and you people don't got nothin' on me."

Hayes reached for the stack of files. He took the uppermost one and opened it in such a way as Nicky couldn't see what he was reading.

"What we got, my friend, is you and Sal Giordano, Frank Bomp, and Vince Caliendo in a warehouse up in the hills back in June of 1938."

"Bullshit. Like I said, I don't even know these guys. What the hell would I be doin' in a warehouse with them?"

Hayes shrugged. "I guess the first thing you'd be doing is talking to Bobby Danza."

Nicky Mariani said nothing. It was barely three or four seconds, but it gave him up as good as any confession.

"Who?" he asked, and though he tried to sound as bullish and confident as ever, there was an audible waver in his voice.

"Roberto Danza. Went missing back in June 1938. Now we know why he went missing and who made him disappear."

"Well, you can go on knowing whatever the hell you think you know. The plain facts are that it has nothing to do with me, and there ain't nothin' you can stick me with."

"I've got the hammer," Hayes said matter-of-factly.

"You've got the what?"

Nicky did better with that one. Maybe he'd overcome the initial shock of how much Hayes appeared to know, and it was now a simple matter of denying everything.

"The hammer, Nicky. The hammer you used to stove Bobby Danza's head in."

Nicky laughed. Had Hayes not known he was lying perhaps it would have sounded genuine. As it was, it just came across as forced and unnatural.

"I don't know what the fuck you're talkin' about," Nicky said. "I don't know Bobby Danza, I wasn't in no warehouse, and I ain't never seen no hammer."

Hayes shook his head. "What the hell is it with you? You're not even Italian. You're Corsican. You've been in LA—what? —seven, eight years?—and already you're indistinguishable from a thousand other cheap wiseass street punks. At least your sister managed to keep some of her class."

"You keep my sister out of this."

"Why would I need to keep your sister out of this? You're telling me that there isn't anything here, Nicky. Why are you concerned about your sister?"

"You know what I mean, man."

"I can guess what you're scared of, Nicky. You brought her over here, right? You made a promise to your folks. You said you'd take care of her, make sure she was fine. Well, seems she is fine. Got herself a husband, a kid, a good little business going on, and then you come along with your bullshit friends and your drug deals and the hookers and the sex-movie stuff—"

Nicky leaned forward. He looked Hayes directly in the eyes and said, "Enough. You have nothing on me. You can talk yourself stupid, but you won't get a single answer out of me." The brash arrogance was gone, as was the punk dialogue. This was Nicolas Mariani, Corsican killer, and there was something altogether chilling about the speed and ease with which the cheap facade had fallen away.

Hayes nodded slowly, and then he reached beneath the desk and produced the evidence bag. He held it above the table for a moment, and then he let it drop. The sound of the object inside hitting the surface was like a gunshot in the confined space of the room.

Nicky blinked, but otherwise there was no reaction. He didn't even look at the bag. He just kept on looking right at Hayes.

"What, you brought supper for us?" he said, his voice calm and unhurried.

Hayes opened the top of the bag. He reached inside and carefully lifted out the hammer by the very end of the shaft. He set the bag on its side, flattened it out, and then laid the hammer on top. He didn't say a word.

Nicky didn't look at the hammer, but he knew it was there. He knew what it was. It smelled of dirt and undergrowth.

"If you look closely," Hayes said, his voice almost a whisper, "you can still see bits of Bobby's skull and brains at the top of the handle."

Nicky smiled like a snake. "If I look really closely I can see a cop with a hammer and a paper bag and a very fertile imagination."

"I got this, and I got someone who will put you right there in that warehouse. June 23, 1938. You remember that date, and you remember this one as well. Today is the day that it all starts falling apart around you, my friend. If you listen closely enough, you can hear the foundations beginning to give way."

"I don't hear nothing," Nicky said. He looked around the room, looked back at Hayes with a sneer. "Fucking silence, my friend. Just silence."

"I'm keeping you overnight," Hayes said.

"The hell you are," Nicky replied.

"Possession of an unlicensed firearm."

"I don't have an unlicensed firearm."

"No, but I do, and I'm gonna lend it to you."

"You can't do that," Nicky said, his tone aggrieved.

"Sure I can," Hayes replied. "I'm police. I can do whatever the hell I like."

"It's a violation of my civil rights."

Hayes smiled and got up. He put the hammer in the bag and set it on top of the stack of files. "Newsflash, scumbag. Your civil rights just got canceled."

Hayes picked up the files and the evidence bag, left the room, stood for moment listening to Nicky Mariani as he hollered up a storm in the interview room. Hayes headed on down the corridor, collared a uniform, said, "Asshole in room three. Stick him in lockup. Give him a cup of water, the worst sandwich you can find, no blankets, and leave him there all night. I'll be back in the morning."

"You got it, sir," the uniform replied.

Hayes went back to his office, locked the files and the hammer in his desk, and then headed out for home. Tomorrow was another day. He would have to let Mariani go, but he would keep on pulling him in time and again until the cracks started to show. Then, with whatever leverage he could gain, he would prize the guy open and get him talking about the people for whom he worked.

As for tonight, it was Valentine's Day, and he was going to take his wife for a late supper. The past few weeks had been intense, and he felt an evening away from it with Carole would give both of them some respite.

As he drove away from Central he thought about where this case might take him. This kind of thing could make a career. Maybe he could finally do something that would make a difference. Maybe Nicky Mariani—crazy son of a bitch that he was—would be the key to some well-deserved changes for the better.

SIXTY-ONE

Nicky Mariani knew that it was Mo Vianelli who'd given him up. It could not have been Vince or Tony Legs. Not a prayer. Mo Vianelli was the only other person who knew about Danza. Mo must have gotten himself picked up for something. That was what had happened. This cop—Hayes—had gotten Mo bang to rights on an assault or something, and Mo, intent on weaseling himself out of it, had given up Nicky for the Danza killing. It was a trade-off. Mo had a yellow sheet longer than Hollywood Boulevard. An assault bust would put him away for a dime, at least. Maybe it'd be three strikes and he'd do life. Hayes would have convinced him of this, Nicky felt sure, and so Mo Vianelli had rolled like a log in a river and told Hayes some bullshit story about how he'd been in that warehouse and seen Bobby Danza get his head bashed in.

Maurizio Vianelli would be taken care of, for sure. He and Vince would find him and straighten it all out for good. But that was not Nicky's priority. Nicky's priority was finding Lucia and getting a lid on this Danza bullshit.

Nicky was released from Central at eight on the Friday morning.

He looked like he'd gotten dressed in a hedge, his mouth was coppery, his eyes gritty after a restless and agitated sleep on a two-inch palliasse. He was more angry than afraid, but he could not deny that the conversation with Hayes had had a deeply unsettling effect. They had the hammer, for Christ's sake. How the hell had that happened? Wasn't it Bomp who'd taken the hammer away? He could not ask him; not ask anyone. Mention a word of this and he'd find himself sharing a bunk with Paulie Belotti. He'd tried desperately to remember the details of that night, but all that came back was the sense of overwhelming power that had accompanied the killing of Bobby Danza. Danza was an asshole. Vianelli was an asshole. Danza was dead, and Vianelli was sure as hell going to join him. But right now it was self-preservation that drove his thoughts and his actions.

Nicky took a cab to the Venus and picked up his car. He drove back to South Coronado. Rita asked him where the hell he'd been.

"Your job is to keep this fucking house, okay? Your job is not to ask me where the hell I've been," was Nicky's response.

Rita knew well enough to leave him alone.

Nicky took a shower, got changed, told Rita to make some coffee and a plate of eggs.

She had to fetch him down to take a call from his sister.

Rita heard just one side of the conversation.

"Hey, what's up?"

"That is really strange you called me. I was just coming over to see you."

"I'll tell you when I get there . . . Sure, sure thing."

"Is Frankie there?"

"No, no reason. Just wondered if he was there."

"Yes, okay. Half an hour maybe."

Nicky ate his breakfast standing and silent, his eyes seemingly unable to focus on anything for longer than a second, his rage of thoughts almost audible. Rita left him to it, went down the street to see her girlfriend. When she got back Nicky was gone.

Nicky arrived at the Madden house just after Frankie had left. Had he seen Frankie's car in the drive he would have waited at the end of the street until he'd gone. He needed Lucia alone.

Their greetings were enthusiastic. They'd not seen each other for some weeks. Nicky made comments about how good the house looked, and when the nanny came through to take Joe for a while, Nicky just laughed.

"What?" Lucia asked.

"Look at you," he said. "All dressed up in that outfit. You got a nanny for Joe. You got this beautiful place. Man, who would have thought it when we got off that boat back in New York?"

"We've worked really hard, Nicky. Frankie does a ten-, twelve-hour day. Works weekends. He's tireless. He's a good man, and we're really happy together."

"Shame he doesn't like me."

"What do you mean? Of course he likes you."

Nicky reached for his cigarettes.

"Nicky, can you not smoke in here? I don't like it around Joe."

Nicky put the cigarettes away. "You are all Suzy Homemaker now, eh? A proper American wife."

"I don't think that's such a bad thing, do you? Isn't that what we came here for?"

"You came here to be a movie star, remember?"

"And I can still be a movie star," she said, but the statement belied her emotions. "Besides, we're not talking about that. We were talking about Frankie and why you think he doesn't like you."

"Arm's length," Nicky said. "Everything is at arm's length with Frankie. If it was his decision, we wouldn't see each other from one Christmas to the next. You see us together, there's no way anyone would think we were family"

"Frankie has his own way of showing how he feels," Lucia said. "He's not over-emotional. He's a quiet man. He's the strong silent type, you know?"

"But he takes care of you, right?"

"He loves me, and he takes care of me."

"Then that's all that really matters," Nicky said. "So, you got some news. What's happening? Why did you call?"

"You first," Lucia said.

Nicky laughed. "No, come on, tell me what's happening."

Lucia paused for just a moment, the excitement so visible in her eyes, and she said, "We're going to have another baby. You're going to be an uncle again, Nicky."

Nicky's eyes widened. "Oh, Lucia," he said, and he was almost moved to tears. He came across and knelt on the floor in front of her. He pulled her close and held her, and he was so happy. "Oh, this is such great news. Oh, this is just amazing."

He leaned back and looked up at her. "I am so pleased for you," he said. He let his sister go and went back to the couch. "If only our parents—"

Lucia raised her hand and Nicky fell silent.

"I don't want to talk about that right now," she said. "We need to go home. We need to see them, Nicky, but now I'm pregnant again and—"

"It's okay," Nicky said. "One thing at a time." For a moment there was tension, and then Nicky dispelled it by saying, "Oh man, this is so fucking cool!"

Lucia scowled. "Nicky! Really, such language isn't necessary."

"Oh, they really got you tamed, haven't they? Where's the tough little Corsican girl that sailed the seas with her big brother, eh?"

"The tough little Corsican girl grew up, Nicky." She shot him a glance that finished the statement without words.

"And I haven't grown up?"

"Did I say that?"

Nicky shook his head. "I'm not fighting with you, Lucia. There's too much good news for us to fight."

"Agreed," she said. "No fighting. So, what news do you have? What did you want to talk to me about?"

Nicky got up and crossed the room to the fireplace. He stood with his hands in his pockets and his head down for a moment, and then he looked at his sister like he'd done as a little boy. Something was wrong, he'd messed up, made a mistake, and his expression said it all.

"What happened, Nicky? Are you in trouble?"

"No," he said.

"Liar," Lucia replied.

"Not in trouble, Lucia. Not yet. Well, it's kind of trouble, yes, but for something I didn't do."

Lucia sighed and shook her head. She sat back in the chair and looked at Nicky without saying a word.

Her thoughts of the previous night seemed to have somehow been prophetic. She knew something was coming, and she knew she would not like it.

"Someone . . . something happened. Something happened to someone I know. Hell, I didn't even know him, but something happened and I was there, and the cops think I had something to do with what happened to him, and now they're giving me a headache about it and saying they're gonna hound me and harass me . . ."

"Nicky."

Nicky stopped talking and looked at Lucia.

"Tell me the truth. I mean, the real truth. Tell me what really happened and how much trouble you're in."

"Me? I'm not in trouble," Nicky lied. It did not surprise him how easily it came, even to his sister. He'd had plenty of practice. "There's a guy I know. You don't need to know his name. He got into a disagreement with another guy that I'd never met. Something about money. Someone owed someone some money. Whatever, it's not important. Anyway, I went with the first guy to see the second guy. Everything was fine, they were working it out, and then the second guy said something and the first guy got mad and they ended up fighting and second guy got hurt real bad and he died."

"He died?"

"He died, yes."

"How did he die?"

"The first guy hit him and he fell down and hit his head."

"And it killed him?"

"Yeah, it killed him."

Lucia shook her head in disbelief. "What is going on with you, Nicky? You know, this is exactly why Frankie keeps you at arm's length. This is why he doesn't want you around unless you really have to be. He's not going to stop you seeing me, and he's not going to stop you being an uncle, but he doesn't want your crazy friends around the family. You understand what I'm saying?"

Nicky was wringing his hands. He needed his sister on his side. He needed to work the fraternal angle for all it was worth. "It was an accident, Lucia. It was an accident. I didn't even know the guy and it wasn't even my argument—"

"I never told you this," Lucia said, "but the police came to see us."

"What?"

"A detective came to see us. Came right to the office just after we'd moved. Back before Christmas. He asked about a girl called Dolores Rayburn. We represent her, but she was arrested in some kind of sex-movie thing. I don't know the details, and I don't want to know. He also asked about another girl, Bernice something-or-other, said that she was hurt by someone whose name I don't remember back in December of 1941. And he asked about you."

"Me?"

"Yes, Nicky. He asked about you. It was just an offhand comment, but I got the impression there was a great deal more going on than just idle curiosity."

Nicky looked dumbstruck. The detective had spoken to Lucia, just as he'd said. They'd asked about the girl Mo Vianelli beat up at the house. Now there was no doubt in Nicky's mind. Mo Vianelli was buying himself out of a hole with this deal.

"You remember the name of this guy who hurt the girl?" Nicky asked.

"No, I don't."

"Try, Lucia. See if you can remember."

Lucia looked irritated, annoyed about such a trivial detail, but she tried nonetheless. "I don't remember, Nicky. It was before Christmas. I don't know . . . I keep thinking of the word 'vanilla' for some reason—"

"Vianelli," Nicky said matter-of-factly.

"Yes," Lucia said. "That sounds right. Vianelli."

"Too many coincidences," Nicky said.

"What are?"

Nicky shook his head. He took a seat and again leaned forward with his elbows on his knees, rubbed his hands together nervously.

"Is this Vianelli guy connected to the trouble you're in now?" Lucia asked.

"I reckon so," Nicky said. "I think they've got him for hurting this girl back in forty-one, and he's trying to buy his way out of it by telling them I did something that I didn't do."

"What is going on, Nicky?" Lucia asked. "How come you're involved with people like this? What have you gotten yourself into?"

"I haven't gotten myself into anything," Nicky said. "I'm trying to manage clubs. I'm trying to run a legitimate business. Unfortunately, the business I'm in means that lowlifes and scumbags come into the clubs. You can't stop them. On the face of it they appear to be good people, but they have other things going on that I don't even know about until it's too late—"

"I really need to know the truth, Nicky," Lucia said. "I need you to look me in the eye and tell me that you didn't do something terrible and that it was someone else."

Nicky was on his knees again, right there on the carpet in front of his sister. He took both her hands in his, he looked her dead in the eyes, and he said, "On my life, on the lives of our parents, I swear to you that I didn't do anything bad. They're after me because they think I can give them some information or something. It isn't right. It's not fair, you know? Whatever they say I did, it was not me."

Lucia looked at her brother for several seconds.

He did not look away.

"Okay," she said. "What do you need from me?"

SIXTY-TWO

Hayes let it lie for forty-eight hours. He wanted Nicky Mariani to simmer a little longer. He knew he was taking a risk, but he felt it was sufficiently calculated to play to his advantage.

Second only to self-preservation, these people were concerned for their reputation. Not socially, not morally—very far from it; the only reputation that concerned them was within their own ranks.

A man could be a thief, a pimp, a drug dealer, a bank robber, a killer, but he could not be a coward or a snitch.

The last thing Nicky Mariani wanted was for his compadres to know he was under investigation. Investigation suggested surveillance, and if that became an issue, then he'd find himself stranded and alone. Nicky Mariani would become the proverbial sinking ship, and the rats would flee for dry land faster than a speeding bullet.

Hayes pulled a couple of favors and got an off-duty uniform on the South Coronado place, another on the Maddens' bungalow in the hills. There was something about this Frankie Madden that bothered him. It was not significant, and it could certainly wait until the business with Mariani was over, but it floated there at the back of his mind. The man had been too defensive when Hayes had asked about his background. Sure, people got nervous around cops, certainly cops who were asking questions, but they only got defensive when there was something to hide. He had made a mental note to look a little more closely into the man's business dealings and associates. He knew some Irish cops, and they had more than enough connections back to the old country to find the truth of anyone's history. If Madden had only been here since '38, then that history was not so far away at all.

Hayes himself kept a weather eye on the Venus and the Starlight as best he could with patrolling black-and-whites and his own industry. By the end of the fifteenth there was nothing to report. Mariani didn't appear to be panicking. It was what Hayes had expected. Mariani was more dangerous than the regular street punks and wannabe button men. He didn't doubt that Mariani had cold-bloodedly dispatched Bobby Danza with a hammer, but without a body, without a weapon, without eyewitnesses, there was nothing he could do to prove or prosecute such a certainty. Mariani was weighing up his options, perhaps baffled as to how Hayes appeared to know so much, paranoia setting in about who might have given him up. If he realized it was Caliendo, then Caliendo would go the way of Bobby Danza. Not that Hayes had any intention of putting in a good word for Caliendo's father at the parole hearing, but the death of the son would be no great loss. One less scumbag on the streets, and Caliendo Senior would rot for however long he had left in San Quentin. That would benefit everyone but Caliendo Senior himself.

Hayes spent Saturday morning and early afternoon at home. Carole noticed there was something different in his manner, as if something tense and wound up had been fractionally released.

She asked him what was happening on the case.

"June of thirty-eight," he said. "Nearly eight years ago now I heard about this character. He was known as Kid Napoleon because he came from Corsica. Where he was before LA I don't know, but he wound up connected to some very bad people. It's hard to imagine, but I've had this guy on my mind all these years, and I think it's now going to come to something."

"The thing with the hammer, right?" Carole asked.

"That was just a ruse, sweetheart. That was just something to unsettle the guy a little."

"Did you do something illegal?"

Hayes smiled and shook his head. "No, I didn't do anything illegal. I was just playing games with the guy. I gave him the notion that I knew exactly what he'd done, how he'd done it, and who he'd done it to. I'm just pushing him in the direction of cooperating. Truth is that I'm not so much interested in him as the people he works for. He's gonna go down, that's for sure, but that's just collateral damage on the way to a bigger bust."

"I really hope it works out," Carole said. "I know how much it's been troubling you."

"It's routine. This is my job."

Carole sat across from her husband at the kitchen table. "Usually I'd agree with you, but this one is different. This has been a bit of an obsession, Louis. I see you having conversations in your head. I know when you've been working on this case, and I really want to see the end of it as well."

Hayes frowned, seemed genuinely surprised. "Really? You think I've been obsessive about it?"

"You talk in your sleep."

"I do not talk in my sleep."

Carole shrugged. "Okay, you don't talk in your sleep."

"Really?"

"Really."

"That's not such a good sign, is it?"

"I was going to suggest some professional help."

Hayes laughed. Carole laughed with him.

He reached out and took her hand. "Smartest decision I ever made, marrying you."

"I know," she said.

"I really do love you."

"And I'm growing quite fond of you," Carole replied.

"Such a wiseass."

"'S what you get for hitchin' up with a smart-as-a-whip San Franciscan."

"I think we should take some time off, you know. Once this thing is done. I really think we should take a week out and go somewhere together."

"I'd really like that, Louis."

"Then it's a deal. I'll close this up and then we go someplace we've never been before."

"You try the kitchen. I'll go to Paris."

"Bring me back something nice, eh?"

"If I remember, sure."

Hayes got up. He walked around the table and stood behind her. He put his hands on her shoulders and she closed her hands over his.

"Luckiest guy alive," he said.

Carole said nothing, just leaned left and kissed his hand.

"I gotta go," Hayes said. "Probably be late again."

"I know," Carole replied.

"Soon I'll stop saying that."

Carole didn't reply. She didn't want to acknowledge her husband's temptation of fate.

Hayes left for Central just after two. This time he figured on finding Mariani himself. He wanted to see the guy's face when he picked him up two times in three days. He knew it would be a war of attrition, grinding down Mariani's resistance, making him feel ever more unnerved and unsettled by showing up at the clubs, at the house on South Coronado, never letting up on the questions. Perhaps this was the least appreciated aspect of police work, but it was also the most familiar and the most necessary. In the main, cases cracked due to pressure and persistence, especially when it came to the closed communities of organized crime.

Hayes found Nicky Mariani at the Starlight. Vincent Caliendo and Tony Leggiero were with him.

"The hell do you want?" was Nicky's opener.

"Nicky," Hayes said. "Good to see you."

Hayes sensed Caliendo's unease. The three of them were sitting at the bar in the back of the club. Leggiero was eating a sandwich.

"Who are these monkeys?" Hayes asked, and then he frowned and indicated Leggiero. "I know you," he said. "You're Anthony Leggiero."

Leggiero sneered. "Well, I don't know you, and I don't think I want to."

"Shame," Hayes said. "I was thinking of making this place my regular."

"Well, you go ahead and try," Leggiero said.

Nicky raised his hand. "Enough," he said. He turned to Hayes. "I don't know what you want, but I don't see you got any reason to be here. Be appreciated if you'd just take whatever business you think you got with me and disappear." He waved Hayes away, as if dismissing a waiter.

Hayes did not let himself get wound up. He had Mariani heading for the ropes, and he was not backing down.

"We need to talk," Hayes said. "I have a few more questions for you, Nicky."

Nicky sighed. His frustration was evident in his body language. This was his territory and the last people he wanted here were the cops.

"My name is Mariani," he said. "Mr. Mariani. You and I ain't buddies, okay? I ain't Nicky and you ain't whatever the hell you're called. You may have plenty of questions for me, but I ain't got no answers for you."

Hayes walked the length of the bar and took a look in the booths at the back. He had no reason to go there; he just wanted to aggravate Nicky as much as possible.

He stopped close to Nicky and smiled. His expression was almost sympathetic.

"We have unfinished business, you and I," Hayes said. "All the stuff you told me Thursday was fine, but some of it doesn't make sense and it's raised a good deal more questions."

"All the stuff I told you Thursday? What the hell are you talking about?"

"You want to do this here, or you want to keep it low-key?"

Nicky slid off the stool. He and Hayes were pretty much the same height, and Nicky stood close, looking right back at Hayes with the tough-guy thing going on.

"You think you can harass me?" Nicky asked. "You think you can intimidate me? You need to back off, my friend. You need to go mind your own business before you start coming here with your bullshit ideas and whatever the hell else you think you got. Like I said before, you got a fertile imagination, and you are taking yourself way too seriously right now."

"June fifteenth, 1938," Hayes said. "A warehouse in the hills. You and Bobby Danza and a hammer, Nicky. I got you right there, I got the weapon, I got a witness, and it's all coming apart at the seams."

Nicky took a step back. He relaxed, frowned, scratched his head. "You got nothing, Mr. Detective man. June fifteenth, 1938, you say?"

Hayes smiled. "June fifteenth, 1938 . . . the day you killed Bobby Danza."

"Well, that would be something, let me tell you," Nicky said. "That would make me some kind of magician. I wasn't anywhere near here on June fifteenth, 1938, so it seems you got me for something that I couldn't possibly have done."

"What, you're gonna tell me you have an alibi now? Is that what you're selling? You're saying you have an alibi for one day nearly eight years ago?"

"I'm sayin' I have an alibi for more than one day, my friend. I was way over in Palm Springs with my sister. We went for a road trip, we stayed in a motel, we saw some sights, you know?"

"Is that so?" Hayes said, and somewhere beneath all his certainties and convictions a tiny shadow of doubt started to invade his thoughts.

Nicky sensed it, perhaps saw something flicker in Hayes's eyes.

"You go ask her, wiseass," Nicky said. "You go ask my sister. She'll tell you exactly where we were and what we were doing all the way from the start to the end of that week. If you got me in a warehouse in the hills, then you got even more imagination than I gave you credit for."

"You can't sell me a bill of goods, Nicky—"

"My name is Mr. Mariani, asshole, and I can sell you whatever the hell I like. Right now you are on private property. You have no warrant, you have nothing to charge me with, and I am telling you to get the hell out of here right now. You wanna know where I was in the middle of June in 1938, you go ask my sister. She is a respectable businesswoman. She will tell you straight. That's the end of it, my friend."

Nicky turned away and went back to the bar.

Caliendo looked ill at ease but covered it as best he could. Leggiero just looked like another smart-mouthed wiseguy with more attitude than sense.

Hayes didn't know what to think. He did not know what to feel. He had made a mistake, and a bad one. He had given Mariani time to get to the sister, and it seemed the sister was going to give him an alibi.

Hayes did his best to hide his anger and outrage, but it showed in the tone of his voice.

"I'll be back to speak with you some more," he said.

"Oh, I don't think so, Mr. Detective man. I don't believe you and I will be seeing each other ever again."

"Don't count on it, Mariani," Hayes said.

"Oh, I'm all done countin', asshole. And like I said before, it's *Mister* Mariani to you."

Leggiero laughed, and then Caliendo joined him.

Hayes looked at Nicky Mariani for as long as he could bear the smug, self-satisfied grin on his face, and then he turned and walked away.

Hayes felt as if some small part of the universe had opened up and swallowed him. By the time he reached the street he felt sick. He looked back at the door of the Starlight. He wanted to go in there, pull his .38, and shoot the three of them. He gathered himself together, he got in the car, and he headed straight for the Maddens' house.

Hayes found Lucy Madden alone with her son. Her cool reception made it clear that he wasn't welcome.

"Can I help you, Detective Hayes?" she asked when she opened the door.

Hayes was surprised that she remembered his name. It had been two months since he'd visited her at the agency offices.

"You remember my name," he said.

"You are not an easy man to forget," Lucy said. "First time I ever met a detective, and you were asking questions about that terrible sex-film business."

"I did, yes."

"And that still hasn't resolved?"

"That's a different matter, Mrs. Madden. That's not why I'm here today."

"Okay . . . then how can I help you?"

"May I come in?" Hayes asked.

Lucy smiled, but it was neither friendly nor welcoming. "I'd rather you didn't, Detective Hayes. Not unless you absolutely have to. I'm about to put Joseph down for his nap. He doesn't do well if I upset his schedule."

"Okay, I understand," Hayes responded, sensing already that he was being wrong-footed.

"So, what is it that I can do for you?"

"I wanted to ask you about your brother," Hayes said. "I've been speaking to him about something that happened some years ago."

Lucy didn't reply. She stood there with her son in her arms, an enigmatic half smile on her lips.

"Have you seen your brother recently, Mrs. Madden?"

"Who, Nicky?" She laughed as if there was some kind of in joke going on. "I don't see Nicky from one Christmas to the next," she said, and Hayes knew in his heart that she was lying. Hayes would have put every dollar he owned or could borrow on the fact that Nicky Mariani came over here as soon as he'd been released from Central.

"Last time I saw him was the day after Christmas. He said he was coming over Christmas Day but he never showed, but then that's just like Nicky."

"You didn't see him today?" Hayes asked. "He didn't come over and see you this morning?"

Lucy frowned. She was almost convincing. Had Hayes not known she was lying he perhaps would have fooled her.

"This morning?" she asked. "No, not this morning. Whatever gave you the idea that he came here this morning?"

"Just a guess," Hayes replied.

"So is that all?"

"No, Mrs. Madden. I wanted to ask you about something that happened eight years ago."

She raised her eyebrows. "Eight years ago? My, I think you're expecting me to have a better memory than I do. I might just disappoint you, Detective."

"I have a feeling you won't," Hayes replied, reconciliation and resignation already audible in his tone of voice.

"So, shoot," she said. "Ask away, and I'll see what I can do."

"June of 1938," Hayes said. "Around the fifteenth, the middle of the month . . . I wonder if you remember where you were."

Lucy laughed dismissively. "Oh my, that was too easy. I remember exactly where I was in the middle of June of that year. I was in Palm Springs."

Hayes closed his eyes for a moment. He took a deep breath.

"And is there any particular reason why you specifically remember being in Palm Springs during that month, seeing as how it was eight years ago."

"We had just arrived in America. Well, we arrived in February of that year, to be honest. We spent some time in New York, and then we came to California at the end of May. We were staying in this dreadful place in Lincoln Heights, and I was quite homesick to be honest, and we wondered whether things might be better for us somewhere else. We went to Palm Springs to see what it was like . . ." Lucy hesitated, and then laughed at some private joke.

"Something's funny?"

"Just why we went to Palm Springs," she said. "We were thinking about San Diego, Santa Barbara, different places, but I insisted on Palm Springs because it sounded the most exotic. It seems foolish now, but that's why we went there first."

"And your brother? He was with you the entire time?"

Lucy seemed genuinely surprised by the question. "Yes, of course he was with me. I was twenty years old, Detective. A young woman on her own in a foreign country? There is no way in the world I would have gone anywhere by myself."

"And your husband? He was with you also?"

"I barely knew Frankie back then. He was here in Los Angeles, but no, he did not come to Palm Springs with us."

Hayes was silent for a moment. He looked at the little boy just a few yards inside the house. He was down on his haunches playing with a police car, of all things.

A quiet sense of sadness overcame Hayes's thoughts. He felt as if he was slowly, silently collapsing. He was made of sand and the tide had finally reached him.

And then he looked at the woman herself. Her expression was artless. If she was not an actress, she should have been. Perhaps she had missed her true calling in life.

Hayes knew he was beaten. Perhaps the war was not over, but this battle was lost. He had been impulsive and foolish. He had tricked Vianelli, even tricked Caliendo, but he had not tricked Nicolas Mariani. Mariani was smarter than his associates, and this was perhaps the very reason that Adamo had given him managerial control of the Venus, the Starlight, and who knew how many other Dragna-owned enterprises.

"And if I speak to your husband, Mrs. Madden?"

"About what?"

"About whether he is aware that you're providing an alibi for your brother?"

"I am sorry. I don't understand. How can I be providing an alibi for my brother?"

"Because I have him right here in Hollywood on June fifteenth, 1938. I know for certain that he was not out in Palm Springs with you."

"You're saying I'm a liar?"

"I'm saying that your loyalties are misguided. I understand family, Mrs. Madden, perhaps not in the same way as you, but I do understand it. I understand that blood is important, and you have a natural instinct to help your brother. But from experience I can tell you that these things never work out well. If you lie for blood, then you die for blood."

"That's very poetic, Detective. Very melodramatic. But it really has nothing to do with me and Nicky, and I can assure that you that every word I have spoken has been the truth."

"Truth is relative," Hayes said, "and in more ways than one."

"Now I don't even understand what you mean," Lucy said, "and I really need to get my son to sleep. It's already way past his nap time."

Hayes smiled wryly. He understood that he'd also been instrumental in the creation of this, that he had been too self-confident, that he had mistaken Mariani's arrogance for bravado and stupidity. The man was anything but stupid, and this was his first hard-won lesson, though perhaps not his last.

"We'll speak again, Mrs. Madden," Hayes said. "I just hope that you understand what you have done, and that your husband—"

"My husband has nothing to do with this," Lucy replied.

"I understand that, but that doesn't make him any less your husband, and you have to account to him as well—"

"I do not concern myself with your business, Detective Hayes," Lucy replied, "and I would be grateful if you didn't concern yourself with mine."

Hayes looked down at his shoes. He buried his hands in his pockets. "Too late," he said. "Your brother already took that decision away from you."

With that he turned toward the street and walked away. Upon reaching the sidewalk, he glanced back at Lucy Madden. She glared at him angrily for a second, and then she stepped back and slammed the front door.

That sound ricocheted back and forth in the airless midafternoon heat like the retort of a gun.

SIXTY-THREE

"Someone's been talking to the cops," Nicky said matter-of-factly.

He was in the back room of the Starlight, there in the small office where business meetings were held.

Vince Caliendo sat to Nicky's left, Tony Legs faced him across a plain deal table. A bottle of rye and three glasses sat between them, and the air was thick with cigarette smoke.

"Nah, man, I don't think anyone is talking to the cops," Caliendo said. "Who the hell is gonna talk to the cops?"

"You didn't hear the questions that asshole was asking me," Nicky replied. "He knows stuff, I tell you, and it ain't come from me."

"So who, Nicky?" Caliendo asked. "Who is doin' this?"

Nicky turned and looked at Caliendo for just a little too long. Caliendo felt his skin crawl, but he could not look away. He thought of his father, and he held on to that thought as he looked right back at Nicky.

"I know who," Nicky said. "Asshole caused trouble for us once already, and he's doin' it again. Cops got him on somethin', and he's buyin' his way out. Tell you now, we should be very fuckin' careful about what we say. You guys—" Nicky indicated both Caliendo and Tony Legs. "You guys gotta be as careful as me. We got a good thing here, and we gotta keep it tight. We fuck it up, then we got Joe Adamo and Jack Dragna to answer to."

"So who?" Tony Legs said. "Who the fuck are you talkin' about, Nicky?"

"Your asshole cousin, that's who," Nicky said.

"What? Mo? You fuckin' serious?" He started laughing, but that laughter died in his throat when he realized that Nicky wasn't joking at all.

"Yeah, I'm serious."

"No fuckin' way, man," Tony said. "Mo may be a dumb asshole, sure he may get a little excitable every once in a while, but he ain't no fuckin' snitch."

"Then how does the cop know about Bobby Danza, huh?" Nicky

asked. "If I didn't tell him, and you guys didn't tell him, then that only leaves Mo, right? We told Mo about that. We got drunk, we talked about it, and we had a good laugh. Who was there? Me, you guys, and Mo fucking Vianelli. I tell you now, he's a snitch. They got him on somethin'. He's beaten up some poor schmooze. He's hurt someone. He's pulled some other dumbass stunt. He's got a yellow sheet. Maybe he's three strikes and lookin' at life, and they gave him a choice. Take the rap or roll over on your buddies. That's what's happened, I tell you now. He's given me up, and now I got this asshole cop all over me like a rash."

Neither Tony Legs nor Vince Caliendo spoke for some time.

Then Tony Legs looked away and shook his head. "Oh fuck," he said, almost a whisper.

"What?" Nicky asked.

"He was bullshitting, man. I figured he was bullshitting me. Way back, before Christmas, he said there was some kid who owed him a bunch of money and he stabbed him. Thought he'd killed the kid, but the kid pulled through."

"When was this?" Nicky asked.

"Like I said, back before Christmas, maybe first week of December."

"You know what happened?"

"He said he stabbed someone. Some kid. At that place . . . the one over near that restaurant . . . Delilah's, right? You know that place?"

"Yeah, I know it," Nicky said. "That's what happened. They got him on something like that and he's turned."

Tony Legs was dumbstruck. His cousin was a snitch. His father's sister's boy—a kid he'd grown up with, a kid he'd known all his life—was talking to the cops and now they were going to have to kill him.

Vince Caliendo sat there with his heart beating through his rib cage. He knew what had happened. He was the only one who knew what had really happened. The true irony wasn't how certain Nicky was of Mo's apparent betrayal, but that Gino Caliendo would have beaten Vince senseless if he'd known that his release had been bought by his son's cooperation with the police. That was not the way things were done. Testament to that fact was Nicky's determination to kill Mo Vianelli based on nothing more than assumption and resultant paranoia.

"So what are we going to do?" Tony asked.

"I am going to speak to Mo," Nicky said. His voice was calm and unhurried. That made his words seem all the more menacing. "I'm going to speak to Mo and we're gonna straighten this out."

Vince knew what he had to do. Mo was going to have to take the fall. If he didn't, if Mo had a chance to speak, to tell the truth, then it would come back to Vince. Only Vince knew that Mo Vianelli was not the reason that Detective Louis Hayes was all over Nicky Mariani. Vince had made that happen. Vince had brought this to their doorstep. Regardless of what Mo Vianelli might or might not have done, maybe it wasn't right that he should die for something he didn't do, but he was going to have to. That was the way of things. It was him or Mo, and when it came to a decision like that there really was no decision. He had to look at it a different way. Deep down, Vince understood that there was such a thing as justice and retribution. Such things rarely came as a result of the law or the federal system. Real justice and retribution came to a man because of his own actions. If Mo died, then Vince believed there were more than enough things in Mo's past to warrant such a penalty. I mean, for Christ's sake, he'd beat that girl up over at the South Coronado house, and then he stabbed the guy at Delilah's.

Vince knew he had to find Mo, not to warn him, but to make sure he didn't get wind of what was happening and flee the city.

"Where the hell is he going to be?" Nicky asked Tony.

"Christ almighty knows," Tony said. "To be honest, I don't see that much of him."

"We go find him," Nicky said. "Call here every hour from a pay phone. If either of you track him down, tell him I want to see him here, that we got a job, good money, but we need to act fast. Call, speak to Max at the bar. Max can be the liaison. That way we don't waste any time."

Vince and Tony sat there, both of them speechless for different reasons.

"So go!" Nicky snapped. "Go find this asshole."

Nicky got up first, perhaps intent on being the one to find Mo, but Vince knew he had to locate him. He knew what he had to do, and the more he thought of it, the more he understood that it was no longer a matter of choice.

Three blocks from the club Vince called Central. He asked for Hayes.

"We got a problem and we gotta solve it," he told Hayes.

"You got a problem?" Hayes said. "Is that so? Well, whatever problem you got, I can guarantee mine is much greater." Hayes could not bring himself to speak of Lucy Madden. He could not tell Vincent Caliendo that Nicky Mariani had been given an alibi on the Danza killing.

"Nicky is convinced that Mo Vianelli turned him in on the Bobby Danza thing. He's got us trying to find him now. Nicky gets hold of him he's gonna kill him, no question. I need whatever you got. I need cars and people and whatever else you can organize to find him before Nicky or Tony Legs get ahold of him."

"You surprise me," Hayes said. "I don't understand why you're so concerned about an asshole like Maurizio Vianelli. He gets nailed for giving up Mariani and you're off the hook."

The lie came so very easily from Vince's lips. Had he heard his own words he perhaps would have believed them. "Not the way it works," he said. "Man has to live with himself, doesn't he? I ain't Mo Vianelli, and I sure as hell ain't Nicky Mariani. I got some kind of conscience, okay?"

"Any idea where he might be?" Hayes asked.

"No clue at all."

"Where are you now?"

"Over near the Starlight."

The thought in Hayes's mind was that he should just let Mariani kill Vianelli. If he couldn't get Mariani for Danza, then some other stiff would serve just as well.

"Okay . . . but you understand what this does now, Vincent? You understand that you are in this as deep as it gets."

"I understand, okay? You think I don't understand? You get my father out. That's your end of the deal. I got to speak to Mo before anyone else. He has to know what's going on."

"I'll get the word out," Hayes said. "Best if you come to Central. Stay off the street."

"I'm not going to Central," Vince said. "Are you fuckin' crazy?"

"Then go somewhere where I can reach you," Hayes replied.

"You know the—"

Vince fell silent.

"Vincent?" Hayes said. "Vincent? You there?"

"I gotta go, man. I just seen him."

The line went dead. Hayes sat there looking at the receiver in his hand.

"What the hell?" he asked no one in particular. "What the god-damned hell is going on?"

Hayes put the phone down, picked it up again, and called the desk.

"Hayes here. Put an APB out for Maurizio Vianelli," he said. "All units, all beats. Need to find this guy as fast as possible. V-I-A-N-E-L-L-I. Start out in the vicinity of the Starlight. I'm going to take a patrol car, so radio me if there's any word of him."

Hayes grabbed his jacket and headed for the stairs. It was a needle in a haystack, but he could not sit at his desk and wait for news.

Hayes drove a patrol car out of the basement lot just after five. He knew the odds were weighed against him finding Vianelli. He also knew that if Mariani found him and their conversation about Billy Resnick was revealed, then Vianelli would be dead by nightfall.

Vince Caliendo had the edge on everyone. He caught up with Mo Vianelli five blocks from the Starlight.

To whatever degree the odds were against Hayes, they seemed to be equally in Vince Caliendo's favor.

"Mo!" he shouted from across the street. "Mo!"

Mo looked back, and for a second there was a hunted expression on his face, almost as if he was expecting someone to come looking for him.

Vince dashed across the street, grabbed Vianelli, and pulled him into a doorway. Vianelli wrestled away from Caliendo.

"What the hell, man? What the fuck are you doing?"

"Mo, you gotta listen to me," Vince said.

"What—"

"You gotta stay tight, man. Shit is going down and you gotta stay close, okay?"

"What's going on?" Mo asked. His words belied his instinctive reaction; it was visible in his eyes.

"There's some asshole cop called Hayes, got everything the wrong way around. He thinks you and me and Nicky killed some asshole called Danza. Says that you stabbed some guy in Delilah's. It's all a fucking mess, man. Anyway, I don't know how, but Nicky's got it in his head that you gave him up. I know that's not true, but we gotta stick together, figure out what the fuck has happened, and how we can all cover each other, right?"

"What the fu—"

"I don't know what the truth is, Mo. All I know is that Nicky's convinced himself that you've rolled over and that you're gonna testify or give evidence or what the fuck. You gotta go face Nicky and straighten this out. You make a run for it, then you got no chance. He'll find you and he'll kill you for sure."

Vianelli became immediately angry and defensive. "Make a run for it? Who the fuck do you think I am? You think I'm gonna run from that asshole? You think Nicky Mariani fuckin' scares me?"

Vince saw it then—the defiance, the arrogance, the violent streak that ran right through Mo Vianelli and out the other side. He'd beaten the hell out of that poor girl at Nicky's place back around Christmas of '41, and stabbed the guy at Delilah's. Christ only knew what else he'd done that Vince didn't know. Maybe this was what was needed—let Mo Vianelli and Nicky Mariani go at each other's throats and see if either was left standing.

"I don't know what you think, Mo. I'm just tellin' you what's going on, and you gotta make your own decisions. Nicky's got this idea in his head and he wants to straighten it out."

Mo Vianelli started to move, and then he hesitated. "So how come you're lookin' to help me out here, Vince? You're all buddy-buddy with Nicky. You and Nicky and Tony Legs are always together. How come you're concerned for my welfare all of a sudden?"

Vince didn't say anything. He just looked back at Mo without flinching.

"You want Nicky's business? Is that it? You want me to get rid of Nicky and you and Tony Legs gonna split everything two ways instead of three. Is that what's going on here?"

Once again, Vince didn't say a word. He let Mo get five from two plus two all by himself.

Mo smiled like a snake. "Tell you something, my friend . . . this turns out the way I think it's gonna turn out, then you and I are gonna have a very different kind of conversation."

"What happens after is what happens after, Mo. You ain't got time to be worryin' about that right now. You go find Nicky and do whatever you gotta do."

Mo smiled. He gripped Vince's shoulder. He didn't say a word, but it was all there in his eyes.

Vince glanced back toward the other side of the street as a black-and-white cruised by. He guessed Hayes had already got people out looking for Mo, and Vince had told Hayes he was down by the Starlight.

Mo went to move. Vince held on to his arm for a second, waited until the cruiser had passed, and then he let go.

"Look after yourself," Vince said.

"Only person who needs to be lookin' after himself is Nicky fuckin' Mariani," Mo said, and with that he stepped out of the doorway and took off.

Vince watched him go. He doubted he could have stopped him, and he did not wish to. He wanted to be done with all of it. He did not want to feel the way he felt. He headed back toward the Starlight, all to set to continue with the search for Mo Vianelli.

SIXTY-FOUR

Hayes had been up all night. He'd called Carole just before eleven, told her that he wouldn't be home. Word had gone out to cruisers, beat cops, other contacts he possessed outside the department, but Mo Vianelli was a ghost. No one had seen or heard word of him for at least twelve hours. Hayes wondered whether he'd been tipped off.

Late on the Saturday night he'd tracked down Vince Caliendo. Caliendo said that Nicky was losing the plot. Nicky had convinced himself that not only had Vianelli snitched, but that he was planning to kill him. The only thing Hayes could think was to bring Mariani in and lock him up, if for no other reason than to flush out Vianelli. But Hayes had nothing, and without something of substance he could not hold Mariani.

Around five a.m., morning of Sunday the seventeenth, Hayes got it into his head that the answer lay with Frankie Madden. If he could convince Frankie Madden that his wife's provision of an alibi for her brother was a real liability to him and his family, then maybe Frankie could convince her to let it go. Frankie had a child to think of, and though Hayes himself was not a father, he knew that there was little else that mattered more than family.

Hayes suspected that Lucy Madden had not told her husband what she'd done. Perhaps Hayes was wrong. There was always that possibility. Perhaps Frankie Madden would stand by his wife no matter what she said or did. Right now, in the absence of any clear alternatives, Hayes believed he had little choice. Slim though it might be, one more shot at getting Nicky Mariani for the Danza killing was something he could not turn down.

Just after seven Hayes headed home. He wanted to shower and change. He tried not to wake Carole, but she was not a heavy sleeper at the best of time.

She got up and made breakfast for him, didn't ask questions, didn't need to know details. It was clear that he was stressed and preoccupied. She did her best to walk on eggshells around him. If he wanted to talk he would do it in his own time.

"It's all fallen apart," he finally said. He was standing near the kitchen door as she washed cups and plates.

Her heart sank. She tried to smile understandingly, but she merely looked anxious.

Hayes reached out his hand. She came toward him and he held her.

"One last shot," he said. "Today . . . now . . . I'm going to see someone, see if I can talk some sense into them, and if that doesn't go, then it can all go to hell."

Carole didn't say a word. She just made her support evident by holding him even tighter.

Though she desperately wanted to see the end of whatever it was that Louis was chasing, she also did not want to see him frustrated. It was a tough job, unforgiving, demanding everything he could give, but it was also his life. Louis was a driven man, and though it hurt her to see him this way, it was something she could not question. Love was unconditional; she'd known what she was getting into right from the start.

"Is there anything I can do?" she asked.

Hayes leaned down and kissed her forehead. "Just be here when I get back."

With that, Hayes took his jacket, his holster and handgun, and he left the house. Before driving away he radioed Dispatch. Still there was no sign of Maurizio Vianelli. Hayes wondered whether he'd already left the city.

Carole watched him from the window. She had so wanted to tell him what was going on with her, with *them*, but she could not say the words. Not yet, not until this thing was done. Not until Louis came home for real—body, mind, and soul.

Hayes headed for the Madden house. Sunday morning, the streets all but empty, and he made good time. The sky was bright and clear; it was somewhere in the midseventies, he guessed. He thought about radioing in to Dispatch one more time, just to see if there was a late report of Vianelli, but he decided against it. Vianelli was gone. Perhaps Mo Vianelli knew what Mariani was capable of even better than Hayes. Perhaps there had been no choice in the matter: Get out or die, as simple as that.

Hayes pulled over to the curb a hundred yards from the Madden place. He did not want to think beyond the conversation with Frankie Madden, and that had yet to happen. There was always the possibility that Madden would refuse to speak with him. As he'd already considered, Lucy might already have explained the situation, secured his agreement on providing an alibi for Nicky, and if that was the case it would be finished, at least for now. Resurrecting anything substantial and probative against Mariani would take a Herculean amount of work. He didn't want to think about it. Hayes would take a trip, just as he'd promised Carole. He would disappear for a while, get some distance from this madness, and then maybe take another tack. He could crack the books, knuckle down hard and get the lieutenancy under his belt. Then he could work toward establishing a specialist unit to tackle Mariani, Leggiero, Caliendo, Adamo, and on up the food chain to Dragna himself. That would be another game altogether, and there was perhaps a way he could—

Hayes stopped midthought.

There was someone coming down the side of the bungalow.

Hayes leaned sideways to get a better view. It was Frankie Madden, no doubt about it, but what the hell was he doing?

Hayes got out of the car. He started walking toward the house. Before he'd gone twenty yards he felt his heart rate increasing. Why was he so afraid?

Madden was approaching his own car, perhaps to fetch something from it, but then he saw Hayes. There was a moment's hesitation before recognition dawned.

Hayes was thirty yards away, raised his hand even as Madden opened his mouth to speak.

Madden frowned, but he still changed direction and approached Hayes.

"Mr. Madden," Hayes said.

"What do you want? What the hell are you doing here?"

"I need to talk to you, Mr. Madden."

"Do you know what day it is, Detective? My family and I are getting ready for church."

"I'm sorry, and I wouldn't be here if it wasn't of real importance."

"And there's some reason you can't come to the door like a regular person?"

"It's about your wife. It's about Mrs. Madden and her brother."

Madden looked at Hayes with an expression Hayes recognized all too well.

It was the expression of someone finding out what they didn't want to know.

Madden didn't speak for a moment. He looked back toward the house. "What about my wife, Detective Hayes?"

"I need you to talk to her, sir," Hayes said. "I need you to talk to your wife about something we were discussing—"

Madden stepped closer. "You have been talking to my wife? When? How come I don't know about this?"

Hayes didn't respond.

"When did you speak to her?"

"Yesterday morning."

"And you didn't tell me? Where did you meet with her?"

"Here," Hayes replied. "I came and spoke with her here in your home."

Madden was clearly surprised, but beneath that there was something altogether more significant. Perhaps his own anxiety, perhaps a sense of things now running outside his control. Madden became agitated. He turned as if to walk back to the house, but then stopped and leaned closer to Hayes.

"You spoke to her about Nicky?"

"I did."

"*What* about Nicky?"

"I have been pursuing a line of inquiry—"

"Just the simple facts, Detective . . . What the hell is going on here?"

"I could be wrong, and I would be the first to admit it, but I believe your wife has provided her brother with a false alibi for something that happened some years ago."

"Specifically?"

"I think this is a conversation we should have elsewhere, Mr. Madden."

Madden shook his head. He was angry, wound up tight. "This is a conversation we are having right now. What exactly happened, and what has my wife said?"

"I cannot give you the details of the investigation, sir—"

Frankie Madden took a step back. When he stepped forward again his fists were clenched and his expression was fierce. He looked like a fighter. He looked like a man all set to step into the ring and slug it out.

"You come to my home, you speak to my wife without telling me, you come again the next day, a Sunday, you tell me that you think my wife is lying to protect her brother—"

"1938," Hayes said. "Something happened back in 1938, and I am convinced that your brother-in-law was responsible. I have witnesses who put him somewhere, but your wife has told me that she was with him in an entirely different part of the state."

"And what is it that my brother-in-law is supposed to have done?"

"I can't—"

Madden took yet another step forward. The man was intimidating, no question about it. Hayes—in that moment—felt physically threatened. Frankie Madden possessed a fearsome presence.

"I am convinced that we are dealing with a murder," Hayes said, knowing that he had crossed the line, that he was divulging confidential information, that the words he had just uttered could lead to a disciplinary tribunal, a conduct review, a—

"Murder," Madden stated matter-of-factly, and there was something about the way he said it that suggested it was no surprise at all.

"I believe so," Hayes said.

"When in 1938?" Hayes asked.

"Mr. Madden, I—"

"*When* in 1938, Detective Hayes," Madden repeated.

"June," Hayes replied. "In June of 1938."

"And Lucy told you what... that she was with her brother somewhere other than Los Angeles during that month?"

Hayes didn't reply. Silence would give Madden the answer he wanted.

Once again Madden turned back and looked at the house. He moved suddenly, and Hayes grabbed his arm.

Madden looked down at Hayes's hand and then shrugged it off.

"I don't want you to—"

"What?" Madden asked. "You don't want me to what? Speak to my wife? Deal with the fact that the police are now coming to my home, asking me questions, getting me and my family involved in things I know nothing about? You don't want me to speak to my wife about this?"

"Mr. Madden, I think—"

"I don't care what you think, Detective," Madden said. "This is my family, my life, and it is my responsibility to deal with this."

Madden marched away, didn't look back at Hayes.

Hayes thought to go after him, but unless invited into the house he would be nothing more than a trespasser.

No, he had come here and spoken to Madden. That was what he had intended to do, and now it was too late to turn back. What Madden would do was unknown to him. Perhaps he would force his wife to tell the truth. Perhaps the Maddens would close ranks with Lucy's brother and that really would be the end of his current investigation into the Danza killing.

Hayes just watched as Madden disappeared back down the side of the bungalow. He asked himself whether he had merely made the situation worse. He wondered whether he had now crossed way too many lines to ever get back to where this had begun. Falsification of evidence, unofficial interviews, operating without the presence of lawyers, not even a partner to corroborate the information he had secured. It was a mess. It was a real mess. Had he just kissed any hope of a lieutenancy away? Had he just kissed goodbye to an entire career?

Hayes turned and walked back to the car. He felt the urge to do nothing but drive somewhere quiet and drink himself into oblivion. He just wanted to run, to escape, to hide. He didn't even want to face Carole. He'd had enough of it, had enough of all of them, these people, these scumbags, these lowlifes, these animals . . .

Hayes looked up at the sound of a door opening.

Madden had left the front of the house. He was halfway down toward the car when Lucy appeared behind him, the child in her arms.

Madden opened the passenger door and stood there. He did not look at his wife. He did not look back at Hayes. He merely stood there until his wife walked down to meet him.

Words were shared, angry it appeared, but Madden just stood resolute and unflinching until his wife got into the car.

Madden walked around and got in on the driver's side.

The engine started and Madden pulled away.

Hayes knew where they were going. He felt sure of it.

There was nothing he could do but follow.

SIXTY-FIVE

If you're born to hang, you'll never drown.

Those were the words that went around and around in Frankie Madden's mind.

Why he thought of something his father had told him he did not know. But thoughts of his father brought with it a wish for the life he had left behind. Frankie felt threatened. That was all he could conclude. What he had created here in America was now being threatened, and it frightened him, as frightened as he'd been that night outside the Garda station.

This was different, so very different, but still the sense of having his life invaded was the same. Lucy had defended her brother. Just that alone would be sufficient to have the police become very interested in who they were, where they had come from, how they could be manipulated to assist in their ongoing investigation of Nicky Mariani.

This was dangerous territory. Frankie knew his life was a house of cards, and it could fall down around his ears without a sound.

The accusations and recriminatory words between him and Lucy had been uttered. Lucy had admitted nothing, but her awkwardness and defensiveness had said it all.

"Frankie, seriously—"

"We're gonna fix this now, Lucy. Enough talking. Nicky is your brother. I get it. I'm not saying that you shouldn't be there for him, but this is beyond—"

"He didn't do anything, Frankie. He's been set up by that detective—"

Frankie laughed dismissively. "I'm sure he has."

"Why are you so quick to judge? Why are you always ready to assume the worst about Nicky?"

"Intuition tells me that if it's a choice between whether he did or didn't do it, he usually did. And it's probably gonna be worse than you thought."

Joe started fussing.

"Enough," Lucy said. "Joe's getting upset now."

"I'll say this much," Frankie said. "We go talk to him now. We find out the truth one way or the other. We have a family. We have another baby on the way, for Christ's sake. What does he think? That he can just use us to get himself out of any situation he gets himself into?"

"Us?" Lucy asked. "What do you mean *us*? You're nothing to do with this—"

"Is that what you think?" Frankie asked, his tone one of incredulity. "You think that my brother-in-law getting my wife to lie to the cops about whether or not he killed someone is nothing to do with me?"

"You know what I mean, Frankie, and Nicky didn't kill anyone."

Joe was crying now, wrestling away from Lucy's hold.

"You don't need to say anything else," Frankie said. "We talk to Nicky, and we fix this once and for all."

"But the thing you don't seem to—"

Frankie turned and glared at Lucy. "Enough!" he demanded. "That's it, Lucy. I don't want to hear another goddamned word until we get to Nicky's house, okay?"

Joe started crying. Lucy didn't respond.

As if it wasn't enough that Hayes had come to their place of business, he was now at their home. He was inside their lives. All because of Nicky. All because of Lucy's asshole brother.

And Lucy, seemingly incapable of separating present from past, her own life from that of Nicky's, had lied to Hayes. Frankie knew it, knew it as well as he knew his own—

And there he had stopped.

There he had caught himself midflight and remembered that he was just as guilty of living a lie as anyone.

He had come to America for killing a man and killed another as soon as he'd arrived, and now he was judging his wife because she wanted to help her brother.

This was his penalty and his penance. That was the very foundation of the house of cards, and it could not have been more fragile.

They left the house without another word. When they reached the car she started again and Frankie told her he was not going to listen to anything she said, not until they were all at Nicky's house.

Frankie kept his eyes on the road and his mind focused on what he had to say to Nicky.

He did not think to look behind him and was unaware that Hayes was half a block away.

Hayes did not need to follow Frankie's car. Hayes knew precisely where the Maddens were going and why. There was going to be a family showdown. Hayes knew he'd been right. Lucy hadn't told her husband what had happened. Frankie had confirmed that no mention had been made of the fact that she and Hayes had spoken the previous morning. The cat was in the chicken coop. Hayes prayed that Frankie Madden had sufficient courage and presence of mind not to buckle under pressure.

The drive was not long. In no time at all the Madden car was turning onto South Coronado.

Hayes slowed down and pulled over before the junction. He parked, got out of the car, and walked to the end of the street. He could see where Frankie Madden had stopped, and before Lucy had time to get out of the car, Frankie was up to the porch of Nicky's house and banging on the door.

"Nicky!" Frankie shouted.

Frankie's voice carried in the still morning air. He looked back to see Lucy getting out of the car. "Stay there!" he shouted. "Stay in the car, Lucy!"

Lucy hesitated, and then she got back in the car with Joe. Joe was struggling. He wanted to go up and see Uncle Nicky.

For a while there was nothing, no sign at all that anyone was home, and then a woman opened the door. She was dressed in a man's shirt, seemingly nothing else, and her hair was mussed.

Frankie went right on in, didn't wait to be invited, didn't stop to answer any questions.

The woman stepped away, looked back toward the street as Lucy got out of the car and started up toward the house with Joe. She was damned if she was going to let Frankie tackle her brother in her absence.

Hayes walked toward the house, didn't know whether to stay or leave. If Nicky and Lucy convinced Frankie to go along with Lucy's story, then he was back to square one. If Frankie demanded that Lucy back down on what she'd told Hayes, then he would have another shot at Nicky for the Danza killing. Hayes would have given anything to be inside and hearing everything that was happening.

Hayes headed back to his car. He sat for a while. He did not see any reason to stay, but he could not leave. He could not go to the house; he could not exacerbate what he had already done, for the actions he had taken thus far were more than sufficient to warrant a harassment case.

Later he would regret it, of course. Later he would ask himself so many questions about what had been said, what had been done, the lines he had pursued, those he had crossed. Hindsight—as always—was the most astute and uncompromising adviser. Hindsight was the richest source of self-criticism, and Hayes stood front and center as those judgments came thick and fast.

Always and forever that same question: *What could I have done to make it different?*

The sound of a car snapped Hayes into the present.

He heard it from behind at first, and before he had a chance to look back, the car had sped past him and turned onto South Coronado. It was going at some rate. Hayes picked up his pace, ran to the corner of the street.

He heard the screech of brakes as the car pulled up.

Something told him—something instinctive and undeniable—that this was trouble.

Confirmation of instinct came with the sight of two men exiting the car and running toward the Mariani house. He could not see their faces, but he knew there was no need to look any further for Mo Vianelli.

They were armed, both of them, and Hayes drew his gun and went after them.

The front door of the house did not delay the men. The first man just landed his foot square in the center and it burst open. It was then that the second man glanced back toward the street. It was Vianelli, no question about it.

Hayes heard shouting before the gunfire started, but when that gunfire came, it was a cannonade. It lasted no more than ten or fifteen seconds, but in Hayes's mind it stretched beyond anything that could be defined. A deep and profound sense of horror filled every atom of his being. He knew that he had been the instigator of this. He knew that people were going to die, and the blood would be on his hands irrespective of who pulled the trigger.

Hayes was at the end of the path, and when he went through the broken doorway he saw Vianelli right there at the foot of the stairs. Vianelli's associate came back through from the kitchen, gun out, and pointed at Hayes. Hayes recognized the second man immediately. Leggiero, Vianelli's cousin. If you live for blood, you wind up dying for it.

"Stop!" he shouted. "Police!"

Leggiero did not lower the gun. He took a step forward, the expression on his face one of resolute determination.

Hayes fired instinctively, caught Leggiero in the upper arm. Leggiero stumbled backward, wounded but not down, and fled back the way he'd come.

Vianelli fled up the stairs, firing back over his shoulder toward Hayes as he went.

Hayes ducked sideways, heard a bullet slam into the edge of the doorframe beside him, and lost his balance.

He landed awkwardly, felt something give in his left shoulder, and then he rolled over onto his side and tried to see where Leggiero had gone.

There were more shots upstairs.

A woman screamed. Hayes did not know if it was Lucy Madden or the girl who'd opened the door. His question was answered immediately. A flash of white in the corner of his field of vision. It was the shirt. The girl in the shirt. She was stumbling backward out of a bedroom doorway. She reached the top of the stairs just as Hayes put his foot on the first riser.

The woman came tumbling down like a rag doll. She landed awkwardly, her neck twisted, her arms out. A wide rush of scarlet soaked through the front of her shirt.

More screaming from up above.

More gunshots.

And then Hayes saw Vianelli. He was running full-tilt as he, too, came from a doorway and across the landing. He did not appear to be armed, and Hayes raised his gun.

Before Hayes could even speak, Frankie Madden was right there behind Vianelli.

Frankie was fast, faster than Vianelli, and Hayes saw a bloom of blood on Vianelli's jacket. Vianelli was wounded, but that was not going to deter Frankie from exacting whatever punishment he saw fit.

Frankie caught Vianelli by the collar of his jacket and lifted him backward and off his feet. Vianelli seemed to fly, his body limp, his arms flailing, and then he came crashing down on his back. Madden was over him then, the fighter's stance, fists clenched, and Hayes could do nothing but watch as Madden let loose with a fusillade of fists to Vianelli's face and upper body.

Hayes moved then, physical instinct overcoming whatever mental reservations he might have possessed.

By the time he reached Madden there was little he could do.

Vianelli's face was a mess of blood and broken bone. His nose was fractured, his cheekbones driven hard into the flesh of his face, his eyes closed with swelling. The man had suffered a terrible beating and was now long past unconsciousness.

Madden paused for just a second. He looked up at Hayes.

Hayes raised his gun, opened his mouth to speak.

Even before Madden snatched the gun away from him, Hayes knew what would happen.

Madden hurled the gun aside. Hayes heard it careen off the wall.

Then Frankie Madden reached down, and with his left hand he gripped Vianelli's jacket lapels. He raised the man's head from the ground, and he pounded his fist again and again and again into Vianelli's face.

Blood sprayed upward and spattered Madden's face and shirt. He didn't stop. He just kept driving those punishing jabs into Vianelli's face. And then, as a final act of rage and hatred, he wrested Vianelli's limp and broken body from the floor, lifted it high, and then hurled the man over the banister to the ground below. The sound of Vianelli hitting the ground below was sickening and utterly final.

It was then that Hayes became aware of the screaming again. It was bloodcurdling, heartrending, desperate.

Hayes stepped back as Madden turned toward him.

Lucy Madden emerged from the door at the far end of the landing.

She looked ahead, her eyes staring, her mouth wide, that terrible sound, ceaseless and chilling, now reverberating back from every wall and filling the house.

It was only then that Hayes understood what he was seeing.

Lucy stumbled forward, regained her balance, the weight she was carrying nearly causing her to lose her footing altogether.

It was the child.

Lucy Madden was carrying the boy.

Frankie looked at Hayes, and there was nothing in the man's expression.

Frankie turned back toward his wife. She held out the lifeless body of their son, his tiny face covered in blood, his feet hanging down, one shoe missing.

Lucy kept on screaming, and that sound went on and on forever as if it would never, ever stop.

SIXTY-SIX

People were lining up outside a small movie theater on West Third. Rita Hayworth was breaking hearts in Vidor's *Gilda*.

The funeral procession went unnoticed, and from the backseat of the limousine Frank and Lucy Madden stared out at different sides of the same street.

Nicky would not be in attendance for Joe Madden's funeral. He was still laid up in Hollywood Hospital with a .38 through-and-through.

Across from Frank and Lucy was the hearse, the tiny coffin within which the body of their son was laid almost buried beneath flowers and wreathes and ribbons.

This would be the third funeral within the space of a week.

Maurizio Vianelli had been buried the previous Friday. Rita Morrison's parents had come from Flagstaff, Arizona, to collect her body. Her funeral had been held there the next day.

Joseph Madden's service had been brief and simple. Neither Frank nor Lucy had been able to present a eulogy. Detective Louis Hayes stood at the back of the chapel, his head down as the Maddens came in, his head down when they left. He had spent enough time with both of them since the South Coronado incident. He was done with questions, and he himself had nothing further to say.

The Danza investigation had been sidelined for a grander spectacle. People had died, among the casualties a small child, and even Hayes—ordinarily so determined—had lost the will to pursue the matter any further.

Meetings with Lieutenant Fuller had moved forward into meetings with Captain Mills. Questions were being asked about Hayes's involvement in the South Coronado incident, about his investigation into Mariani. Possessing no internal department or personnel equipped to investigate the actions of officers or their conduct, it was left to Fuller and Mills to make recommendations or take action. As yet little had been decided, and even less had been done. The only agreement made was that Hayes would take a month's paid leave. Hayes went willingly. He was exhausted, mentally, physically, emotionally, every which way it was possible to be exhausted.

He'd told Carole that they would go away as planned, but only after the child's funeral.

And so it was done. The service was over and the small procession made its way out along Santa Monica Boulevard to the Hollywood Memorial Cemetery. Here amid celebrities and nobodies, Joseph Saveriu Madden was buried, not yet four years of age. The names of studio owners, directors, producers, and movie stars were every which Hayes looked, but he only looked because he could not face the scene before him. That tiny coffin, no longer than two feet, disappeared silently into the earth. Lucy Madden sobbed and gasped and held on to her husband as if to let go would see herself also disappear.

And when it was done they all went their separate ways.

No one spoke. Not a single word was shared.

Some people indeed lived by blood, and died for it as well.

Some people, it seemed, died for no good reason at all.

SIXTY-SEVEN

The morning of Friday, first of March broke clear and bright.

Vince Caliendo was pulling up near the back of Hollywood Hospital, right there where he and Nicky and Paulie Belotti had delivered Grigor Zakarian all those years before.

Tony Legs had been driving back then. Vince hadn't even known Maurizio Vianelli. And now? Well, now Mo Vianelli was dead and Tony was running for his life.

Vince parked at the curb opposite the ambulance bay. He let the engine idle, ready to move if a cop showed up. He'd visited Nicky pretty much every day, brought him food, spent time with him, and never once had Nicky said a word about the death of his nephew. He'd also said nothing about Vince himself. There was nothing about Nicky's manner that gave Vince the feeling that he knew what Vince had done. It was all about Mo Vianelli. Mo was the one who'd wanted a war. Mo was the one who had started this. Hell, Nicky was even somewhat understanding of Tony Legs's position.

"Mo was his fuckin' cousin. Family shit. What the fuck are you gonna do, eh? Maybe Mo's father made him go along with it. I don't fuckin' know. I ain't jumpin' to any conclusions. As far as I'm concerned, Tony is gone and he ain't comin' back. I sure as hell ain't gonna go chasin' him."

Vince knew that this was only half the story. Tony Leggiero was connected, always had been, always would be. No made man, but he'd been on the way. Nicky would never get an inside look on the thing because he wasn't Italian. Those were the breaks. Nicky was smart enough to know that killing Tony wasn't something you did without permission. Chasing him down and killing him for siding with his cousin was a different story. That was political. That was family stuff, and Nicky knew not to tread on that hallowed ground without asking permission of high-up people. Nicky wanted to make it look like he was letting it lie, but to kill Tony Leggiero he'd have had to get Joe Adamo's blessing, maybe even the nod from Jack Dragna. That wasn't going to happen in a month of Sundays.

When Vince saw Nicky make his way from the back of the building, he got out of the car and went to meet him. The bullet he'd taken had gone right through the side of his body, just inches from his stomach. He'd been lucky. A little way to the left and it'd have been a gut shot—messy, painful, a long time to heal; a couple of inches further and it would have been his spine.

"Jesus Christ, I am starving," Nicky said once they were in the car and the engine was running. "Let's go to the Venus. I want pasta and steak, some wine as well. The shit they feed you in there, it's... well, it's shit is what it is."

Vince pulled away. He was too busy listening to Nicky to notice the car that headed out a little way back and started following them.

Nicky was like his old self by the time they reached the Venus. Every other thing that came out his mouth was some wiseguy comment about something. He even made a joke. Vince laughed, and the laughter was genuine. He was certain now that Nicky had no idea that he'd talked to Hayes at Central. He was in the clear, and that was like being given a second shot at life.

Nicky went into the Venus first, Vince right behind him, and it was only as he stepped through into the dimly lit interior of the club that he was aware of the man behind him.

Before Vince even had a chance to turn, the man had gripped the back of his neck with such force that he could barely breathe. He gasped. Nicky turned, and there was an expression on his face that was both one of inevitability and surprise.

"You carrying a weapon?" Frankie asked.

"Hell, no," Nicky said. "I just got out of hospital."

Frankie ran his hand around Vince's midriff, under his arms, found a .38 tucked in the back of his waistband. He took it out, pocketed it, and pushed Vince forward.

Vince stumbled, collided with Nicky. Nicky lost his balance and fell awkwardly against a table. The guy at the bar looked ready to act.

Frankie pointed at him. "Stay right where you are," he said, his voice hard and cold.

Nicky turned and looked at the barkeep. He nodded. The barkeep took a step back, seemed to just disappear from view.

"In the back," Frankie said.

Nicky turned, started walking, Frankie urging Vince along behind him.

They took a booth in the semidarkness at the back of the club.

Nicky and Vince slid along the seat. Frankie took a chair from a nearby table and sat facing them.

"What's his name, Nicky?"

"Who? What are you talking about?"

"The guy with Vianelli? What is his name?""

"Hell, how should I know—" Nicky started.

Frankie took out Vince's gun and cocked it. He held it up, pointed right at Vince's face, mere inches away.

Vince's hands went up instinctively. "Jesus Christ, man, what the—"

Frankie turned the gun sideways and cracked the chamber against Vince's nose. Vince howled. His nose streamed blood immediately.

Vince lowered his head and his hands came up to defend himself against further injury, but Frankie seemed to have done what he intended.

The gun was now aimed unerringly at Nicky Mariani.

"His name, as you know all too well, is Anthony Leggiero," Frankie said matter-of-factly. "They call him Tony Legs. That is his name, and you are going to find him and kill him for me."

Nicky started laughing.

Frankie was as fast as he'd ever been. He just whipped his left arm around and caught Nicky along the jawline with the heel of his hand.

Nicky fell sideways into Vince. Vince's nose was still streaming. There was blood all down the front of his shirt and jacket. There were now bloody handprints on the table.

"Jesus Christ, Frankie, enough!" Nicky said. "I can't just go out there and kill someone."

"You can, Nicky. Sure you can. You've killed before, and you'll do it again. Those people murdered my son, and you're to blame. You brought this into our lives, and now you are going to do this thing for us. You are going to find this guy and kill him."

"I'm so sorry about Joe. You cannot even begin to imagine how sorry I am for what happened, but you don't understand—"

Frankie took the gun and hit Vince in the side of the head. Vince howled in pain again, held his hands over his head. "Jesus Christ, what the hell are you hitting me for?"

"Because you are fucking expendable," Frankie said, his voice calm and detached. "You, I don't need. I just need Nicky here. I need you to do what I ask, Nicky, or I'm going to shoot this asshole in the face, and then I'm going to shoot you. If I have to do that, so be it. I don't want to, for Lucy's sake, but I will, believe me."

"You don't want me to kill anyone, and I know for sure that Lucia doesn't want me to—"

Frankie pushed the gun barrel against the side of Nicky's throat.

Nicky fell silent.

"Look at me, Nicky. Look at me real hard. I am going to say this again just once. You find this Tony Leggiero guy and you kill him. You kill him or I'm going to kill you and this asshole here and anyone else who gets in the way, you understand?"

Nicky didn't speak.

"Do you understand me, Nicky?"

"Yeah, Frankie . . . yeah, I understand you."

Frankie withdrew the gun. He got up from his chair and looked down at the two men facing him.

"You have no goddamned idea what you're—" Vince started.

Frankie Madden clenched his fist and hit Vince Caliendo square in the face. It was a haymaker, and Vince's head snapped back and struck the wall. He was out cold before he even knew what had happened.

"I'm not gonna wait long," Frankie said. "You got twenty-four hours." He turned and started away toward the door.

Nicky started to get up. "Frankie—"

Frankie didn't look back. "Twenty-four hours, or I'm coming back to kill both of you. Do not doubt me, Nicky. Really . . . do not even think of doubting me."

SIXTY-EIGHT

There were ghosts now.

Perhaps they had always been there, but it was only now that he had begun to perceive their presence.

Bobby Durnin, Aleksy Bodak, and now Joseph, his own flesh and blood, his firstborn. His son.

A life barely begun, a life that was almost no life at all, snuffed out like a candle flame.

The smoke from that extinguished flame would always be there, always present, haunting him, following him, and no matter how fast he ran, it would always arrive before he did.

Conscience was a country you could never escape.

Frankie lay beside his wife. She slept as if dead herself. She had been taking tranquilizers. At first just one, now two and three at a time. She disappeared for twelve, fourteen hours into whatever chasm of forgetting she could find, rising only to shuffle around the house in her gown, eating almost nothing, muttering a handful of words, the look in her eyes one of someone irretrievably lost, perhaps never to return.

Frankie was afraid that not only had he lost his son, but he would now also lose his wife. If not in body, then surely in mind and spirit. He looked at her and she was a hollow shell. The light had gone out, and he feared it would never come back.

It had been merely hours since he'd spoken with Nicky, but already the fear was eating away at him.

Could he bear the burden of another man's death on his hands?

He had begun to believe that he could not do this. The grief was endless, but could he really take another life? If he did, he wondered if what was left of his sanity might finally leave him to some endless nightmare.

Frankie rose and went through to the kitchen. He sat at the kitchen table. He could feel his heart in his chest, his blood in his veins. At one point he felt as if he had disconnected from his body entirely and was watching himself from the other side of the room.

The house seemed like someone else's. The life he had created with Lucy was now no life at all, and yet there was another child on the way. He was concerned also for Lucy's sanity, for whether she was even capable of being a mother again, whether the pills she was taking would do some irreparable damage to the unborn child. Would that be another penalty . . . to lose not only the child they had, but the child that had not yet arrived?

Was he challenging God, seeing who was strongest, seeing whether he could withstand whatever punishment was assigned to him for what he had done in Ireland, in New York?

Frankie's thoughts raged ferociously. He wanted silence. Needed it. He could hear Bobby Durnin's voice. He could see Bodak's lifeless body there on the dirty floor of a disused warehouse, the smell of rot and sweat and blood all around him.

Who was he? What kind of life was this, that he had to carry this conscience with him?

He was Daniel McCabe. He was a son, a brother, a fighter, a killer.

He was no more Frank Madden than all the other Hollywood dreamers who walked these streets and sat in restaurants and made believe that the world they lived in was not the world they saw.

If he did this, if he really went through with this, then what would happen to them? Could he risk it? And for what? To feel he had achieved some kind of retribution? How short-lived would that feeling be, and what would it solve? It wouldn't bring Joseph back, and it wouldn't change the depth of grief that he and Lucy were even now drowning in.

Frankie got up and paced. He walked to the window and looked out into the street.

The lights cast a sickly yellow glow onto the sidewalks.

This was not his city, not his country, not his home.

He caught his own spectral reflection in the glass, and he knew then that he could not go through with this. His heart could not be home to yet another ghost.

Frankie Madden got dressed and left the house. It was after three in the morning, Saturday, March second.

He drove straight to South Coronado, walked around the back of Nicky's house, and knocked on the window until the lights came on up above.

Nicky came down. He looked like a man both hunted and haunted. He stood in the darkened kitchen and saw his brother-in-law in the backyard.

Frankie had never seen the man so scared in his life.

Nicky forced himself to move, forced himself to unlock the back door.

"Frankie... Jesus..."

"Don't do it," Frankie said. "The other guy. Leggiero. Leave it be. Don't kill him."

Nicky looked at Frankie out of a dream.

"Let it go, Nicky. Too many have died already. I don't want another killing on my conscience."

The relief on Nicky's face was immediate. He looked as if every muscle and sinew and nerve had suddenly been released from a tremendous pressure.

Frankie stood there for a second, and then he lowered his head and started to sob.

"My boy..."

"Christ, Frankie," Nicky said. "Come into the house, man... Come into the house..."

Frankie looked up at his brother-in-law, and the tears streamed down his face.

"My son is dead, Nicky... My son is fucking dead..."

Nicky reached out toward Frankie, and Frankie pushed his hand away.

"You are not my family," Frankie said. "You are not my life. You have to leave me be... You have to let me go..."

"What are you talking about? What the hell is going on?"

Nicky took a step out onto the back porch.

"Get the fuck away from me. Leave me the fuck alone. Leave me and my wife the fuck alone..."

Frankie backed up.

Nicky took another step and Frankie raised his fists.

Frankie seethed through gritted teeth. "Take one more step and I will beat you to death right where you stand."

Nicky backed up. His eyes wide, his face blanched of color, and he didn't dare move. He knew what Frankie Madden was capable of. He remembered the first day they met, the way he took Cova and Altamura down without even breaking a sweat. Most of all he remembered Aleksy Bodak.

"I hear you," Nicky said.

Frankie looked at Nicky a moment longer, and then he turned and walked away.

*

A few moments later Nicky heard the sound of Frankie's car. He stood there on the back porch and went on listening until the engine had faded into silence.

He went back upstairs, but he could not sleep.

He lay awake and thought about his sister, his brother-in-law, the son they had lost.

Collateral damage. That was the phrase that came to mind. Collateral damage.

And then the phone rang.

Nicky's heart stopped. He did not want to answer it.

It rang so loud, and it kept on going, and he knew he could not ignore it.

"Nicky."

"Lucia?"

"Listen to me, Nicky . . . Don't ask any questions. Just listen to me . . ."

SIXTY-NINE

Detective Louis Hayes arrived in the early evening of Monday, March 4. He had come alone.

Frankie saw the car pull up to the curb. He knew who it was.

Hayes killed the engine. He sat there for several minutes before exiting the vehicle. Even then he seemed to hesitate, standing and looking up toward the house as if waiting for some reason to move.

Eventually he walked around the car and headed up the path.

Frankie opened the front door. He said nothing.

"Mr. Madden."

"Detective Hayes."

"I wondered if you and your wife had a few moments."

Frankie stepped aside, let Hayes pass him, and then he closed the front door and showed Hayes through to the kitchen.

Lucy was there. She was washing plates. She tried to smile, but it didn't come easily. She started to dry her hands, and Hayes said, "Please, don't let me stop you."

"What's happening?" Frankie asked. "Why are you here?"

"I came to tell you about the other man," Hayes said. "The one who was with Maurizio Vianelli at Mr. Mariani's house when . . ."

"I know when," Lucy said. "I know who you mean."

"What about him?" Frankie asked.

"We found him dead, Mr. Madden. This morning. We found him dead in a disused tenement building. I felt you should know."

"Jesus Christ," Frankie said. "It just doesn't stop, does it?"

"It's justice," Lucy said quietly, and then she turned back to the sink and continued washing plates.

"Perhaps," Hayes said, "but still we need to investigate it. And I need to ask you some questions."

"No more questions," Lucy said without turning around. "We don't have to answer any of your questions, Detective. We don't have to and we don't want to. We just want to put all of this behind us and get on with our lives." She glanced over her shoulder at her husband. "Isn't that so, Frankie?"

Frankie hesitated for a heartbeat.

"Isn't it, Frankie?" Lucy repeated. "We just want to get on with our lives now."

"Yes," Frankie said.

"You're right," Hayes said. "You're not obliged to answer any more questions—"

Lucy smiled, but it was cold and emotionless. "Good. Then that's settled. Was there anything else, Detective Hayes?"

Hayes looked taken aback. "Er . . . er, no, Mrs. Madden. There isn't anything else."

"Frankie will show you out," she said, and she turned away once more without wishing Hayes goodbye.

Hayes hesitated on the porch. He looked at Frankie Madden as if trying to see inside him.

"Tell me that you had nothing to do with Tony Leggiero's death," he said.

Without a moment's hesitation, Frankie said, "I had nothing to do with Tony Leggiero's death."

"And your wife? Can you vouch for her—"

"My wife," Frankie said, "is the kindest and most decent person I have ever known."

"That's not an answer to my question."

"Take care of yourself, Detective," Frankie said. "You look tired. Maybe you should take a vacation or something."

"I will . . . but when I come back you and I will have words. I don't believe you've told me the truth about any of this . . . not what happened with your brother-in-law, not about your wife, and not about who you are. I saw you in that house. I saw behind the facade. You're no more a Hollywood businessman than I am. You have a history, Mr. Madden, and I think you have ghosts."

Frankie Madden remained implacable. He looked at Hayes for just a moment more, and then he stepped back and quietly closed the door.

Louis Hayes, once again challenged and frustrated in his efforts to find the truth, stayed right where he was for a few moments and then he walked back to the car.

As for the death of Leggiero, Hayes believed Frankie Madden. But he did not believe Lucy. He knew she'd given her brother an alibi for the Danza killing. He suspected she'd then called the debt in.

Anthony Leggiero had not been found in a tenement building

at all. He'd been found in a warehouse full of costumes and stage props up in the hills.

He'd been tied to a chair and his head had been bashed in. From the shape and depth of the injuries, it appeared that Tony Legs had been beaten to death with a hammer.

Hayes knew that this had happened before, and he knew—knew with everything he possessed—that it would happen again. Nicolas Mariani, this self-styled Kid Napoleon, had only just started. This arrogant Corsican son of a bitch was all set to steal the world. There would be more killings. Hayes knew this for sure. Hayes had crossed paths with Mariani, and this time Mariani had slipped away. Next time... Well, next time Hayes would be better prepared.

He started the engine. He pulled away from the curb.

The sun was setting over Hollywood. The roads were all but empty. He made good time and found Carole waiting, dinner on the table.

"All good?" she asked.

"All good," Hayes replied. He kissed her. She smiled, pulled away, but he pulled her back and held her a moment longer.

"What's that for?" she asked.

"Because I love you, and I know I've been neglectful recently. I'm sorry, okay? It's not you. Sometimes work just—"

"Work is done for a while," Carole said. "We're out of here tomorrow. You have no idea how much I am looking forward to this. Two weeks' vacation. I can't even remember when I took two weeks' vacation."

"Open a bottle of wine," Hayes said. "I'm taking a shower before dinner."

"We should celebrate," Carole said, "but I'm not going to join you."

Hayes frowned. "Why? You not feeling good? What's up, sweetheart?"

"I just don't think I should be drinking... not in my condition..." She left the sentence hanging in the air.

Hayes looked at her.

Carole smiled.

Hayes understood.

"Oh my God," he said.

Carole stepped toward him and he opened his arms wide. He held her against him, and he knew then that everything he'd ever wanted was right within his reach.

SEVENTY

Frankie stood in the kitchen. He watched his wife as she finished at the sink. For just a fleeting moment it was like watching a stranger.

He wanted to ask, but he didn't dare.

He knew what had happened. She'd reached Nicky. She'd told him that Leggiero needed to die. She, too, had now crossed the line. They were in this together, whatever *this* was.

"We let him in," Frankie said, "and he will never leave."

Lucy did not respond.

"Lucy, I mean it . . . We let Nicky in and he will never leave. You know what he is, right? You know what he's capable of."

Lucy turned and smiled. "I love you, Frankie. I love you with all my heart."

"I love you just the same."

"I love my brother, too. He's family. Family you can never forget."

Frankie thought of his own family, of Erin, of the life he had left behind.

"I understand that . . . I really do," he replied.

Lucy set down the dishtowel and came around the kitchen table. As she passed Frankie she leaned up toward him.

"Then don't make me choose between you," she whispered.

And then she kissed him, and headed for the stairs without another word.